DEADLY MISSION

"Looks like you'll have to climb," Seregil whispered, squinting up. "Be careful going over; most of these places have the walls topped with spikes or sharp flints."

"Hold on!" Alec tried to make out Seregil's expression through the darkness. "Aren't you coming with me?"

"It's a one-man job; the fewer the better," Seregil assured him. "Would I send you in alone if I didn't think you could handle it? Best leave your sword, though."

"What if someone sees me?"

"Honestly, Alec! You can't just go hacking your way out of every difficult situation that arises. It's uncivilized."

Alec unbuckled his sword and started up the garden wall. He was halfway to the top when Micum called softly, "We'll meet you back here when you've finished. Oh, and look out for the dogs."

"Dogs?" Alec dropped down again. "What dogs? You didn't say anything about dogs!"

Seregil tapped himself sharply between the eyes. "Illior's Fingers, what *am* I thinking of tonight? There's a pair of Zengati hounds, snow-white and big as bears."

"That's a fine detail to forget," growled Micum.

"Anything else I should know?"

"Let's see, the spikes, the dogs, the servants— No, I think we covered it. Luck in the shadows, Alec."

"And to you," Alec muttered, starting up the wall again.

Praise for *Luck in the Shadows*
by Lynn Flewelling

Luck in the Shadows

Lynn Flewelling

Bantam Books
New York Toronto London Sydney Auckland

LUCK IN THE SHADOWS
A Bantam Spectra Book/September 1996
SPECTRA and the portrayal of a boxed "s" are trademarks of Bantam Books,
a division of Random House, Inc.

ISBN 0-553-57542-2
Published simultaneously in the United States and Canada

Bantam Books are published by Bantam Books, a division of Random
House, Inc. Its trademark, consisting of the words "Bantam Books" and
the portrayal of a rooster, is Registered in U.S. Patent and Trademark
Office and in other countries. Marca Registrada. Bantam Books, 1540
Broadway, New York, New York 10036.

PRINTED IN THE UNITED STATES OF AMERICA

OPM 10 9 8

This one's for you, Doug,
for all the best reasons.
LBF

ACKNOWLEDGMENTS

Like many first novels, this one wouldn't be complete without acknowledgments. Those of you who don't know me can skip this part, if you like. Really. I don't mind.

With deepest gratitude to those hardy early readers who believed in this project long before I did myself: Mom, Fran, and kid sister Sue, God love 'em; Gram, God rest her; Jeffs K. & A.; sisters of the heart Darby, Laurie, the Other Lynn, and Nancy; Bonnie; Cheryl; Marc and the whole BookMarc's gang; Cathie Pelletier, for her guidance and support; Greta, Sandy F., Gary, Bill & Dorothy, Maria, Sabine, Scott & Julie, Marc & Lisa, Todd, Jen, Gail N.; Suzannes K. & C.; and Pete "The Organmeister" K. and Debbie C., who materialized out of the electronic ether at the nicest possible time. Apologies to anyone I missed.

Love also to Matt and Tim, who've heard, "Not now, Mom's writing," far too often; and to my dad, who's probably bragging me up in Heaven, because he always did.

And finally, special thanks to my literary midwives, Lucienne Diver, Eleanor Wood, and Anne Groell, who made it all come real.

Author's Note

The ancient Hierophantic calendar is based on a lunar year divided into twelve 29-day months and four seasonal festivals, which account for an additional twelve days.

Winter Solstice—observance of the longest night and celebration of the lengthening of days to come. (Mourning Night and Festival of Sakor in Skala.) Followed by:
>Sarisin
>Dostin
>Klesin

Spring Festival—preparation for planting, celebration of fertility of Dalna. (Festival of the Flowers in Mycena.) Followed by:
>Lithion
>Nythin
>Gorathin

Summer Solstice—celebration of the longest day, followed by:
>Shemin
>Lenthin
>Rhythin

Harvest Home—finish of harvest, time of thankfulness. (Great Festival of Dalna in Mycena.) Followed by:
>Erasin
>Kemmin
>Cinrin

LUCK
IN THE
SHADOWS

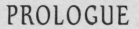

PROLOGUE

Mouldering bone crumbled beneath their boots as Lord Mardus and Vargûl Ashnazai lowered themselves down into the tiny chamber beneath the earthen mound. Oblivious to the pervasive odor of swamp and old death, to the dank earth filtering down the back of his neck and into his hair, Mardus crunched across more bones to a rough stone slab at the back of the chamber. Brushing aside brittle ribs and skulls, he reverently lifted a small pouch from the stone. The rotted leather fell to pieces at a touch, spilling eight carved wooden disks across his palm.

"It appears you've accomplished your purpose, Vargûl Ashnazai." Mardus smiled and the scar beneath his left eye tightened.

Ashnazai's sharp, sallow face was ghostly in the uncertain light. With a nod of satisfaction, he passed a hand over the disks and for an instant their form wavered, giving hint of their true shape.

"After all these centuries, another fragment reclaimed!" he exclaimed softly. "It's a sign, my lord. The time draws nigh."

"A most propitious sign. Let us hope that the remainder of our quest is as successful. Captain Tildus!"

A black-bearded face appeared in the

rough opening at the top of the mound. "Here, my lord."

"Have the villagers been gathered?"

"Yes, my lord."

"Good. You may begin."

"I shall make preparations for the safe conveyance of these," Vargûl Ashnazai said, reaching to take the disks.

"And what could *you* do that the ancients have not already done?" Mardus inquired coldly, pocketing them as casually as if they were gaming stones. "There's nothing so safe as that which appears to be worthless. For the time being, we will trust in the wisdom of our ancestors."

Ashnazai quickly withdrew his hand. "As you wish, my lord."

Mardus' soulless black eyes met and held his as the first screams erupted above them.

Vargûl Ashnazai was the first to look away.

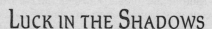

1

LUCK IN THE SHADOWS

Asengai's torturers were regular in their habits—they always left off at sunset. Chained again in his corner of the drafty cell, Alec turned his face to the rough stone wall and sobbed until his chest ached.

An icy mountain wind sighed through the grating overhead, carrying with it the sweet scent of snow to come. Still weeping, the boy burrowed deeper into the sour straw. It scratched painfully against the welts and bruises that bloomed across his bare skin, but it was better than nothing and all he had.

He was alone now. They'd hanged the miller yesterday and the one called Danker had died under torture. Alec had never met either of them before his capture but they had treated him kindly. Now he wept for them, too, and for the horror of their death.

As the tears subsided, he wondered again why he'd been spared, why Lord Asengai repeatedly told the torturers, "Don't mark the boy too badly." So they hadn't seared him with red-hot irons or cut off his ears or opened his skin with knotted whips as they had with the others. Instead, they'd beaten him skillfully and dunked him until he thought he was drowned. And no matter how many times he'd screamed out the truth, he couldn't seem to convince his captors that he'd wandered onto

Asengai's remote freeholding seeking nothing more than the pelts of spotted cats.

His only remaining hope now was that they would finish him off quickly; death loomed like a welcome release from the hours of pain, the endless stream of questions that he didn't understand and couldn't answer. Clinging to this bitter comfort, he drifted into a fitful doze.

The familiar tread of boots jerked him awake sometime later. Moonlight slanted in through the window now, pooling in the straw beside him. Sick with dread, he pulled himself into the deeper shadow of the corner.

As the footsteps came closer a highly pitched voice suddenly burst out, shouting and cursing over the sounds of a scuffle. The cell door banged open and the dark forms of two warders and a struggling captive were framed for an instant against the torch-light from the corridor beyond.

The prisoner was a small, slightly built man but he fought like a cornered weasel.

"Unhand me, you cretinous brutes!" he cried, his furious words marred somewhat by a noticeable lisp. "I *demand* to see your master! How *dare* you arrest me! Can't an honest bard pass unmolested through this country?"

Twisting an arm free, he swung a fist at the warder on his left. The larger man blocked the blow easily and pinned his arms sharply back again.

"Don't fret yourself," the guard snorted, giving the prisoner a sharp cuff on the ear. "You'll meet our master soon enough and wish you hadn't!"

His partner let out a nasty chuckle. "Aye, he'll have you singing loud and long before he's through." With this, he struck the smaller man quick, harsh blows to the face and belly, silencing any further protests.

Dragging him to the wall opposite Alec, they manacled him hand and foot.

"What about that one?" one of them asked, jerking a thumb in Alec's direction. "They'll be taking him off next day or so. How 'bout a bit of sport?"

"No, you heard the master. Be worth our hides if we spoiled him for the slavers. Come on, the game'll be starting." The key grated in the lock behind them and their voices faded away down the corridor.

Slavers? Alec curled more tightly into the shadows. There were no slaves in the northlands but he'd heard tales enough of people carried off to distant countries and uncertain fates, never to be seen again. Throat tight with renewed panic, he tugged hopelessly at his chains.

The bard raised his head with a groan. "Who's there?"

Alec froze, regarding the man warily. The pale wash of moonlight was bright enough for him to see that the man was dressed in the gaudy clothing common to his kind: a tunic with long, dagged tippets, the striped sash and hose. Tall, muddy traveling boots completed the garish outfit. Alec couldn't make out his face, however; the fellow's dark hair hung to his shoulders in foppish ringlets, partially obscuring his features.

Too exhausted and miserable to attempt idle conversation, Alec pressed into his corner without reply. The man seemed to be squinting hard in his direction, but before he could speak again they heard the guards returning. Dropping flat in the straw, the bard lay motionless as they dragged in a third prisoner, this one a squat, bull-necked laborer in homespun garments and stained leggings.

Despite his size, the man obeyed the warders in terrified silence as they chained him by the feet next to the bard.

"Here's another bit of company for you, boy," one of them said with a grin, setting a small clay lamp in a niche over the door. "Someone to help you pass the time 'til morning!"

The light fell across Alec. Dark bruises and welts showed darkly against his fair skin. Clad in little more than the tattered remnants of his linen clout, he returned the man's gaze stonily.

"By the Maker, boy! What did you do that they dealt with you so?" the man exclaimed.

"Nothing," Alec rasped. "They tortured me, and the others. They died—yesterday? What's the day?"

"Third of Erasin, come sunrise."

Alec's head ached dully; had it really only been four days?

"But what did you arrest you for?" the man persisted, eyeing Alec with obvious suspicion.

"Spying. But I wasn't! I tried to explain—"

"It's the same with me," the peasant sighed. "I've been kicked, beaten, robbed, and not a word will they hear from me. 'I'm Morden Swiftford,' I tell 'em. 'Just a plowman, nothing more!' But here I am."

With a deep groan the bard sat up and struggled awkwardly to untangle himself from his shackles. After a considerable effort he finally managed to arrange himself with his back resting against the wall.

"Those brutes will pay dearly for this indignity," he snarled weakly. "Imagine, Rolan Silverleaf a spy!"

"You, too?" asked Morden.

"It's too absurd. There I was, performing at the Harvest Fair at Rook Tor only last week. I happen to have several powerful patrons in these parts and believe me, they shall hear of the treatment I've endured!"

The fellow prattled on, giving an encyclopedic recital of the places he'd performed and the highly placed people to whom he looked for justice.

Alec paid him little heed. Wrapped in his own misery, he huddled morosely in his corner while Morden gaped.

The jailers returned within the hour and hauled the frightened plowman away. Soon cries of an all-too-familiar nature echoed up the hallway. Alec pressed his face against his knees and covered his ears, trying not to hear. The bard was watching him, he knew, but he was beyond caring.

Morden's hair and jerkin were matted with blood when the guards dragged him back and chained him in his place again. He lay where they flung him, panting hoarsely.

A few moments later another guard came in and handed out meager rations of water and hard biscuit. Rolan examined his bit of biscuit with obvious distaste.

"It's maggoty, but you should eat," he said, tossing his portion across to Alec.

Alec ignored it and his own. Food meant dawn was close and the start of another grim day.

"Go on," Rolan urged gently. "You'll need your strength later." Alec turned his face away, but he persisted. "At least take a bit of water. Can you walk?"

Alec shrugged listlessly. "What difference does it make?"

"Perhaps a great deal before long," the other man replied with an odd half smile. There was something new in his voice, a calculating note that was decidedly out of place with his dandified appearance. The dim light of the lamp touched the side of his face, showing a longish nose and one sharp eye.

Alec took a small sip of the water, then downed the rest in a gulp as the needs of his body took over. He'd had nothing to eat or drink in more than a day.

"That's better," murmured Rolan. Getting to his knees, he moved out as far as the leg chains allowed, then leaned forward until the manacles drew his arms back tautly. Morden raised his head, watching with dull curiosity.

"It's no use. You'll only bring the guards back," Alec hissed, wishing the man would keep still.

Rolan surprised him with a wink, then began to flex his hands, spreading the fingers and straining the thumbs about. From across the cell Alec heard the soft, sickening snap of joints separating. Rolan's hands slipped free of the manacle rings. Falling forward, he caught himself on one elbow and quickly relocated the joints at the base of each thumb.

He wiped the sweat from his eyes with the end of one tippet. "There, and now the feet." Pulling down the top of his left boot, he extracted a long, bodkinlike instrument from an inner seam. A moment's work on each of the leg iron locks and he was free. Taking up Morden's water cup and his own, he came over to Alec.

"Drink this. Slowly now, slowly. What's your name?"

"Alec of Kerry." He sipped gratefully at the extra ration, hardly believing what he'd just seen. For the first time since his capture, he felt the beginnings of hope.

Rolan watched him closely, looking as if he'd reached a not entirely agreeable decision. At last he sighed and said, "I suppose you'd better come with me." Pushing his hair impatiently back from his eyes, he turned to Morden with a thin, unfriendly smile.

"But you, my friend, you seem to set remarkably small value on your life."

"Good sir," Morden stammered, cowering back, "I'm only a humble peasant but I'm certain my life means as much to me—"

Rolan cut him off with an impatient gesture, then reached forward to thrust his hand into the neck of the man's grimy jerkin. He yanked out a thin silver chain and dangled it in Morden's face.

"You're not very convincing, you know. Louts though they are, Asengai's men are far too thorough to miss a bauble like this."

His voice is different! Alec thought, watching the strange confrontation in confusion. Rolan wasn't lisping at all now; he just sounded dangerous.

"I should also tell you, by way of instruction, that tortured men are usually extremely thirsty," the bard continued. "Unless they smell of ale, as you do. I trust you and the guards had a pleasant supper together? I wonder what sort of blood is it you're smeared with?"

"Your mother's moon flow!" Morden snarled, his simple expression vanishing as he pulled a small dagger from his legging and lunged at Rolan. The bard dodged the attack and drove his clenched fist against Morden's throat, crushing his larynx. A swift jab of his elbow to Morden's temple felled the man like an ox; he collapsed in the straw at Rolan's feet, blood flowing from his mouth and ear.

"You killed him!" Alec said faintly.

Rolan pressed a finger to Morden's throat, then nodded. "Seems I did. The fool should've yelled for the guards."

Alec cringed back against the clammy stone as Rolan turned to him.

"Steady now," the man said, and Alec was surprised to see he was smiling. "Do you want to get out of here or not?"

Alec managed a mute nod, then sat rigidly while Rolan unlocked his chains. When he'd finished he went back to Morden's body.

"Now let's see who you were." Sliding the dead man's dagger into his boot, Rolan pulled up the soiled jerkin to examine the hairy torso beneath.

"Hmm, that's no great surprise," he muttered, probing at the left armpit.

Curious in spite of his fear, Alec crept just close enough to peer over Rolan's shoulder.

"See here?" Rolan showed him a triangle of three tiny blue circles tattooed into the pale skin where the arm joined the body.

"What does it mean?"

"It's a guild mark. He was a Juggler."

"A mountebank?"

"No," Rolan snorted. "A keek, a ferret. The Jugglers carry out any sort of dirty mischief for the right price. They swarm around petty lords like Asengai the way blow flies gather on a midden." Tugging the dead man's jerkin off, he thrust it into Alec's hands. "Here, put this on. And hurry! I'll say this just once; fall behind and you're on your own!"

The garment was filthy and soaked with blood at the neck, but Alec obeyed quickly, pulling it on with a shudder of revulsion. By the time he'd gotten it on, Rolan was already at work on the lock.

"Rusty son of a whore," he remarked, spitting into the keyhole. The lock gave way at last and he opened the door a crack, peering out.

"Looks clear," he whispered. "Stay close and do what I tell you."

Alec's heart hammered in his ears as he followed Rolan out into the corridor. Several yards down lay the room where Asengai's men carried out their tortures. Beyond that, the door to the warder's room stood open and they could hear the noise of a rowdy game of some sort in progress.

Rolan's boots made no more noise than Alec's bare feet as the two of them crept up to the open doorway. Rolan cocked his head, then held up four fingers. With a quick motion he indicated that Alec should cross the doorway quickly and quietly.

Alec stole a glance inside. Four guards were kneeling around a cloak on the floor. One cast the knucklebones and coins changed hands amid much good-natured cursing.

Waiting until their attention was focused on the next toss, Alec slipped across to the other side. Rolan joined him soundlessly and they hurried around a corner and down a stairway. A lamp burned in a shallow niche at the bottom. Rolan took it and set off again.

Alec knew nothing of the lay of the place and quickly lost all sense of direction as they made their way along a succession of twisting passageways. Halting at last, Rolan opened a narrow door and disappeared into the darkness beyond, whispering for Alec to watch his step just in time to save the boy from tumbling down more stairs that descended less than a pace from the door.

It was colder down here, and damp. The wavering circle of light from Rolan's lamp skimmed across lichen-stained stonework. The floor was stone as well, rough and broken with neglect.

A final, crumbling set of stairs brought them to a low,

iron-strapped door. The paving beneath Alec's bare feet was frigid. His breath puffed out in rapid little clouds. Handing him the lamp, Rolan went to work on the heavy lock that hung from a staple in the door frame.

"There," Rolan whispered as it came free. "Blow out the light and leave it."

They slipped out into the shadows of a walled yard. The lopsided moon was low in the west; the sky behind the stars showed the first hint of predawn indigo. A thick rime of frost coated everything in the yard: wood stack, well, farrier's forge—all glinted softly in the moonlight. Winter was coming early this year, Alec thought. He could smell it on the air.

"This is the lower stable yard," Rolan whispered. "There's a gate beyond that wood stack, with a postern beside it. Damn, but it's cold!"

Scrubbing a hand back through his ridiculous curls, he looked Alec over again; except for the filthy jerkin, the boy was all but naked. "You can't go traveling all over the country like that. Get to the side door and open it. There shouldn't be a guard, but keep your eyes open and be *silent*! I'll be right back."

Before Alec could protest, he'd ghosted away in the direction of the stables.

Alec crouched by the doorway for a moment, hugging himself against the cold. Alone in the darkness, he felt his brief burst of confidence ebbing away. A glance at the stables showed no sign of his strange companion. Genuine fear stirred just below the fragile threshold of his resolve.

Fighting it down, he forced himself to concentrate on gauging the distance to the dark side of the wood stack. *I haven't come this far to be abandoned for weakness,* he berated himself. *Maker Dalna, hold your hand over me now!*

Drawing in a deep, silent breath, he darted forward. He got within arm's length of the wood stack before a tall figure stepped from the shadow of the forge a scant few feet away.

"Who's that?" the man demanded, pulling something from his belt. "Stand and speak, you!"

Alec dove for the stack, throwing himself down behind it. Something hard dug into his chest as he landed. Grabbing at it, he closed his hand around the smooth haft of an ax. Then he was rolling to avoid the heavy club the man was swinging at his head.

Gripping the ax like a quarter staff, Alec managed to deflect the sentry's arcing swing. He was badly overmatched, however, and what little strength he had left after days of mistreatment soon faded as blow after blow rained down. Leaping back, he caught sight of Rolan near the stable door. Instead of coming to his aid, however, the bard faded back into the shadows.

That's it then, he thought. *I got into trouble and he's left me.*

Driven by fury born of utter despair, Alec flew at the startled sentry, driving the man back with wild swings of the ax's double blade. If he was going to die in this terrible place, he'd go down fighting under an open sky.

His adversary recovered quickly and was pressing in for the kill when they were both surprised by a clattering uproar nearby. The stable door slammed back and Rolan burst out mounted bareback on an enormous black horse. A pack of ostlers, stable boys, and guards spilled out after him, raising the alarm.

"The gate, damn it! Open the gate!" Rolan shouted, leading his pursuers in a fool's chase around the courtyard.

Distracted, the sentry made a clumsy parry and Alec sprang under his guard with a savage swing. The blade struck home and the man went down screaming. Dropping the ax, Alec dashed to the gate, heaved the heavy bar out of its brackets, and pushed the doors wide.

Now what?

Looking around, he found Rolan occupied at the far end of the yard.

A guard had him by one ankle, and a stable hand was leaping for the horse's bridle. Spotting the open gate, he reined the horse back on its haunches and kicked the beast into a furious gallop straight across the yard. His mount sprang effortlessly over the well and bolted for the gate. Hauling back on the reins, Rolan twisted the fingers of one hand into the black's mane and leaned over its neck, other arm extended.

"Come on!" he yelled.

Alec reached up just in time. Rolan's fingers clamped around his wrist, wrenching him off his feet and across the horse's broad back. Clambering upright, he locked his arms around Rolan's waist as they thundered though the gate and down the road beyond.

They skirted the little village nestled against the walls of the keep and flew on along the road down the wooded mountainside below Asengai's domain.

After several miles, Rolan left the road and plunged into the thick forest that flanked it. Safe among the trees, he reined their mount to a halt.

"Here, take these," he whispered, shoving a bundle of some sort into Alec's hands.

It was a cloak. The coarse fabric smelled rankly of the stable but the boy wrapped himself in it gratefully, drawing his bare feet up against the horse's steaming sides to warm them.

They sat in silence, and after a moment Alec realized that they must be waiting for something. Presently they heard the clatter of hooves approaching. It was too dark to count the riders as they passed, but judging by the sound, there were at least half a dozen. Waiting until they were all well past, Rolan turned the black again to the road and started back in the direction of the keep.

"We're going the wrong way," Alec whispered, tugging at Rolan's sleeve.

"Don't worry," his companion replied with a soft chuckle.

A few moments later he turned aside from the main road, this time onto a badly overgrown track. The ground fell away sharply, and branches whipped at their faces as they cantered along under the cover of the trees. Halting again, Rolan claimed the cloak and threw it over the horse's head to keep the beast quiet. They soon heard the riders again, moving slower now and calling back and forth to one another. Two riders ventured down the track, passing within ten yards of where Rolan and Alec stood holding their breath.

"He must've been a wizard, I tell you!" one was saying. "Killing that southern bastard the way he did, disappearing out of the cell, and now this!"

"Wizard be damned," the other retorted angrily. "You'll wish you was a wizard if Berin don't catch up with 'em down the road. Lord Asengai'll skin the whole bunch of us!"

A horse stumbled and reared.

"Bilairy's Guts! This way's hopeless in the dark. They'd have broke their necks by now," the lead man grumbled. Giving up, the riders turned back the way they'd come.

Waiting until all was quiet, Rolan mounted in front of Alec and handed him back the cloak.

"What do we do now?" whispered Alec as they headed down the mountain track again.

"I left some supplies a few miles from here. I just hope they're still there. Hang on tight. We've got a rough ride ahead of us."

2

ACROSS THE DOWNS

Alec opened his eyes to the noonday light. For a drowsy moment he blinked up at the branches overhead, trying to recall where he was and wondering why the scratchy roughness of the blankets felt so good against his skin.

Then a sudden onslaught of memories slapped him fully awake. Scrambling to his knees, he pulled the blankets around him and looked about in alarm.

Rolan was nowhere in sight, but their stolen horse was still in the little clearing, along with the bay mare and the battered leather pack Rolan had cached here before venturing into Asengai's domain. Burrowing back beneath the blankets, Alec closed his eyes again and waited for his heartbeat to slow.

He was amazed that Rolan had been able to find his way back here at all. To Alec, exhausted beyond measure, the ride had seemed one long, impossible series of difficulties: thickets, streams, and a skree field they'd crossed on foot. Never faltering, Rolan had urged him on with promises of hot food and warm blankets. By the time they'd reached the clearing, Alec had been too tired and cold to do more than collapse onto the bracken pallet that lay ready beneath the shelter of a thick fir.

The last thing he remembered was listening to Rolan curse the cold as he joined him beneath their shared pile of blankets and cloaks.

It was bitterly cold now, despite the brightness of the sun. Long crystals of frost thrust up through the mossy loam next to his pallet, like bundles of tiny glass blades. Overhead, mackerel-striped clouds ribbed the hazy sky. There'd be snow soon, the first of the year.

Their camp lay next to a small waterfall, and the sound of it had gotten into his dreams. Pulling the stolen cloak around his shoulders, he went into the bushes to relieve his bladder, then walked down to the edge of the pool below the falls. Every bruise and welt protested as he dipped up a handful of icy water, but he was too happy to care; he was alive and he was free! Whoever, whatever this Rolan Silverleaf was, Alec owed him his life.

But where was the man?

Branches rattled on the opposite side of the pool as a doe stepped from the trees to drink. Alec's fingers itched for the taut pull of a bowstring.

"Maker keep you fat until we meet again!" he called softly. Startled, the deer sprang away on slender legs and Alec set off to see what he could forage.

It was an old forest. Towering firs had long since choked out all but the most persistent undergrowth, so that a man could easily have driven a cart between their thick, straight trunks. High overhead, the dense canopy of interlaced boughs filtered the sunlight to muted underwater tones. Moss-crusted boulders studded the slope. Between them, patches of dead ferns whispered dryly as he passed. Finding a few late mushrooms, he gathered them, nibbling at one as he went along.

As he passed a large boulder, he was surprised to find a rabbit dead in a snare. Hoping this was Rolan's work, he freed the carcass and sniffed it. It was fresh. Mouth watering at the first prospect of hot meat in days, he headed eagerly back to the camp. As he neared the clearing he heard the knock of steel against a flint and hurried on to show Rolan their breakfast.

Stepping from the shelter of the trees, he froze in terror.

O Dalna, they found us!

A rough-clad stranger was standing with his back to Alec, looking out over the pool. His tunic of green homespun and leather

breeches were unremarkable; it was the long scabbard slung low
on the intruder's left hip that caught the boy's attention.

Alec's first thought was to melt back into the woods, find
Rolan. As he took a cautious step back, however, his heel struck
a dry stick. It snapped loudly and the man whirled about, sword
drawn. Dropping the rabbit and the mushrooms, Alec turned to
bolt. A familiar voice behind him brought him to a halt.

"It's all right. It's me. It's Rolan."

Still poised to run, Alec took a wary look back and realized
his mistake. It was Rolan, after all, though he bore little re-
semblance to the foppish coxcomb of the night before.

"Good morning," Rolan called. "You'd better go get that co-
ney you dropped. I've only got one other and I'm famished!"

Alec's cheeks flushed hotly as he hastily gathered up the
rabbit and mushrooms and brought them to the fire.

"I didn't recognize you," he exclaimed. "How can you look so
different?"

"Just changed my clothes." Rolan pushed back the thick
brown hair that hung now in damp waves over his shoulders. "I
don't suppose you got a very good look at me before, racing
around in the dark as we did."

This was true, Alec reflected, sizing his companion up. Rolan
somehow seemed taller in the daylight, though he was not a large
man at all. Rather, he was slender and fine-featured, with large
grey eyes set over high cheekbones and a long, narrow nose. His
mouth was fine, almost thin, and tilted at the moment in a lopsided grin that made him look younger than Alec would have
guessed before.

"I don't know, Rolan—"

"Oh, and about the name." The grin tilted a bit higher. "It isn't
actually Rolan Silverleaf."

"What do I call you, then?" asked Alec, not particularly
surprised.

"You can call me Seregil."

"How's that?"

"*Ser*-ah-gill."

"Oh." It was an odd-sounding name, but Alec sensed it was
all he was going to get for the moment. "Where were you?"

"Checking to see if anyone tracked us. There's no sign of
Asengai's men yet, but we'd better move on soon in case they get
lucky. We'll eat first, though. You look starved."

Alec knelt by the fire, inspecting the two lean coneys with a rueful smile. "We'd be eating venison if I had my bow. Those bastards took everything I owned. I don't even have a knife! Lend me one and I'll clean these."

Reaching into the top of one tall boot, Seregil handed him a long poniard.

"Maker's Mercy, that's a beauty!" Alec exclaimed, running a thumbnail appreciatively along the edge of the narrow, triangular blade. As he set about cleaning the first rabbit, however, it was Seregil's turn to be impressed.

"You're pretty handy at that sort of thing," he remarked as Alec opened the belly with a single quick stroke.

Alec offered him a purplish-brown lobe of liver. "You want some of this? Good for your blood in the winter."

"Thanks." Accepting the morsel, Seregil sat down by the fire and watched him thoughtfully.

Alec colored a little under that frank gaze. "Thank you for saving my life last night. I'm in your debt."

"You handled yourself well enough. How old are you, anyway? You look young to be roaming around all by yourself."

"Sixteen last summer," Alec replied a bit gruffly. He was often taken for younger than he was. "I've lived my whole life in the woods."

"But not alone, surely?"

Alec hesitated, wondering how much he really wanted to reveal to this odd stranger. "My father died just after the summer solstice."

"I see. An accident, was it?"

"No, he had the wasting sickness." Tears stung Alec's eyes and he bent lower over the rabbit, hoping Seregil wouldn't notice. "It was a hard death. Even the drysians couldn't help him in the end."

"You've been on your own all of three months, then?"

"Yes. We missed the spring bird trade, so I had to spend the summer in Stone Tor working off our debt to the inn where Father lay sick. Then I came out for the fall trapping, like we always did. I already had a whole string of pelts, good ones, when I ran into Asengai's men. Now, with no equipment, no horse, nothing, I don't know—"

He broke off, his face grim; he'd walked the thin line of starvation before.

"Don't you have a family somewhere?" Seregil asked after a moment. "Where's your mother?"

"I never knew her."

"Friends?"

Alec handed him the dressed rabbit and took up the second. "We kept to ourselves mostly. Father didn't like towns."

"I see. So what will you do now?"

"I don't know. In Stone Tor I worked in the scullery and helped out the ostler. I guess I'll have to go back to that for the winter."

Seregil made no comment and Alec worked in silence for a moment. Then, watching the steam from the open carcass rise between his fingers, he asked, "All that back there last night—was it you they were looking for?"

Seregil smiled slightly as he skewered the first rabbit on a long stick and propped it over the fire. "That's a dangerous question to ask a stranger. If I was, I'd probably kill you just for asking. No, I'm just a wandering collector of tales. I've picked up a lot that way."

"So you really are a bard, then?"

"Sometimes. I was up above Kerry not long ago, collecting stories of the *Faie* who were supposed to have lived up in the Ironheart Mountains beyond Ravensfell Pass. Being from that region yourself, you must know something about them."

"The Elder Folk, you mean?" Alec grinned. "Those were always my favorite stories. We used to cross trails with a skald who knew all about them. He said they were magic folk, like trolls or centaurs. When I was little I used to look for them in the shadows of the trees, though Father said it was foolish. 'Those tales are nothing but smoke from a liar's pipe!' he'd say—"

Alec's voice faltered and he broke off, rubbing at his eyes as if smoke had blown into them.

Seregil tactfully failed to notice his distress. "Anyhow, a few days ago I ran afoul of Asengai, same as you. I'm off Wolde now. I've got a bit of singing lined up there in three days' time."

"Three days?" Alec shook his head. "You'd have to go straight over the Downs to get there that quickly."

"Damn! I must be farther west than I thought. I hear the Downs are a dangerous place for anyone who doesn't know where the springs are."

"I could show you," Alec offered. "I've been back and forth

across them most of my life. Maybe I could turn up some work there, too."

"Do you know the town?"

"We traded there every fall at the Harvest Fair."

"Sounds like I've found myself a guide." Seregil extended his hand. "What's your price?"

"I can't take your money," Alec protested. "Not after what you did for me."

Seregil waved this aside with a crooked grin. "Honor's for men with money in their pockets; you've got a long, cold winter ahead. Come now, name your price and I'll pay it gladly."

The logic was indisputable. "Two silver marks," Alec replied after a moment's calculation. Reaching to clasp hands on it, however, his father's voice spoke in the back of his mind and he drew back, adding, "Hard money, and half now."

"Very prudent of you."

As they shook on the bargain, Alec felt a curving edge against his palm and drew his hand from Seregil's to find himself holding a large silver coin. Two fingers wide and covered with fine designs, it lay heavy against his palm.

"This is too much!" he protested.

Seregil shrugged. "It's the smallest I have. Keep it and we'll settle up in Wolde. It's a pretty thing, don't you think?"

"I've never seen anything like it!" What little currency Alec had seen were crude lozenges of copper or silver, distinguished only by weight and a few crude symbols struck in. The designs on this coin were better than anything he'd seen in a jeweler's stall.

One side bore the slim bow of a crescent moon, tipped on its side like a smile with five stylized rays fanning out beneath it to the lower edge of the coin. Cradled within the crescent was the figure of a flame. The obverse showed a crowned woman. She wore a cuirass of some sort over her flowing gown, and held a large sword upright before her face.

"How did you get it into my hand?" he asked.

"Telling spoils the trick," replied Seregil, tossing him a square of wet sacking. "I'll tend to the cooking. You go clean yourself up. A quick swim should help."

Alec's smile disappeared. "Bilairy's Balls, it's nearly winter and you want me to take a *bath*?"

"If we're going to share blankets over the next few days, yes.

No offense, but dungeon life hasn't done much for your general ambience. Go on, I'll mind the fire. And get rid of those clothes! I've got clean ones for you."

Dubious but not wanting to appear ungrateful, Alec picked up a blanket and went to the pool. Noting the lacy edgings of ice that still rimmed the stones, however, he decided that gratitude only went so far. Stripping off his rags, he gave himself a cursory scrubbing and pulled the blanket around his waist. As he bent to duck his head under the water, the sight of his reflection froze him, crouched and trembling, on the wet stones. Only the day before, Asengai's men had strapped him to a plank and titled him into a water butt, holding him under again and again until he thought his lungs would burst. He'd had enough of water for now, thank you very much.

Seregil smiled wryly to himself as he watched the boy's hasty ablutions. These northerners seemed to develop a genuine aversion to water over the winter. Tugging open his pack, he rummaged out an extra tunic, breeches, and a belt.

Alec hurried back to the fire and Seregil tossed him the clothes. "These should do for you. We're almost of a size."

"Thanks." Shivering, Alec went off a few feet and turned away before letting the blanket drop.

"Asengai's men did a thorough job on you, I see," said Seregil, running a critical eye over the bruises on the boy's back and thighs.

"Dalna's Hands, there's such a thing as modesty," the boy muttered as he struggled into the breeches.

"Never had any use for it, myself, and I don't see why you're so bothered with it either. Under those bruises and that scowl, you're fairly pleasing to look at." Seregil's expression betrayed nothing more than the thoughtful concentration a man might show when sizing up a horse he was about to buy.

Indeed, Alec was well favored, Seregil thought, amused by his companion's discomfort. The boy was lightly built and supple, with dark, intelligent blue eyes in a fair face that blushed easily and concealed little. This last was easily remedied, though at times an honest face was useful. The ragged, honey-gold hair looked like it had been trimmed with a skinning knife, but time would fix that, too.

Still, there was something more than Alec's appearance that intrigued him. The lad was neat-handed, and there was a familiar quickness about him that had little to do with training. And he asked questions.

Alec finished dressing and reached to put the silver coin Seregil had paid him into a pouch on his borrowed belt.

"Wait a second. Watch this," said Seregil, producing another like it from his own purse. Balancing it on the back of one hand, he gave a quick snap of his wrist, pulled his hand out from under it, and caught the coin before it dropped half an inch. "Want to try?"

Puzzled but intrigued, Alec tried the trick. On the first attempt he dropped his coin. On the second and third try it bounced off his fingertips. The fourth time, however, he grasped it before it had fallen more than a few inches.

Seregil nodded approvingly. "Not bad. Now try it with your left."

When Alec could do the catch with either hand, Seregil had him try it using only his thumb and forefinger, and finally to perform the trick with his eyes shut.

"Ah, but this is too simple for you," Seregil said at last. "Here, give this a try."

He placed his coin on the ground beside him and rested his hand to the left of it, an inch or so away. With a subtle twitch of his little finger, he swept it beneath his palm without even disturbing the dust. When he raised his hand, the coin was gone. Shaking it from the sleeve of his tunic with a comic flourish, he demonstrated how the snap was done. Again Alec managed it after only a few tries.

"You've got the hands of a born thief," Seregil observed. "Perhaps I'd better not show you any more of those just now!"

Left-handed compliment that it was, Alec returned the grin as he snapped the coin up his sleeve a final time.

They ate quickly, then covered all signs of their camp, burying the fire and tossing their refuse into the pool. As they worked, Seregil found himself again pondering what he'd seen of Alec so far, wondering what he could make of such a boy. Alec was quick and surprisingly well spoken. His nature—a blend of stubborn persistence and appalling openness—made for an interesting mix. With a bit of polishing, a little training—?

Shaking his head, Seregil pushed the thought away.

As they mounted to leave, a tiny owl flew across the clearing and perched in a dead tree. Blinking in the afternoon light, it fluffed up and let out a mellow *too too too*.

Seregil gave the saw-whet a reverent nod; the Lightbringer's own bird seen in daylight was no small omen.

"What do you suppose he's doing out so early?" Alec remarked.

Bemused, Seregil shook his head. "I have no idea, Alec, no idea at all."

A cold wind carried the first light snow down through the trees as they set off down the mountainside.

Giving the bay a loose rein, Seregil scanned the forest around them for any sign of Asengai's soldiers as he rode along behind Alec. Without a saddle, the boy had to cling on with knees and hands. He managed well enough, but it was hard going and made for little conversation.

They reached the edge of the Downs by late afternoon and cantered from the shelter of the trees. Before them monotonous, dun-colored grasslands rolled away to the distant horizon. The wind moaned steadily over the waste, sweeping the fine, gritty snow up into feathery gusts. A rumpled grey blanket of clouds had sealed itself across the sky.

"Illior's Finger, but I hate the cold!" Seregil exclaimed, stopping to secure his hood and tug on a pair of gloves.

"And you the one all for bathing," Alec chided. "This is nothing compared to what it will be come next—" He broke off suddenly, staring at Seregil. "You swore by Illior!"

"And you swear by Dalna. What of it?"

"Only southerners swear by Illior. Are you from the south? The Three Lands?"

"As a matter of fact, I am," Seregil replied, enjoying the boy's guileless astonishment. To most northerners the Three Lands were hardly more than places of fancy in a bard's tale; he might as well have said, "I'm from the back of the moon." "Do you know much of the south?"

"A little. The Gold Road goes down from Wolde all the way to the country of Mycena. Most of the caravaneers I've met have been Mycenians, though there have been a few Skalans, too. Skala's near there, isn't it?"

"Yes, it's a huge peninsula between the Inner and Osiat seas, west of Mycena. To the east is Plenimar, which lies on another peninsula to the east of Mycena, along the coast of the Gathwayd Ocean. The Gold Road, as you call it, is the main trade route between the Three Lands and the northern freeholdings."

"Which country are you from?"

"Oh, I travel around."

If Alec noticed the evasion, he let it go. "Some of the traders claim that there are dragons in the south, and powerful wizards. I saw a wizard once at a fair." His face brightened at the memory, easy to read as a tavern bill. "For a price she'd hatch salamanders from hen's eggs and make fires burn blue and red."

"Indeed?" Seregil had performed those tired fakeries a few times himself. Still, he understood all too well the wonder they could evoke.

"A Skalan trader tried to tell me the streets of his cities were paved with gold," Alec went on. "I didn't believe him, though. He was the one who tried to buy me from Father. I was only eight or nine. I could never figure out what he wanted me for."

"Really?" Seregil lifted a noncommittal eyebrow.

Luckily, Alec was more interested in the matter at hand. "I've heard that Skala and Plenimar are always at war."

Seregil gave a wry smile. "Not always, but often."

"Why?"

"That's an old question, and a complicated one. This time, I suspect it'll be to gain control of the Gold Road."

"This time?" Alec's eyes widened. "They're going to have another war? And way up here?"

"Looks that way. There are those that believe Plenimar means to drive out the Skalan and Mycenian merchants and extend their own political influence over the northern freeholds."

"You mean by conquering them?"

"Given their past history, I imagine that will be Plenimar's solution."

"But why haven't I heard any of this before? In Stone Tor, even at the Harvest Fair, nobody was talking of war!"

"Stone Tor is a long way from the main trading routes," Seregil reminded him. "The fact is, very few northerners are aware of it at the moment, except those who already have a hand in it. As it stands now, no one will be able to make a move until spring."

"But Asengai and that man Morden, are they part of it?"

"An interesting question." Seregil pulled his hood forward again. "I think the horses have walked long enough, don't you? We need to make some distance before dark!"

The Downs made for smooth riding. Alec knew of a spring they could camp by and set a steady pace until dark.

He knew the landmarks well, but could imagine what it must look like to his companion. Seregil was clearly uneasy as they left the mountains behind, and kept looking back over his shoulder as if trying to use the distant peeks to gauge their progress.

But the mountains were quickly obscured by the lengthening darkness and windblown snow. The sun, never more than a pale hint behind the lowering clouds, was their only guide.

"We'll have to make your food last," Alec remarked when they'd halted for the night. "Most of the summer game has moved south—not that I'd be able to get anything without my bow anyway," he added bitterly.

"I've got cheese and sausage enough for both of us," Seregil told him. "Good with a bow, are you?"

"Good enough." In truth, Alec felt like he was missing a limb without one. The bow he'd lost at Asengai's had been the best he'd ever made.

Dismounting, they scavenged around for firewood but found nothing except low, resinous bushes that burned too quickly, giving off more light than heat. Bundling up as best they could against the wind, they sat close together over their cold supper.

"You said that the fighting between Skala and Plenimar is an old question," Alec said at last. "What did you mean?"

"That's a long story," Seregil said with a chuckle, pulling his cloak tighter. "But a long story can make a long night seem shorter, I suppose. To begin with, did you know that the Three Lands were once one country?"

"No."

"Well, they were, and they were ruled over by a priest king called a Hierophant. The first Hierophant and his followers came from somewhere far across the Gathwayd Ocean over two thousand years ago. It's from them that your Dalna the Maker comes, along with Astellas and the others. They made their first landfall

on the Plenimaran peninsula. Benshâl, the capital city of Plenimar, stands on the site of the Hierophant's first city."

Alec's eyes narrowed skeptically at the thought of a city that
old, or his familiar patron deity having such exotic origins. He
kept his doubts to himself, though, not wanting to interrupt
the tale.

"Over the years, these people and their religion spread around
the Inner and Osiat seas, founding what eventually became
Mycena and Skala," Seregil went on.

"And it was these people who brought the worship of Dalna
north?"

"That's right. The Hierophant's people worshiped the Sacred
Four: Dalna the Maker and Astellus the Traveler, whom you
know; and Illior Lightbearer and Sakor of the Flame, who never
caught on up in these parts.

"But getting back to the subject at hand, the unity of the
Three Lands didn't last. As centuries passed the different regions
developed ways of their own. The Plenimarans, for instance,
stayed by the great Gathwayd Ocean, a body of water larger than
you've ever dreamed of. They're still great sailors and explorers.
It was the Plenimarans who sailed south beyond the Strait of Bal
to discover the Aurënfaie—"

"Hold on! Aurën*faie*? Like the Faie up beyond Ravensfell?"
Alec broke in excitedly, then felt his cheeks go warm as Seregil
chuckled.

"That's right. Your Elder Folk, properly called the Hâzadriëlfaie,
are said to be the descendants of a group of Aurënfaie who went
into the northern lands before the time of the Hierophant. Aurënen
lies south of the Three Lands, across the Osiat and beyond the
Ashek Mountains."

"Then the Aurënfaie aren't human, either?"

"No. *Faie,* in their tongue, means 'people' or 'belonging to,'
while *Aura* is their name for Illior; hence, *Aurënfaie,* the People
of Illior. But that's another story altogether—"

"But they *are* real?" Alec persisted; this was more than
Seregil had let on previously. "Have you ever seen any? What are
they like?"

Seregil smiled. "Not so different from you and me, really. No
pointy ears or tails, anyway. They're a handsome folk, for the
most part. The main difference between Aurënfaie and humans is
that the 'faie generally live for three or four hundred years."

"No!" Alec snorted, certain this time that his companion was pulling his leg.

"Think what you like, but that's what I've understood to be true. More important, however, is the fact that they were the first to possess magic. Not that they're all wizards, of course."

"But priests have magic," Alec interjected. "Especially the drysians. Long ago, when the Maker still lived among the people, Dalna came to a woman named Drysia and revealed to her all the secrets of the land and its proper use. The drysians can draw on the power of the earth and they know the secret uses of herbs and stones. Some even know the speech of beasts."

Seregil regarded him with that peculiar tilted grin again. "You've got a touch of the skald, too, I see. You're correct about priests having magic, but it's not the same as true wizardry. If you ever see a real wizard at work, you'll recognize the difference."

"So all wizards are really Aurënfaie?"

"Oh, nothing of the sort. But they did mix blood with the Tírfaie."

"Tírfaie?"

"Sorry. A good story teller should always know his audience. *Tírfaie* is the Aurënfaie word for outsiders. Roughly translated, it means 'the people of short lives.' "

"I guess they'd think so, if they live as long as you say," Alec allowed.

"Just so. Anyway, during the years when the Aurënfaie had open commerce with the Three Lands, the peoples mingled and many of the half-blood children were born with magic. Some stories even claim that Aura—or Illior, depending on which side of the Osiat you're from—sent a messenger in the form of a huge dragon to teach these half bloods how to use their powers."

"Dragons are real, too?" breathed Alec, more wide-eyed than ever.

Seregil grinned. "Don't get your hopes up. As far as I know, no one's seen a dragon in Skala since then."

"Skala? But I thought the Plenimarans were the ones who found the Aurënfaie."

"And I thought you hadn't heard this story before," Seregil countered dryly.

"I haven't, but you said that the Plenimarans—"

"They did, but the Aurënfaie got on best with the Skalans in the end. Most of those who stayed in the Three Lands settled there. But that was a very long time ago, more than eight hundred years. Eventually most of the Aurënfaie withdrew to their own land again."

"Why did they leave?"

Seregil spread his hands. "As with anything, there were many reasons. But their legacy remains. Wizard children are still being born and they still go to Rhíminee for training. That's the capital city of Skala, by the way."

"Rhíminee." Alec savored the exotic sound of it. "But what about the wizards? Have you ever seen one?"

"I know a few. We'd better get some sleep now. I suspect we've a hard few days ahead of us."

Although Seregil's expression scarcely changed, Alec sensed once again that he'd strayed into forbidden territory.

They settled down for the night, sharing what warmth they could beneath their blankets and cloaks as the wind wailed across the Downs.

The following morning Alec tried the coin catches again but his cold fingers were too stiff.

"As soon as we get to Wolde we'd better find you some gloves," said Seregil, hovering over their meager fire. He lifted his hands to show Alec the fine leather gloves he wore. He'd had them on yesterday, too, the boy realized. "Let me look at your hands."

Turning Alec's palms up, he clucked disapprovingly as he examined the cracks and calluses that covered them.

"Too much rough living. No delicacy of touch." Pulling off a glove, he slid his palm across Alec's. The skin was surprisingly smooth.

"I can tell gold from silver in the dark just by the feel of it. Looking at my hands, you'd think I'd never done a day's work in my life. But you! We could dress you up like a gentleman dandy and your hands would give you away before you ever opened your mouth."

"I doubt I'll ever have to worry about that. I like those tricks, though. Can you show me something else?"

"All right. Watch my hand." Without lifting his arm from where it rested across his knee, Seregil moved the fingers quickly in a smooth ripple, as if drumming briefly on an invisible tabletop.

"What's that?" Alec asked, mystified.

"I just told you to have the horses ready. And this—" He raised his right index finger as if to scratch under his chin, then looked slightly to the left, drawing the finger back a little toward his ear. "That means we're in danger from behind. Not every sign is that simple, of course, but once you learn the system you can communicate without anyone being the wiser. Say we were in a crowded room and I wanted to tell you something. I'd catch your eye, then lower my chin once just a bit, like this. Now you try it. No, that's too much. You might as well shout! Yes, that's better. Now the horse sign. Good!"

"Do you use this a lot?" asked Alec, trying the danger sign with indifferent results.

Seregil chuckled. "You'd be surprised."

They set off at a brisk canter. Seregil still found the terrain distressingly featureless, but Alec seemed to know what he was doing. Finding the spring the previous night had been heartening evidence of Alec's abilities as a guide and Seregil kept his doubts to himself.

Keeping one eye on the sky, the boy scanned the horizon for landmarks Seregil could only guess at. Left to himself, Alec was rather quiet by nature. There was nothing reticent or strained about it—he simply seemed content to concentrate on the business at hand.

This soon proved not to be the only thing on his mind, however. Reining in at another small spring just before noon, he turned to Seregil as if they'd only paused for breath in an ongoing conversation and asked, "Will you be working as a bard in Wolde?"

"Yes. Around the Woldesoke I go by the name Aren Windover. Perhaps you've heard of me?"

Alec gave him a skeptical look. "*You're* Aren Windover? I heard him sing last spring at the Fox, but I don't recall him looking like you."

"Well, I guess I don't look much like Rolan Silverleaf, either, just now."

"That's true," Alec admitted. "Just how many names do you go by, anyway?"

"Oh, whatever suits. And if you won't take my word that Aren and I are one and the same, I'll prove it. Which of my songs did you like the best?"

" 'The Lay of Araman,' " Alec answered at once. "The tune stuck in my head for weeks after but I could never remember all the verses."

" 'The Lay of Araman' it is, then." Seregil cleared his throat and launched into the song, his voice a rich, lilting tenor. After a moment Alec joined in. His voice wasn't as fine, but he could carry a tune.

> *"Across the sea sailed Araman,*
> *a hundred men he led.*
> *His ship was black as Death's left eye,*
> *her sails were deep bloodred.*
> *They sailed to Simra's distant shore*
> *to answer Honor's call.*
> *A hundred men sailed out to sea,*
> *but none sailed home at all.*
>
> *For Honor's price is blood and steel*
> *and Death will be your brother.*
> *A soldier's life is full of strife,*
> *but I swear I'd have no other!*
>
> *On the city walls stood King Mindar,*
> *he watched the ship draw nigh.*
> *Five hundred men were at his back*
> *and gave the battle cry.*
> *Then marched they to the battle plain*
> *to meet the seaborne foe,*
> *While Araman and his hundred men*
> *came all ashore below.*
>
> *For Honor's price is blood and steel*
> *and with your life you'll buy it.*
> *But the ladies love a fighting man*
> *and there's none that will deny it!*

Then Araman strode on the field
  and Mindar stepped to meet him.
'Your lying tongue has brought us here!'
  cried Araman to greet him.
'I see your force is greater,
  you have numbers on your side,
But by my sword, I'll see you dead
  'ere the turning of the tide.'

For Honor's price is blood and steel
  though flesh won't stop a sword.
The glory of a soldier's death
  will be your last reward!

Then on the plain the armies met
  and sword rang out on shield.
Helms were cloven, limbs were hacked,
  yet neither side would yield,
Until the generals found themselves
  alone upon the plain.
Six hundred soldiers, brave and bold,
  would never fight again.

For Honor's price is blood and steel
  and well the widows know
The worth of Honor to the lads
  now lying down below!

Then toe to toe and blade to blade
  the two fierce warriors fought.
To steal the heart's blood of his foe
  was each one's only thought.
From their wounds the blood flowed down
  to stain the trampled sward
And when the tide was turning
  Mindar fell to Araman's sword.

For Honor's price is blood and steel
  for churl and lord as well
And generals often lead their men
  down to the gates of hell!

Bold Araman, the victor now,
  lays his blade aside.
From his wounds his life flows out
  just like the sea's great tide.
The price of Honor paid in full
  with blood and steel and lives,
On an empty plain by an empty shore
  the rightful victor dies.

For Honor's price is blood and steel
  so harken well, my son.
Honor's a damned expensive thing
  if you're dead when the battle's won!"

"Well sung!" Seregil applauded. "With a good apprenticeship, you might make a passable bard yourself."

"Me?" Alec said with an embarrassed grin. "I can imagine what Father would have said to that!"

So can I, Seregil thought, having decided that the dead man must have been a pretty dour sort.

They passed much of the afternoon ride trading songs. As soon as Seregil discovered how Alec blushed at the bawdy ones, he made a special point of including plenty of those.

For two days they traveled hard and slept cold, but the time passed quickly. Seregil proved as fine a wayfaring companion as Alec could have hoped for, happy to fill the long hours of riding with tales, songs, and legends. The only subject he proved stubbornly reticent about was his own past, and Alec quickly learned not to press. Otherwise, however, they got on well enough. Alec was particularly intrigued by stories of life in the south.

"You never finished telling me about why the Three Lands fight so often," he said, hoping for another story after a particularly long silence that afternoon.

"I do tend to get sidetracked, don't I? What would you like to know?"

"About that priest king and all, I guess. It used to be all one country, you said, but now they're three. What happened?"

"Same thing that always happens when someone thinks someone else has more land and power than they do—there was a war.

"About a thousand years ago, the various territories got restless under Hierophantic rule. Hoping to hold his people together, the Hierophant granted them dominion, dividing them up into pretty much what are now Skala, Mycena, and Plenimar. Each had its own regent, appointed by him, of course.

"It was a logical split, geographically speaking, but unfortunately Plenimar got the short end of the stick. Skala controlled the sheltered plains below the Nimra Range. Mycena had fertile valleys and established outposts to the north. But Plenimar, earliest settled of the three, lay on a dry peninsula with diminishing resources. To make matters worse, the first rumors of gold soon came back from the north and Mycena controlled the routes. What Plenimar did have, though, were warriors and ships, and it wasn't long before they decided to use them. Just two centuries after the division, they attacked Mycena and started a war that lasted seventeen years."

"How long ago was this?"

"Nearly eight hundred years. Plenimar probably would've won, too, if Aurënen hadn't come into the fight in the last years."

"The Aurënfaie again!" Alec cried, delighted. "But why did they wait so long?"

Seregil shrugged. "The doings of the Tírfaie were of little concern to Aurënen. It was only when the fighting neared their own waters that they officially allied themselves with Skala and Mycena."

Alec thought a moment. "But if the other countries had all the gold and land and everything, how come they weren't stronger than Plenimar?"

"They should have been. The wizards of Skala were at the height of their powers then, too. Even the drysians were enlisted to the fight and, as I'm sure you can imagine, they are a force to be reckoned with when they want to be. Some old ballads speak of Plenimaran necromancers and armies of walking dead that could be driven back only by the strongest magicks. Whether or not these tales are true, it was the most terrible war ever fought."

"And Plenimar didn't win?"

"No, but they came close. In the spring of the fifteenth year of the war, Hierophant Estmar was killed; this sundered the Three Lands forever. Luckily, the black ships of Aurënen sailed through the Straits of Bal just after this and attacked at Benshâl, while the Aurënfaie army and their wizards joined the fighting at Cirna. Whether it was by magic or simply the force of fresh troops, the power of Plenimar was finally broken. At the Battle of Isil, Krycopt, the first Plenimaran ruler to call himself Overlord, was killed by the Skalan queen, Ghërilain the First."

"Hold on!" Reaching into his purse, Alec brought out the silver coin. "Is this her, the woman on the coin?"

"No, that's Idrilain the Second, the present queen."

Alec turned the coin over and pointed to the crescent and flame symbols. "And what do these mean?"

"The crescent stands for Illior; the flame above is for Sakor. Together they form the crest of Skala."

Skala! thought Alec as he tucked the coin away. *Well, at least I know now where you're from.*

3

SEREGIL MAKES AN OFFER

Their third morning on the Downs dawned clear.

Seregil woke first. It had snowed heavily the night before. Luckily, Alec had spotted an abandoned burrow just before sunset and they'd spent the night inside. The hole still stank of its former inhabitants, but it was large enough for the two of them to stretch out in. With the pack and Seregil's saddle jammed in the opening as a windbreak, they'd managed to keep warm for the first time since they'd come onto the Downs.

Cramped but warm, Seregil was tempted to let Alec's soft, even breathing lull him back to sleep. Looking down at him as he slept, he examined the planes of the boy's face.

Am I only seeing what I want to see? he wondered silently, feeling again the instinctual twinge of recognition. But there would be time for all that later; for now he had to concentrate on Wolde.

Giving Alec a nudge, he wriggled out of the burrow. Golden pink light washed across the unbroken expanse of snow surrounding them, its brightness dazzling after several days of sullen weather.

The horses were pawing at the snow in search of forage and Seregil's belly growled sympathetically at the sight; tired as he was of tough sausage and old cheese, this morning's scant breakfast would exhaust the last of the food.

"Thank the Maker for a sight of the sun!" Alec exclaimed, crawling out behind him.

"Thank Sakor, you mean," yawned Seregil, pushing his hair back from his eyes. "Of the Four— Oh, hell, it's too early for philosophy. Do you think we'll make Wolde today?"

Alec peered hard to the south, then nodded. "Before sundown, I'd say."

Seregil waded over to the horses and scratched his bay under the forelock. "Oats for you tonight, my friends, and a hot bath and supper for me. If our guide's worth his silver, that is."

Seregil was uncharacteristically quiet as they rode along that morning. When they stopped to rest the horses at midday, however, Alec sensed something was up. Seregil had that same bemused look about him that Alec remembered seeing when he'd offered to rescue him from Asengai's keep, as if he wasn't certain what he was about to do was the wisest move.

"The other night I joked about an apprenticeship for you," he said over his shoulder as he adjusted his saddle girth. "What do you think of the idea?"

Alec looked at him in surprise. "As a bard, you mean?"

"Perhaps apprenticeship isn't exactly the right term. I'm not a guildsman of any sort, much less a bard. But you're quick and smart. There's a lot I could teach you."

"Like what?" Alec asked, a little wary now but interested.

Seregil hesitated a moment, as if sizing him up, then said, "I specialize in the acquisition of goods and information."

Alec's heart sank. "You're a thief."

"I'm nothing of the sort!" Seregil frowned. "At least not in the sense you mean."

"Then what?" Alec demanded. "A spy like that Juggler fellow you killed?"

Seregil grinned. "I'd be insulted if I thought you knew what you were talking about. Let's just say for the moment that I'm acting as an agent of sorts, engaged by an eminently respectable gentleman to collect information regarding certain unusual occurrences here in the north. Discretion prevents me from saying more, but I assure you the goal is noble—even if my methods don't always seem so."

Hidden somewhere in his companion's suddenly high-flown, convoluted discourse, Alec suspected he'd just admitted to being a spy after all. Worse, he had nothing but Seregil's word that what he was telling, or half telling him, was the truth. Still, the fact remained that Seregil had rescued him when he could more easily have left him behind, and had since offered him nothing but friendship.

"I imagine you're already fairly skilled in tracking and that sort of thing," Seregil went on casually. "You say you're a fair shot with a bow, and you made good use of that ax, now that I think of it. Can you handle a sword?"

"No, but—"

"No matter, you'd learn quickly enough, with the right teacher. I know just the man. Then, of course, there'd be palming, etiquette, lock work, disguise, languages, heraldry, fighting—I don't suppose you can read?"

"I know the runes," Alec retorted, though in truth he could only make out his own name and a few words.

"No, no, I meant proper writing."

"Hold on, now," cried Alec, overwhelmed. "I don't mean to be ungrateful—you've saved my life and all, but—"

Seregil waved this aside impatiently. "Given the circumstances of your capture, getting you out of there seemed the least I could do. But now I'm talking about what *you* want, Alec, beyond tomorrow, beyond next week. Honestly, do you really mean to spend the rest of your life mucking out stalls for some fat innkeeper in Wolde?"

Alec hesitated. "I don't know. I mean, hunting and trapping, it's all the life I've known."

"All the more reason to give it up, then!" Seregil declared, his grey eyes alight with enthusiasm. "How old did you say you are?"

"Sixteen."

"And you've never seen a dragon."

"You know I haven't."

"Well, I have," Seregil said, swinging up into the saddle again.

"You said there weren't any more dragons!"

"I said there weren't any more in Skala. I've seen them flying under a full moon in winter. I've danced at the great Festival of

Sakor and tasted the wines of Zengat, and heard mermaids singing in the mists of dawn. I've walked the halls of a palace built in a time beyond memory and felt the touch of the first inhabitants against my skin. I'm not talking legend or imagination, Alec, I've done all of that, and more than I have breath to tell."

Alec rode along in silence, overwhelmed with half-realized images.

"You said you couldn't imagine yourself as anything more than what you've been," Seregil went on, "but I say you've just never had the chance to try. I'm offering you that chance. Ride south with me after Wolde, and see how much world there is beyond your forests."

"But the stealing part—"

Seregil's crooked grin held no trace of remorse. "Oh, I admit I've cut a purse or two in my time, and some of what I do could be called stealing depending on who you ask, but try to imagine the challenge of overcoming incredible obstacles to accomplish a noble purpose. Think of traveling to lands where legends walk the streets in daylight and even the color of the sea is like nothing you've ever seen! I ask you again, would you be plain Alec of Kerry all your life, or would you see what lies beyond?"

"But is it an honest living?" Alec persisted, clinging to his last shred of resolve.

"Most of those who employ me are great lords or nobles."

"It sounds like a pretty dangerous line of work," Alec remarked, aware that Seregil had once again side-stepped the question.

"That's the spice of it, though," cried Seregil. "And you can end up rich!"

"Or at the end of a rope?"

Seregil chuckled. "Have it your way."

Alec gnawed absently at a thumbnail, his brow creased in thought. "All right, then," he said at last. "I want to come with you, but first you've got to give me a few straight answers."

"It's against my nature, but I'll try."

"This war you spoke of, the one that's coming. Which side are you on?"

Seregil let out a long sigh. "Fair enough. My sympathies lie with Skala, but for your safety and mine, that's as much as I'll say on the matter for now."

Alec shook his head. "The Three Lands are so far away. It's hard to believe their wars could reach us here."

"People will do quite a lot for gold and land, and there's precious little of either left in the south, especially in Plenimar."

"And you're going to stop them?"

"Hardly," scoffed Seregil. "But I may be of some help to those who can. Anything else?"

"After Wolde, where would we go?"

"Well, home to Rhíminee ultimately, though first—"

"What?" Alec's eyes widened. "You mean to say that you live *there*? In the city where the wizards are?"

"What do you say?"

Some small, final doubt held Alec back a moment longer. Looking Seregil in the eye, he asked, "Why?"

Seregil raise one eyebrow, perplexed. "Why what?"

"You hardly know me. Why do you want me to come with you?"

"Who knows? Perhaps you remind me just a bit of—"

"Someone you used to know?" Alec interjected skeptically.

"Someone I used to *be*." The crooked grin flashed again as Seregil pulled off his right glove and extended his hand across to Alec. "So it's settled?"

"I guess so." Alec was surprised to catch a glimpse of what looked like relief in his companion's eyes as they clasped hands. It was gone in an instant and Seregil quickly moved on to new plans.

"There are a few details to take care of before we reach town. How well known are you in Wolde?"

"My father and I always stayed in the trader's quarter," replied Alec. "We generally put up at the Green Bough. Except for the landlord, though, most of the people we knew wouldn't be there this time of year."

"Just the same, there's no use taking chances. We'll need a reason for you to be traveling with Aren Windover. Here's a lesson for you; give me three reasons why Alec the Hunter would be in the company of a bard."

"Well, I guess I could tell how you rescued me and—"

"No, no, that won't do at all!" Seregil interrupted. "First of all, I don't want it known that I—or rather Aren—was anywhere near Asengai. Besides, I make it a rule never, never, *never* to use the truth unless it's the last possible option or so outlandish that nobody would believe you anyway. Keep that in mind."

"All right then," said Alec. "I could say I was attacked by bandits and you—"

Seregil shook his head, motioning for Alec to continue.

Alec fidgeted with the reins, sorting through various inspirations. "Well, I know it's sort of the truth, but people would believe that you hired me as a guide. Father and I hired out sometimes."

"Not bad. Go on."

"Or"—Alec turned to his companion with a triumphant grin—"perhaps Aren has taken me on as *his* apprentice!"

"Not bad, for a first effort," Seregil conceded. "The rescue story was very good, actually. Loyalty to one who saves your life is well understood and seldom questioned. Unfortunately Aren's reputation is such that nobody would believe it. I'm afraid he's a bit of a coward. The guide story, however, is seriously flawed. Aren Windover is a well-known figure in the Woldesoke; if bards make their living as wanderers, why would he need to engage a guide in the territory he's familiar with?"

"Oh." Alec nodded, a bit crestfallen.

"But the apprentice idea should do nicely. Luckily, you can sing. But can you think like a bard?"

"How do you mean?"

"Well, suppose you're in a tavern on the highroad. What sort of customers would you have?"

"Traders, wagoneers, soldiers."

"Excellent! And suppose there's a great deal of drinking going on and a song is called for. What would you choose?"

"Well, probably something like the 'The Lay of Araman.' "

"A good choice. And why?"

"Well, it's about fighting and honor; the soldiers would like that. And it's widely known, so everyone could join in. And it has a good refrain."

"Well done! Aren's used that song many times, and for just those reasons. Now suppose yourself a minstrel in a lord's hall, performing for fat barons and their ladies."

"Maybe 'Lillia and the Rose'? There's nothing coarse in it."

Laughing, Seregil leaned across to clap Alec on the shoulder. "Perhaps you should take Aren on as apprentice! I don't suppose you play an instrument?"

"Afraid not."

"Oh well. Aren will just have to apologize for your green skills."

They spent the rest of the afternoon extending Alec's repertoire as they rode along.

By late afternoon the Downs gave way to the rough, sloping terrain of the Brythwin River valley. In the distance they could make out the squares of bare fields and distant farmsteads that marked the boundary of the Woldesoke district. The river itself, a black, tree-fringed line far below, flowed into Blackwater Lake several miles east of the waterfront town. Bordered along its northern shore by the great Lake Wood, the shimmering expanse of water stretched unbroken to the far horizon.

"You say the Gathwayd Ocean is bigger than that?" asked Alec, shading his eyes. He'd hunted along the Lake's shores all his life and couldn't imagine anything larger.

"By quite a margin," replied Seregil cheerfully. "Let's move on before we lose the light."

The late-afternoon sun cast a mellow glow across the valley. Picking their way down the stony slope, they struck the main road leading along the river toward Wolde. The Brythwin was low, its course laced with gravel spits. Stands of ash and willow grew thickly along the banks, often screening the river from view.

A mile or so before reaching the lake shore, the road curved away from the river to skirt a dense copse of trees. Reining in, Seregil studied the wall of branches for a moment, then dismounted and motioned for Alec to follow.

Bare willow branches stroked over them, catching at hoods and harness as they pushed their way through to a clearing beside the river. A tiny stone cottage surrounded by a wattle and daub fence stood on a rise close by the water's edge.

As Seregil approached the gate a brindle hound came rushing at them from around the corner of the cottage, growling and showing its teeth. Alec retreated hastily back in the direction of his horse, but Seregil stood his ground. Muttering a few low words, he made some sort of sign with his left hand. The dog skidded to a halt on the other side of the gate, then skulked back the way it had come.

Alec gaped. "How did you do that?"

"Just a little thief's trick I picked up somewhere. Come on, it's perfectly safe."

A very old, very bald little man answered Seregil's knock.

"Who's that?" he demanded, peering blankly past them. A deep scar, faded white against the old fellow's leathery skin, ran in a ragged line from the top of his skull to the bridge of his nose.

"It's me, old father," Seregil replied, slipping something into his outstretched hand.

The old man reached to touch Seregil's face. "I thought as much when Crusher went quiet like that. And not alone this time, eh?"

"A new friend." Seregil guided the blind man's hand to Alec's cheek.

The boy remained still as the dry fingertips ran swiftly over his features. At no point were names exchanged.

The old fellow gave a rheumy chuckle. "Beardless, but no girl. Come in both of you, and welcome. Sit yourselves by the fire while I fetch something to eat. Everything's as you left it, sir."

The little house consisted of a single room with a loft overhead. Everything was neat and spare, the old man's simple belongings arranged with care on shelves along the walls.

Seregil and Alec warmed themselves gratefully at the cheerful blaze on the hearth while their host shuffled about with practiced efficiency, setting out bread, soup, and boiled eggs for them at the scrubbed wooden table.

Seregil wolfed his supper and disappeared into the loft. When he came down again he was dressed in a bard's embroidered tunic and striped hose. A traveler's harp of dark wood inlaid with silver was slung over his shoulder. He'd washed again, too, Alec noted in mild surprise. He'd never met anyone who set such store by washing.

"Do you recognize me now, boy?" Seregil asked in a haughty, slightly nasal voice, giving Alec an elaborate bow.

"By the Maker, you really are Aren Windover!"

"You see? What you remembered about Aren wasn't his face so much as his flamboyant manner, the gaudy clothes, and the affected way he spoke. Believe me, I do all that with good reason.

When you get right down to it, aside from the fact that Aren and I are physically identical, we're nothing alike at all."

Their host let out a dry cackle from his corner by the fire.

"As for your appearance," Seregil continued, "I've set out some things for you upstairs. Go clean yourself up, then we'll see about your hair. Aren would never allow any apprentice of his to look so unkempt."

The loft was as sparsely furnished as the room below, containing only a bed, washstand, and clothes chest. A dusty candle burned in a dusty sconce and by its light Alec saw a broadsword hanging on the wall above the bed, its scarred scabbard blackened with age. On the bed lay a tunic of russet wool, a new cloak, a pair of soft doeskin breeches, and a belt with a sheathed dagger and a pouch. Opening the latter, Alec found ten silver pennies. A pair of high leather boots sagged against the bedpost. Both clothing and boots were clean but worn—more of Seregil's castoffs, no doubt.

Lucky for me I met up with someone my own size, Alec thought, inspecting the boots more closely. As he'd expected, there was a dagger pocket stitched inside the left one. Pulling on the boots, he slipped his Skalan coin and five of the pennies into the knife pocket as a precaution against cutpurses; his father had taught him never to carry all his money in one place when he went into a town.

As he dressed, he could hear Seregil plucking away at the harp below. After a moment there came a light ripple of notes and scattered snatches of melodies.

He plays as well as he sings, thought Alec, wondering what other talents would reveal themselves as he got to know Seregil better. Below the music, however, he suddenly caught the sound of quiet conversation. After a moment's hesitation, he crept to the edge of the loft and strained to hear more. Both men were keeping their voices low and he could make out only bits and pieces.

". . . days ago. They seem peaceful enough, but why so many?" the blind man was saying.

"No doubt . . ." Seregil's voice was harder to hear. "I suppose, with the mayor."

"Aye, calling himself Boraneus, claims to be a trade envoy for the Overlord."

Overlord? thought Alec. He'd heard that term before! And hadn't Seregil as much as said he'd been sent north to see what the Plenimarans were up to? Holding his breath, Alec inched closer to the edge, trying to pick up the thread of the conversation.

"Did she know him?" Seregil was asking.

". . . last evening . . . dark, well favored . . . a sword cut . . ."

"Which eye?"

"Left, she said."

"Illior's Fingers! Mardus?" For an instant Seregil sounded genuinely startled. The old man muttered something, to which Seregil replied, "No, and I'll do my best to see that he doesn't . . . more demon than . . ."

Both men were silent for a moment, then Seregil called out, "Alec! Have you fallen asleep up there?"

Alec quickly rolled his old clothes into a bundle, then paused a moment longer for the guilty blush to pass.

The look that Seregil gave him as he hurried down the ladder betrayed only impatience, but he was certain he could feel Seregil's eyes on his back as he busied himself with packing away their traveling clothes.

Seregil tucked his harp under one arm and went to take leave of their host.

"Luck in the shadows," the blind man said, clasping hands with them at the door.

"And to you," Seregil returned.

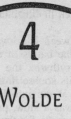

4

WOLDE

Wolde—largest of the isolated trade centers scattered across the northlands—owed its prosperity to the Gold Road, a narrow span of the Gallistrom River, and a tiny yellow flower.

The Gold Road began to the north in the foothills of the Ironheart Mountains, where gold had been mined from time out of mind. At Kerry, the precious metal was smelted and molded into round, flat ingots called baps and sewn into square sheepskin bales stuffed with wool. This wool, shorn from the mountain sheep native to the region, was especially soft and fine and had since become another source of wealth for the region. The original purpose of the bales, however, was merely to protect the gold, for the road was fraught with hazards, not the least of which were bandits. Weighing as much as two men, the bales were difficult to steal but floated if they were lost in one of the many rivers that crossed the route. Loaded onto ox-drawn wagons, the bales were carried on to Boersby, where they were packed onto flatboats and taken down the Folcwine to the Mycenian seaport of Nanta.

The country between Kerry and Boersby was desolate except for a few settled districts. The caravaneers traveled in large groups with hired swordsmen and archers to protect them.

The last safe refuge between Blackwater Lake and Boersby was the town of Wolde on the banks of the Gallistrom River.

Unlike the placid Brythwin, the Gallistrom was dangerous, deep, and broad. From its source in the Ironheart, it swept down through the great Lake Wood into Blackwater Lake. Originally the only safe crossing was a slow, precarious system of ferries. Wagons waiting on the shore for the next raft across were easy prey for bandits. Many others were lost to the river itself when strong spring currents overturned the rafts, sweeping away men, oxen, and gold.

At last a wide stone bridge was constructed and the tiny settlement that had sprung up around the ferry site grew into a village. The area had riches of its own, as it turned out. Dye-yielding plants of many sorts grew in profusion between the lake and the forest, among them the yellow wolde from which the town took its name. With these plants nearly any color could be produced, many in rich hues superior to anything produced in the south. Dyers, weavers, fullers, and felters set up shop there and suddenly the wool of Kerry was in great demand. Bolts of soft, lustrous "Wolde cloth" were now sought almost as eagerly in the south as the golden baps. By Alec's day, Wolde was a wealthy guild town centered around the bridge and protected by a stout wooden palisade.

The sun was nearing the western horizon when Alec and Seregil rode up the lake shore to the town walls. Across the water they could see the many colored sails of fishing boats making their way back to town for the night.

"It's early for the gates to be closed, isn't it?" remarked Seregil as they reined in. "Any time I've been here before they've been kept open until well after dark."

Alec looked the palisade over. "The walls are higher, too."

"State your names and business, if you please," a disinterested voice called from overhead.

"Aren Windover, a bard," Seregil announced, dropping into Aren's slightly pompous manner. "I am accompanied by my apprentice."

"Windover, is it?" The sentry leaned over the parapet for a better look at the newcomers. "Why, I remember you! You played at the summer fair and was the best of all the bards that come. Pass through, sir, and your boy."

A horse postern swung inward. Alec and Seregil ducked their

heads and rode inside. The sentry, a youngish man in a leather jerkin, extended a long-handled toll basket down to them.

"That's one copper a horse and a silver half penny for each rider, sir. We've not seen a proper bard or skald since you was here last, you know. Where'll you be staying this time through?"

"I mean to start at the Fishes, but hope for better before I leave," replied Seregil, motioning Alec to pay the toll. "By my recollection, it's early in the day for the gates to be locked. Aren't there more guards than usual?"

"That there is, sir," the man replied, shaking his head. "There's been three raids on the caravans within the last couple of months, two of 'em within ten miles of the town. The caravaneers are mad as scalded cats over it, claiming the town's supposed to guard the road. But the mayor, he's more worried about Wolde itself being attacked. We've been building up the palisade and standing extra watches ever since. It all seems to have calmed down, though, since them southerners showed up."

"Southerners?" Seregil's feigned surprise was not lost on Alec.

"Oh, aye. Plenimarans, of all people! An envoy called Lord Boraneus come to set up trade, as I hear it."

Boraneus? Alec stole a glance at Seregil; this was one of the names he'd picked up eavesdropping at the blind man's cottage—that and another, something starting with *M*.

"Brought a mess of soldiers with him, too," the gatekeeper went on. "Must be two score or more. We didn't know what to make of it when word first come that they was on the way, but it turned out to be a good thing. They made short work of them bandits, I can tell you! The taverners claim they're a rough lot, but they pay well, and in silver. I warrant you'll pick up a good piece of trade with 'em yourself."

"I have the greatest hopes." Throwing back his cloak, Seregil produced a silver coin from his own purse and flipped it to the man. "Thank you for your most helpful information. I hope you'll drink my health at the Three Fishes."

Pocketing the coin happily, the sentry waved them through.

Within the palisade the road wound through the center of the town toward a market square that spanned both sides of the bridge.

The streets here were stained with the colorful, foul-smelling runoff of dyers' shops. In the more prosperous lanes, raised wooden walkways had been built to prevent patrons from stain-

ing their garments with the mud. Gatherers' carts trundled from
shop to shop all day, loaded with shipments of pigment-bearing
plants and minerals. The poorest of children had bright rags on
their backs; even the pigs and dogs that wandered the neighborhood displayed a startling diversity of color. The clack and
thump of the weavers' looms filled the air and lengths of freshly
dyed cloth, hung to dry on racks strung between buildings and
over the streets, gave the area a perpetually festive appearance.

This was familiar territory to Alec, and he felt a twinge of
sadness as he looked around. The last time he'd been here his father had been alive.

"That's the mayor's hall there, where that Boraneus fellow is
staying," he said as they entered the open square at the center of
the town. Too late he recalled that his knowledge of Boraneus'
whereabouts had also been gleaned while eavesdropping.

Seregil looked over at him, an unreadable expression on his
face, and Alec added quickly, "Important visitors always lodge
with the mayor. It's the custom here."

"I'm lucky to have so well versed a guide," Seregil replied
with quiet amusement.

The large, elaborately decorated hall stood beside the Dalnan
temple. Guildhalls and craftsmen's shops lined the sides of the
square on this side of the bridge. The Temple of Astellus commanded the other side of the river, and with it the fishermen's
guild, a tavern, more shops, and several inns.

Seregil took the lead here, riding across the bridge into the
Lake Quarter. As they neared the waterfront, the streets grew
narrower and more winding. The stink of the dyers' quarter was
replaced by the pungent odors of fish and damp nets.

"Father and I never came down into this part of town," Alec
said, looking nervously around at the weathered building overhanging the street and the shadowed alleys between.

Seregil shrugged. "People know how to mind their own business here."

The taverns were coming alive now; the sounds of shouting
brawls and snatches of drunken song echoed from all directions.
Someone hissed a soft invitation to them from a shadowed doorway as they rode by. After several more turns, they came out at
the waterfront.

The palisades extended out into the water on both sides of the
town. Within their embrace lay long wharves, warehouses, and

taverns, all built on posts above the slope of the shingle. Looking out over the water, Alec again tried to imagine how big an ocean must be to outstrip this. On either side, the shore seemed to curve away endlessly, the far shore visibly only on the clearest of days.

Seregil hurried them along down the street to a narrow building squeezed in among the wharves. The sign over the open door displayed three intertwined fish, and from inside came the raucous clamor of a tavern crowd. A small knot of loafers had gathered beneath the windows with pipes and mugs.

Dismounting, he handed Alec his harp and pack.

"Mind the part I've given you," he whispered, keeping his voice low. "From here on you're the apprentice of Aren the Bard. You've seen what he's like; react accordingly. If I'm abrupt with you, or order you about like a servant, don't be resentful—it's Aren's way, not mine. Frankly, I don't envy your position. Ready?"

Alec nodded.

"Good. Then the act begins." With that, Seregil stepped back and became Aren.

"Take the horses to the stable around the side," he ordered, raising his voice for the benefit of the onlookers. "Make certain they're properly looked after. Then see the tavern keeper about a room. Tell him I'd have the one at the top of the house, overlooking the lake, and don't let that villain charge you more than a silver mark for it, either! When you've taken care of the baggage, bring my harp to the common room. Be quick, now."

With this, he disappeared into the warmth of the tavern.

"By the Old Sailor, I guess you been told, boy!" laughed one of the loiterers, much to the amusement of his cronies.

Scowling, Alec led the horses around to the stable. In spite of Seregil's hasty explanation, he wasn't sure he liked this turn of events. When the horses had been seen to, he gathered up the pack and Seregil's saddle and hurried into the steamy bustle of the kitchen.

"I'm looking for the tavern keeper," he said, catching a harried serving girl by the sleeve.

"Taproom," she snapped, nodding curtly toward a nearby doorway. Leaving the gear by the door, he went on into the taproom and found himself faced with a portly, red-faced giant in a leather apron.

"I need lodgings for my master and myself," Alec informed him, endeavoring to imitate Aren's imperious manner.

The taverner scarcely looked up from the tapping of a fresh barrel. "Big room at the top of the stairs. Shouldn't be no more than three or four to a bed tonight."

"My master prefers the room at the top," Alec said.

"Does he indeed? Well, he may have it for three marks a night."

"I'll give you one," Alec countered. "We'll be here for several nights and I'm certain my master—"

"Your master be damned!" the taverner growled. "That's my best room, and I couldn't let the mayor himself nor the whole of the damned Guild Council have it for less than three! Not when there's all these southern strangers lolling about with more money than brains. I could get five a night from any one of them."

"Begging your pardon," Alec chose his words with care, "but I think my master, Aren Windover, and I could bring you in ten times that each night we're here."

Satisfied with the set of the tap, the taverner shoved his hands into his belt and glowered down at Alec. "Well! Begging *your* pardon, my young whelp, but just how do you think you could do that?"

Alec held his ground stubbornly; his father'd had a knack for dickering. Thinking back, he asked, "Do you make more profit from your rooms or your ale?"

"From the ale, I suppose."

"And how much do you charge for that?"

"Five coppers for a flagon, a half silver for a jug. What of it?"

Sensing the man's growing impatience, Alec quickly came to the point. "What you need, then, is something to attract men to drink. And what attracts drinking men more than a good bard? You may not know Aren Windover, but a good many in town do. You put it about that he's playing at your tavern and I think you'll have to send out for more ale. I can probably coax a few soldiers in here, and they'll bring their friends the next night. You know how fighting men can drink!"

"Aye, used to be one m'self," the tavern keeper nodded, looking Alec up and down. "Come to think of it, I believe I have heard of this Windover chap. He's the one drew such a crowd over at the Stag and Branch last year. Perhaps I could let you have the room for two and a half."

"I can pay in advance," Alec assured him. Then carried away with the success of his own invention, he added for good measure, "Master Windover is to play for the mayor, you see."

"The mayor, eh?" the tavern keeper grunted in surprise. "Why didn't you say so! Playing at the mayor's, and the Fishes as well? All right, then. Go and tell your master that the room is his for two marks."

"Well—" Alec mused stubbornly.

"Damn you, do you want my blood? One and a half, then, but I've got to make a profit, don't you see?"

"Done," Alec conceded. "But that does include candles and supper, right? And the bed linens had better be fresh! Master Windover is very particular about his bed linens."

"You do want my blood," the landlord growled. "Yes, yes, he'll get his dinner and he'll get his cursed bed linens. But by the Old Sailor, he better be all you say or the fishermen will have the pair of you for bait."

Alec paid out two nights in advance for good faith, then toiled upstairs balancing their gear and a candlestick.

Passing the common sleeping room on the second floor, he climbed a steeper stairway to the attic. A short, windowless corridor led to a door at the far end.

Tucked in the peak of a gable, the room Seregil had specified was small, with sloping walls on either side. The narrow bed and washstand nearly filled the cramped space. Alec found a cheap tallow candle in a cracked dish on the stand and lit it from his own, then pushed back the shutters of the window over the bed. The back of the tavern stood out over the water on pilings. Looking out, Alec found a sheer drop down to the water below.

A thick crescent moon cast a glittering trail across the lake's black surface. It was pleasant up here at the top of the house, quiet and warm. It occurred to Alec that he could probably count on one hand the times he had ever been alone inside a proper house, and never in a room so high. After pausing a moment to savor the new sensation, he sighed and headed back down the stairs.

Looking out over the noisy commotion of the tavern, he spotted Seregil talking with the host and was struck once more by the difference between "Aren" and Seregil; their movements, their stance, the set of their mouth, all as distinct as if they really were two separate men.

Seregil glanced up just then and motioned impatiently for him to come. Dodging past servers with flagons and wooden trenchers, Alec made his way through the crowd.

"Of course, we have only just arrived in town," Seregil was saying, "but I shall present myself to your most honored mayor tomorrow." Coughing delicately into his fist, he added, "I seem to have taken sore in the throat today, but I'm certain a night's rest will repair my voice. In the meantime, I am certain that you will be pleased with my apprentice's abilities."

The landlord darkened noticeably at this, and Alec gave Seregil a startled glance, which he pointedly ignored.

"You mustn't fear," Seregil went on airily. "This lad is constantly surprising me with his rapid progress. Tonight you shall have a demonstration of his talents."

"We shall see, Master Windover," the taverner growled doubtfully. "Your boy claims he'll be good for business, so the sooner you start, the better."

Though he made a sort of bow to Seregil, Alec was certain he caught a glint of malevolent humor in the man's eye as he left.

"You've been busy," Seregil remarked dryly as he checked the tuning of his harp. The crowd shifted restlessly around them, anticipating entertainment.

"There's nothing wrong with your voice!" Alec whispered in alarm.

"There are a few things I need to do tonight that don't allow me to be the center of attention for the whole evening. You'll be fine, don't worry. I understand you beat our landlord down to one and a half for the room. I didn't think you'd bring the old robber down below two. I *am* curious, however, as to how you propose to bring in Plenimarans."

"I don't know," Alec admitted, "it just seemed like a good thing to tell him at the time."

"Well, hopefully we'll be on our way before we have to keep too many of your promises. But in case we're not, a word of caution—stay clear of the soldiers, especially if you're out alone. These are Plenimaran marines, and there's not much most of them aren't capable of, if you take my meaning."

"I don't think I do," said Alec, puzzled by Seregil's tone.

"Then try this. They have a saying among them: 'When whores are few, a boy will do.' Got that?"

"Oh." Alec felt his face go hot.

"Anyway, consider yourself warned. Now I think it's time for you to prove yourself, my bardling."

Seregil rose and cleared his throat before Alec could make further objections.

"Good people," he announced, gesturing for their attention. "I am Aren Windover, a humble bard, and this lad is my apprentice. While journeying to reach your fair town, I fear I have contracted a temporary inflammation of the throat. Nonetheless, I pray you will allow us to offer you entertainment."

He resumed his seat amid enthusiastic cheering and pounding of mugs. Favorite ballads were called for, and more ale.

Alec's mouth went dry as a roomful of expectant faces turned his way. He'd sometimes been a member of such gatherings, but never the focus of one.

Seregil passed him a mug of ale with a mischievous wink.

"Don't worry about this lot," he whispered, "they've got full bellies and half-empty jugs."

Alec took a long swallow and managed a weak grin in return.

Seregil knew the extent of Alec's repertoire and chose requests accordingly, striking up first with "Far Across the Water Lies My Love."

Alec's voice, though hardly of bardic quality, was good enough for this audience. He sang all the fishermen's songs he knew, and made a passable job of several of the story ballads Seregil had taught him on the Downs. This, together with Seregil's excellent playing, soon endeared them to the crowd. When his voice began to weaken Seregil pulled out a tin whistle and struck up a dance tune for variety.

More customers appeared as word spread, pushing in and calling for ale and songs. Among the newcomers were half a dozen men in brigandine leather armor and brimmed helmets. Heavy swords were slung from their belts. Alec didn't need Seregil to point these out as the marines he'd been warned against. They looked like rough customers.

Alec sang for over an hour before Seregil stopped to beg leave for a small rest.

"Stay and mind the harp," he told Alec, thrusting the instrument into the boy's hands. "And see that you get some water to wet your throat with. Ale's good for the spirit but bad for the voice. You're doing splendidly!"

"But where are—"

"I'll be back soon."

Alec watched as Seregil made his way toward the far corner of the room where a tall, broad-shouldered man sat by himself. The fellow's face was shadowed by a deep hood, but by his worn leather cuirass and the long sword at his belt Alec guessed he made his living as a caravan guard. Seregil exchanged greetings with the stranger and was invited to join him on the bench. They were soon deep in conversation.

Having clearly been dismissed for the moment, Alec let his gaze wander over the rest of the crowd and discovered a drysian sitting near the door. Distinguished by her plain robe and the bronze serpent lemniscate pendant she wore on a leather thong around her neck, she was already surrounded by a small crowd of people seeking healing. They stood quietly, watching with a mixture of hope and awe as she examined an infant lying on her lap. Curious as ever, Alec headed over to join them.

The dark braid that fell over her shoulder as she leaned forward was well streaked with grey, her weathered face set in stern lines, but her hands were steady and gentle as she examined the baby. She ran her hands over the little body, then lifted the child and put her ear to its chest and belly. Grasping the staff that leaned against the bench at her side, she spoke a few soft words over the child, then handed it back to its mother.

"Boil one of these in a cup of clear water each morning," she instructed, counting out six dried leaves from a pouch at her belt. "Add a little honey and some milk. Cool it and give it to her through the day. When the last leaf is gone, the child will be well. On that day place three copper marks on the altar at Dalna's Temple and give thanks. You will give me one mark now and the Maker's Mercy be with you."

She then went on to deal with the others, sometimes dispensing herbs or charms, sometimes merely praying over the sufferer. Several fishermen ventured near when she had finished with the children, and finally a wealthy merchant couple who timidly presented their young daughter. After the usual examination, the drysian gave the mother a bunch of herbs and charged her to give a silver offering rather than copper, as she had all the others. Without a word, the husband paid her the money and the family left.

Alec was about to turn away when the drysian looked straight at him and asked, "Why do you suppose I charged them more?"

"I—I don't know," Alec stammered.

"Because they could afford to pay more," she stated, and startled him further by giving him a knowing wink. "Perhaps I could be of some service to your master. You're lodging here tonight?"

"Yes, in the room at the top," Alec replied, wondering what she would make of Seregil's sham illness. "Can I tell him your name?"

"That won't be necessary. Tell him I'll attend to him later."

She stood to stretch and her staff slid sideways, clattering to the floor. Without thinking, Alec retrieved it and held it out to her. In the brief moment that both their hands were on it, he felt a strong and not altogether pleasant tremor pass through the wood.

"The blessings of the Maker be with you this night," she said and disappeared into the crowd.

The singing went on until midnight. Though Alec's modest repertoire was exhausted long before that, the drinkers called on Seregil to keep playing and a number of them stood to lead the song. When at last the owner announced that he must put the shutters up, the crowd gave the bard and his apprentice a rousing round of applause and most left a coin or two on the table near the door. Well pleased with his investment, the taverner poured them each a final mug of ale and, drinks in hand, they went upstairs.

Collapsing on the bed, Seregil inspected the night's earnings and passed half the coins to Alec. "We did well. Thirty coppers, two silver. You met Erisa, I noticed."

"Who?"

"The drysian. What do you make of her?"

"She seemed like any of the others. Sort of—" He paused, seeking the proper word.

"Unsettling?"

"Yes, that's it. Not frightening, just unsettling."

"Believe me, drysians can be pretty damn frightening when they choose to." Before he could expound on the subject, however, the latch lifted and Erisa herself slipped quietly in.

"I thought you'd keep the poor lad at it all night," she scolded. "I suspect you're not really in need of my ministrations?"

Seregil shrugged, grinning crookedly. "I could hardly expect to fool you. Alec, run down to the kitchen, will you? We both need something to eat after all that ale, and I'm certain Erisa's had no time for supper."

"Just tea and a little bread for me," said Erisa, folding her arms. Clearly they were both waiting for him to leave.

Ordered about again! he thought as the door closed firmly behind him. He was more intrigued than irritated, however. This drysian must be the mysterious "she" spoken of by the blind man, but who was the hooded swordsman?

Halfway down the passage he hesitated, then crept back as silently as he could to the door.

"A force of fifty was reported heading into the Western Barrens above Wyvern Dug," Erisa was saying. "Connel spotted them near Enly Ford on the seventh of Erasin, but there's been no sign of them since."

"I can understand them courting the mountain lords and trying to get a hold on the Gold Road," said Seregil, "but there's nothing in that direction but a few barbaric tribes. What in the world are they after up there?"

"That's what Connel hoped to learn. He set out to follow them as soon as we heard what was going on. Unfortunately, nothing's been heard from him, either— Alec, please do hurry with my tea."

An unpleasant tingling sensation that had nothing to do with the burning of his cheeks engulfed Alec briefly as he hurried downstairs. He took his time heating the water, dreading having to face her again. When he returned to the room, however, she simply thanked him and took her leave.

"Well now, this is a good enough bed, but only wide enough for one. Where are you going to sleep?" Seregil yawned, stripping off his tunic. Apparently he had nothing to say on the subject of Alec's eavesdropping.

"As your apprentice, I guess I'd be expected to sleep in the stable," Alec ventured, not relishing the prospect.

"You're thinking like a tinker's brat. What good would you be to me out there? Your place is in front of the door in case we have any visitors in the night. Make yourself a pallet."

As they settled down to sleep, Alec found himself thinking of the drysian again.

"Have you known her long?" he asked, looking up into the darkness.

"Erisa? Oh, yes."

It became evident after a moment's silence that Seregil considered this sufficient reply. Alec decided to press on.

"How did you meet her?"

For a moment he thought Seregil had gone to sleep or was refusing to answer, but then he heard the bed ropes creak.

"I had business at Alderis," Seregil told him. "That's in Mycena, near the coast. It was a difficult job and I was new at my trade, very young. Anyway, I botched it and got caught. My captors expressed their displeasure most emphatically and discarded what was left of me rather far from the town. They thought I was dead; I remember having a few doubts on the matter myself. When I woke up several days later, I was in a hut and there was Erisa."

"I'll bet she has powers beyond just healing," Alec said, remembering the sharp tingle from her staff.

"She can control people if she chooses. I've seen her do it, though she dislikes the power for the most part. I'll tell you something, though. She's saved my life several times, and I hers, but I'm a little nervous around her. You seldom know what a drysian's thinking, or how they see things."

"She knew I was listening."

Seregil chuckled in the darkness. "She'd have known if *I* was listening. Don't worry, you do it very well for a beginner. Now you'd better get some rest. We have a busy day tomorrow. You need outfitting, and I want a good look at those soldiers."

Alec heard the bed creak again. Below their window, waves lapped softly at the pilings, lulling him into a comfortable doze. He was just drifting off when Seregil's sudden laugh startled him awake again.

"And you've got us singing for the mayor!"

5

FRIENDS MET, ENEMIES MADE

Alec sat up blinking as Seregil threw open the shutters early the next morning. Cold air and early sunlight flooded the room.

"I doubt you'd have heard a prowler in the night, but you blocked the door nicely," Seregil observed, tucking his harp under his arm. "While you've been snoring the morning away, I've been thinking. Your idea of singing for the mayor was an inspiration. That's where this Boraneus fellow is staying, after all. I have a few things to attend to at the market. Find yourself something to eat and meet me there later so we can see about getting you properly outfitted. Look for me at the swordsmith Maklin's in an hour if you don't see me sooner. Now out of my way!"

As soon as he was gone Alec rose and pulled on his boots. Outside, the sun shone across the calm surface of the lake, shimmering around the distant sails that dotted the waters to the horizon.

Anxious as he was to catch up with Seregil, the scents of porridge and frying sausage that met him as he hurried downstairs were too good not to investigate.

"You're the bard's 'prentice, ain't you?" a woman asked as he paused in the doorway. "Come in, lad! Your master was just here and said I was to see you have all you want."

Seregil must have been generous, Alec thought as she piled his trencher with plump sausages and oat porridge, then fetched a pitcher of milk and some hot ash cakes to go with it.

"However did you get so thin with a master as kind as that, eh?" She smiled, watching with satisfaction as Alec tucked in to her cooking.

"He only just took me up," Alec told her around a mouthful. "I had some hard times before."

"Well, you stick by him, love. He'll make an honest fellow of you."

Alec nodded agreeably, though he still had certain reservations on the matter. Leaving a coin of his own on the table when he'd finished, he set off for the market.

"All I have to do is go back the way we came in last night," he told himself, setting off on foot. But for all his skill in the wilds, Alec had always found towns rather baffling. One narrow, twisting street looked very much like another in daylight and before long he was so turned around he couldn't even find his way back to the waterfront. Cursing all towns and those who built them, he gave up and decided to ask directions.

Unfortunately, there were few people about. The fishermen had long since gone out, and most of their women were at the market at this hour, or indoors behind their shutters. He'd passed several gangs of children earlier, but the street he found himself in now came to a dead end in a cluster of warehouses and was quite deserted. Nothing to do, it seemed, but retrace his steps and hope for the best.

Turning a corner, he spotted a tavern and decided to try his luck there. He'd almost reached it when the door swung open and a knot of Plenimaran marines spilled unsteadily out into the street. There were five of them, staggering and singing drunkenly in their foreign tongue. Spotting Alec before he could duck back out of sight, they ambled over in his direction.

Giving them a polite nod, Alec tried to hurry past but one caught the edge of his cloak and yanked him roughly into their midst. His captor, a round-faced man with a scar twisting his lower lip, rattled off some sort of challenge, punctuating it by poking Alec in the chest with his finger.

"Stupid drinker!" a taller fellow with a black beard growled, pushing Scar-Lip away and throwing an arm heavily around

Alec's shoulders. His accent was thick but he made himself understood. "What my Soldier Brother says, you is a likely looking man-child to be a marine. Why you don't join us up?"

"I don't think I'd make much of a soldier," Alec replied. Several of them casually felt their daggers. "What I mean is, I'm not old enough, big enough—like you!"

A one-eyed soldier fingered the sleeve of Alec's tunic. "Nice, nice. You too good be Soldier Brother?"

"No!" Alec cried, turning within the circle of men. "I respect Soldier Brothers. Brave men! Let me buy you a drink."

Without warning, One-Eye and Round-Face pinioned his arms. The bearded soldier tore Alec's purse from his belt, emptying the contents into his hand.

"Sure, you buy us all many drinks!" he said, grinning as he inspected the coins. Suddenly his face darkened, and he thrust something up before Alec's eyes.

It was the Skalan coin; he'd had it out the night before and forgotten to put it back in his boot.

"Where you got this, man-child?" the bearded Plenimaran snarled. "You don't look no filthy Skalan! What you do having filthy bitch queen money?"

Before Alec could answer, the man punched him hard in the stomach and spat out, "Filthy spy, maybe?"

Maker's Mercy, not that again!

Gasping for breath, Alec doubled over and they knocked him down into the half-frozen mud of the street. Someone kicked him in the back and his vision blurred with dazzling sparks of pain. Struggling up onto his knees, he prayed that his cloak hid the motion of his hand as he reached for his dagger.

"You, Tildus! It's early in the day to be out torturing children, isn't it?"

Alec couldn't see who'd spoken, but the man's deep voice carried a welcome north country accent. The marines paused in their sport as the bearded man turned.

"Micum Cavish, greetings! Not torturing at all, just questioning spy."

"That's no spy, you damned fool, that's my brother's son. Let him go before you strain our friendship!"

Astonished, Alec craned his neck for a better look at this Micum Cavish. Catching sight of the man, he began to understand.

Cavish was the hooded man Seregil had spoken with the night before. The hood was thrown back now to reveal a freckled, strongly featured face under a thick mane of auburn hair. Heavy reddish brows overshadowed his pale blue eyes, and an even heavier mustache drooped over the corners of his mouth. His stance was relaxed, but his right hand, hooked casually into his belt, was in easy reach of his sword hilt. The fate he was out-numbered five to one was apparently not of the slightest concern to him.

"You must forgive," Tildus was saying, "there is much drink in us. When we see money of the bitch queen here, we get mad, you see?"

"Since when does a single coin make anyone a spy?" Micum Cavish's tone was bantering, but his hand remained at his belt. "He got himself 'prenticed to a bard not long ago. They pick up all kinds of coins along the caravan route. Up here silver's silver, no matter whose face it has on it."

"Mistake, eh?" Tildus grinned tightly, motioning for the others to get Alec on his feet. "Not hurt so much, eh, man-child? You singer, maybe we come hear you sing. Give you good Plenimaran silver! Come, Brothers, we sober up now and not get into some more trouble." With that he gathered his glowering men and lurched off down the alley.

"Thanks," Alec said as they gathered his strewn money. At closer range, he was surprised to see that the man's hair was sprinkled with silver around the temples. "So you're my uncle Micum?"

The big swordsman grinned. "First thing that came to mind. It's lucky I happened along when I did, too. That Tildus is a nasty bastard to begin with, and worse when he's drinking. What are you doing wandering around here alone?"

"I was heading for the market, but I got lost."

"Just go back up the street, turn left and keep straight 'til you get there." Favoring Alec with a knowing wink, he said, "I think you'll find Aren at the second tailor's to the right of the corner."

"Thanks again," Alec called after him as Micum strode away. The tall man raised his hand in a brief salute and disappeared around the corner.

● ● ●

Alec found Seregil busy haggling over the price of some tunics. Taking in Alec's disheveled appearance, he broke off quickly and stepped away from the booth.

"What have you been up to?"

Alec's tale was quickly told. Seregil raised an eyebrow at the mention of Micum's intervention but made no further comment.

"There's a good deal of activity in the square today," he told Alec. "Seems we got here just in time. The Plenimarans are leaving tomorrow and the mayor is holding a banquet tonight in their honor, quite a grand affair. He is, however, somewhat at a loss for entertainment. I've just been working out a way to make myself conspicuous."

"What are you going to do, sing on the steps of his house?"

"Nothing so obvious. There's a very pleasant fountain right across the street from it. I think that's close enough, don't you?"

He concluded his business with the tailor and they set off across the bridge to Armorers Street.

The clamor of hammer on metal there was almost more than Alec could stand, but as they came abreast of a bowyer's shop, he paused, face brightening noticeably.

"I don't know much about that sort of thing, but I've heard Corda's the best," Seregil remarked.

Alec shrugged, not taking his eyes from the display of bows. "Corda's are fancy enough, but they don't have the range of Radly's. Either way, though, they're beyond my means. I'd like to stop in at Tallman's, if you don't mind. I don't feel comfortable traveling without a bow."

"Certainly, but first I want to see Maklin about a sword."

Somewhere behind the front room of the swordsmith's shop, hammers rang down on steel and Alec had to resist the impulse to put his fingers in his ears. Seregil, however, poked happily through the gleaming collection of swords and knives that covered the walls. Most of these weapons were the swordsmith's own work, but one section was given over to an assortment of older weapons traded in for new. Seregil paused to look these over, pointing out those of antique or foreign design, as well as certain clever modifications. Alec could scarcely hear him.

Mercifully, the din lessened suddenly as a portly man in a stained leather apron stepped in through a doorway at the back of the shop, shouting a greeting to Seregil.

"Well met, Master Windover! What can I do for you today?"

"Well met, Master Maklin," Seregil shouted back. "I need a blade for my young friend here."

"For me?" Alec asked in surprise. "But I told you—"

The swordsmith turned an appraising eye on Alec. "Ever held a sword before, lad?"

"No."

Pulling out a set of calipers, the smith set about measuring Alec's various dimensions. Kneading his arm muscles with a serious expression, Maklin bellowed, "I've just the thing for him!" and disappeared into the workshop again. He returned with a sheathed long sword cradled in the crook of one arm. Presenting the hilt to Alec, he motioned for him to draw it.

"He has the height and span to wield it," Maklin remarked to Seregil. "It's a good blade, well balanced and easy to cast about with. I made it special for a caravaneer, but the bugger never called back for it. Not overly fancy, but it's a lovely bit of steel. I slaked it in bull's blood during the forging, and you know there's nothing finer than that short of magicking."

Even Alec could see that the swordsmith was being modest. The gleaming blade felt like a natural extension of his arm. It wasn't light, but he felt a certain natural flow to the movements as Maklin had him hold his arm this way and that. The hilt was wire-bound, with a round, burnished pommel. The bronze quillons arched gently away from the hilt, terminating in small flattened knobs carved to look like the tightly curled head of an unopened fern. The blade was unadorned but mirrored the light with a faintly bluish sheen.

"A pleasing design," Seregil remarked, taking the sword in his hands and fingering the quillons. "Not fancy, as you said, but not cheap-plain, either. See how the quillons curve away from the grip, Alec? Just the thing to snap your enemy's sword out of his hand or break his blade, if you know what you're doing."

Drawing his own sword, he held the two up together to show Alec the similarity between them. For the first time Alec noted that the quillons of Seregil's weapon, which ended in worn dragon's heads, were notched and scarred with use.

"It's a fine blade, Maklin. How much?" asked Seregil.

"Fifty marks with the sheath," the smith replied.

Seregil paid his price without quibbling and Maklin threw in a sword belt, showing Alec how to wrap it twice around his waist and fix the lacings so that the blade hung at the proper angle against his left hip.

Back in the street again, Alec tried to thank Seregil.

"One way or another, you'll repay me," Seregil said, brushing the matter aside. "For now, just promise me that you won't draw it in public until you've learned how to use it. You hold it just well enough for someone to give you a fight."

As they passed the bowyer shops again, Seregil paused in front of Radly's.

"There's no point going in there," Alec told him. "A good Radly bow costs as much as this sword."

"Are they worth it?"

"Well, yes."

"Then come on. If it comes down to you protecting our lives with it, I for one don't want you using some three-penny stick."

Alec's heart beat a bit faster as they entered the shop. His father, a competent bowyer himself, had often pointed the place out with uncommon reverence. Master Radly, he'd told his son, had gifts beyond the natural for bow making. Alec had never imagined that he'd enter the place as a customer.

The master bowyer, a stern, grizzled man, was instructing an apprentice in the finer points of fletching as they came in. Inviting them to look about for a moment, he continued on with his instruction.

Alec was in his element here, inspecting the array of bows with the same relish that Seregil had obviously felt at the swordsmith's.

Great longbows, six feet tall unstrung, hung on cords from the ceiling. Crossbows of various types were displayed on wide shelves, along with lady's hunters, composite horse bows—nearly every type common in the north. But Alec's eye settled on those known simply as the Black Radly.

Somewhat shorter than the regular longbow, these were fashioned from the Lake Wood's black yew, a difficult wood to work. Less experienced bowyers were likely to ruin half a dozen staves for every bow they came out with, but Radly and his apprentices had the knack. Rubbed with oil and beeswax, the black bows gleamed like polished horn.

Seven of these lay on a long table in the center of the shop and Alec inspected each one, checking the straightness of the tapered limbs, the smoothness of the nocks and the ivory maker's plate set flush into the back of the grip. Then, choosing one, he grasped it on either side of the grip and twisted sharply; the lower limb of the bow came free in his hand.

"What are you doing?" Seregil hissed in alarm.

"It's a wayfarer's bow." Alec showed Seregil the steel ferrule on the end of the limb, with its tiny pin that locked in place inside the sheath of the hand grip. "They're easier to carry in rough country, or riding."

"Easier to conceal, too," Seregil noted, fitting the sections back together. "Is it as powerful as a longbow?"

"They can have better than eighty pounds pull, depending on the length."

"And what, pray tell, does that mean?"

Alec picked up another bow and held it out in front of him as if to draw. "It means that if you could get two men to stand one in front of the other, you could shoot a broadhead arrow through the both of them. These'll take down most anything from a hare to a stag. I've heard they can even shoot through chainmail."

"They'll draw heart's blood from a brass weathercock!" said Radly, joining them at last. "Sounds like you know something of archery, young sir. What do you think of 'em?"

"I like these." Alec indicated the two he'd laid aside. "But I'm not certain on the length."

"We'd best check your draw," Radly said.

Alec held out the bow and drew an invisible string back to his ear while the bowyer stretched a measuring line between the back of his left forefinger and the angle of his jaw below his right eye.

"Either of these would do for you," Radly concluded, "or that there." He pointed to one on the table that Alec had passed over.

"I'll go with these two," Alec said, sticking by his first choice.

Radly held the bows up side by side. "Have a look at the plates."

The shop mark, a black yew scrimshawed into the ivory, seemed almost identical until he pointed out a tiny "R" visible in the crown of the tree on both of Alec's choices, indicating that they were the work of the master bowyer and not one of his assistants.

"You've a good eye for a youngster," said the bowyer. "Come and try them."

Radly strung the bows, then led the way out through the workshop and into the alley beyond.

At the far end, several targets had been set up. The first was a simple bull's-eye painted on a cross section of a large log. The second was another bull, but to reach the center of it the arrow had to pass straight through three iron rings hung from wickets between the target and the archer. The last was simply eight long willow wands stuck upright in the ground.

"What's all this?" Seregil whispered as the bowyer went to adjust the wands.

"I've heard it said that he won't sell a Black to anyone who can't hit all three targets," Alec whispered back, strapping a leather guard to his left forearm.

Returning, Radly handed him a quiver of arrows. "Now then, let's see you shoot."

Selecting his first shaft with care, Alec sent it straight into the center of the first bull. Using the second bow, he repeated the feat easily, shaving some of the fletching off the first shaft.

At the next target, his first arrow glanced off a ring and fell short. Looking up at the clear blue sky, he drew in a deep breath, letting the necessary calm flow through him. On the second try he shot true, then repeated the shot just to be sure. Switching to the other bow, he made three clean shots in quick succession.

It was a good day for shooting, he decided, relaxing into the almost supernatural sense of calm and well-being that came over him at such times. Moving to face the last target, he let fly four arrows in quick succession, hitting every other wand and nipping each off at nearly the same height.

Behind him, Seregil let out a low whistle of appreciation, but Alec kept his eye on the targets.

Changing bows, he quickly hit the remaining wands, shearing them off at a different height. As he lowered the bow, applause erupted behind him and he turned to find Seregil, Radly, and several apprentices grinning approval.

Blushing, he muttered, "I guess I'll take this one."

Seregil's afternoon foray was a success; he returned with the news that they were to entertain at the mayor's banquet that evening. As soon as he'd made apologies to the innkeeper, he dragged Alec off to a nearby bathhouse, then back to their room to put the final touches on his grooming.

"You look better in this than I do," Seregil remarked as he adjusted Alec's sash.

Alec wore "Aren's" second-best garments: a long tunic of fine blue wool edged with embroidered bands along the hem and sleeves. One of the scullery girls had been paid to burnish his boots to a respectable shine.

Seregil himself was magnificent in a crimson tunic bordered with an intricate black and white pattern at neck, sleeves, and hem. His dark hair was bound back with a thin band of scarlet and black silk twisted into an elaborate knot at the back. Draping a new cloak of rich midnight blue gracefully over one shoulder, he pinned it in place with a heavy silver brooch.

"While I was striking the bargain for our wages with the mayor's bailiff I was able to quiz him on the guests," Seregil told him. "Lord Boraneus, ostensibly a trade envoy, is the head of the Plenimaran expedition. There's another noble, a Lord Trygonis, who also seems to have some pull, though he doesn't say much. With a little sweet talk to one of the house maids I also found out that Boraneus and Trygonis are housed in the best front rooms on the second floor. Besides the usual honor guard at the banquet, I imagine there'll be plenty of soldiers scattered around outside. Now, are you absolutely certain you understand what we have to do tonight?"

Alec was trying with little success to arrange the folds of his cloak in imitation of Seregil's. "We sing until everyone is well into the wine. You'll pause to tune the harp and break a string. Then I'm sent home for a new one and you step out for some air. There's a small servants' stairway at the back of the house that takes us up to the second floor. I meet you there and we go up together."

"And you have the extra string with you?"

"In my tunic."

"Good." Seregil reached into the pack lying on the bed and pulled out something wrapped in a bit of sacking. Unrolling it, he showed Alec a handsome dagger. The handle was fashioned from black horn inlaid with silver. The slender blade was deadly sharp.

"This is for you," said Seregil, balancing the dagger across his palm for a moment. "It caught my eye while Maklin was fussing over you. It's longer than your other one and better balanced. A little fancy for a bard's apprentice, perhaps, but nobody's going to see it in your boot. If we do our job right tonight, you shouldn't need it anyway."

"Seregil, I can't—" the boy stammered, overcome. "I can never repay you as it is and—"

"Repay me for what?" Seregil asked in surprise.

"For this, for all of this!" Alec exclaimed, sweeping a hand around the room. "The clothes, the sword, the bow—I haven't ever made enough in my life to repay all this. Maker's Mercy, I haven't known you a week yet and—"

"Don't be silly. These are the tools of the trade. You'd be useless to me without them. Don't give it another thought or insult me with talk of repayment. I can't think of anything that means less to me than money; it's too easy to come by."

Shaking his head, Alec slid the dagger into the pocket of his boot and grinned. "It fits."

"Well, let's get to work, then. And may Illior watch over us tonight."

The stars were out by the time they set off for the mayor's hall. A cold wind cut in off the lake and they pulled their cloaks around them against the cold. As promised, Seregil had found Alec a pair of gloves, and he suspected the boy was grateful now for their warmth.

Not for the first time that day Seregil asked himself what he was doing dragging a green boy he'd known for less than a week's time off on a burglary job. Or what Alec was doing going along with him, for that matter. Shrewd as he was in some matters, the boy seemed to place an alarming amount of trust in him. Never having been responsible for anyone but himself, Seregil wasn't quite certain what to make of it, except that taking Alec on as a partner of sorts out on the Downs had seemed like a good idea at the time. However much logic might dictate otherwise, looking at Alec striding along beside him, Seregil's intuition told him he'd somehow stumbled into a fortuitous decision.

At the mayor's house they were taken to the kitchen for the customary meal. The tapestry over the door had been pulled back and they could see the guests in the hall being entertained by a juggler. When the last of the platters had come back to the kitchen and the wine and fruit had been passed, Aren Windover was announced.

The great hall was ablaze with firelight and wax tapers. The trestles had been set up in a U facing the hearth and the company, made up mostly of rich merchants, guild masters, and craftsmen of Wolde, clapped approvingly as Seregil and Alec took their places on a small platform set up there. Alec handed Seregil the harp with a flourish he'd learned less than an hour before, then stepped back deferentially.

In Aren Windover's most flowery manner, Seregil introduced himself and made a brief speech of gratitude to the mayor and his lady. His words were well received and he struck up the first song amid a flutter of applause. He captured his audience at once with a rousing hunting lay, then moved on to a succession of love songs and ballads, throwing in a raucous ditty here and there once he saw that the ladies approved. Alec took frequent turns at the harmonies and fetched ale for his master as the occasion demanded.

The one calling himself Boraneus sat in the place of honor to the right of the fat mayor and Seregil studied him surreptitiously as he played. Boraneus was tall, with the high coloring and thick, blue-black hair of a true Plenimaran. He was younger than Seregil had expected, no more than forty, and extremely handsome despite the thin scar that ran from the inner corner of his left eye to the cheekbone. His black eyes sparkled rakishly as he shared some joke with the mayor's wife, but when the smile faded his face had a veiled, unreadable quality.

By the Light, that's Duke Mardus—whatever he calls himself here, Seregil thought as he played. Though he'd never seen Mardus before, he knew him both by description and reputation. The most highly placed officer of the Plenimaran intelligence system, he was also known to be a sadistically ruthless inquisitor. Seregil felt an involuntary chill as Mardus' impassive gaze rested briefly on him. To have such a person study your face was the worst sort of luck.

The other envoy didn't look like he amounted to much. A narrow, whey-faced fellow with lank dark hair, Trygonis was apparently doing his dour best to avoid being drawn into conversation with the garrulous matrons seated on either side of him. Splendidly dressed as he was in the regalia of a Plenimaran diplomat, to Seregil's practiced eye his pale skin and silent, peering manner told a different tale. He had more the look of one who spent his life huddled over books in rooms where sunlight never penetrated.

Seregil played on for nearly an hour before he judged the time to be right. Pausing to tune the harp, he snapped the string and, after a tense, whispered exchange with Alec, rose and bowed to the mayor.

"My most gracious host," he said, affecting an air of barely concealed irritation while Alec did his best to appear shame-faced. "It seems my apprentice has neglected to bring extra strings for my instrument. With your kind permission, I will send the boy back to my lodgings for replacements."

Comfortably into his cups, the mayor waved agreeably and Alec hurried out.

Seregil bowed again. "If I may ask your further indulgence, I will take this opportunity to freshen my throat with the cool night air."

"By all means, Master Windover. I think it may be some time before we let you go. Your fine singing goes well with the wine."

Once outside, Seregil made a show of clearing his lungs and admiring the stars. Spotting a Plenimaran guard posted near the front of the building, he asked after the privy and was directed to the yard in back of the house. As soon as he was safely around the corner, he pressed into the shadows and checked again; no guards back here. Alec was waiting for him beneath the servants' stairs.

"Did anyone see you?" Seregil whispered.

Alec shook his head. "I went across the square, then doubled back to the other side of the house."

"Good. Now stay close and pay attention. If anything goes wrong, you're on your own, understand? If it comes to that, I'll do my best to come back for you, but your best guarantee is to not get into trouble in the first place. All right?"

Looking rather less than reassured by this advice, Alec nod-ded gamely and followed him up the stairs to the second level of the house.

The door was locked, but Seregil produced a long pick. Be-yond they found a dimly lit service passage. Seregil signed *Quickly* and moved to a door at the far end. Beyond it, they could hear sounds of the revelry below. Opening it the merest crack,

Seregil found that they were near the upper landing of the great staircase.

Just as they were about to make a dash for the guest rooms, a black-clad marine came upstairs from the hall and disappeared into one of the rooms overlooking the street. Emerging a moment later with a small chest, he went back downstairs. Seregil counted slowly to ten, then drew Alec behind him into the hall. Moving quickly to the room the soldier had entered, they found the door unlocked.

"This is Trygonis' room," whispered Seregil. "Keep watch, and if you touch something, *anything,* be sure to leave it exactly as you found it."

Against the right wall stood a carved bedstead with a clothes chest at the foot. A tall wardrobe and a writing table stood by the window.

"This first, I think," Seregil murmured, kneeling in front of the chest. After a moment's examination he drew a small leather roll from his tunic and spread it out in a workmanlike fashion on the floor beside him; it contained an impressive collection of various lock picks and other implements, each in a narrow pocket of the roll. The chest's heavy padlock came open on the first attempt.

Except for a brass map tube, the chest contained little more than the usual mundane articles of clothing and equipment, all seeming to confirm that the man was a diplomat rather than a soldier. Quickly shaking out the rolled parchment from the tube, Seregil moved to the thin sliver of light at the door and unrolled it to find a map of the northlands. Alec peered over his shoulder for a moment, then went back to his watch-keeping while Seregil studied it more closely, committing the details to memory.

Small red points had been inked in next to the Gold Road towns of Wolde, Kerry, and Sark. Several other points marked remote freeholdings along the Ironheart foothills, Asengai's among them.

Nothing so surprising there. Seregil rolled up the map and replaced the contents of the chest as he'd found them. The desk yielded nothing of value, but in the wardrobe he found a small silk pouch containing a golden disk hung on a golden chain.

One side of the pendant was smooth; on the other a peculiar, abstract device of intricate lines and swirls stood out in raised relief. Try as he might, Seregil couldn't make sense enough of it to reproduce it later. Mildly annoyed, he replaced it and joined Alec at the door. No more than five minutes had elapsed.

The next room was very much like the first, except for a dispatch box sitting on the table. It was banded with nailed strips of brass and secured with an internal lock rather than a hasp. Moving to the light again, he examined the lock plate, noting tiny imperfections in the metal around the keyhole. A less experienced thief might have dismissed them as pits in the metal; Seregil recognized the needle holes lightly plugged with wax and brass dust. Anyone attempting to force the lock while the device was engaged would end up with at least one tiny but no doubt heavily poisoned needle embedded in his hand. Running sensitive fingertips over the brass nail heads, he found one on the back left corner that depressed with a barely audible click. Double-checking to be sure he hadn't missed any others, he picked the lock and raised the lid.

On top was a sheaf of documents written in cipher. Setting these aside, he found a map much like the larger one, but with only two red points marked on it: one deep in the heart of the Blackwater Fens at the southern end of the lake, the other apparently somewhere in the Far Forest. The point in the Fens was circled.

Beneath the map was a leather pouch containing another of the golden pendants.

What in the name of Bilairy are these? he wondered, frustrated again at not being able to make sense of the design.

At the clothes chest he felt carefully down through the layers of tunics and robes until his fingers encountered studded wood near the bottom. Lifting the clothing out, he found a rectangular casket a foot long and perhaps half that deep, its lid secured only by a hook. His mouth twisted into a humorless smile as he cautiously opened it; inside lay a collection of small but effective torture instruments and several earthenware vials. More certain than ever that his man really was Mardus, Seregil took extra care to replace the box as he'd found it. As he was replacing the clothing, however, another leather pouch dropped from the folds of a robe. Probing inside, he found a few Plenimaran coins, two rings, a case knife, and some small wooden disks.

There were eight in all, fashioned from some dark wood and pierced through the center with a square hole. They had a slightly oily feel, and each was carved on one side with the same frustrating design he'd seen on the gold pendants.

Now here's a piece of luck at last, he thought. These crude things didn't look like something anyone would miss in a hurry. He pocketed one for later study.

He'd just locked the chest when Alec made a frantic gesture at the door. Someone was coming.

With Alec at his heels, Seregil moved smoothly to the window. Swinging the casement wide, he looked up to find the overhang of the roof within easy reach.

He'd already pulled himself up onto the slates above before he noticed the two guards lounging near the fountain. For a brief second his breath caught in his throat; he was in plain sight if they looked up. The noise from the hall must have covered his scramblings, however, or perhaps they were drunk, for neither of them did.

Alec snaked out the same way, and Seregil caught his wrists to help him up. The boy looked scared, but still had presence of mind enough to gently push the window shut with his foot on the way up.

The slick slate roof was steeply pitched, but they managed to get over to the back side, reaching the servants' stairway without mishap. At the bottom Seregil grasped Alec's shoulder for a moment in silent approval, then pointed him off toward the kitchen door.

Alec was nearly there when a tall figure reached from the shadows and caught him by the cloak. Seregil tensed, hand stealing to his dagger. Alec jerked back instinctively and the man laughed. Just as Seregil was about to spring to his aid, however, he heard the man speak and realized this must be one of the soldiers who'd accosted the boy earlier that day.

"Hey, you sing good in there," the man exclaimed. His tone seemed friendly enough, but he hadn't released his grip on Alec's cloak. "You sing more for me now maybe?"

"I've got to get back in." Stepping away as far as he could, Alec pulled the harp string from his tunic and waved it like a pass. "My master needs this. I'll be in trouble if I make him wait."

"Trouble?" The man squinted at the string. "No trouble for you, Cavish's man-child. Go sing some more for the fat mayor and my master!" Turning Alec loose, he sent him on his way with a resounding slap on the back.

Letting out a soundless sigh of relief, Seregil waited until the way was clear, then skirted back through the shadows to reappear from the direction of the mayor's privy.

It was after midnight before they returned to the Three Fishes. Nonetheless, Seregil insisted on making ready to leave at first light.

"You did well tonight," he said as he finished strapping up his pack. "That was quick thinking, with the window."

Alec grinned happily at the praise and continued checking over his new equipment. Master Radly had included an oilskin bow case and a covered quiver in the price of the bow, to which Alec had added a score of arrows, linen twine and wax for bow-strings, and packets of red and white fletching.

Seregil was just turning to say something more when they both were startled by the sound of someone pounding up the stairs. Micum Cavish burst into the room. Panting, he said, "I don't know what you did this time, Seregil, but a pack of Plenimaran marines are on their way here right now!"

Somewhere below they heard a door bang open, then the sounds of heavy feet.

"Grab your things, Alec!" Seregil ordered, throwing back the shutters.

A moment later Tildus and a dozen Plenimaran soldiers burst into the room, only to find it dark and empty.

6

ALEC EARNS HIS BOW

From the inn window the three of them dropped thirty feet into water cold enough to knock the breath from their lungs.

Alec floundered, gasping as he tried to hang on to his gear and keep his head above water. A strong hand closed over his wrist; Micum hauled him to a handhold on the slimy pilings supporting the building.

"Quiet!" Seregil whispered against his ear.

Working their way back to the shallows, they crawled out onto a narrow mud bank and huddled there as the sounds of a violent search rang out overhead.

"I doubt you two will be welcome again at the Fishes," Micum whispered through chattering teeth.

It was a miserably cold vigil they kept, and dangerous. At one point several marines found their way under the building, forcing the three fugitives to turtle back into the icy water until they were gone. It was over an hour before Micum judged that it was safe to go.

They made a sorry trio as they staggered from the shadows of the tavern. Covered in mud, their hair and clothing stiffened into fantastic configurations, they moved as fast as their numbed legs would allow, heading for the market square.

Micum led the way to the Temple of Astel-

lus that stood next to the Fisherman's Guildhall on the square. It
was a plain, windowless structure, but the large double doors at
its front were elaborately carved with boats and water creatures.
The lintel above displayed the stylized wave symbol of Astellus
the Traveler. By custom, the doors of the temple were never
locked, and they slipped inside without challenge.

Alec had never been inside the place before, though he'd
passed it often enough. The plastered walls of the central room
glowed with fanciful underwater scenes and icons showing several of the patron deity's more noteworthy labors.

Near the central shrine a young acolyte dozed at his post.
Passing quietly, they found their way to a door at the back of the
temple and into the storeroom beyond.

Offerings, sacks of food for the priests, and oddments of furniture were stacked carelessly about. Alec sat down on an up-
ended crate while Micum cast about, looking for something.

"Isn't it over to the left more?' asked Seregil.

"I've got it." Micum pulled open a trapdoor in the floor.

Looking over his shoulder, Alec saw a ladder descending into
the darkness. Cold, earth-smelling air rose up the shaft.

"Let's hope the mayor neglected to tell his visitors about this
route," Seregil muttered.

Micum shrugged. "A good fight puts the fire of Sakor in your
blood. I think we could all use the warmth!"

Seregil cocked a wry eyebrow at Alec. "He works as hard to
find trouble as I do avoiding it."

With a derisive chuckle, Micum climbed down the ladder.
Alec followed while Seregil took a moment to prop several small
crates to fall over the door when it closed.

Once down, Micum rummaged in a belt pouch and drew out
a small glowing object. Its pale radiance spilled out through his
fingers, spreading a small circle of light.

"Magic?" Alec asked, leaning closer.

"A lightstone," Seregil told him. "I lost mine in a dice game
two months ago and I've been fumbling around with flint and
steel ever since."

"Too bad it doesn't give off any heat," Micum said, chaffing
his arms as he led the way down the tunnel.

"Where are we?"

"An escape tunnel leading out of town," Micum explained. "It
has openings near the lake shore and another just inside the

woods. The Temple of Dalna has one, too. The idea was to be able to evacuate the town secretly if it was ever besieged. I doubt it would work, though—most likely bring you right up in front of the enemy. But it was thought up by merchants, not generals. As it is, Seregil and I have probably made the best use of them over the last few years."

"Where to now? The cave?" Seregil was shivering visibly now as he tried to pull his stiff cloak more closely about him.

"That's the closest place."

The passage ran in a fairly straight line back from the river. It was hardly wide enough for two men to pass, and the roof was so low that Micum had to stoop in places. The damp earthen walls, shored up at intervals with timber, gave off an unpleasant chill. Blotches of lichen and pale fungi sprouted from the support beams. After some time, the tunnel branched.

Taking the right fork, Micum drew his sword and whispered over his shoulder, "Look sharp, boy, in case we have company."

Alec moved to draw his own blade but Seregil nudged his hand away from the hilt. "Never mind that," he said. "You couldn't get by to fight and if you stumbled, you'd probably run Micum through. If we meet anyone, fade back with me and stay out of the way."

But they met nothing except a few rats and slow-moving salamanders, and soon the tunnel began to slant upward, ending at a narrow cave. It was hardly more than a thin cleft in the rock and the floor of it narrowed sharply to a V, making for uncomfortable going.

Barking shins, hands, and heads against sharp-edged stones, they clambered up the fissure. Micum pocketed the lightstone as they reached the top and they pushed their way through a dense thicket of bramble at the mouth of the cave.

Looking around, Alec saw that they were somewhere in the woods; stands of oak, birch, and fir grew thickly around them. The sinking moon cast netted shadows through the canopy of branches overhead, curling darkness beneath the firs. Dawn was a few hours away and all was still.

Seregil was trembling more violently than the others.

"You never could stand the cold," Micum said, unclasping his cloak. When Seregil moved to shrug it away, Micum stopped him with a stern look and swung it around his shoulders himself.

"Save your pride for warmer days, you damn fool. The boy and I are bred to it. Your blood's too thin. Come on."

Still scowling, Seregil tied the cloak strings under his chin without further protest.

Moving quietly over the snowy ground, they headed deeper into the forest. The ground rose and fell sharply, and the shadows were thick, but Micum went along as confidently as if they were hiking a highroad.

Halfway up a hillside, they reached another cave. It was larger than the last and its opening lay in plain sight. High-roofed and shallow, it narrowed at the back to a tiny passage leading farther into the hillside. Alec and Seregil were slim enough to pass through sideways without much trouble, but Micum grunted and swore as he worked his way in.

"I don't recall you having so much trouble a few years back," observed Seregil.

"Shut up, you," Micum wheezed, pulling free at last.

The crevice twisted sharply several times, threatening to close altogether, but finally opened into a wider space. Micum brought out his light again, and Alec saw that they were in another cave, this one quite large.

Wood lay arranged for a fire in a circle of stones. Hunkering down beside it, Seregil found a small jar among the logs and shook what appeared to be hot coals onto the tinder.

"More magic for you." Grinning, he handed Alec the jar. Small chips of stone glowed bright as embers but, like the lightstone, gave off no heat.

"Those are fire stones," he explained. "Be careful with them. They won't hurt skin but the second they touch anything that will burn—cloth, wood, parchment—they ignite. I've seen too many accidents to carry them traveling."

Flames licked up through the dry wood, dispelling the chill and darkness. The natural chamber narrowed overhead to a crevice, and by some trick of the draft the smoke was drawn neatly up this natural chimney.

Firewood, folded blankets, and a number of pottery jars lay on various ledges around the caves. Piles of dry bracken and fir boughs were formed into rough pallets against the walls.

"This is snug camp," said Alec, admiring it.

"Micum found it a while back," Seregil said, huddling over

the flames as closely as he dared. "Only we and a few friends know about it. Who was here last?"

Micum inspected the stone shelf that held the jars and held up a black feather. "Erisa. She must have stopped here before going into town. Let's see what she's left in the larder."

Carrying a few of the jars to the fire, he inspected some marks carefully incised on the wax seals. "Let's see. There's a bee on these, that's honey. A wheat stalk, that's hard biscuit. A bee and a cup—mead. What've you got?"

"I'm not certain." Seregil held a jar closer to the light. "Dried venison. And here's some tobacco for you."

"Bless her kind heart." Micum took a pipe from somewhere inside his tunic and filled it. "I left my pouch behind in all the scuffle."

"And these two must be herbs," Seregil continued. "Looks like yarrow and fever bane. Well, thanks to our good friend Micum Cavish, we're in no need of healing. I just want to get dry!"

Stripping off their filthy garments, they spread them by the fire and wrapped up in blankets.

Too cold to concern himself with modesty for once, Alec noticed that both of his companions had a number of scars, though Micum's were by far the more numerous and serious. The worst was a pale rope of tissue that began just beneath his right shoulder blade. It curved down around his back to end just short of his navel. Noticing the boy's interest, he turned to the light and ran a thumb proudly over the end of the welt.

"Closest I ever came to Bilairy's gatepost." Lighting his pipe, Micum puffed out a few rings of mellow smoke. "It was nine winters ago, wasn't it, Seregil?"

"I believe it was." Seregil gave Alec a wink. "A group of us were traipsing up around the Fishless Sea and ran into a particularly unfriendly bunch of nomads."

"Unfriendly!" snorted Micum. "I'd never seen their like before—great hairy giants. We still don't know where they came from. They were too busy trying to kill us to answer questions. We stumbled across their camp by accident one evening, and figured we'd say hello and try to trade for supplies. But just as we reached the pickets, a whole pack of them—big as bears and twice as mean—came charging out of nowhere at us on foot. We were mounted, but they had us surrounded before we realized what was going on. The weapons they used looked something like a big flail; a long haft with several lengths of chain attached, each two or three feet long. Only the links of the chains were flattened and the edges ground keen as razors. Of course, we didn't know about that until after we'd started to fight. Cyril lost an arm, cut clean off, and Berrit was blinded and died soon after. One of the bastards took the front legs off my horse and then laid into me. That's when I got this beauty." He ran a hand over the knotted ridge of flesh again. "I was all tangled up in the stirrups, but I managed to get my sword up in time to block his swing— all but one of the chains, and that laid me open to the bone right through my jerkin. If I hadn't blocked the rest, I believe he'd have cut me in half. Seregil popped up from somewhere and killed him just as he was going for another stroke. It's lucky we had the drysian Valerius traveling with us, or I'd have crossed over right then and there."

"I suppose this was my worst," said Seregil, showing Alec deep indentations in the lean muscle on either side of his left thigh.

"I was exploring an abandoned wizard's keep. She'd been dead for years, but a lot of her wards were still in place. I'd been very careful, spotted all the symbols, disarmed device after device. She'd been something of a genius in that way and I was feeling pretty proud of myself. But no matter how good you are, there's always a trap with your name on it somewhere, and I found one that day. I missed a trigger of some sort—never did see it—and the next I knew my foot went through the floor. An iron spike shot across, pinning my leg like a speared fish. Half an inch to the left and I'd have bled to death. I couldn't reach far enough into the hole to free myself, short of cutting off my leg. I've no stomach for pain. From what little I remember, I did a lot of yelling and fainting until Micum found me and carried me out. Not a very heroic tale, I'm afraid."

Alec had stripped the oilskin cover from his bow to check for damage. Without looking up from his work, he ventured shyly, "Still, you were brave enough to do all that."

"You've got a short memory all of a sudden," Seregil scoffed, passing him the mead jar. "Aren't you the same half-starved lad who survived Asengai's dungeons and followed me out, not to mention what we did tonight? That's a lot to claim before you're even grown."

Alec shrugged, embarrassed. "That wasn't bravery. There just wasn't anything else to do."

Micum laughed grimly. "By Sakor, then you've learned the secret of being brave. All you need is some training."

Reaching over the fire, he retrieved the mead jar from Seregil. "So what will you do now?"

Seregil shook his head. "I'd planned to blend into some caravan and take the Gold Road all the way to Nanta, but now I'm not so sure. What was all that fracas about tonight? I was certain nobody saw us."

"I was watching the house from the square. Everything was quiet until well after you left. The party broke up soon after, the guests went home, and the lamps inside were mostly out. I was just about to leave myself when all hell broke loose. Someone started yelling, then there were lights all over the place, and soldiers running everywhere. I got as close as I could—which wasn't too hard with all the excitement—and looked into the hall. That big fellow, Boraneus, had the mayor cornered. All I heard was that anyone who'd been at the feast was to be arrested and brought back immediately. That's when I lit out after you. Those Plenimarans are a damned well-organized bunch. I didn't think I was going to get to you in time."

Seregil tapped his chin with one long forefinger. "If someone had actually seen us, then they wouldn't be arresting all the guests. That's a bit of luck, I'd say."

"And what, exactly, *did* you steal?"

"Just this." Seregil dug into his belt pouch and handed Micum the wooden disk. "I wanted to show Nysander the pattern."

Micum turned it over on his palm and tossed it back to him. "Looks like a gaming piece to me—not the sort of thing anyone would make that kind of fuss over. You know, I think you might not have been the only ones ghosting around there tonight. Could be one of the guards got a case of light fingers."

"We saw one coming out of Boraneus' room before we went in, carrying a box," Alec recalled. "And someone nearly caught us in the other room as we were leaving. It could have been one of them."

"I suppose so." Seregil frowned into the fire for a moment. "At any rate, we've certainly made ourselves look guilty enough, leaving the way we did. I say we avoid the Gold Road. We'll find some horses—"

"Find?" Micum interjected wryly.

"—and head cross-country to Boersby Ford," Seregil went on, ignoring the remark. "That should be far enough to shake loose of any pursuit. Then we can take passage down the Folcwine to Nanta. With any luck, we'll be there in less than a week. If the weather holds, we can get a ship across to Rhíminee."

"I think I'd better stay clear of Wolde until the Plenimarans are well gone," Micum said, stretching out on a pallet and yawning until his jaws cracked. "I'll go back with you as far as Boersby, in case there's any trouble."

"Did they get a good look at you?"

"I'm not sure they didn't. They were right on my heels all the way to the Fishes. Better safe than dead, eh?"

Sheltered in their hidden cave, they slept deeply until afternoon.

"We'd better wait until dark to move on," said Seregil, squinting up at the narrow crack of light from the smoke hole. Pulling his harp from its case, he satisfied himself that it had survived the dunkings of the previous night, then set about tuning it. "We've still got a few hours to kill. Micum, how would you like to give my young apprentice a few lessons in swordsmanship? He'll benefit from learning your methods as well as my own."

Micum winked at Alec. "What he means is that my ways aren't as dainty as his, but I manage to make my way well enough."

"Come on now, old friend," Seregil demurred, "I'd be hard pressed if I had to face you in a fight."

"That's true—but it would be the time I *wasn't* facing you that I'd worry about! Come on, Alec, I'll show you daylight methods."

Micum began with the basics, teaching Alec how to grip the weapon so that it balanced to his advantage, what stances presented the smallest target to an opponent, and simple slash and parry maneuvers. Seregil finished his tuning and lazily plucked out a tune, pausing occasionally to offer advice or argue points of style.

As Alec moved slowly through Micum's drills, he began to suspect that he was learning from two masters of uncommon ability. His arm was soon aching as he tried to deflect Micum's mock attacks. Though Micum's blade was of a heavier make than his own, the man flashed it about as if it weighed no more than a glove.

"I'm sorry," Alec said at last, slicking sweat from his forehead. "It's hard, moving so slow."

Micum flexed his shoulders. "It is, but you have to learn to control the movements and direct the blade, not just wave it about until it hits something. Come on, Seregil, let's show him how it's done."

"I'm busy," replied Seregil, working on a tricky bit of fingering.

Moving to stand over him, Micum growled, "Put away that twopenny toy, you tit-sucking coistril, and show me the length of your blade!"

Seregil laid his harp aside with a sigh. "Dear me, that sounds rather like a challenge—"

Lunging swiftly past Micum, he sprang to his feet and drew his sword, then swung a flat-bladed attack at Micum's sword arm. Micum blocked and countered. Grinning fiercely and showering each other with blistering insults, they battled around the confines of the cave, leaping over the fire pit and threatening to trample Alec underfoot until he wisely retreated to the narrow crevice at the back. From there he watched with delighted admiration as the two of them moved over the uneven floor, graceful as acrobats or dancers.

At first it seemed to him that Seregil spent more time avoiding attacks then returning them—his movements seemingly effortless as he sprang here and there, his sword flashing up to block a blow, then dodging away, making Micum change his stance to follow him. But Micum was no clumsy bear, either. There was a powerful grace to his motions, a steady, implacable rhythm as he pressed his attacks. Soon Alec couldn't have said if Micum was driving or chasing, if Seregil was leading or being driven.

The mock battle ended in a draw of sorts; choosing his moment, Micum side-stepped an attack, slapped Seregil's blade away, and skewered a loose fold of his tunic.

At the same moment, however, the wickedly slender poniard appeared somehow in Seregil's left hand, its tip pricking through Micum's jerkin just below his heart. They stood frozen for an instant, then broke away laughing.

"So arm in arm we tumble down to Bilairy's gate!" Micum said, sheathing his sword. "You marred my jerkin, I see."

"And you ventilated my new tunic."

"By Sakor, it serves you right for pulling that rat-sticker in the middle of a proper sword fight, you sneaky bastard!"

"Isn't that cheating?" Alec inquired, emerging from his crevice.

Seregil gave the boy a wink and a crooked grin. "Of course!"

"It's no wonder you swear by Illior's Hands," Micum growled in mock exasperation. "I always have to keep an eye on both of yours."

"Illior and Sakor." Alec shook his head. "You say they're like my gods, but that they've been forgotten in the north."

"That's right," said Seregil. "Dalna, Astellus, Sakor, and Illior; all part of the Sacred Four. You'll need to know more of them, down in Skala."

Micum rolled his eyes. "We could be here the rest of the week now. He's worse than a priest on such things!"

Seregil ignored the protest. "Each one of them rules a different part of life," he explained. "And they possess the sacred duality."

"You mean like how Astellus helps with birth and guides the dead?" asked Alec.

"Exactly."

"But what about the others?"

"Sakor guards the hearth and directs the sun," Micum told him. "He's the soldier's friend, but he also inflames the mind of your enemy and brings on storms and drought."

Alec turned back to Seregil. "And you always swear by Illior."

"Where's that coin I gave you?" Taking it, Seregil turned it to the side with the crescent moon. "This is the most common sign of Illior. It symbolizes the partial revelation of a greater mystery. The Lightbearer sends dreams and magic, and watches over seers and wizards and even thieves. But Illior also sends madness and nightmares.

"All the Four are a mix of good and ill, bane and blessing. Some even speak of them as both male or female rather than one or the other. The Immortals show us that it's the natural way of things that good and ill be mixed; separate one from the other and both lose their significance. That's the strength of the Four."

"In other words, if some must be priests, then others must be murderers," Micum noted wryly.

"Right, so my cheating in a fight is actually a sacred act."

"But what about the other gods?" asked Alec. "Ashi, and Mor of the Birds, and Bilairy and all?"

"Northern spirits and legends, for the most part," Seregil said, rising to gather his belongings. "And Bilairy's just the gatekeeper of souls, making certain that none go in or out before the time appointed by the Maker. As far as I know, there was only one other god great enough to challenge the Four—an evil, dark one."

"Seriamaius, you mean?" said Micum.

Seregil made a hasty warding sign. "You know it's bad luck to speak the name of the Empty God! Even Nysander says so."

"Illiorans!" the big man scoffed, nudging Alec. "They've got superstitious streaks a mile wide. It was all legends anyway, started by the necromancers back in the Great War. And good true steel took care of them."

"Not without considerable help from drysians and wizards," Seregil replied. "And it took the Aurënfaie to put an end to it."

"But what about this other god?" asked Alec, feeling a chill go up his back. "Where did it come from if it wasn't part of the Four?"

Seregil snugged down the straps of his pack. "It's said the Plenimarans brought the worship of the Empty God back from somewhere over the seas. It's supposed to have been a pretty unpleasant business, too—all kinds of nasty ceremonies. This deity was said to feed off the living energy of the world. He did grant uncanny powers to the faithful, but always at a terrible price. Still, there are always those who will seek such power, whatever the risk."

"And this Empty God is supposed to have started that great war?"

"The worship of that god would have been well established by that time—"

"Sakor's Flame, Seregil, a man could grow old waiting for you to draw breath once you start talking!" Micum interrupted impatiently. "We've a long ride ahead of us, and horses to 'find.' "

Seregil made him a rude gesture, then went to the supply shelf and left a few coins. "We don't have much for the larder, but I think this will do." He replaced Erisa's feather token with a bit of knotted cord.

Micum fished a fir cone from a pouch and added it to the collection. "We'll need a sign for you, now that you know the place," he said to Alec. "It's good manners to let others know when you've been here."

Alec found a bit of fletching and placed it with the other things.

Micum clapped him on the shoulder approvingly. "I guess I don't need to ask you to keep our secrets."

Alec nodded awkwardly and turned to pick up his gear, hoping the others didn't see his embarrassed blush. Whoever these men really were, it felt good to have their trust.

They left the woods as soon as it was dark and made their way back to the edge of the farmland surrounding the town. It was impossible not to leave a trail across the snow-covered fields, so they kept to the back roads and lanes as much as possible, eyeing each farm as they passed.

As the last lights in the distant town winked out, Seregil paused on a rise overlooking a prosperous steading.

"That's what we want," he said. "Dark house, big stable."

"Good choice," said Micum, rubbing his hands cheerfully. "That's Doblevain's place. He breeds the best horses in the area. You see to the animals. Alec and I will find the tack."

"All right," Seregil agreed. "Alec, we'll continue your education with a lesson in horse thieving."

Keeping to the road and the trampled ground of the corral, they managed to leave almost no trail at all as they approached the stable. Just as they reached the door, however, two large mongrels came out of the shadows and advanced on them with raised hackles.

Facing them calmly, Seregil spoke softly and made the left-handed sign Alec had seen him use on the blind man's dog a few days earlier, with nearly the same effect. Both curs halted for a moment, then trotted forward to lick Seregil's hand, tails whipping happily. He scratched their ears, murmuring to them in a friendly tone.

Micum shook his head. "What I wouldn't give to be able to do that! He's got a drysian's own touch with animals. Must come from his—"

"Come on, we haven't got all night," Seregil interrupted

impatiently, and Alec thought he saw him make some sign to Micum, though he couldn't make out what it was.

The stable shutters were down, so they decided to risk a light. Micum reluctantly cracked his lightstone into two pieces, handing half to Seregil. By the light of the remaining half, he and Alec located the small tack room and began pulling down saddles and gear.

Seregil soon emerged from the rich, sour darkness of the stalls leading three glossy horses, the dogs still padding contentedly at his heels.

Snowflakes were spiraling down again as they led their mounts away from the farm. When Seregil judged they were out of earshot, they mounted and set off at a gallop over the fields, trusting the new snow to cover their tracks.

By sunup they'd covered the miles of open hill country between Wolde and the Folcwine Forest. They came within sight of Stook at the forest's northern border but avoided the town, heading instead down the highroad through the forest.

New snow lay deep on the road and weighed heavily on the boughs of the trees that flanked it. The sky overhead was a stolid, even grey.

Seregil and Micum rode slightly ahead of Alec, deep in conversation. Studying their profiles, Alec wondered at how his old life sometimes seemed years gone already, and with it the simple hunter he'd been.

Lost in his own thoughts, it took a few seconds for him to make the connection between the searing pain that suddenly burned across the top of his left thigh, and the arrow protruding from his horse's side just in front of the girth strap. The animal screamed and threw him, then bolted down the road.

The snow cushioned his fall. Dumbfounded, he reached down and felt the shallow gash in his leg. The wound was minor, but the suddenness of it all seemed to numb him momentarily. It wasn't until he'd struggled up to check his bow that he truly understood what was happening. As if time had paused and was now resuming its normal course, the air around him was instantly filled with an angry hail of arrows.

"Alec, get down!" Seregil shouted from somewhere nearby.

Clutching his bow and quiver, Alec dropped and scrambled on

his belly to the nearest trees. Rolling into their shelter, he peeked
cautiously around a tree trunk, realizing too late that he was on
the opposite side of the road from Micum. Four archers stood in
the road less than two hundred feet away, sending out a volley of
arrows. Alec also caught a glimpse of others working their way
through the trees in his direction.

The archers kept up their steady attack; arrows sang in the air,
nipping off a hail of twigs around him, thudding into the trees he
sheltered behind. There was no sign of Seregil except a third
track snaking off through the snow into the trees beyond Micum.
Left more or less on his own, Alec knew what his next step had
to be.

His heart pounded sickeningly as he fitted an arrow to the
string and took aim at a man for the first time in his life. A tall
archer standing boldly at the edge of the road presented an easy
target, but try as he might, Alec couldn't seem to hold steady.
Startled by a horse's scream, he released the shaft high and it
sped off uselessly into the trees. Micum's gelding drove itself
into a heap just in front of him, a shaft protruding from its throat.
Another arrow slammed into the beast's chest and it gave a final
bellowing groan.

"The bastards know their business, killing the horses," Micum
called over to him. "I hope you have a few shafts left—I'm
pinned down here!"

Nocking a second arrow, Alec drew the fletching to his ear
and tried again.

"O Dalna!" he whispered as his bow arm wavered again. "Let
me pull true!"

Damn, he can't do it, Micum thought in alarm, watching
Alec's face.

Before he could decide how to get across to help him, however, a bandit with a sword rushed him from the trees. Silently
commending Alec to whatever gods he had, Micum turned to
meet the attack.

It was his habit to look into his opponent's eyes as he fought;
in this scarred, swarthy face he read no fear. Their swords rang
out a steady, grim music as each, conscious of the uncertain footing beneath the snow, tried to draw the other into a clumsy misstep. Suddenly Micum saw the man's gaze flicker to the left.

Jumping aside, he faced the second swordsman before the man had time to swing at his back. Thinking Micum had off-balanced himself, the first man overextended a lunge and Micum's blade took him under the ribs.

Even as he jerked the blade free, he caught movement out of the corner of his eye and barely avoided a slicing cut at his shoulder from a third swordsman. Drawing a long dagger with his left hand, Micum moved back, trying to keep them both in front of him. These two were younger, less sure of themselves than the first, but they knew their trade. Leering like wolves, they stayed wide apart, making it difficult to defend from both at once. One would cut at him to draw a parry, while the other tried to hamstring him on his open side. But Micum had been in too many fights like this to be drawn. Using his sword and dagger, he managed to fend off their attacks and return a few thrusts of his own.

Pinking one of them on the arm, he said easily, "I think it's only fair to tell you that my purse is far too light for you to go to such trouble to take it." His attackers exchanged a quick glance but made no reply, grimly pressing to break his guard.

"Suit yourselves, then."

The man to his right feinted forward strongly, managing to nick Micum on the ribs just deeply enough to make him regret leaving his mail shirt behind in Wolde. Springing back, however, the man missed his footing in the churned snow and staggered. Micum killed him before he'd regained his balance and was just turning to address his final opponent when a sharp blow from behind knocked him to his knees. Looking down, he found a bloody arrowhead protruding from the front of his leather shirt just beneath his right arm. The two swordsmen, unable to break through his defense, had managed to push him out onto the road and into the archers' range.

Serves me right for not paying attention, he thought angrily, seeing the final stroke coming down. Before it could, though, the bravo fell backward with a red-fletched arrow squarely through his chest.

Ducking for cover again, Micum looked across the road. Alec knelt behind the dead horse, returning the archers' shots with a singing volley of his own. Two lay dead already, and another dropped as Micum watched.

"By the Flame," Micum gasped. "By the *Flame*!"

• • •

Seregil disappeared into the forest at the first sign of ambush. Making a wide circuit, he outflanked three swordsmen headed in Alec's direction and then worked his way into their path, concealing himself behind a fallen tree until they came abreast of him. When all three had passed, he jumped out and swung at the hindmost, killing him with a slash across the back of the neck. The second man turned in time to catch Seregil's blade in the throat.

Unfortunately, the third man—a great, heavyset villain armed with a broadsword—had ample time to face him. He caught Seregil's first blow at midblade, throwing it back in an attempt to wrench it free. Seregil maintained his grip, but the force of the blow sent an unpleasant shock up his arm. He considered a timely retreat into the woods, but the snow was too deep for sprinting. Springing back a pace, he sized up his opponent.

Evidently the other man was doing the same; he gestured derisively at the slender blade Seregil carried, spat into the snow, then launched a mighty swing at his head. Hoping for the best, Seregil pulled a dagger and ducked under the blade, throwing himself at his adversary's knees. The unexpected move caught the man off guard just long enough for Seregil to bury the knife in his thigh. With a bellow of pain, the man tumbled backward, dragging Seregil with him, and immediately rolled to pin him.

Caught face down under the larger man's bulk, Seregil choked on the powdery snow. Try as he might, he couldn't break free. Then the weight shifted and cold, callused hands were around his throat, cutting off his wind and shaking him like a rat. Summoning all his will, he managed to draw up his leg to reach his boot top. A sizzling haze of stars swam before his eyes, but practiced fingers found the grip of his poniard. With the last of his strength, he drove it back between his assailant's ribs.

The big man let out a startled grunt, then crumpled over on top of him, still pinning him down. Gasping for air, Seregil heaved the body aside and staggered to his feet.

"Illior's merciful today," he panted, bending to make certain the man was dead.

Something buzzed past his head like an angry wasp and he flung himself down, pulling his poniard free of the body. But it was Alec, another arrow ready on the string, who stepped from the trees. The boy's left thigh was bloody and he looked decidedly pale. Micum Cavish was with him, holding a bloodstained wad of cloth against his side.

"Behind you." Micum nodded past Seregil's shoulder.

Turning, Seregil found another ambusher sprawled dead in the snow not four feet from his back, a red-feathered arrow through his throat.

"Well," he gasped, standing up to brush off the snow, "I believe you just repaid me for that bow."

"By Sakor, this child can shoot!" Micum grinned. "He just put me in his debt back at the road, then picked off two more as easy as you please. I saw another take off through the trees when Alec was coming over to tend me."

"Damn," Seregil muttered as he collected his weapons and searched the dead men scattered around. "Get your arrow from that one, Alec."

Alec approached the dead man and gingerly tugged on the shaft protruding from his neck. As he pulled it free, the man's head rolled to the side, his open eyes seeming to fix on his killer. Alec backed away from him with a shudder, carefully wiping the arrowhead in the snow before dropping it into his quiver.

Back at the road they gathered the other bodies into a heap. Alec pulled the arrow from the first man he'd shot, but before he could clean it, Micum took it from him.

"That was your first man, wasn't it?" he asked.

"Micum, it's not his way," Seregil warned, knowing what his friend was up to.

"It's best to do these things proper," Micum replied quietly. "I did it for you, remember? It's you should be doing it for him."

"No, it's your ritual," Seregil sighed, slouching against a tree. "Go ahead, then. Get it over with."

"Come here, Alec. Stand facing me." Micum was uncommonly serious as he held up the arrow. "There's a twofold purpose in this. The old ways, the soldier ways, say that if you drink the blood of your first man, none of the others you ever kill will be able to haunt you. Open your mouth."

Alec shot a questioning look to Seregil, who only shrugged and looked away. Under Micum's commanding gaze, Alec opened his mouth. Micum laid the arrowhead briefly against his tongue, then withdrew it.

Seregil saw the boy grimace, remembered the salt and copper

taste that had flooded his own mouth years before when Micum had done the same with him. His stomach stirred uneasily.

When it was over, Micum patted Alec's shoulder. "I know you didn't enjoy that much, any more than you enjoyed killing those fellows. Just remember that you did it to protect yourself and your friends, and that's a good thing, the only good reason to kill. But don't ever get so that you like it, any more than you liked the taste of the blood. You understand that?"

Alec looked down at the steaming crimson stains spreading out from the bodies in the snow and nodded.

"I understand."

7

SOUTH TO BOERSBY

In spite of his wound, Micum agreed with Seregil that they should bolt through as quickly as possible to Boersby. Giving wide berth to the few steadings and inns that lay along the road, they kept up a steady pace for as long as Micum could stay in the saddle, slept in the open, and ate whatever Alec shot.

Micum's wound didn't fester, but it was giving him more pain than he cared to admit. More aggravating still, however, was Seregil's increasing silence during the day and a half it took to reach the banks of the Folcwine. From past experience, Micum recognized this as a sure sign that something was amiss; Seregil's black mood could go on indefinitely if something didn't happen to shake him out of it.

They rode out of the forest at late afternoon and sat looking out over the broad course of the Folcwine. Micum was bleeding again, and it left him faint and irritable.

"Bilairy's Guts, Seregil, come out with it before I knock you down!" he growled at last.

Scowling down at his horse's neck, Seregil muttered, "I wish we'd taken just one of them alive."

"One of—oh, hell, man! Are you still brooding about that?" Micum turned to Alec. "A nest of forest bandits—hardly a rarity in the Folcwine—surprises him, and instantly there's some dark plot afoot. I think he's just piqued that he didn't hear them coming."

Alec looked down at his hands, apparently finding it politic not to comment.

"All right, then." Seregil turned in the saddle to face Micum. "We searched the bodies. What did we find?"

"Nothing out of the ordinary," Micum snapped. "Not one solitary thing!"

"That's right. But think again, what *did* they have?"

Micum snorted with exasperation. "Cloaks, boots, belts, tunics, all local stuff."

"Swords and bows," Alec ventured.

"Locally made?"

"The bows were. I don't know about the swords."

"Looked to be," Micum said slowly, thinking back. "But what in the name of all—"

"Everything was new!" Seregil exclaimed, as if they should immediately understand. "Did they have gold, jewelry, fancy clothes?" he demanded. "Not a scrap! A little silver in their purses, but not so much as a luck charm or knucklebone otherwise. So what we're left with is a gang of ruffians in new local clothing, carrying new local weapons, who are either so inept at their trade or of such austere temperament that they forgo any of the usual adornments."

With that he sat glowering at the others, thin mouth twisted in an exasperated grimace.

He looks like a filthy young lordling berating dim-witted servants, thought Micum, again resisting the temptation to knock his friend off his horse.

Alec suddenly straightened in his saddle. "They weren't bandits at all. They were just rigged out to look like it!"

Seregil's features relaxed into something like a smile for the first time that day. "But more than that, they were foreign to the area. Otherwise, they'd have had no need to buy everything new."

"When we searched the bodies there weren't any guild marks, were there?" asked Alec. "You know, like that Juggler at Asengai's?"

"No, at least none that I recognized. But that may not be significant in itself."

Micum smiled to himself, watching them go over the details

of the ambush again like two hounds on a fresh scent. The boy was hooked for certain.

"So who are they?" he broke in at last. "Plenimarans? Even if they tracked us, which I doubt, how could they get far enough ahead of us to set up an ambush?"

"I don't think they could," said Seregil. "These fellows were already in place, waiting for us."

Micum stroked down the corners of his heavy mustache. "But that still means they'd have to have gotten word of who we were and which way we were coming."

"That's right," Seregil agreed. "It could have been by magic, or pigeon. In any case, it means there's a good deal more afoot here than we thought. All the more reason for staying off the main roads and getting to Skala as soon as possible. Time may be shorter than we think."

"If the Overlord's forces—" Micum began, but Seregil cut him short with a quick glance toward Alec.

"Sorry, Alec," he said, "we trust you well enough, but we answer to others in this matter. It's probably safer this way anyhow."

Seregil looked up at the lowering clouds. "We're losing the light fast, but we're too close to town for me to spend another night outside. What do you say, Micum? Are you well enough to press on?"

"Let's press on. You've got contacts there, don't you?"

"At the Tipsy Frog. We'll stay the night there."

The lamps were lit by the time they reached the town.

Unlike Wolde, Boersby was a rough and ragged wayside town consisting almost entirely of establishments catering to the traders. Jumbled together at the water's edge like thirsty cattle, inns, taverns, and warehouses competed for frontage with the long docks stretching out into the river.

With winter coming on, the town was crowded with the last rush of traders trying to make a profit before the roads closed until spring.

Seregil led the way to a dubious-looking hostelry at the edge of town. The battered signboard over the door displayed a bilious green creature—no doubt intended by the artist to be a frog—draining a hogshead.

A sizable crowd milled about in the dim confines of the main room, hollering back and forth and pounding on tables for service. A fire smoldered on the large hearth, filling the room with an eye-stinging haze. A heavy plank laid across two barrels served as the bar, and behind it stood a lean, pasty-faced man in a leather apron.

"Any rooms?" Seregil inquired, giving the taverner a discreet hand sign.

"Only got one left at the back, nothin' fancy," the taverner replied with a quick wink. "One silver penny per night, in advance."

With a curt nod Seregil tossed a few coins on the bar. "Send up some food—whatever you've got and lots of it—and water. We're just off the trail and hungry as wolves."

The room was hardly more than a lean-to built onto the back of the tavern. A sagging bedstead against the far wall, its linen hinting broadly of previous lodgers, was the only furnishing. A scruffy lad appeared a moment later with a candle stand and a covered firepot, closely followed by another with a platter of roast pork and turnips, and pitchers of ale and water.

A soft knock came at the door as they were eating. It was the landlord this time. Without a word, he handed Seregil a bundle and left.

"Come along, Alec," said Seregil, tucking it under his arm. "Bring the pack. There's a bathhouse next door and I could do with a wash. What about you, Micum?"

"Good idea. I doubt I could stand the three of us in a closed room tonight." He rubbed a hand ruefully through the thick, coppery stubble on his cheeks. "I could do with a good shave, as well, not that either of you would understand!"

The bathhouse was a drafty establishment. After some determined haggling with the woman who owned it, Seregil saw to it that the two splintery wooden tubs the place boasted of were emptied of their murky contents and refilled with clean water. For an additional fee she heated two buckets of water to take off the chill. As they stripped down, she brought in towels and coarse yellow soap, then took their clothes away to be washed. No stranger to naked customers, she greeted Alec's hot-cheeked discomfort with open disdain.

"You've got to get over that, you know," Seregil remarked as he and Micum settled in their tubs.

"What?" Alec huddled closer to the room's tiny fire, waiting his turn.

"This modesty of yours. Or at least the blushing part."

Micum sank back with a sigh, letting the tepid water soften the crusted blood around his wound. Seregil scrubbed himself quickly head to foot and climbed out again.

"All yours, Alec. Use the soap and have a care for your nails. I've a notion to elevate our station in life by tomorrow." He was shivering as he scrubbed the ragged towel over his hair and shoulders. "Illior's Hands!" he grumbled. "I swear when I get back to Rhíminee I'm going to head for the nearest civilized bath and stay there a week!"

"I've seen him fight through fire, blood, starvation, and magic," Micum remarked, speaking to nobody in particular, "but deny him a hot bath at the end of it and he fusses like a kept whore."

"A lot you'd know about that." Unrolling his bundle, Seregil shook out a coarse woolen dress and pulled it on over his head.

Alec gaped in astonishment, and Seregil give him a wink. "Time for another lesson, I think."

He quickly plaited his hair back into a loose braid and pulled a few strands free to hang untidily around his face. Greyish powder from small pouch dulled his hair and skin. Unwrapping the rest of the bundle, he pulled out a huge striped shawl, battered wooden clogs, and a leather girdle. Satisfied with his work, he tucked the smallest of his daggers out of sight under his belt and turned away for a moment, rearranging his body beneath the loose gown to give the impression of the stooped frailty of age. When he turned back again, Alec and Micum saw an unremarkable little servant woman.

"Would the two gentlemen be good enough to give an opinion?" Seregil asked in an old woman's voice heavy with the soft accent of Mycena.

Micum gave his nodded approval. "Well met, gramma. Where are you off to in that getup?"

"Less said, less heard," Seregil replied, going to the door. "I'm off to see which way the wind blows. If anyone asks, just say I had other clothes, which of course," he added, dropping a rusty curtsy and flashing his best crooked grin, "I do!"

• • •

When their clothes came back, Alec and Micum returned to their room at the Frog. The candles were lit and the firepot glowed cheerfully on its tripod in the center of the room.

"How's your side feel now?" Alec asked.

"Better, but I'll rest easier on the floor," Micum said, eyeing the sagging ropes showing beneath the bed frame. "Just be a good lad and help me make up a pallet with the cloaks here next to the door."

Alec laid down blankets and cloaks for him and Micum sat down gratefully, sword across his knees.

"Bring your sword over and I'll show you how to keep a proper edge on it," he invited, taking out a pair of whetstones.

They worked in silence for a while, listening to the singing of metal against stone. Bone-tired, Alec was grateful to find Micum a person easy to be quiet with. The man's uncomplicated good nature demanded no idle chatter.

He was rather startled, therefore, when Micum said without looking up from his task, "You're as quiet as a stump. You might not think it, but I'm just as nosy as Seregil in my way."

When Alec hesitated, he continued, not unkindly, "I never imagined him taking on an apprentice at all, and certainly not a simple young woods colt like you. Not that I mean any offense, mind you. It's just that you've more the look of a gamekeeper's son than a spy. So tell me, what do you think of our friend?"

"Well," to be honest, I'm not quite sure what to think. From the first he's treated me like—as if—"

He stopped in confusion; he'd seldom been consulted about his opinions, and had to search for the words to frame them. Besides, while Micum's open, jovial manner invited candor, it was clear that he and Seregil were close friends.

"It's as if he knows all about me," he managed at last. "And sometimes like he assumes I know all about him. He's saved my life, clothed me, taught me all sorts of things. It's just that every so often it occurs to me that I don't know much about him. I tried asking him about his home, his family—that sort of thing—but he just smiles and changes the subject. He's good at that."

Micum gave a knowing chuckle.

"Anyway," Alec continued, "he seems to think he can make me into whatever it is that he is, but it makes me nervous sometimes. I don't know enough about him to know what he expects of me! You're his friend and all, and I wouldn't ask you to break a confidence, but isn't there something you can tell me about him?"

"Oh, I think so." Micum ran a thumbnail along the edge of his sword blade. "We first met years ago up near the Gold Vein River. We got on well enough and when he went south to Rhíminee again, I went with him.

"He has an old friend there, Nysander, and it was from him that I learned most of what I know about our closemouthed friend. Where he came from and why he left is for him to tell you. I don't know much of it myself, except that he has some degree of noble blood that connects him to the Skalan court. He was hardly older that you are now when he came to Skala, but he'd seen some trouble already. Nysander's a wizard, and he took Seregil on as an apprentice. It must not have worked out, though—Seregil's no wizard, for all his tricks with animals—but they've stayed friends. You'll meet him when you get there. Seregil always visits him first thing when he comes home from a jaunt."

"A wizard! What's he like?"

"Nysander? He's a good old soul, kind as the Maker on a summer's day. A lot of the other wizards act pretty grand and mighty, but let old Nysander get a drink or two in him and he's likely to start conjuring green unicorns or setting the knives to dancing with the spoons, for all that he's one of the old ones."

"Old ones?"

"Wizards live as along as Aurënfaie, and Nysander's been around a good long time. He must be pushing three hundred these days. He knew Queen Idrilain's grandmother, and Idrilain's a grandmother herself now. He's a great favorite of hers. She has him to her chambers frequently, and he's always at banquets."

"Seregil said there were a lot of wizards at Rhíminee."

"There's a whole place full of them, called the Orëska House—though it's more like a castle than a house. Like I was saying, a lot of them are pretty full of themselves and take him for a doddering old fool, snub him even. But you just wait until you meet him, then make up your own mind.

"As for Seregil, don't worry about him. He's not the trusting type, so if he's chosen to take you along with him, you can be sure he's pleased with you—whatever his reasons. One thing I can tell you for certain is that he'll lay down his life for a friend, and never leave a comrade in the lurch. *Never.* He may tell you different—and once you see how he lives in Rhíminee, you may wonder—but I know him and he's as true as the sun in the sky. The one thing he can't forgive is betrayal; you'll do well to remember that. Somewhere, back before he came to Skala, someone betrayed him badly somehow and it's left a mark on him for life. He'll kill anyone who betrays him."

Alec mulled this over for a moment, then asked, "What's Rhíminee like?"

"It's the most beautiful city in the world. It's also rotten with intrigue. The royal family has more branches than a willow and they're always scheming against each other for a higher place on the tree. Political plots, old feuds, secret lovers, and who knows what else. And more often than not, when one of them needs a document stolen or some token delivered in the dead of night, it's our friend Seregil who does the job. The people who hire him never actually meet him, mind you, but those who want his services know how to contact him. You ask for the 'Rhíminee Cat.' He's the best and worst kept secret in the city."

"It's all so hard to imagine." Alec shook his head ruefully. "He thinks I can do that sort of thing?"

"I told you before, if he wasn't certain you could, you wouldn't be here. I wager he sees something in you that neither you nor I do. Oh, he'd have rescued you anyway, no matter what, but there must be something else that's caused him to keep you on with him."

Micum caught his eye and winked. "Now there's a mystery for you to solve, for I doubt you'll ever hear it from Seregil. In the meantime, though, don't worry about pleasing him. Just keep your eyes open and follow his lead."

Slipping back into the room, Seregil threw his shawl aside and sprawled across the bed to ease the kinks from his back. Micum and Alec looked at him expectantly.

"There's a price on Aren Windover's head, and yours, too, Alec," he informed them. "There was also mention of an unknown third man. I trust this information was furnished by the man who got away on the road the other day."

"Don't start on that," Micum warned. "Who's offering this reward? Our good mayor of Wolde?"

"Supposedly. The message came by pigeon yesterday, saying that we've carried off the guild money box or some such nonsense."

"How much is Aren worth this time?"

"Twenty silver marks."

"Bilairy's gateposts!" Micum gasped. "What the hell have you gotten into?"

"Damned if I know." Seregil scrubbed a hand wearily through his hair. "Where's my pouch?"

Alec tossed it to him and he took out the wooden disk, regarding it with a puzzled scowl. "This is the only thing we took. I can't figure what would make it worth all this trouble, but I guess we'd better keep a close guard on it, just in case."

Threading a length of leather lacing through the square hole in its center, he stared at it again for a moment, then tied the thong around his neck. "If they want it back that badly, I'm all the more determined to get it to Skala."

"And how much do they want for me?" Alec asked. "It's the first time I've been an outlaw."

"Twenty marks, same as me. Not bad for one of your tender years. They only offered half that for Micum."

"You're certain there was no mention of me by name?" asked Micum.

"None at all. Seems you got away clean."

"I've always come and gone as I pleased around there, so I won't be missed. Are we in danger here?"

"I don't think so. If they had agents in Boersby, they wouldn't have involved the locals. It sounds like they sent similar messages all over: Stook, Ballton, Ösk, even Sark. Whoever they are, they've lost us and they're not pleased. Just the same, I think we'd best be very careful."

"If they're looking for two men and a boy, I say we split up." Micum stroked his mustache thoughtfully. "I believe I'd like to circle back anyway, have a look at that place you saw marked on the map, down in the Blackwater Fens. I'll head out before first light."

"Are you sure you're up to it?"

"I'll ride easy."

"Take our horses with you when you go and send word as

soon as you can. I've already booked passage for Alec and myself down to Nanta. If you need to find us, we'll be aboard a
river trader called the *Darter*. She's got a black hull with a red
cutwater. Ask for Lady Gwethelyn of Cador Ford."

"Lady Gwethelyn?" Micum grinned. "It's been a while since
I've heard from that good lady. You're in for a singular treat,
Alec my lad!"

8

THE CAPTAIN AND THE LADY

"That's a warm-lookin' wench, even if she is a bit past her prime, eh, Captain Rhal?" the helmsman remarked.

The *Darter's* triangular sail was bellied out in the brisk wind, and Rhal moved to the rail for a better view of his passenger, still seated in the prow.

The captain was a stocky, dark-haired man of middling years. Though somewhat balding, he was still comely enough in a rakish, weather-beaten sort of way to attract the graces of a good many women in a good many ports—a fact he was glad to capitalize on.

"That she is. I've always fancied a trim-cut wench," he agreed, discounting Skywake's appraisal of her age; coming from him that meant anything over the age of fourteen. Though the lady in question was clearly past the first blush of youth, she was no beldam. Perhaps twenty-five?

Lady Gwethelyn and her young squire had come aboard at dawn. After seeing her gear stowed in the small passenger cabin, she'd asked the captain if she might sit in the prow, as she was prone to seasickness and thought that the breeze might help ward it off until she became accustomed to the motion of the ship. Her soft, low voice and gentle manner had charmed him right down to his boots.

The trip downriver might not be so monotonous this time, after all.

Studying her in the morning light, Rhal found no cause to alter his first assessment. Her carefully draped wimple framed a demure, fine-boned face. Under her mantle she wore a high-necked traveling gown that showed to advantage a slender waist and gently rounded bosom. She might be a bit thin through the hips for some, but as he'd remarked to Skywake, he liked his women trim. The chill wind off the water had brought out the roses in her pale cheeks, and her wide grey eyes seemed to sparkle as she leaned toward her traveling companion to point out some detail on the distant bank. Perhaps she was closer to twenty?

The *Darter*'s primary cargo was generally furs and spices, but years ago Rhal had found it lucrative to add an extra cabin below decks, and he often ferried passengers up and down the Folcwine. The previous evening, an old servant woman had booked passage as far as Nanta for the lady and her squire. In return for a glass of ale, the old gossip was happy to extol the beauties of her mistress and bemoan the frailty of health that forced her to spend the harsh winter months with her relations in the south.

This was common enough; many of the more well-to-do merchants in the northlands found themselves southern wives, and often these ladies preferred to migrate back to their warmer homelands before the icy grip of the northern winter brought all normal activity to a halt.

Seeing to it that the sail was properly trimmed, Rhal went forward to con the river. The Folcwine was broad and generally forgiving, but this was the season for gravel bars.

His new position afforded him a better view of his passengers, and he found himself distracted again. The ever-present squire—scarcely more than a raw boy for all his livery and sword—had stepped to the rail. The woman sat gazing pensively toward the shore, hands clasped in her lap.

Her dress, her manner, the large garnet ring she wore on one gloved forefinger, all confirmed her a lady of quality, but Rhal found himself again wondering about her reasons for traveling. She'd come aboard with nothing but a large hamper and one none-too-heavy trunk. The squire had a battered old pack that weighed nearly as much; hardly the baggage of a gentlewoman. That, together with her lack of women servants and the late hour at which her passage was booked, suggested a more interesting possibility. Could it be she was a runaway wife? One could always hope, and, by Astellus, he had a week to find out!

While Seregil would have been more than pleased with the impression he had made upon the captain, his pensive mood was no ruse.

The previous night, he'd found suitable clothing for himself and Alec, then checked Micum's wound and tried unsuccessfully to get him to take the bed. When all efforts had failed, Seregil had tumbled into it beside Alec and fallen asleep almost at once. Aside from the fact that he was worn out from the events of the last few days, he knew it was the only way to escape Micum's thunderous snoring.

Sometime later, he'd awakened with the sense of something amiss. A strong wind had come up in the night. It gusted around the corners of the building, sighing through the cracks in the walls. The firepot had died to a dim glow and he was cold except for the warmth of Alec's naked back resting lightly against his own. This in itself was odd, he'd thought, because together with the fact that he didn't remember disrobing, the boy's persistent modesty would hardly have allowed him to sleep naked with anyone else.

Yet that wasn't it, he decided sleepily. By the faint light of the firepot, he could make out Micum's bulk on the pallet by the door. Something wrong there, something obvious—if only his foggy brain would clear.

Sliding out of bed, he crossed softly to where Micum lay, disliking the feel of the rough, cold boards under his bare feet. The sense of unease grew stronger as he crouched beside him; he had never known Micum to sleep so quietly.

His friend lay curled on his side, facing away from Seregil so that he could scarcely hear the man's breathing. In fact, he couldn't hear any breathing at all.

"Micum, wake up," he whispered, but his throat was so dry that hardly a sound came. Dread—thick and palpable—pressed around him and he grasped his friend's shoulder, suddenly desperate for him to wake up, to speak.

Micum was as cold to the touch as the floor beneath Seregil's feet. Jerking his hand away, he found it darkly stained with blood. Micum slumped slowly onto his back, and Seregil saw the gaping wound in his friends throat where his own poniard was still lodged. Micum's eyes were open, his expression one of terrible surprise and sadness.

An anguished cry welled in Seregil's throat. He lurched back and pushed himself away from the body, snagging tender skin on the rough planking.

The wind mounted a sudden assault on the house, slamming one of the window shutters back in a frigid blast of air. Fanned by the draft, the coals blazed up for an instant, and by their brief illumination, Seregil caught sight of a tall figure standing in the corner nearest the window. The man was closely muffled from head to knees in a dark mantle but Seregil recognized the implacable straightness of back, the slightly inclined head, the sharp thrust of a cocked elbow under the cloak as an unseen hand rested on belt or pommel. And, with an utterly unpleasant mingling of precognition and memory, he knew exactly how their conversation would begin.

"Well, Seregil, this *is* a pretty state I find you in."

"Father, this isn't how it appears," Seregil replied, hating the pleading note he heard in his own voice—the very echo of a past self who'd uttered these same words in a situation not unlike the present one—but powerless to sound otherwise. But his older self was also uneasily aware of his empty weapon hand.

"It *appears* that you have a dead friend on your floor and a catamite in your bed." His father's voice was just as he remembered: dry, sardonic, full of calculated disapprobation.

"That's only Alec—" Seregil began angrily, but the words died in his throat as the boy rose naked from the bed with a wanton grace completely unlike his usual manner. Coming to Seregil, he pressed warmly against him and exchanged an arch glance with his father.

"Your choice of companions has not improved."

"Father, please!" A dizzying sense of unreality closed in on Seregil as he sank to his knees.

"Exile has only strengthened your baser tendencies," his father sneered. "As ever, you are a disgrace to our house. Some other punishment must be found."

Then, with that rare gentleness that had always taken Seregil off guard, he shook his head and sighed. "Seregil, my youngest, what am I to do with you? It has been so long! Let us at least clasp hands."

Seregil reached to take his father's hand. Shameful tears burned his eyes as he peered up into the depths of the hood, hoping for a glimpse of the well-remembered face. Yet even then a tiny, sickening tendril of doubt uncurled at the back of his mind. Alec's hands tightened on his shoulders as his father's hand closed around his.

"You're dead!" Seregil groaned, trying too late to pull away from the fleshless grasp that held him. "Nine years ago! Adzriel sent word. You're dead!"

His father nodded agreeably, pushing back his hood. A few strands of dark hair clung to the shriveled scalp. The sharp grey eyes were gone, leaving two black craters in their place; the bridge of his nose was eaten away. Shriveled lips twisted into the parody of a smile as he inclined his ruined face, engulfing Seregil in a sullen, mouldy odor.

"True, but I am still your father," the thing went on, "and you shall be properly punished!"

A sword flashed from under the cloak and he stepped back, holding Seregil's severed right hand in his—

—and Seregil had bolted up in the bed, drenched in sweat, clutching both hands to his heaving chest. There was no wind, no open shutter. Micum's snoring rose and fell in a comforting rumble. Beside him, Alec stirred and mumbled a question.

"It's nothing, go back to sleep," Seregil whispered, and with his heart beating much too quickly, he'd tried to do the same.

Even now, with the sunlight glancing off the water and the rapid chuckle of the current beneath the bow, the ominous, disorienting feel of the dream haunted him. He'd certainly had nightmares before but never about his father, not since he'd left home, and never one that had left him with such a throbbing headache the next day. A cup of mulled wine at the tavern had helped, but now it was creeping back, hammering at his temples and bringing a bitter taste into his throat. He wanted desperately to rub his eyes, but the carefully applied cosmetics prevented even this slight relief.

"Are you still unwell, lady?"

Seregil turned to find the captain towering over him.

"Just a bit of headache, Captain," he replied, modulating his voice to the softer tones he'd adopted for this particular role.

"That's probably from the sun off the water, my lady. Come around behind the mast. You'll still feel the breeze, but the sail will shade you from the glare. I'll have one of the men heat some wine for you; that should put you right."

Offering his arm, Rhal led his fair passenger back to a bench attached to the deckhouse. To his ill-concealed annoyance, Alec followed them back and took up a station at the starboard rail.

"That boy keeps a close watch on you," Rhal observed, seating himself next to "Gwethelyn" rather more closely than the span of the bench required.

"Ciris is a kinsman of my husband's," Seregil replied. "My husband has entrusted him with my safety. He takes his task very seriously."

"Still, it doesn't seem that a slip of a boy could be much protection." A sailor appeared with a pitcher of wine and a pair of wooden cups. Rhal served Seregil himself.

"I'm certain you have nothing to fear on my account. Ciris is a fine swordsman," Seregil lied, sipping delicately at his wine; it had not escaped his notice that his cup was a good deal fuller than the captain's.

"Just the same," Rhal replied gallantly, leaning closer, "I'm making it my duty to watch over you until we reach port. If there's any service I can render, day or night, you've only to call on me. Perhaps you would do me the honor of taking supper with me in my cabin tonight?"

Seregil lowered his eyes demurely. "You're very kind, but I'm so weary from my journey that I shall retire quite early."

"Tomorrow night, then, when you're rested," the captain parried.

"Very well, tomorrow. I'm sure you've many tales that will entertain my squire as well as myself. We will be honored."

Captain Rhal rose with a slight bow; the fleeting look of frustration Seregil caught as he turned away assured him that, at least for the moment, he'd held the day.

• • •

"Captain Rhal's out to seduce me," Seregil announced in their little cabin that evening, applying fresh cosmetics while Alec held the lantern and a small mirror.

"What are you going to do?"

Seregil winked. "Go along with him, of course. Up to a point, anyway."

"Well, you could hardly let him, you know—" Alec gestured vaguely.

"Yes, *I* know, though I rather wonder if you do." Seregil raised an appraising eyebrow at his young companion. "But you're right, of course. Letting him under my skirts now would certainly spoil the illusion I've worked so hard to create. Still"—dropping into the manner of Lady Gwethelyn, he looked up at Alec through his lashes—"this Captain Rhal is a handsome rogue, wouldn't you say?"

Alec shook his head, unsure whether Seregil was being serious or not. "Are you going to sleep with all that on your face?"

"I think it might be wise. If the man is determined enough to invite a married woman to his cabin on the first day, I certainly wouldn't put it past him to find some excuse to wander in here during the night. That's why I'm also going to wear that."

He gestured toward the fine linen nightgown on the bed. "The key to successfully traveling in a disguise is to maintain it at all times, no matter what. Unlace me." Standing up, he held his hair to one side while Alec undid the back of the gown. "The practice may come in handy for you someday."

From this angle, Alec was uneasily aware of the completeness of Seregil's disguise. Throughout the day, watching from across the deck as Seregil played Gwethelyn for the captain and crew, he'd been halfway taken in himself.

The illusion was considerably diminished, however, as the gown fell away and Seregil began untying his false bosom. It was his own creation, he'd explained proudly—a sort of close-fitting linen undershirt, the modest breasts consisting of domed pockets stuffed with balls of soft wool.

"Better than some real ones you'll run across," he said with a grin. "I think I can do without that for now, though." He tucked the garment carefully away in the chest. "As the defender of my honor, it's up to you to keep our good captain from discovering their loss, should he appear."

"You'd be safer with Micum along."

"Micum hates working with me when I go as a woman. Says I'm 'too damned pretty by half' and it makes him nervous."

"I can understand that," Alec replied with a self-conscious grin. "Lady Gwethelyn" sounded a troubling chord in him, as well. Seregil's convincing illusion stirred up a confusion that Alec hadn't the philosophy to put into words.

"You'll do fine. Besides, a lady is allowed some protection of her own." Smiling, Seregil pulled a small dagger from the sleeve of his discarded gown and tucked it under his pillow. "I've heard that Plenimaran women are expected to use these on themselves if some stranger invades their bedchamber, so as to protect their husband's honor. I call that adding injury to insult."

"Have you ever been to Plenimar?" Alec asked, sensing the opening for a tale.

"Just along the borders and territories, never into the country itself." Seregil pulled on the nightdress and set about braiding his hair over one shoulder. "Strangers don't pass unnoticed there. Unless you have some good honest reason for going there, it's better to stay away. From what I've heard, spies there have extremely short lives. I find more than enough to keep me busy in Rhíminee."

"Micum says—" Alec began, but was interrupted by a heavy knock at the door.

"Who's there?" Seregil called in Gwethelyn's voice, wrapping himself in a cloak and signaling for Alec to retreat to the curtained servant's alcove.

"Captain Rhal, my lady," came the muffled reply. "I thought some tea might help you to sleep."

Alec peeked out of his alcove, and Seregil rolled his eyes. "How very thoughtful."

Alec stepped forward on cue as Rhal came in, taking the steaming pitcher with a bow that effectively blocked further progress into the room.

"I was just about to put out the candle," Seregil said with a yawn. "I shall have a cup, and I'm sure I shall go directly to sleep. Good night."

Rhal managed a strained bow and left, but not before shooting a decidedly unfriendly glance in Alec's direction.

Alec closed the door firmly and turned to find Seregil shaking with silent laughter.

"By the Four, Alec, you'd better watch your back," Seregil

whispered. "My new swain is jealous of you! And the way you met him at the door—"

He broke off, wiping his eyes. "Ah, I'll sleep soundly tonight knowing my virtue is so well guarded. But I believe your constancy deserves a reward. Pour the tea and we'll have a tale!"

When they'd settled comfortably on either end of the bunk with their cups, Seregil took a long sip and said expansively, "So, what would you like to hear about?"

Alec thought for a moment; he had so many questions, it was difficult to know where to begin. "The warrior queens of Skala," he replied at last.

"Excellent choice. The history of the queens is the essence of Skala itself. You recall me saying that the first of these queens appeared during the first great war against Plenimar?"

Alec nodded. "Queen Gera-something."

"Ghërilain the First. The Oracle's Queen, she's sometimes called, because of the circumstances of her crowning. At the start of the war Skala was ruled from Eros by her father, Thelátimos. He was a good leader, but Plenimar was at the height of her strength and by the tenth year it looked as if Skala and Mycena were going to fall. Plenimar had overrun Mycena as far as the Folcwine River years before and controlled the farmlands and territories to the north. With their superior sea power and ample resources, they had every advantage."

"And they had the necromancers," Alec interjected. "And their armies of walking dead, you said."

"I see that certain subjects stick in your mind. I believe I said that legends mention *rumors* of such things. The Plenimarans are known for their brutality and thoroughness both during battle and after. It's a short step from there to monsters, wouldn't you say?"

Noticing that Alec looked a little crestfallen, he added kindly, "But it's important to have a good ear and a sharp memory; you're well equipped in those respects. In our trade you have to sift every tale, separate the true weave from the embroidery, as it were.

"But to resume my tale, things looked quite hopeless that tenth winter of the war. In desperation, Thelátimos resolved to consult the Afran Oracle. This meant making a long, dangerous journey to Afra, which lies in the hills of central Skala. But he reached the precinct by the solstice and asked what he should do. The royal scribe who accompanied him took down the Oracle's reply word for word. Thelátimos later had it inscribed on a golden tablet that is displayed to this day in the throne room at Rhíminee. It reads: 'So long as a daughter of Thelátimos' line defends and rules, Skala shall never be subjugated.'

"Those words changed the course of history forever. Since the Afran Oracles were renowned for the accuracy and wisdom of their prophecies, Thelátimos, though rather surprised, decided to follow the edict. The divine covenant was proclaimed and his four sons duly stepped aside in favor of their sister Ghërilain, a girl just your age and the youngest of his children.

"There was a great deal of controversy among the generals as to whether the Oracle meant for an untried girl to take over the actual leading of the armies. Thelátimos meant to follow the letter of the prophecy. Declaring his daughter Queen, he instructed his commanders to prepare her for war. As the story goes, they had other ideas. They gave her a bit of training, dressed her up in fine armor, and stuck her in the center of a sizable bodyguard at the rear of the army. During the next battle, however, young Ghërilain rallied her guard, led them to the front, and personally killed the Overlord Krysethan the Second. Although the war continued another two years, her actions that day bought Skala and her allies enough time for the Aurënfaie to arrive. From that day no one doubted Ghërilain's divine right to lead."

"And there have been queens ever since?" asked Alec. "No one ever questioned the Oracle's words?"

"Some did. Ghërilain's son Pelis secretly poisoned his sister when he was passed over as king, then took the throne, claiming that the Oracle had really meant 'so long as the daughter of Thelátimos rules' rather than 'a daughter of the line of Thelátimos.' Unfortunately for him, there was a devastating crop failure during his second year of rule, quickly followed by an outbreak of plague. He died, along with hundreds of others. As soon as his niece, Agnalain, took the throne things began to improve."

"But what if a queen had no daughters?"

"That's come up a few times over the last eight hundred years. Queen Marnil was the first. She had six fine sons but no acceptable successor. In desperation she journeyed to Afra where the Oracle instructed her to take another consort, specifying that she choose a man on the basis of bravery and honor."

"What about her husband?" asked Alec.

"That did present a problem, since the Oracle wasn't very specific. Since then, various queens have interpreted the directive in a number of ways. Some even used the office as a sort of reward. Queen Idrilain's grandmother, Elesthera, had more than thirty 'consorts,' but even the Skalans considered this rather eccentric."

"How could a queen produce legitimate heirs if she slept with any man who took her fancy?" Alec exclaimed, looking scandalized.

"What does legitimate mean, after all?" Seregil said with a laugh. "A king may be cuckolded if his wife can fool him into thinking that her lover's child is his own, not a difficult thing to do. But any child a queen bears is her own, no matter who the father was, and therefore a legitimate heir."

"I guess so," Alec conceded with obvious disapproval. "Were there any bad queens?"

"The usual mix over the years. Divinely instituted or not, they're still human."

Alec shook his head, grinning. "All these stories and histories. I don't see how you remember all that!"

"One has to, to do any sort of business among the Skalan nobles. Importance is judged by which branch of the line one is related to, how far back you can trace noble blood, which consort one is descended from, whether your ancestor was directly descended from a female or male branch, whether or not they were legitimate—I could go on, but you get the idea."

He set his cup aside and stretched. "And now I think we'd both do well to turn in. I've a busy day tomorrow dealing with our good captain, and you've got your work cut out for you defending my honor!"

9

THE LADY IS INDISPOSED

Seregil jerked awake just before dawn, a strangled groan crawling up his throat. He tried to choke it back, but the muffled croak was enough to bring Alec from his alcove.

"What is it? What's wrong?" the boy whispered, groping his way across the cramped cabin.

"Nothing, just a dream."

Alec's hand found his shoulder. "You're shaking like a spooked horse!"

"Strike a light, will you?" Seregil clasped his arms tightly around his knees, trying to quell the fit of trembling that shook him.

Alec quickly lit a candle at the companionway lantern and regarded Seregil with concern. "You're pale as anything. Sometimes the quickest way to make a nightmare pass is to tell it."

Seregil let out a long, slow breath and motioned for him to draw up the cabin's single chair; he was certainly in no hurry to sleep again.

"It was morning," he began softly, staring at the candle flame. "I was dressed and about to go on deck. I called for you but you weren't around, so I went alone.

"The sky was a hideous, boiling purple, the light through the clouds harsh and brassy—

you know, the way it is just before a thunderstorm? The ship was in ruins. The mast was snapped off, with the sail hanging down over the side, the deck all littered with wreckage. I called out again, but there was no one on board but me. The river was black as oil. There were things floating in the water all around the ship, too—severed heads, hands, arms, bodies—"

He scrubbed the back of one hand across his mouth. "What I could make out of the shore was a desolate waste, the land burned and torn up. Smoke from ruined fields flowed out over the water and as I watched it seemed to gather itself, moving toward the ship in great coils and billows. As it came closer I began to hear sounds. At first I couldn't make out their direction, but then I realized it was all around me. It was the—the things in the water. They were all moving, limbs flexing and kicking, the faces twisting into horrid expressions as they rolled in the water."

He heard a small gasp of revulsion from Alec; to a Dalnan, there was nothing more horrible than a desecrated corpse. Seregil drew another shaky breath and forced himself to continue.

"Then the ship lurched and I knew that something was climbing up the torn sail. I couldn't see what it was but it jerked the vessel around like a fishing float. I clung to the far rail, waiting for it. I knew that whatever it was, it was unspeakably vile—that the very sight of it was going to shatter me. Yet even in the midst of my terror, a small, sane part of my mind was screaming that there was something terribly important that I should be remembering. I didn't know if it would save me, but it was imperative that I think of it before I died. And then I woke up."

He managed a faint, self-mocking laugh. "There it is. Sounds rather silly, telling it like that."

"No, it was a bad one!" Alec shuddered. "And you still don't look too well. Do you think you can sleep some more?"

Seregil glanced at the brightening square of the window. "No, it's almost morning. You go back to bed, though. No sense both of us losing sleep over nothing."

"Are you sure?"

"Yes, you were right about telling it. It's fading already," Seregil lied. "I'll be fine."

. . .

As Seregil moved through the details of the morning, the nightmare did begin to fade, but in its wake came a strong sense of unease. His headache had returned, too, shortening his patience and unsettling his stomach. By noon he was so out of sorts that he retreated to his place by the cutwater, hoping to be left alone. Alec seemed to sense that he would do well to make himself useful elsewhere, but the captain was not so easily put off.

Traveling in disguise always posed complications, but Seregil was finding his current role more restrictive than usual. Rhal's inopportune attentions were more than he felt up to dealing with in his present state. The captain found frequent opportunities to make himself available to Lady Gwethelyn, noting points of interest along the shore, inquiring after her comfort, suggesting innumerable diversions for her young squire. He accepted her apologies graciously enough, but was firm in his intention to entertain them at supper that evening.

Soon after the midday meal, Seregil excused himself and spent the remainder of the afternoon dozing in the cabin. By the time Alec roused him to prepare for dinner he was feeling considerably better.

"Sorry to leave you on your own up there," he apologized as Alec worked at a knotted lacing on his gown. "Tomorrow we'll find a way to get in some training. Lady Gwethelyn can keep to her cabin with her squire in attendance. Swordplay would be rather awkward down here, but I'm sure we can come up with something. More signing and palming tricks, maybe. That's something you have to keep at or you'll lose it."

Wriggling out of the wrinkled garment, he lifted a fresh gown from the trunk and dropped it over his head. When Alec had pulled the lacings snug, he carefully draped a gauzy wimple over his hair, binding it with a silk cord and arranging the folds to spread gracefully over his shoulders. In addition to the garnet ring, he added a heavy chain of twisted gold and large pearl earrings.

"Illior's Fingers, I'm famished," he said as he finished. "I hope I can manage to eat in a ladylike fashion. What's for supper? Alec?"

The boy was regarding him with a perplexed expression. Blushing a bit, he blinked and replied, "We're having stewed fowl. I dressed out the birds for the cook while you were asleep."

He paused, then added with a grin, "And from what I heard from the sailors today, this disguise of yours is working."

"Oh? What did they have to say?"

"The cook claims he's never seen the captain so taken with a woman. Some of the others are taking bets on whether he'll have his way with you before we reach Nanta."

"Highly unlikely. I trust you to see to your duty, Squire Ciris, until we're safely ashore."

Rhal opened the door at their knock. He'd donned a fusty velvet coat for the occasion and had given his beard a proper trimming as well. With an inward groan, Seregil presented his hand and allowed himself to be escorted in.

"Welcome, dear lady!" Rhal exclaimed, pointedly ignoring Alec as he drew Seregil's arm through his own. "I hope you'll find everything to your liking."

A small table stood neatly set for three, the wine already poured, fine wax candles alight in place of the malodorous oil lanterns.

"Why, you look fresh as a spring rose at dawn," he went on, seating Seregil with practiced courtesy. "It pained me to see you looking so peaked this afternoon."

"I'm much better, thank you," Seregil murmured. Alec gave him a quick wink behind Rhal's back.

Both fowl and wine proved to be excellent. Conversation during the meal was somewhat strained, however. Rhal made little effort to include Alec, and replied somewhat stiffly when the boy made several pointed allusions to Lady Gwethelyn's fictitious husband. Having grown accustomed to his part, Alec was clearly beginning to revel in it.

"You must give us news from the south, Captain," Seregil interjected when a particularly grim pause threatened.

"Well, I suppose you've heard about the Plenimarans?" Rhal took a large, blackened pipe from a nearby rack. "With your permission, my lady? Thank you. Before we sailed from Nanta the week before last, news came through that the old Overlord, Petasárian, was ailing again and not expected to last long. That bodes ill for the rest of us, if you ask me. Being Skalan born, I don't care much for the Plenimarans, but Petasárian has held to the treaties these last five years. That heir of his, young Klystis, is another matter. They say he's been ruling in all but name this last year, and it looks to most like he's sharpening up the swords again. Rumor has it that he may even have a hand in the old man's illness, if you take my meaning. What I pick up along the coast is that there's a good many in Plenimar who think the Twelfth Treaty of Kouros should never have been signed, and that those who say so are anxious to get Petasárian out of the way so his son can set things to rights."

"Do you think there could be a war?" Seregil effortlessly counterfeited feminine alarm.

Rhal puffed sagely at his pipe. "Skala and Plenimar hardly know what to do with themselves when they're not killing each other off, though I hold the Plenimarans are generally the ones to kick the beehive. Yes, I think they're getting ready to go at it again, and mark my words, this time it'll be a bad one. Those that have business over that way say that there's an uncommon amount of ship building going on in Plenimaran ports. The press gangs are out in force, too. Sailors are getting shy of taking shore leave there."

This was fresh news to Seregil, but before he could pursue it further they were interrupted by the cabin boy who'd been sent in to clear the table. While the cloth was being changed, Rhal unlocked a small cabinet over his bunk and brought out a dusty decanter and three small pewter cups.

"Aged Zengati brandy. Quite rare," he confided as he poured. "My trade connections in Nanta give me access to a good many luxuries of this sort. Come, Squire Ciris, let's drink the health of our most excellent lady. May she continue to delight the eye and gladden the heart of those privileged to look upon her."

Though he spoke to Alec, his gaze never left Seregil's face as he raised his cup to his lips.

Seregil lowered his eyes modestly, sipping at the fiery spirit.

Alec lifted his cup again, adding with apparently ingenuous gallantry, "And to the fair child she carries, my next cousin!"

Rhal choked on his brandy, going into a brief coughing fit. Seregil looked up in startled amusement, but managed to compose himself by the time Rhal recovered.

"I would not have spoken of it had not my dear cousin, in his youthful enthusiasm, broached the indelicate subject," Seregil murmured, setting his cup aside. Mycenian ladies of quality were noted for their modesty and discretion.

But Rhal was clearly less put off than Alec had intended. Seregil could guess at the new train of thought behind those dark eyes. *After all, if a woman's already plowed and planted and still has a pleasing shape, what harm can be done?*

"My lady, I had no idea!" he said, patting her hand with renewed warmth.

The cook entered with a tray of covered bowls and Rhal set one in front of him. "No wonder you've been off your feet. Perhaps the dessert will be more to your liking."

"Indeed?" Seregil lifted the lid from his dish with a small expectant smile, then froze, the color draining from his face. Inside maggots writhed over severed ears, eyes, and tongues. A hot wave of nausea and panic rolled over him. Dropping the lid with a clatter, he rushed from the room.

"Don't be alarmed, boy!" he heard Rhal say behind him. "It's quite common in her condition—"

Reaching the rail, he sagged over it and vomited up his supper, dimly aware that Alec was at his side.

"What's wrong?" the boy demanded in an urgent whisper when he'd finished.

"Get me below," groaned Seregil. "Get me below *now!*"

Alec half carried him down the companionway to their cabin, where Seregil collapsed on the bunk and buried his face in his hands.

"What happened?" Alec pleaded, hovering anxiously over him. "Should I go for the captain, or fetch some brandy?"

Seregil shook his head violently, then raised his head to look up at the boy. "What did you see?"

"You ran out!"

"*No!* In the bowls. What did you see?"

"The dessert, you mean?" Alec asked in confusion. "Baked apples."

Striding to the cabin's single small window, Seregil threw it open and inhaled deeply. Fear, keen as a dagger's point, coursed through him; every instinct screamed for him to arm himself, watch his back, run somewhere, *anywhere*. His head was pounding again, too, twisting his empty belly into a painful knot.

Turning to face Alec again, he said softly, "That's not what I saw. The dishes were full of a steaming mess of—" He stopped, wondering at the terrible, inexplicable anxiety that had overwhelmed him at the sight. "Never mind. It's not important. But it wasn't baked apples."

A convulsive shudder racked him and he sagged against the cabin wall.

More alarmed than ever, Alec drew him to the bunk and made him sit down again. Seregil curled into the corner at the head of the bunk, back pressed to the wall. But he was still master of himself enough to send Alec to Captain Rhal with Lady Gwethelyn's apologies; it seemed that in her present state, she could not bear the odor of certain foods.

When Alec returned, he found Seregil pacing restlessly in the narrow confines of the cabin.

"Bolt the door and help me out of this damned dress!" Seregil hissed, but could scarcely stand still for the unlacing. When Alec had finished, he pulled on his leather breeches beneath his nightdress, wrapped a mantle about his shoulders, and returned to his corner of the bunk, sword hidden between the pallet and the wall behind him.

"Come here," he whispered, motioning for Alec to sit beside him.

Pressed shoulder to shoulder with Seregil, Alec could feel the occasional fits of trembling that still seized him, and the feverish heat of his body.

But Seregil's voice was steady, though barely audible. "Something's happening to me, Alec. I'm not sure what, but you should know about it because I don't know how I'm going to end up."

With that said, he told Alec of his latest nightmare, and of the unreasoning dread that had come over him before.

"It's either magic or madness," he concluded grimly. "I'm not sure which would be worse. I've never felt anything like this. The—things in the bowls? I've seen sights a hundred times worse and scarcely given it a second thought. I may be a lot of things, Alec, but I'm no coward! Whatever this is, I imagine things are going to get worse before they get better—if they get better." He tugged distractedly at the wooden disk hanging around his neck. "If you want to move on without me, I'll understand. You don't owe me anything."

"Maybe not," Alec replied, trying not to think about how

frightened he suddenly felt, "but I wouldn't feel right about it. I'll stay on."

"Well, I won't hold you to that, but thank you." Drawing up his knees, Seregil cradled his head on his arms.

Alec was about to retreat to his alcove when he felt another shiver rock through Seregil. Leaning back against the wall, he stayed silently by him well into the night.

10

SEREGIL DESCENDING

Seregil struggled free of another nightmare just before dawn. Throwing open the window, he dressed quickly, then sat watching the sky brighten. The anxiety of the dream gradually faded, but the first hint of a renewed headache seemed to grow with the light. Before long he heard Alec moving around in the alcove.

"You've had another bad night," the boy said, not bothering to make it a question.

"Come hold the mirror for me, will you?" Seregil opened a pouch of cosmetics and set to work. Dark circles stood out like bruises under his eyes; the hand holding out the mirror was not as steady as it had been a week before.

"I think Lady Gwethelyn will keep mostly to her cabin today. I'm not up to lengthy dissemblements," he said, inspecting his handiwork when he'd finished. "Besides, it will give us a chance to get on with your training. It's high time you learned to read. In fact, you can hardly manage our trade without it."

"Is it difficult?"

"You've caught on to everything else I've thrown at you," Seregil assured him. "There's a lot to it, but once you know the letters and their sounds, it comes quickly. Let's take a short walk on deck first, though. I could use the air before attempting breakfast. Let the captain see how ill I look and perhaps he'll leave us alone."

It was snowing in earnest this morning; wet, heavy flakes draped into a heavy curtain about the ship, deadening sound and making it impossible to see much farther than the end of the bow. Every rope and surface was outlined in white, and the deck was a mass of slush. Captain Rhal stood by the mast, giving orders to several men at once.

"Tell Skywake to keep her in the middle of the channel if he can figure out where it is!" he called to one sailor, jerking a thumb in the direction of the helmsman. "Keep dropping that lead until this clears. We're less likely to get hung up so long as we stay well out in the channel. By the Old Sailor, there's not enough breeze to fill a virgin's— Well, good morning to you, my lady. Feeling better, I trust?"

"The motion of the ship is most unsettling," Seregil answered, leaning on Alec's arm for good effect. "I fear I shall have to spend the remainder of our journey below."

"Aye, it's filthy weather, and damned early for it this far south. At this rate we'll be lucky to reach Torburn by dark tomorrow. It's going to make for a long day, so if you'll excuse me— Ciris, why don't you fetch your mistress some hot wine from the galley?"

With this, he strode off toward the helm.

"I don't know whether to be relieved or insulted!" Seregil chuckled under his breath. "Go fetch us some breakfast. I'll meet you below."

Despite the strange visions of the previous night, Seregil wasn't prepared for what he saw in the porridge Alec brought back. Pushing his bowl away, he retreated to the bunk.

Alec frowned. "It's happening again, isn't it?"

Seregil nodded, not caring to describe the slithering mass he saw in the bowl, or the stench that wafted up out of the teapot. Gathering up the dishes, Alec carried them away and returned with a mug of water and a bit of bread.

"You've got to get at least this into you," he urged, pressing the cup into Seregil's hand.

Seregil nodded and downed it quickly, doing his best to ignore the disturbing sensations that skittered across his tongue.

"You won't last long on that," Alec fretted. "Can't you manage a little bread? Look, it's fresh from the ship's oven."

Alec unwrapped a napkin and showed him the thick slice. Sweet, yeasty steam curled up in the sunlight and Seregil's empty belly stirred at the fragrance. As he reached for it, however, maggots erupted out of the bread, tumbling through the boy's fingers onto the table.

Seregil averted his eyes with a grimace. "No, and I think it might be better if you took your meals elsewhere until this is over.

They commenced the writing lesson later that morning. Seregil's battered leather pack yielded up several small rolls of parchment, quills, and a pot of ink. Crowded together over the small table, Alec watched Seregil draw the letters.

"Now you try," he said, handing Alec the quill. "Copy each letter underneath mine and I'll tell you its sound."

Alec knew as little about handling a quill as he did about swordplay, so they paused for a brief lesson in penmanship. He was soon inked to the wrists, but Seregil saw progress being made and held his tongue. After he'd mastered the characters, Seregil took the quill and swiftly spelled out their names, then the words for bow, sword, ship, and horse. His script flowed graceful and elegant next to Alec's smudgy scrawls.

Alec watched all this with growing interest. "That word there; that means me?"

"It means anyone named Alec."

"And this is 'bow.' It's as if these little marks have power. I look at them and the things they stand for just pop into my head, like magic. That one there doesn't look anything like a bow, yet now that I know the sounds of the letters, I can't look at it without seeing a bow in my head."

"Try this." Seregil wrote out 'Alec's Black Radly bow' and read it aloud, pointing to each word in turn.

Alec followed along, grinning. "Now I picture my own bow. Is it magic?"

"Not in the sense you mean. Ordinary words simply preserve ideas. Still, you have to be careful. Words can lie, or be misunderstood. Words don't have magic, but they have power."

"I don't understand."

"Well, the mayor of Wolde wrote a letter to the mayor of Boersby and it said something like 'Aren Windover and his apprentice stole my money. Capture them and I'll reward you.' Because the mayor of Boersby knows the mayor of Wolde, he reads and believes. Did we steal the money?"

"No, we just went through those rooms and you—"

"Yes, yes," Seregil snapped, cutting him short. "But the point is that a few words on a piece of paper were all it took to convince the mayor of Boersby that we did!"

Seregil stopped suddenly, realizing he was practically shouting. Alec shrank back, looking as if he expected a blow. Seregil pressed his palms down on his knees and took a deep breath. The headache was back from wherever it had been lurking, and with the pain came an extraordinary surge of anger.

"I'm not feeling very well, Alec. Why don't you go above for awhile?" It was an effort to speak calmly.

Jaw set in a stubborn line, Alec strode out without a word.

Sinking his head into his hands, Seregil wrestled with the sudden, inexplicable surge of conflicting emotions. He wanted to go after him, try to explain and apologize, but what was he going to say?

Sorry, Alec, but for just a moment there I really wanted to throttle you?

"Damn!" He stalked around the confines of the tiny cabin. The pain in his head swelled to a blinding ache. Beneath the pain, a vague urge began to resolve itself into an almost sensual feeling of need. It flowed through him, drawing his lips back from his teeth in a terrible, vulpine smile, filling every fiber of him with the desire to lash out. He wanted to grasp. He wanted to strike. He wanted to rend and tear—

He wanted—

And then, in a final searing flash, it was gone, taking the worst of the headache with it. When his vision cleared he found himself grasping the hilt of the penknife they'd been using. Somehow he'd driven it into the tabletop with such force that the little blade had snapped in two.

He didn't even remember picking it up.

The room seemed to spin slowly around him as he stood looking down at the broken knife. "Illior help me," he whispered hoarsely. "I'm going mad!"

• • •

Hurt and confused, Alec paced the deck. Until last night Seregil had treated him with nothing but kindness and good humor; if not always communicative, he'd certainly been even-handed and generous.

Now out of the blue, this coldness.

The shock of the morning's events gradually faded, allowing worry to replace his anger. This was what Seregil had been trying to warn him of last night, he realized. Of course, he had only Seregil's word that this was some new aberration; what if he'd been crazy all along?

And yet he couldn't forget his conversation with Micum Cavish back in Boersby. Alec had trusted Micum from the start, and this behavior just didn't fit with what he'd told him that night. No, Alec decided, Seregil wasn't to blame for this behavior.

He didn't have to get me out of Asengai's, he reminded himself sternly. *I've said I'll stand by him through this and I will!.*

Nonetheless, he couldn't help wishing that Micum had come south with them.

Alec wandered the deck disconsolately that night, ignoring the questioning looks the sailors exchanged as he passed.

Seregil's erratic behavior had continued throughout the day. Still unable to eat that evening, he'd grown more agitated and irritable as the night wore on. Alec had tried to talk to him, calm him, but only succeeded in upsetting him more. Seregil had finally ordered him out again, speaking slowly through clenched teeth.

It was too cold to sleep above, so Alec retreated to the companionway, his back to the cabin door. He was just dozing off when Rhal came below.

"What are you doing out here?" the captain asked in surprise. "Is something amiss with your lady?"

The lie he'd rehearsed earlier came out smoothly enough. "My snoring disturbed her sleep, so I came out here," Alec replied, rubbing his stiff neck.

Rhal frowned down at him a moment, then said, "You're

welcome to my bunk. It doesn't look like I'll be needing it, not with this weather."

"Thank you, but I think I better stay close, in case she needs me," Alec replied, wondering at this unexpected generosity.

Just then a hoarse cry came from inside the cabin, followed by what sounded like a struggle.

Scrambling to his feet, Alec tried to prevent Rhal from rushing in. "No! Let me—"

The burly captain thrust him aside like a child. Finding the door bolted, Rhal kicked it open and took a step inside.

Behind him, Alec watched with alarm as the man stopped abruptly, then reached for the long knife at his belt.

"What the hell is this?" growled the captain.

Alec let out a small groan of dismay.

Haggard and white, Seregil stood swaying in the far corner, sword in hand. His nightgown was torn down the front, effectively dashing any illusion of Lady Gwethelyn. For a moment it looked as if he might attack. Instead, he shook his head slightly and tossed his sword down on the bunk. Waving one thin hand, he motioned for them to enter. Alec moved to Seregil's side. Rhal remained where he was by the broken door.

"I'll ask you this once," he said slowly, his voice dark with anger. "Whatever it is you're up to, has it endangered my ship or my crew?"

"I don't believe so."

Rhal sized the two of them up for a long moment. "Then what in the name of Bilairy are you doing waltzing around in women's rigging?"

"There were some people I needed to get away from. If I tell you any more, then you *will* be in danger."

"Is that so?" Rhal looked skeptical. "Well, I'd say it was either political or you've got one angry husband after you. The *Darter* wasn't the only ship at Boersby that night. Why load this onto me?"

"I heard you were a man of honor—"

"Horse shit!"

Seregil smiled slightly. "But it's no secret that you've no great love for Plenimar."

"That's true enough." Rhal took another long look at him. "I see what it is you're aiming to make me believe. Assuming I buy it, which isn't saying I do, it still doesn't explain all the mummery that's gone on since you came aboard. You've played me for a cully, and I don't care much for that!"

Seregil dropped wearily onto the bunk. "I'm not going to explain my motives; they don't concern you. As for your attentions to the late Lady Gwethelyn, the boy and I both did everything we could to discourage you."

"I'll grant that, I suppose, but it's still my inclination to escort the pair of you over the side."

"You'd have a bit of explaining to do to your crew, wouldn't you?" Seregil suggested with a meaningful lift of an eyebrow.

"Damn you!" Rhal ran a hand over his beard in frustration. "If any of my men find out about this—the story would travel the length of the river before spring!"

"That's easily avoided. We dock at Torburn tomorrow. Lady Gwethelyn can disembark there, pleading ill health. I understand there are some wagers riding on whether or not she'll give you a tumble? If you like, I can be seen emerging from your cabin in the morning, winsome smile playing about my lips—"

Rhal darkened again. "Just see to it that both of you keep to your cabin until we arrive. Play your parts until you're out of sight of my ship and don't ever let me set eyes on either of you again!"

Striding furiously out, he collided with the first mate in the hall. Before the man had time to do more than grin, Rhal snarled, "See to your duties, Nettles!" and slammed into his own cabin.

"Well, that was undoubtedly one of the most embarrassing moments of my life," Seregil groaned, bravado falling away. "It's no easy matter, facing down a big, angry sailor in nothing but a woman's nightgown."

"You threw your sword away!" Alec exclaimed in disbelief, pushing the door back into place.

"We'd have fought if I hadn't. Win or lose, you and I couldn't afford the results. How would we have explained things if I'd killed him, eh? You defending my virtue? The crew would kill you in an instant, and Illior only knows what they'd do with Lady Gwethelyn. If he'd killed me, things would turn out just about the same. No, Alec, it's best to talk your way out whenever you can. As it stands, I don't think our secret could be in safer hands. Besides, he interests me. Blustering rogue that he is, I suspect he's intelligent and shrewd enough when women aren't involved. You never know when someone like that might be useful."

"What makes you think he'd ever help you?"

Seregil shrugged. "Intuition, maybe. I'm seldom wrong."

Alec sat down and rubbed his eyes. "What was all that commotion before we came in?"

"Oh, just another of those nightmares," Seregil replied, affecting a nonchalance he didn't feel. He didn't like to think what might have happened if Alec had been in the cabin with him when he'd thrashed his way up out of this latest one.

Sitting up, he reached for his cloak on top of the trunk. The torn nightdress slipped off his shoulder, revealing a patch of reddened skin on his chest, just above the breastbone.

"What's this?" asked Alec, reaching to move the wooden disk aside for a better look.

Icy fingers clamped around Seregil's heart. Overwhelmed by a sudden, inexplicable fury, he caught Alec by the wrist and shoved him roughly away. "Keep your hands to yourself!" he snarled.

Yanking the cloak around his shoulders, he retreated into the corner of the bunk. "Go to bed. *Now!*"

Hunched in his alcove much later that night, Alec heard Seregil stir.

"Alec, you awake?"

"Yes."

A long pause followed, then, "I'm sorry."

"I know." Alec had been thinking and already had the beginnings of a plan. "Micum said you know a wizard at Rhíminee. Do you think he could help you?"

"If he can't, then I don't know who can." There was another pause. Alec heard something like a dark chuckle, and the sound raised the hair on the back of his neck.

"Alec?"

"Yes?"

"Be careful, will you? Tonight, for just an instant—"

Alec tightened his grip on the sword lying across his knees. "It's all right, now. Go back to sleep."

Their last day aboard the *Darter* was a long one. Seregil spent the morning staring morosely out the window.

Alec maintained a careful distance, preoccupied with his own plans. By afternoon, he was ready to chance Rhal's displeasure and went above.

He settled behind the cutwater, hood pulled up against the wind. By the time they neared Torburn just before sundown, he'd managed to speak with the helmsman and several of the other sailors without their captain noticing. If it was up to him to get them both to Rhíminee, then he had to know how to get there.

To Rhal's relief, Lady Gwethelyn did not appear until the ship had put in at Torburn. The first mate's tale, already gleefully if discreetly spread among the crew, had amply explained both the silence of the lady and his sudden coolness toward her. Surreptitious nods and nudges were exchanged all around the deck when she finally came above to disembark.

No one but Rhal noticed, however, when the lady slipped a small something into his palm as he handed her down the gangway. Unwrapping the little silk square later that night in his cabin, he found the garnet ring his strange passenger had worn.

"A peculiar character, and no mistake." he exclaimed under his breath. Shaking his head in bemusement, he hid the ring safely away.

11

DARK PURSUIT

The cart bumped along over the rutted dirt road through the rolling Mycenian countryside. Seregil sat huddled in his cloak beside Alec on the single rough bench. It wasn't as cold here yet as it had been in the northlands, but snow wasn't far off and the chill seemed to get into his bones.

He found that if he stayed very still he could clear his mind, holding both the pain in his head and the increasingly frequent fits of irrational rage at a manageable level. It was exhausting work. In his more lucid moments he was relieved at how well Alec was managing, though the fact that the boy had not yet slipped away, despite ample justification and opportunity, continued to baffle him.

Their first night ashore in Torburn, they'd taken a tiny room near the riverfront and changed back into their stained traveling clothes. It was then that Alec had calmly outlined his plan.

"You're sick," he began, looking very deliberate. "Since you think this Nysander is the only one who can help, I say we push on for Rhíminee."

Seregil nodded.

Taking a deep breath, Alec continued, "All right then. The way I understand it, the fastest route this time of year is to go overland to

Keston, then take a ship to the city—one that goes by way of a canal at somewhere called Cirna. I don't know where any of those places are. You can help me or I'll ask directions as we go, but that's what I mean to do."

Seregil began to buckle on his sword. After a moment's hesitation, however, he handed it instead to Alec. "You'd better take this, and these."

He gave Alec his belt dagger and a small, razorlike blade from the neck of his cloak.

Alec took them without comment, then said almost apologetically, "There's one more."

"So there is." Seregil drew the poniard from his boot and handed it over, fighting back another twinge of hot rage as he did so.

It was an uncomfortable moment for both of them, each knowing perfectly well that these precautions would be useless if Seregil made up his mind to retrieve his weapons. Alec, Seregil noted, kept his own weapons about him.

"How many days will it take to reach Keston?" Alec asked when they were done.

Seregil lay back on the bed and fixed his gaze on the rafters. "Two, if we ride hard, but I doubt I'll be able to do that."

His head hurt again; how long now until another fit came on? A brisk walk in the night air might have helped, but he was too sick to attempt it. Better to concentrate on helping Alec with the details at hand.

"I'll need money," Alec said. "What do you have left?"

Seregil tossed him a purse containing five silver marks and the jewelry he'd worn aboard the *Darter*. Turning out his own pouch, Alec added two copper halfs and the Skalan silver piece.

"Hang on to the jewels for now," Seregil advised. "You're not dressed well enough to hawk them without attracting notice. Sell the clothes, though."

"They won't bring much."

"Illior's Hands, money's not the only way to get something! I should think you've been around me long enough to have learned that."

• • •

It was dark by the time Alec entered the Torburn market-place. Only a few of the booths around the square were open, but he finally found a clothier. The dealer proved to be a shrewd bargainer and he came away with a disappointing four silver pennies.

He let out a harsh sigh, tucking the coins away. "That's not going to make my task any easier."

Passing a woman frying sausages on a brazier, he paused longingly, then moved on still hungry.

An hour later, after some hard bargaining, he was the owner of a battered pony cart. Though hardly more than a large box set on a single axle, it looked sturdy enough. This, and the purchase of a few modest provisions, left him with exactly two copper halfs and the Skalan coin. Buying a horse was clearly out of the question.

Time I turned thief for good, he thought, still stinging from Seregil's parting admonition. He returned to the inn for a few hour's sleep, then slipped quietly downstairs just before dawn. Letting himself out a side door, he pulled on his boots and headed for the stable.

Great droves of silver-gilded clouds moved slowly past the sinking moon. Alec's heart hammered uncomfortably in his chest as he lifted the latch on the stable door. With a silent prayer to Illior, protector of thieves, he crept in.

A guttering night lantern gave enough light for him to avoid the drunken stable hand snoring in an empty stall. Moving on, a shaggy brown and white pony caught his eye. Throwing a halter around its neck, he led the beast out to the nearby alley where he'd hidden the cart and harnessed it. With this completed, he hurried back to the room.

Seregil was awake and ready to go. One look told Alec that his night had not been a peaceful one.

Despite this, he eyed Alec's cart and pony with a shadow of his old crooked smile, his face just visible in the failing moonlight.

"Which one did you pay for?" he asked softly.

"The cart."

"Good."

• • •

By sunrise they were well on their way to Keston. The road wound through rolling winter-bare farmland and countryside and they met only a few wagons and an occasional patrol of the local militia. With the harvest in and the Gold Road closing down until spring, Mycena would be a quiet place through the winter.

Seregil sank deeper into gloomy silence through the day, answering Alec's few attempts at conversation in such a dispirited manner that he soon gave up. When they stopped for the night at a wayside inn, Seregil retired immediately, leaving Alec to sit alone over his ale in the common room.

By the next morning Seregil's hunger had faded to a hollow ache; even the thought of water nauseated him.

Worse still, he was feeling guilty about Alec. The boy had proved too honorable to run off, but how he must be regretting his vow to stay. Seregil was trying to gather the strength for pleasant conversation as they road along when a hint of motion caught his eye off to the left. He turned quickly, but the field was empty. He rubbed at his eyes, thinking it was a trick of his weakened body, but the flicker came again, just on the edge of his vision.

"What's the matter?" asked Alec, giving him a puzzled look.

"Nothing." Seregil scanned the empty countryside. "Thought I saw something."

The annoying flicker came repeatedly as the day went on, and by afternoon he was more tense and withdrawn than ever. It might be some new quirk of the madness growing in him, he thought, but well-tried instincts counseled otherwise. Another violent headache had also grown through the day, leaving him too dull-witted and queasy to give the matter proper consideration. Pulling his cloak tight against the cold wind, he kept watch and fought off the desire to sleep.

They spent that night in the hayloft of a lonely farmstead. Seregil's nightmares returned in force and he woke up bathed in a cold sweat at dawn. An undefined sense of anxiety gnawed at him; he couldn't recall the details of the dream, but the wary sidelong glances he caught from Alec suggested that he'd been more restless than usual. He was just considering asking the boy about it when he thought he saw motion in a dark corner of the barn. Alec was busy with the harness and didn't see him brace, reaching for the sword that no longer hung at his side.

There was nothing there.

This will be his fourth day without eating, Alec thought as they rattled off down the road again. Wan and hollow-eyed as Seregil looked, he was bearing up better than Alec had imagined possible. Physically, that was; Seregil's odd behavior was increasingly alarming.

Today he sat hunched over like an old man, despondent except for occasional bursts of intent alertness. At those moments, a terrible glitter came into his eyes and his fists would clench until it seemed his knuckles must surely break through the skin. This new development, coupled with the strange events of the previous night, did not bode well.

Alec was beginning to be as frightened of Seregil as he was for him.

He hadn't intended to sleep the previous night, but the exhaustion of the past few days caught up with him and he'd dozed off. In the middle of the night he'd awakened to find Seregil crouched less than a foot away, eyes shining like a cat's in the dark, his breathing was so harsh it was almost a growl. Motionless, he simply stared at Alec.

Alec wasn't certain how long they'd remained frozen like that, staring each other down, but Seregil finally turned away and threw himself down in the straw. Alec had spent the remainder of the night keeping watch from a safe distance.

In the morning neither of them spoke of the incident. Alec doubted whether Seregil recalled it at all. But that, together with Seregil's nervous vigilance today, strengthened his resolve to not close his eyes again until he could lock his companion safely in a ship's cabin at sea.

Driving along in daylight, however, Alec could see all too clearly how Seregil was suffering. Reaching behind the bench, he pulled out one of their tattered blankets and laid it over his shoulders.

"You're not looking so good."

"Neither are you," Seregil croaked through dry lips. "If we drive through the night, we might make Keston by tomorrow afternoon. I could probably manage the reins for a while—if you need to sleep."

"No, I'll be fine!" Alec replied quickly. Too quickly, it seemed, for Seregil turned away and resumed his morose vigil.

The sense of pursuit grew stronger as the day dragged on. Seregil was beginning to catch glimpses of whatever it was that stalked him, a glimmer of movement, the blur of a dark figure that disappeared in the blink of an eye.

Just after midday he started so violently that Alec laid a hand on his arm.

"What is it?" he demanded. "You've been doing that since yesterday."

"It's nothing," Seregil muttered, but this time he was certain he'd caught sight of someone on the road far behind them.

Soon after, they topped the crest of a hill and came upon a Dalnan funeral. Several well-dressed men and women and two young children stood by the road, singing as they watched a young farmer driving an ox and plow in the middle of an empty field. The winter soil gave way grudgingly before the plowshare, coming up in frozen plates of earth. An elderly woman followed the driver, scattering handfuls of ash from a wooden bowl into the fresh furrow. When the last of it was gone, she carefully wiped out the inside of the dish with a handful of earth and poured it out onto the ground. The farmer turned the ox and plowed slowly back over it. A dusting of snow floated down as Alec and Seregil rattled past in their cart.

"It's the same as in the north," Alec remarked.

Seregil glanced back listlessly.

"The way they plow the ashes of the dead back into the earth, I mean. And the song they were singing was the same."

"I didn't notice. What was it?"

Encouraged by his companion's show of interest, Alec sang:

> *"All that we are is given by you, O Dalna, Maker and Provider.*
> *In death we return your bounty and become one with your wondrous creation.*
> *Accept the dead back into the fertile earth that new life may spring from the ashes*

*And at the planting and at the harvest will the dead be re-
membered.*
Nothing can be lost in the hand of the Maker.
Nothing can be lost in the hand of the Maker."

Seregil nodded. "I've heard that—"

Breaking off suddenly, he lunged for the reins and yanked the
pony to a stop. "By the Four, look there!" he gasped, looking
wildly across the field on their left. A tall, black-swathed figure
stood less than a hundred yards from the road.

"Where? What is it?"

"Right there!" Seregil hissed.

Even at the distance of a bow shot Seregil could see something amiss in the lines of the figure, some profound wrongness
of proportion that disturbed him more than the fact that Alec obviously could not see it himself.

"Who are you?" Seregil shouted, more frightened than angry.

The dark figure regarded him silently, then bowed deeply and
began a grotesque dance, leaping and capering about in a fashion
that would have been ridiculous if it wasn't so horrible. Seregil
felt his whole body go numb as the nightmarish performance
continued.

Shuddering, he shoved the reins into Alec's hands. "Get us
away from here!"

Alec whipped up the pony without question.

When Seregil looked back, the weird creature had vanished.

"What was *that* all about?" Alec demanded, raising his voice
to be heard over the rattling of the cart.

Trembling, Seregil gripped the edge of the seat and said nothing. A few moments later he looked up to find the thing walking
in the road ahead of them. At this range he could see that it was
too tall to be a man. And there was too much distance between
the shoulders and the head, not enough between shoulders and
hips, so that the arms appeared immensely long, its movements
graceless but powerful. It looked back over one sloping shoulder
and beckoned to him, as if to hurry him toward some destination.

"Look there!" Seregil cried in spite of himself, gripping
Alec's arm as he pointed. "All in black. Bilairy's Eyes, you *must*
see it now!"

"I don't see anything!" Alec replied, the edge of fear clear in
his voice.

Seregil released him with a snarl of exasperation. "Are you blind? It's as tall as a—"

But even as he pointed again it vanished with a parting wave of its arm. An icy wave of fear rolled over him.

Throughout the remainder of that leaden afternoon his dark tormentor toyed with him, playing an evil game of hide-and-seek. First Seregil would spy it far off, spinning madly in the middle of a bare field. A moment later it would appear beside him, striding beside the cart close enough to touch. A troop of Mycenian militia rode by and he saw it lurching along unnoticed in their midst; soon after it rode past in the opposite direction on the back of a farm wagon.

Alec clearly could not see it and Seregil soon gave up calling his attention to it; whatever the visitations meant, they were for him alone.

The worst came just as the sun was stooping to the horizon. He hadn't seen the specter for nearly half an hour. Suddenly a wave of appalling coldness engulfed him. Jumping unsteadily to his feet, he whirled to find the creature crouched in the tail of the cart, arms outstretched as if to gather both Alec and him to its breast. The hem of its black sleeve actually brushed Alec's head.

Then it laughed. An obscenely rich chuckle bubbled up from the depths of the black hood and with the sound came a charnel stench so revolting that Seregil retched dryly even as he grappled with Alec for the boy's sword.

Obviously convinced that Seregil had gone completely mad at last, Alec fought him for it and they both toppled over the side.

They came down hard with Seregil on top. The pony continued on a few yards, then shuffled to a stop. Looking up, Seregil saw that the cart was empty.

He rocked back on his heels and drew in deep, shuddering breaths, one hand pressed to his chest.

"Look at me!" Alec demanded angrily, scrambling up to grasp him by the shoulders. "Never mind about the pony. It's not going anywhere. You've got to tell me what's going on! I want to help you, but damn it, Seregil, you've got to talk to me!"

Seregil shook his head slowly, still staring over his shoulder at the cart. "Get us off the road before dark!" he whispered. *"Aura Elustri málrei—"*

"Tell me what you saw!" Alec cried, shaking him in frustration.

Seregil focused on Alec then, clutching at the front of the boy's tunic in desperation. "We must get off the road!"

Alec regarded him for a long moment, then shook his head resignedly. "We will," he promised.

They came to a ramshackle crossroads inn just before dark. Seregil's legs buckled as he stepped down from the cart and Alec had to help him inside.

"I want a room. No, two rooms," Alec told the innkeeper curtly.

"Top of the stairs." The man eyed Seregil nervously. "Is your friend here sick?"

"Not so sick that I can't pay," Seregil said, forcing a smile. It took all his concentration to make it convincing and as soon as he was out of the man's sight he dropped the pretense, sagging against Alec as they climbed the narrow stairs.

Suddenly he was tired, so tired! He was already half asleep as Alec lowered him onto a bed.

He dozed, woke, dozed again. Alec was there for a time. He tried to help Seregil drink, but he wasn't thirsty, just tired. Presently, Alec left and Seregil heard a key turn in the lock. It was all very strange, but he was too sleepy to think about it anymore. Turning onto his side, he drifted deeper into a murky doze.

He woke up shivering sometime later. The room had grown cold and Alec was crowding him off the bed against the wall, digging an elbow into the small of his back in the process. Twisting a bit, he tried to reclaim some space, but it was just too cold to sleep. Could the window be open? Did this room have a window? It seemed to him it didn't.

Giving up, he opened his eyes to check and found the night lamp still burning.

"Damn it, Alec, move—"

The words died in his throat.

It wasn't Alec pressing against him, but his tormentor, the black specter. It lay face up, arms crossed over its breast in the frightful parody of a tomb effigy. It remained perfectly motionless as Seregil dragged himself over the foot of the bed and scrambled for the door. Too late he remembered hearing the key turn; he was locked in.

"Alec! Alec, help me!" he shouted, pounding on the door. Dizzying panic constricted around his chest like bands of iron.

"No one will hear you."

The creature's voice was like a high wind rushing through the naked branches of winter trees—sardonic, inhuman, the embodiment of desolation. Seregil turned and the dark thing sat up, its upper body levering in a single rigid motion like the folding of a clasp knife. In the same unnatural fashion it bent forward slightly and stood up. It seemed to fill the cramped room.

Seregil tried to cry out again, but no sound came out.

"He can't help you now." Waves of frigid cold radiated from the figure, and with it the same terrible stench.

"What are you?" Seregil demanded in a strangled whisper.

The specter advanced a step, halving the distance between them. "You led a good chase," it replied in its soft, moaning voice. "But there is no escape, no forgiveness for such as you."

Seregil flattened himself against the wall, eyes darting about the room for some cover, finding none. "What do you *want*?"

"Don't you know? Such a pity to die in ignorance. But it is all one to us. You are a thief, and we want back what you have stolen. You can elude us no longer."

"Tell me what it is!" Anger and despair mingled with his fear to recall a tentative shred of courage.

Stretching its arms out across the ceiling, the loathsome thing wheezed out another blast of sepulchral fetor.

He was going to die; not knowing why seemed the final injustice.

The figure laughed again as it reached down for him, the sound of its voice tugging at the last roots of his sanity.

"No!" Snarling, Seregil sprang at it.

For a brief second his hands seemed to grasp at some distorted form, then he slammed into the far wall. When he whirled about, the creature was standing by the door.

Another of the strange fits of blood lust came over Seregil then and this time he welcomed it, opening himself to the strength it lent. He ached with it, was driven mad with it as he flew at the dark thing. The night candle was kicked over and went out but still he fought on, finding the creature with his hands, feeling the chill of it slip away again and again.

Suddenly his fingers found purchase. The form grew solid

and he clawed at it, seeking a throat with his hands. It toyed with him, fending him off without returning his blows.

The game did not last long, however. Huge talons sank suddenly into his chest and the world erupted in a searing blast of pain. Mercifully, his mind went out.

Alec lay half strangled on the cold floor beside Seregil. In the darkness he couldn't see what had happened to his hand, but it hurt like hell.

"What's going on up there?" the landlord shouted angrily from the far end of the passage. "I'll not have my house torn up in the middle of the night, do you hear?"

"Bring a light. Hurry!" Alec gasped, struggling one-handed to his knees.

The landlord appeared in the doorway, candle in one hand, a stout cudgel in the other. "Sounds like someone's bein' murdered up—"

He stopped short as his light fell over them. Seregil lay unconscious or worse, blood staining the breast of his shirt and his throat. Alec realized he probably didn't look much better. His nose was bleeding where Seregil had struck him, and his face and neck were badly scratched. Cradling his left hand against his chest, he saw what looked like a round, raw burn in the center of his palm.

"Hold the light down," he told the innkeeper. Kneeling over Seregil, he made certain his friend was still breathing, then pulled the neck of his shirt open and gasped in dismay.

The last time he'd seen the reddened area on Seregil's chest had been aboard the *Darter*. Now there was a bloody wound in the same spot. Holding the palm of his throbbing hand to the light again, Alec saw that his burn and this mark were exactly the same size and shape.

On the floor beside Seregil lay the wooden disk, the useless trinket he had stolen from the mayor's house because it wouldn't be missed. Picking it up gingerly by the broken leather thong, Alec compared it to the strange burn on his palm and the one on Seregil's chest.

It matched perfectly. Looking closer, he could even make out the print of the small square opening in its center.

It was right in front of us all the time! he thought in silent anguish. *How could he not have known? Why didn't I see?*

He'd been awakened by the sound of Seregil crashing about in the next room and gone to see what was the matter. In his haste he forgot the lamp and cursed angrily to himself as he'd fumbled the key into the lock of Seregil's door. The hallway was dark, the room inside darker still. In spite of the noise, he'd been unprepared for the attack that came the moment he stepped in.

When cold fingers grasped at his throat, Alec's only thought was how he could defend himself without injuring Seregil. He was trying to get a better grip on Seregil's tunic when his hand slipped inside the neck of it. Finding the thong under his hand, he'd grabbed for it, felt it sliding away as Seregil drew back. Then the terrible pain.

"What sort of foolishness is this?" the landlord demanded, looking over Alec's shoulder. Then the man was backing way, making a sign against evil. "You've killed him with sorcery!"

Alec thrust the disk out of sight. "He's not dead. Come back here with that light!"

But the man fled. Cursing in frustration, Alec stumbled to his own room and struck a light.

What was he to do with the cursed disk? Throwing it into the fire seemed to be the wisest course of action, yet doubt stayed his hand; Seregil had thought it valuable enough to steal, and later had said he was determined to get it to Rhíminee.

Handling it only by the leather lacing, he found a patched tunic in Seregil's pack and rolled the disk up in it. Shoving it to the bottom of the pack, he carried their gear downstairs and hurried back for Seregil. The innkeeper and his family had barricaded themselves in the kitchen storeroom and, despite his various pleas and assurances, refused to come out.

In the end he had to get Seregil down by himself, carrying the unconscious man across his shoulders like a slaughtered deer. Once downstairs, he laid him on a table and went through the kitchen again to the storeroom.

"You in there!" he called through the door. "I need a few supplies. I'll leave money on the mantelpiece."

There was no reply.

A candle stood in a dish on the sideboard. Lighting it with an ember from the banked fire, he cast about for food. Most of it was locked in the storeroom with its owner but he still managed to come away with a basket of boiled eggs, a jug of brandy, half a wheel of good Mycenian cheese, some new bread, and a sack of pippins. Going out to the well, he discovered a jar of milk let to cool and added that to his haul.

Stowing everything beneath the seat of the cart, he used their blankets and a few from the inn to make a pallet in the back.

When everything was ready, he carried Seregil out to the makeshift bed and carefully wrapped him up. Except for his labored breathing, Seregil looked like a dead man on a bier.

"Well, he won't get any better sitting here," Alec muttered grimly, slapping the reins over the pony's rump. "I said we were going to Rhíminee, and that's where I mean to go!"

12

ALONE

*—d*id the dead sleep within death? Some vestige of his living consciousness sensed the passage of time. There was a change of some sort, but what? Slowly he became aware of pain but it was muted, experienced at a distance.

Very odd.

Smells came with the pain, the smell of illness, infection, the unwashed odors of his own body from which his fastidious nature recoiled even as he rejoiced in the ability to discern them. Perhaps he wasn't dead, after all? He had neither explanation for his predicament nor memory of his past and now even the pain was slipping away again. Silently, helplessly, he willed it back, but it was gone.

He was alone. And lonely—

Alec drove as hard as he dared, determined to reach the seaport by the following day. He stopped only to rest the pony and tend Seregil's wound.

The burn on his own hand made his arm ache to the elbow, but it was scabbing over already. Inspecting Seregil's breast in daylight, however, he found that the wound there was still raw, with angry lines of infection fanning out from it.

He stopped at the next farmstead they came to, hoping to beg a few herbs and some linen. The old wife there took one look at Seregil and disappeared back into her kitchen, returning a few moments later with a basket containing yarrow salve and aloes, clean linen rags, a flask of willow bark tea and one of milk, fresh cheese, bread, and half a dozen apples.

"I—I can't pay you," he stammered, overwhelmed by such generosity.

The old woman smiled, patting his arm. "You don't need to," she said in her thick Mycenian accent. "The Maker sees every kind deed."

The countryside fell away into gentle slopes as Alec drove westward toward Keston. By the following afternoon they came down into more settled country.

There was a different scent on the breeze here. It was a water smell, but with an unfamiliar tang. Gulls wheeled overhead, much larger than the little black-headed ones on Blackwater Lake. These birds had long yellow beaks and grey wings tipped with black. Great flocks of them flew overhead or picked their way over empty fields and rubbish heaps.

Topping a rise, Alec saw in the distance what could only be the sea. Awestruck, he reined in and stared out over it. The sun was low. The first golden stain of sunset spread a glittering band across the silver-green water. A scattering of islands lay like knucklebones cast along the coastline, some dark with trees, others bare chunks of stone thrusting above the waves.

The road wound on down to the coast, ending in a sprawling town that hugged the shore of a broad bay.

"You must be an inlander."

An old tinker had come up beside the cart. Wizened and bandy-legged, the fellow was bowed nearly double under the large pack he carried. What Alec could see of his face beneath the brim of his battered slouch hat was dark with stubble and dust.

"You've the look of an inlander finding the sea for the first time. Sitting there gape-mouthed like that, you couldn't be nothin' else," the old relic observed with a rusty chuckle.

"It's the biggest thing I ever saw!"

"Looks even bigger when yer in the middle of 'er," the tinker said. "I was a sailor in me youth, before a shark took me leg for dinner."

Twitching his dusty cloak back, he showed Alec the wooden peg strapped to the stump of his left leg. Cleverly carved to resemble the limb it replaced, the end of it was made in the shape of a wooden clog that neatly matched the real one on his other foot.

"Trampin' all the day, I don't know which foot gets more sore. Might you offer a fellow traveler a ride into town?"

"Climb up." Alec reached to aid him.

"Much obliged. Hannock of Brithia, at your service," the tinker said, settling himself on the bench. There was an expectant pause.

"Aren. Aren Silverleaf." Alec felt a bit silly giving the old man a false name, but it was becoming a habit.

Hannock touched a finger to the brim of his hat. "Well met, Aren. What happened to your friend in the back here?"

"A bad fall," Alec lied quickly. "Tell me, do you know Keston town?"

"I should say I do. What can I do for you there?"

"I need to sell this cart and find passage to Rhíminee."

"Rhíminee, is it?" Hannock rubbed at his bristly chin. "By the Old Sailor, you'll be damned lucky to find passage this close to winter. It'll come dear, too. More than you're likely to realize from this contraption and a spavined pony. But don't fret yourself, boy. I've a friend or two in most any port you can name. Leave it to old Hannock."

Alec was soon glad of the tinker's company. Keston was a bustling town, full of rambling streets laid out with no rhyme or reason that he could make out; the lanes that Hannock directed him down were little more than broad pathways between the tenements that stood cheek by jowl with warehouses and taverns. Gangs of sailors, reeling with high spirits of one sort or another, jostled in the dark alleyways and snatches of songs and curses seemed to come from all directions.

"Yes, I've still a friend or two along the quays," said Hannock as they reached the waterfront. "Let me ask around a bit and I'll meet you back at the Red Wheel. You con the sign yonder? Two shops down from that, at the next warehouse, there's a drayman, name of Gesher. He'll probably take this rig off your hands. It'll do you no harm to mention my name in the bargaining."

Hannock's name notwithstanding, Drayman Gesher ran a bleak eye over the cart, the exhausted pony, and its equally exhausted driver. "Three silver trees, not a penny more," he said gruffly.

Alec had no idea what the relative worth of a silver tree might be, but was happy enough to unload the rig and be done with it. With the understanding that they would close the deal when Alec brought the cart back, he hurried off to the Wheel. Leaving Seregil well covered, he went inside.

He found the old tinker seated at a long table joking with a weathered man in seafaring garb.

"Here's the lad himself," Hannock told his companion, pushing a pot of beer Alec's way. "Sit down, boy. Aren Silverleaf, this is Captain Talrien, master of the *Grampus*. As fine a mariner as you can hope to find on the two seas, and I should know. We first sailed together with Captain Strake, me as mate and him but a green slip of a cabin boy. He's agreed to work out a passage for you and your unfortunate friend."

"So you're short on jack, eh?" Talrien grinned, getting right to the point. His skin, brown as an old boot from salt and sun, contrasted sharply with his pale hair and beard. "How much have you got?"

"I can get three silver trees for the pony and the cart. Is that a good price?"

Hannock shrugged. "No, but it's not a bad one, either. What do you say, Tally? Will you take the lad?"

"That's scarce a single passage. Mighty important that you get to Rhíminee, is it?" Talrien drawled, settling back in his chair. When Alec hesitated a moment too long, he laughed, holding up a hand.

"Never mind, then, it's your own business. Tell you what I'll do. I'm short a man this time out; for three silver I'll take your friend and you can work your passage. You'll have to bunk in the hold, but you're in luck there, for the cargo is grain and wool. Last voyage we carried granite cobbles. If that's agreeable to you, let's cross palms on it and call it done."

"Done it is," Alec replied, clasping hands with him. "Many thanks to you both."

Talrien had a longboat moored at the quay. After loading in his few remaining possessions, Alec and Talrien carefully lifted Seregil into the bottom of the boat.

Seregil was paler than ever. His head lolled limply from side to side as wavelets nudged the longboat against the stone footing of the quay. Tucking a wadded cloak behind his friend's head, Alec looked down at him with a pang of fear. *What if he dies? What will I do if he dies?*

"Don't you worry, lad," Talrien said kindly. "I'll see to it he's made comfortable. You go sell your wagon and I'll send the boat back for you."

"I—I'll be here," Alec stammered, suddenly reluctant to leave Seregil in the hands of strangers. But what else was there to do? Clambering into the rickety cart for the last time, he flicked the reins over the pony's dusty rump.

Mycenian silver trees turned out to be rectangular lozenges of silver, each with the rough shape of a tree struck into it. Clutching the coins, he ran back as fast as he could to the docks.

As he came within sight of the deserted quay, a sudden thought stopped him in his tracks. Before they'd left the *Darter,* hadn't Captain Rhal spoken of Plenimaran press-gangs working the ports?

"By the Maker," he groaned aloud, dread settling like heavy ice in his belly. In his haste and weariness, had he handed Seregil over to a clever pair of rogues? Cursing himself, he stamped up and down in the cold, squinting into the darkness for any sign of movement. He hadn't even thought to ask Talrien which of the ships was the *Grampus*!

It was a still night. Waves lapped gently against the quay. The faint sounds of men singing happily over their mugs in nearby taverns made his vigil all the more lonesome as he stood in the darkness. A bell sounded aboard one of the ships at anchor, its tone muted and distant.

He was just calling himself ten kinds of fool when he caught sight of a light moving toward him over the water. It disappeared for a moment, obscured by the hull of some ship, then reappeared, still bobbing steadily his way with the splash of unseen oars.

A wiry, redheaded sailor scarcely older than himself brought the little craft neatly alongside the dock. Alec didn't know much of press-gangs, but this didn't have the look of one.

"You the new hand for the *Grampus*?" the boy inquired, shipping his oars and looking up at Alec with a brash grin. "I'm Binakel, called Biny by most. Haul in then, 'less you fancy spending the night on the jetty, which I don't. By the Old Sailor, it's colder'n a cod's balls tonight!"

Alec had hardly clambered down onto the stern bench before Biny was pulling away. He talked a steady stream as he rowed, needing no prompting or encouragement as he rattled on with hardly a pause for breath. He had a tendency to jumble one topic in with another as things occurred to him, and a good deal of it was profane, but Alec managed to sift out enough to set his mind at rest by the time they drew alongside the sleek hull of the *Grampus*. Captain Talrien was a good-tempered master, according to Biny, whose highest praise was that he'd never known his captain to have a man flogged.

The *Grampus* was a coastal trader. Carrying three triangular sails on tall masts, she could deploy twenty oars on each side when need be, and ran regularly between the port cities of Skala and Mycena.

The crew was in a fury of preparation on deck. Alec had hoped to speak with Talrien again, but the man was nowhere to be seen.

"Your friend's down here," Biny said, leading him below.

Seregil lay asleep in a deep nest of wool bales. More bales and plump sacks of grain were packed into the long hold for as far as Alec could see by the light of Biny's lantern.

"Mind the light," Biny warned as he left. "A spark or two in this lot and we'll go up like a bonfire! Keep it on that hook over your head there, and if ever we meet with rough seas, be sure to snuff it."

"I'll be careful," Alec promised, already searching for fresh bandages. Those covering Seregil's stubborn wound were badly stained.

"Cap'n sent down food for you, and a pail of water. It's there around the other side," Biny pointed out. "You ought to speak to Sedrish tomorrow about that hurt of your friend's. Old Sedrish is as good a leech as he is a cook. Well, g'night to you!"

"Good night. And give my thanks to the captain."

The bandage lint had stuck to Seregil's wound and Alec carefully soaked it loose, lifting aside the stained pad to find the raw spot looking worse than ever. There was no evidence that the old woman's salve was doing any good, but Alec applied it anyway, not knowing what else to do.

Seregil's slender body had quickly failed to gauntness. He felt fragile in Alec's hands as he lifted him to wrap the fresh bandage. His breathing was less even, too, and now and then caught painfully in his chest.

Laying him back against the bales, Alec brushed a few lank strands of hair back from Seregil's face, taking in the deepening hollows in his cheeks and at his temples, the pallid whiteness of his skin. A few short days would bring them to Rhíminee and Nysander, if only Seregil could survive that long.

Warming the last of the milk over the lantern, Alec cradled Seregil's head on his knee and tried to spoon some into him. But Seregil choked weakly, spilling a mouthful down his cheek.

With a heavy heart Alec set the cup aside and stretched out beside him, wiping Seregil's cheek with a corner of his cloak before pulling it over both of them.

"At least we made it to a ship," he whispered sadly, listening to the labored breathing beside him. Exhaustion rolled over him like a grey mist and he slept.

—a stony plain beneath a lowering leaden sky stretched around Seregil on all sides. Dead, grey grass under his feet. Sound of the sea in the distance? No breeze stirred to make the faint rushing sound. Lightning flashed in the distance but no rumble of thunder followed it. Clouds scudded quickly by overhead.

He had no sense of his body at all, only of his surroundings, as if his entire being had been reduced to the pure essence of sight. Yet he could move, look about at the grey plain, the moving mass of clouds overhead that roiled and churned but showed no break of blue. He could still hear the sea, though he could not tell its direction. He wanted to go there, to see beyond the monotony that surrounded him, but how? He might well take the wrong direction, moving away from it, deeper into the plain. The thought froze him in place. Somehow he knew that the plain went on forever if you went away from the sea.

He knew now that he was dead and that only through Bilairy's gate could he escape into the true afterlife or perhaps out of any existence at all. To be trapped for eternity on this lifeless plain was unthinkable.

"O Illior Lightbringer," he silently prayed, "shed your light in this desolate place. What am I to do?"

But nothing changed. He wept and even his weeping made no sound in the emptiness—

13

Inquiries Are Made

"Oh, yes, they was here all right. I'm not soon likely to forget them!" the innkeeper declared, sizing up the two gentlemen. The sallow one would try and stare it out of him, but the comely, dark-complected gentleman with the scar under his eye looked to be a man who understood the value of information.

Sure enough, the dark one reached into his fine purse and laid a thick double tree coin on the rough counter between them.

"If you would be so good as to answer a few questions, I would be very grateful." Another of the heavy rectangular coins joined the first. "These young men were servants of mine. I'm most anxious to find them."

"Stole something, did they?"

"It's a rather delicate matter," the gentleman replied.

"Well, you've missed 'em by nigh onto a week, I'm sorry to say. They was a bad sort, I thought, when first I laid eyes on 'em. Ain't that so, Mother?"

"Oh, aye," his wife assured them, eyeing the strangers over her husband's shoulder. "Never should have taken them in, I said after, empty rooms or no."

"And she was right. The yellow-haired one tried to murder the other in the night. I locked me'self and the family in the storeroom after I caught 'em at it. In the morning they was both gone. Don't know whether the sickly fellow was living or dead in the end."

The innkeeper reached for the coins but the dark man placed a gloved fingertip on each of them.

"Did you, by chance, observe the direction they took?"

"No, sir. Like I said, we stayed in the storeroom 'til we was certain they was gone."

"That's a pity," the man murmured, relinquishing the coins. "Perhaps you would be so good as to show us the rooms in which they stayed?"

"As you like," the innkeeper said doubtfully, leading them up the stairs. "But they didn't leave nothin'. I had a good look 'round right after. It was damned odd, that boy wanting the key to the outside of the other's door. Locked him in, I guess, then took after him in the dead of night. Oh, you should have heard the noise! Thumpin' and caterwauling— Here we are, sirs, this is where it happened."

The innkeeper stood aside as the two men glanced around the cramped rooms.

"Where was the fight?" the pale one asked. His manner was not so obliging as that of his companion, the innkeeper noted, and he had a funny sort of accent when he spoke.

"This here," he told him. "You can still see a few dibs of blood on the floor, just there by your foot."

Exchanging a quick look with his companion, the dark man drew the innkeeper back toward the stairs.

"You must allow us a few moments to satisfy our curiosity. In the meantime, perhaps you would be so kind as to carry ale and meat to my servants in the yard?"

Presented with the opportunity for further profit, the innkeeper hustled back downstairs.

Mardus waited until the innkeeper was out of earshot, then nodded for Vargûl Ashnazai to begin.

The necromancer dropped to his knees and took out a tiny knife. Scraping at the spots of dried blood scattered over the rough boards, he carefully tapped the shavings into an ivory vial and sealed it. His thin lips curved into an unpleasant semblance of a smile as he held the vial up between thumb and forefinger.

"We have them, Lord Mardus!" he gloated, lapsing into the Old Tongue. "Even if he no longer wears it, with this we shall track them down."

"*If* they are indeed those whom we seek," Mardus replied in the same language. In this instance, the necromancer was probably correct in his assumptions, but as usual, Mardus made no effort to encourage him. They all had their roles to play.

With Vargûl Ashnazai trailing dourly behind him, Mardus returned downstairs and gave the innkeeper and his wife an eloquent shrug.

"As you said, there is nothing to be found," he told them, as if abashed. "However, there is one last point—"

"And what would that be, sir?" asked the innkeeper, clearly hoping for another lucrative opportunity.

"You said they fought." Mardus toyed with his purse strings. "I am curious as to the cause. Have you any idea?"

"Well," replied the innkeeper, "as I said, they was at it hammer and tongs before I got up there at all. Time I got the lamp lit and found my cudgel, the young one already had the other fellow laid out. Still, just from what I saw looking in, it 'peared to me they was fighting over some manner of necklace."

"A necklace?" exclaimed Vargûl Ashnazai.

"Oh, it was a paltry-looking thing, weren't it?" the wife chimed in. "Nothing to kill a fellow over!"

"That's right," her husband said in disgust. "Just a bit of wood, 'bout the size of a five-penny piece, strung on some leather lacing. Had some carving done on it, as I remember, but still it didn't look like anything more than some frippery a peddler would carry."

Mardus offered the man a bemused smile. "Well, they were a bad pair, just as you say, and I suppose I'm well rid of them. Many thanks."

Tossing a final coin to the innkeeper, he went out to the yard where his men stood ready.

"Have you any doubts now, my lord?" Ashnazai whispered, trembling with suppressed rage.

"It seems they've eluded us once again," Mardus mused, tapping a gloved finger thoughtfully against his chin.

"He should have been dead a week ago! No one could survive—"

Mardus smiled thinly. "Come now, Vargûl Ashnazai, even you must see that these are no ordinary thieves we are pursuing."

Casting an approving eye over the empty country surrounding the crossroads inn, he turned to the group of armed men. "Captain Tildus!"

"Sir?"

Mardus inclined his head slightly toward the inn. "Kill everyone, then burn it."

14

SAILING SOUTH

Alec felt like cheering aloud as the mainland slipped under the horizon their first
day out. The sheer emptiness that surrounded the ship—the endless sky, the
biting cold of the wind, and frozen spume
thrown up by the prow as the *Grampus* raced
gaily along under full-bellied sails—all this
seemed to cleanse him down to the bone.

He worked hard, to be sure. The sailors
relegated him to the lowliest tasks, not out of
any meanness but because he would not be
with the ship long enough to be worth training. Though his hand was still sore and both
hands were soon cracked from the salt and
cold, he worked with a good will at any task
he was assigned: sanding decks, hauling slops,
and helping in the scullery. Whenever he
could find a free moment, he went below to
tend to Seregil.

Despite Alec's diligent care, however, his
companion was clearly failing. The infection
was spreading across Seregil's thin chest, and
hectic fever spots bloomed over his cheekbones, giving his face its only color. A sickly
odor clung about him.

Sedrish, the ship's cook and surgeon, gave
Alec what help he could, but none of his
remedies seemed to have any effect.

"At least you can still get something into

him," Sedrish observed, watching Alec patiently coax a sip of broth between Seregil's cracked lips. "There's hope so long as he'll drink."

Alec was working his way through a tangled pile of rope their third day out when the captain happened by. The weather was holding fair and Talrien appeared to be in a high good humor.

"It's too bad you're leaving us at Rhíminee. I believe we could make a pretty passable sailor of you," he remarked, bracing easily against the rail. "Most inlanders spend their first voyage heaving their guts over the side."

"No problems that way," Alec replied, brightening up a bit. "Just some trouble finding what Biny calls my 'sea legs.' "

"I noticed. That first day when the swells were heavy you rolled around like a keg in the bilge. When you set foot on land again, it'll be just as bad for a bit. That's why sailors always head straight for the taverns, you know. You sit and drink long enough, and pretty soon you feel like you're back on the rolling deep. Makes us feel more at home."

Just then a cry came down from the masthead. "Land sighted, Captain!"

"We've made good time," Talrien said, shading his eyes as he looked across the water. "See that dark line on the horizon? That's the isthmus. By tomorrow morning you'll see one of the great wonders of the world."

Alec woke feeling queasy the next morning. The motion of the ship felt different, and he couldn't hear waves against the hull.

"Hey, Aren," called Biny, sticking his head down the hatchway. "Come above if you want to see something."

On deck, Alec found they were riding at anchor in a narrow harbor. A crowd had gathered at the rail.

"What do you think of that?" Biny asked proudly.

A thin mist steamed up from the surface of the sea. The first rose-gold light of dawn shone through it, bathing the scene before them in a layer of pale, shifting fire.

Sheltering cliffs soared up out of the mists on either side of the harbor. At its head lay Cirna, a jumbled collection of square, white-plastered buildings that clung like swallow's nests to the steep slopes above the jetties.

Catching sight of him, Talrien waved an arm. "That's one of the oldest cities in Skala. Ships were putting in here before Ero was built. You can see the mouth of the Canal over there, to the left."

Looking across the water, Alec saw that a huge channel had been cut through the cliffs at the head of the bay. Flanking the mouth of it were enormous pillars carved in relief. Each reached five hundred feet or more from the waterline to the top of the cliff and was surmounted by an elaborate capital. At this early hour, flames and black smoke still issued from the huge oil flares that topped them.

"How would you make anything that big?" Alec exclaimed, trying to grasp the scale of what he was seeing.

"Magic, of course," scoffed Biny.

"And hard work," Talrien added. "Queen Tamír the Second built it when she founded Rhíminee. They say it took a hundred wizards and a thousand workmen two years to build the Canal. Of course, that was back in the old days, when there were enough magicians about to be spared for such labor. It's five miles from end to end, but less than three hundred feet wide. And those beacons, atop the pillars there? You can see them for miles. We steered in by them last night." Turning, he waved a hand at the gathered crew. "Come on, you lot! We've got work to do."

The *Grampus* carried cargo for Cirna, and they put in alongside one of the docks that jutted out from the shore. Alec saw to it that Seregil was moved to an out-of-the-way nook in the hold, then went above to watch the bustling activity on shore. At closer range he could see that the tops of the great pillars were not alike. The one on the left was carved in the form of a fish emerging from a wave. Even from across the harbor he could make out the scales on its sides, the graceful curve of the fins. The capital on the right appeared to be a stylized flame.

"Why are they different?" he asked Sedrish, shading his eyes.

"Those are the pillars of Astellus and Sakor, of course," the cook replied as if amazed at his ignorance. "Illior and Dalna are at the other end. They say those old builders figured if they were

going to muck up the natural lay of the land so, they'd better tip
their caps to the gods when they got all done."

Talrien stood at the top of the gangplank with one of the sailors, calling out cargo numbers for the man to record in the log.
On the dock below, the various merchants to whom the cargo belonged kept similar track.

Alec studied them with interest. Instead of tunics, they wore
long belted coats that reached below the knee and leather
breeches like those that Seregil favored. Many wore broad-
brimmed hats with a long colorful feather or two stuck at an
angle in the band.

Another vessel was unloading at a neighboring wharf; a single
glimpse of their cargo was enough to draw Alec down for a
closer look. Ducking through a throng of sailors and dock hands,
he joined the crowd gathering around a makeshift corral that had
been roped off for the horses that were being led ashore. He'd
seen plenty of horses in his life, but never the match of these.

These creatures were as tall as the black mare he'd left behind
in Wolde, but not so heavily made. Their legs were long, tapering
from rounded haunches to dainty hooves, and they bore their
proud heads on well-arched necks. Their coats and manes had
none of the rough shagginess Alec was accustomed to, but shone
in the morning sun as if they'd been polished. Despite the commotion around them, the animals showed no skittishness as they
milled about. Most were bays, with a few chestnuts and blacks
mixed in. The one that immediately caught Alec's fancy, however, was a glossy black stallion with a white mane and tail.

"They're something, ain't they?" Biny remarked, appearing at
his elbow.

"They are that," Alec agreed. "I've never seen anything like
them!"

"I shouldn't think so. Them's Aurënen horses, just come up
from the south."

"Aurënen!" Alec grabbed Biny's arm and pointed toward the
ship. "Are there any Aurënfaie there? Do you know what they
look like?"

"Nah, that's a Skalan ship. The Aurënfaie don't come up here.
Ships like that one trade in Virésse and bring the cargo—horses,
jewelry, glass, and the like—back to the Three Lands to sell for
theirselves."

Virésse. Seregil had once mentioned that only one port in Aurënen was open to foreigners.

"Horses like them are only for the nobles and the rich," Biny went on. "I heard once that the Queen herself wouldn't never ride no other kind in battle, nor the Princess Royal, neither. And her the head of all the cavalry in Skala."

The stallion Alec had admired came near and he couldn't resist reaching out to it. To his delight, the beast pushed its slim head against his hand and nickered contentedly as he stroked its velvety nose and forelock. Lost as he was in admiration of the horse, it wasn't until a gloved hand reached out to stroke the stallion's neck that he noticed Biny and the rest of the crowd had melted back. Turning, he found himself face-to-face with a young woman as exotic as the horse itself.

Dark chestnut hair, drawn back from a sharp widow's peak, hung in a thick braid down the back of her mud-spattered green cloak. A few strands of it had escaped to frame her heart-shaped face in soft, curling wisps. As she turned to Alec, frozen in awe beside her, he saw the startling blue of her eyes, the flush of healthy color in her cheeks. For a moment his only thought was that here stood the most beautiful woman he'd ever seen. And an extraordinary one at that, for instead of a gown she wore close-fitting doeskin breeches beneath a green tabard edged in white. The front of the tabard was richly embroidered with the emblem of a pair of crossed sabers supporting a crown. A heavy silver gorget at her throat flashed in the sunlight, and a long sword hung from a military baldric slung across her chest.

"He's a beauty, isn't he?" she remarked.

"Uh, yes." Alec hastily turned his gaze back to the horse.

"Were you thinking of buying him?" she asked as the horse leaned over the rope to rub his chin on Alec's shoulder. "He's certainly taken to you."

"No! Oh, no—no, I was just looking." Alec stepped back acutely aware of how filthy and worn his own clothing was. "I just never saw Aurënfaie horses before."

Her sudden smile made her look girlish in spite of the sword. "I spotted him right off, but I didn't want to buy him away from you if you'd already made up your mind." Stroking the horse's nose, she spoke softly to it. "What do you say, my fine fellow? Shall I take you home?"

As if in answer, the stallion snorted and pushed his head against her hand.

"I guess that settles it," said Alec, pleased that his favorite should get such a fine mistress.

"I'd say so," she agreed. The horse dealer had been hovering nearby and at her gesture came over to them, bowing deeply. "Your horses are as fine as ever, Master Roakas. This gentleman and I have decided that I should take the black with white. What are you asking?"

"For you, Commander, two hundred gold sesters."

"Fair enough. Captain Myrhini has the purse."

"Many thanks, Commander. Will that be all this time?"

"No, I still have to pick out a few for the Guard, but I wanted to grab this one before someone else did. Would you ask one of my escort to saddle him for me?" Turning back to Alec, she smiled again. "Thanks for your help. You must tell me your name."

"Aren Silverleaf."

Another soldier in green and white led the saddled stallion back. Swinging lightly up, she reached into the wallet at her belt.

"Silverleaf, is it? Well, good luck to you, Aren Silverleaf." She tossed him a coin that glittered yellow as it spun through the air. He caught it deftly, hardly taking his eyes from her to do so. "Drink my health. It'll bring me luck."

"I will, thanks," Alec called after her as she rode away. Turning quickly to the soldier, he asked, "She's beautiful! Who is she?"

"You didn't know?" the man exclaimed, looking him up and down. "That was Princess Klia, youngest daughter of the Queen. Quite a day for you, eh boy?"

The crowd surged forward to the corral again and several strangers clapped Alec on the back, envying him his brush with royalty.

Biny elbowed his way through the press. "What's that she tossed you?"

Alec held up the gold coin. Smaller than his Skalan silver piece, it was stamped on one side with the same design of crescent moon and flame and on the reverse with the profile of a man.

"A half sester? You could drink her health for a couple of days on that!" Biny gave him a playful jab in the ribs.

"A princess!" Alec marveled, shaking his head.

"Oh, we see her all the time up here. She's second in command of the Queen's Horse Guard now, under her brother, and has quite an eye for the beasts. Come on, they've started loading already. We'd better start back."

With their own cargo dispatched, Talrien's crew was now stowing slender clay wine jars below deck. After these came crates of chickens that Talrien ordered lashed down amidships on deck. The rest of their voyage would be enlivened by the cackling and crowing of the birds, as well as their stink and the clouds of feathers they shed.

By late morning everything was secured and they sailed out to join the other vessels waiting to enter the Canal; ships were carefully spaced out to avoid any mishaps that might block the narrow channel. Soon after they dropped anchor, a skiff sailed up to them and a stout little man in a greasy slouch hat climbed aboard. Talrien spoke briefly with the harbor master and paid out the tariffs for anchorage and passage. When he'd gone, Talrien waved Alec over.

"One-hour wait," he said. "Tell Sedrish to get a meal up, will you?"

Alec relayed the message, then took hot water and some broth down to Seregil. By the time he came up again, several of the ships ahead of them had passed into the Canal's dark opening. A bright mirror flash came from the heights near the top of the Astellus column and the stout galley moored next to them hauled anchor, unfurled a single sail, and glided off into the dark cleft.

At last the lookout called down, "There's our signal, Captain!"

"That's it, men!" Talrien shouted. "Break out the oars and stand to your locks."

While the anchor was being raised, several of the sailors set up torches fore and aft. Others pulled back a section of the deck and brought out the long oars stored there. Each oar was passed through a round, rope-padded lock in the ship's rail, twenty to a side. At the captain's signal, the mate climbed up on a hatch and began to sing. Picking up the rhythm he set, the oarsmen pulled in practiced unison and the ship slid smoothly forward over the calm face of the bay. Captain Talrien stood at the tiller, steering her into the echoing dimness beyond the pillars.

The sun had already passed noon, and little sunlight penetrated far into the chasm. It was colder inside and smelled of
salt-drenched stone. Alec was standing with Sedrish when he
happened to look up.

"Are those stars?" he asked in amazement. The narrow strip
of sky was pricked with faint points of light.

"It's the high walls, shutting out the sun. I fell down a well
when I was a lad and it was just the same. About the only time
there's much light in here is at high noon."

Rough stone towered overhead on either side, seeming to bear
down over the vessel. Small freshets of water flowed down here
and there, tumbling off the uneven rock face. In places, the surface of it gave back a glassy reflection that puzzled Alec.

"That's from the magicking," Sedrish explained. "In places it's
shiny smooth like that; others, like over there, the rock just
dripped and ran like wax down the side of a candle. I wouldn't
have liked to been in here when them wizards was blasting away,
I can tell you!"

Their passage was a quiet affair. The narrow space around
them gave back every whisper and splash and the effect seemed
to subdue even Biny. When the lookout at last shouted, "Half
way sighted, Captain," his voice reverberated in a succession of
ghostly echoes up and down the canal.

Alec was wondering how on earth anyone could tell distance
in such a place when he caught sight of something white against
the right wall up ahead. As they drew nearer, he could see that
it was a huge statue of polished marble standing in a shallow
niche carved into the wall. The figure glowed like a pale lantern
in the dimness.

"Who's that?" Alec asked.

"Queen Tamír the Second." Sedrich touched a hand respect-
fully to his forelock as they passed. "Skala's had good queens
and bad, but old Tamír was one of the best. Even the balladeers
can't improve much on the life she led."

Alec squinted through the gloom as they passed the statue.
The sculptor had visualized his subject striding into the wind;
her long hair streamed behind her, and the robes she wore were
molded to the gracious curves of her form. Much of her left side
was covered by an oval shield and in her right hand she raised a
sword as if saluting the passing vessels. Her face was neither ex-

ceedingly beautiful nor terribly plain, but her proud stance and fierce expression spoke across the centuries.

"After the Plenimarans destroyed the old eastern capital of Ero, she just up and moved the survivors across to the other side and had this Canal cut through," Sedrish went on, lighting his pipe from a lantern. "That must be better than six hundred years ago now. Aye, there was no stopping her, they say. She was raised as a boy up in the mountains because her uncle had seized the throne. No good come of that, of course; that's what got Ero destroyed. When he was killed in battle, this nephew of his steps forward and says, 'By your leave, I'm a girl.' Her uncle had murdered just about everyone else of the blood, so they crowned her on the spot. During her reign she beat back the Plenimarans, was lost at sea during a battle, then turned up a year later and took back the throne and ruled 'til she was an old woman. Quite a character, she was. Queen Idrilain's said to be a good deal like her."

As they sailed out into Osiat waters at the western end of the Canal, Alec craned his neck to see the carved tops of the pillars flanking this entrance. He recognized the representation of Dalna; a sheaf of grain bound with a serpent. The other, a coiled dragon crowned with a crescent moon, must be that of Illior.

The *Grampus* turned south down the coast with a good following wind. The winter sea shone like polished steel in the late-afternoon sunlight.

Rocky, steep-sided islands of all sizes punctuated the coastline, rising out of the water like ruined fortresses. Some were overgrown with copses of dark fir or oak; those with any sort of harbor were inhabited by colonies of fishermen. A few trading ships were still plying this route and Talrien hailed back and forth with them using a speaking trumpet.

The Osiat was alive with more than sea traders. Alec soon spotted his first school of porpoise. Leaning over the rail, he watched dozens of them leap and sport alongside the ship, their dark backs arching through the waves as they escorted the ship for several miles. Soon after, he saw another school leaping in flight before the dire form of the ship's namesake, a grampus. Though not large as whales go, it looked positively enormous to Alec. The thought of such monsters swimming about under their very keel left him with a decidedly uneasy feeling.

The western shore of Skala presented a rugged face. The harsh granite bones of the country lay exposed at the coastline and again in the peaks of its mountainous spine. Between these two stony extremes lay fertile terraces and valleys, the forests and harbors where the Skalan people had found purchase centuries before. Above the surf-scoured ledges of the shore, the higher ground sloped back from the sea in a series of ascending undulations to meet the inland mountains.

Looking shoreward, Alec could make out wagons and riders moving along a coastal highroad. A company of horsemen gave off glints of metal through the cloud of dust that half obscured their numbers.

"That there's the Queen's Highroad," Biny informed him. "It runs all 'round the peninsula, then up the isthmus and clear to Wyvern Dug."

That evening they put in at a little harbor to unload a shipment of wine and some of the poultry crates, taking on a consignment of copper bars in exchange.

When the hold was quiet again, Alec settled down next to Seregil, hoping to get a little more broth into him. But after a few spoonfuls he choked and Alec gave up. Seregil's breathing was harsher now, rattling in his throat as his chest slowly rose and fell. As he listened, Alec felt despair crystallizing into a hard lump in his throat. Unable to bear it any longer, he dug down into Seregil's battered pack and found the knotted scarf containing the jewelry. Stuffing it into his tunic, he hurried above in search of the captain and Sedrish.

"You've got to look at him," he told them, trying to keep his voice from wavering. "I don't think he'll make it at this rate."

In the hold Sedrish bent over Seregil's still form, then shook his head. "The boy's right, Captain. The man's sinking."

Talrien felt Seregil's pulse, then sat down on a barrel frowning. "Even if we make straight for the city, passing all ports of call, I don't know that it will be soon enough."

"But you could do that?" Alec asked.

Meeting Alec's bleak, determined gaze, Talrien nodded. "I'm master of this ship. I say when she sails and where. It won't do my business any good to come in a week late—"

"If it's money, then maybe this will help." Alec pulled the handkerchief from his tunic and handed it to him.

Opening it, Talrien found the heavy gold chain, earrings, and the gold half sester Klia had given Alec.

"I wasn't supposed to sell those things—he didn't want me to." Alec gestured anxiously in Seregil's direction. "If it's not enough, I think he can more than repay you once we reach the city."

Talrien retied the cloth and handed it back. "I'll have you in Rhíminee by noon tomorrow. We can talk about price later on. Sedrish, fetch this boy some ale."

When they'd gone, Alec lay down next to Seregil and pulled both their cloaks over them, hoping to lend the sick man some of his warmth. Seregil's skin was moist and cold, his eyes deeply sunken beneath bruised-looking lids. For an instant Alec thought he saw a faint expression of pain across his features.

With tears stinging behind his own eyes, Alec grasped one cold hand and whispered, "Don't let go! We're too close now, don't let go."

Again he thought he caught the faintest flicker of emotion in that still face. Probably it was only a trick of the light.

—the plain again. Unchanging emptiness and moaning wind.

Ah, it was all too maddening! He wanted to curse, yell, kick, strike out. All he could do was spin around and around like an idiot, sweeping the horizon for some sign.

But in the midst of his fury he caught sight of a dark figure in the distance. The dark stalker, his final adversary in life, had it followed him even here?

But no, even across the gulf of distance that separated them he could make out the figure of a man, the hood of his dark cloak drawn back to reveal the pale oval of a face. And the man was calling to him.

No, singing!

He could not catch the words but the melody was so lovely, so filled with welcome and promise, that tears sprang to his eyes. How far? How long to reach him? Impossible to judge distance in this cursed barren place, but no matter. He would run to him, for he suddenly felt wondrously light as he skimmed over the dead grass and stones. He was running—no, he was flying! The feeling of release, of joyous movement was dizzying. The ground beneath him blurred and the figure ahead waited with open arms to receive him. Too soon and not soon enough he reached him, was caught by him and held above the ground, for suddenly he had form again, as the man stopped his song and smiled kindly upon him. And such a face! It was as beautiful and serene as a god's. The skin had the color and sheen of purest gold and gathered in supple folds at the corners of his eyes and mouth as he smiled. One eye was covered with a patch, but even this failed to mar the perfection of those features. The other eye, deep and richly blue as a sapphire or a summer sky, gazed at him with depthless love.

"You have come at last, my wounded one."

The voice held the very embodiment of all the love and tenderness he had ever hoped to find in his short, violent life.

"Help me, take me from this place!" he begged, grasping at the being's arms, cold and rigid as stone beneath his hands.

"Of course," answered the god, for surely that must be what he was—Bilairy or Illior, come to rescue him from this terrible place.

Gathering him close, the god cradled him like a child against his chest, stroking him with his cold, gentle hand. "We will pass through the gates and over the sea together, you and I. Give to me the gift you have brought and we shall go at once."

"Gift? But I brought no gift," he stammered, his heart suddenly hammering like a sharp, tiny fist in his chest.

"But you did." The god's hand stroked his head, his shoulder, opened his shirt to lay bare his chest, which ached with the thundering of his pulse. "There, you see?"

The sickly odor rose in his nostrils again as a searing shaft of pain impaled him. Looking down, he saw the small wound that gaped just over his heart; from it, as if from a bloody socket, peered an eye as wonderfully blue as that of the god. A perfect match. And suddenly he was struggling in vain against the iron grip that held him as the golden-skinned god reached to reclaim it—

The *Grampus* pounded south through the night. Coming on deck just after dawn, Alec saw towering grey cliffs off the port bow and a cluster of islands lying close to shore ahead of them.

"Rhíminee harbor, just inside those islands," Talrien shouted over the wind.

Rhíminee was the largest of the western ports, and the most heavily fortified. A series of long granite moles had been constructed between three smaller islands that ranged across the harbor mouth, leaving two openings to allow for the passage of friendly vessels. As the *Grampus* passed through one of these sea gates, Alec saw that the broad causeways bristled with catapults and ballistas. A similar arrangement of moles joined two smaller islands within the harbor itself, dividing it into inner and outer zones like the bailey of a keep.

The sailors furled all but one sail and they glided into the outer harbor, steering past scores of vessels already anchored there. Long, swift war galleys with scarlet sails and two banks of oars were moored near the causeways, their bronze ramming beaks just visible at the waterline. Merchant ships, square barges, and small, high-prowed caravels rode at anchor by the dozens.

The sea gate to the inner harbor had been constructed as a wide chute that afforded no cover to any vessel entering its constricts. Ballistas were mounted on either side and the facing walls of the chute were built in a series of tiers, so that companies of archers could harry any enemy ship that breached this inner defense.

The land embracing the harbor itself rose sharply back on all sides. Even before they had cleared the inner fortifications, Alec caught sight of the citadel above. It was huge; the main city spread over the tops of several hills set half a mile back from the water, and he judged it must be three miles wide at least. Sheer stone walls surrounded the city, hiding from view all but a few glittering domes and towers visible over the parapet.

The only approach from the harbor seemed to be a twisting road enclosed between long stone walls. Alec was no tactician, but recalling that Rhíminee had been built to replace a city destroyed in war, it looked to him as if the Skalans didn't intend to lose a second capital.

Beyond the inner moles, a jumbled sprawl of buildings clung to the base of the cliffs below the citadel. As the ship was rowed toward an empty wharf, Alec looked with growing dismay at the bustling waterfront, the relief he'd felt at reaching the city quickly giving way to alarm at the prospect of trying to find a single wizard somewhere in the incomprehensible city before him.

He caught Biny by the sleeve as the young sailor hurried by. "Have you heard of a place called the Orëska House?"

"Who ain't?" Biny exclaimed, jerking a thumb at the upper city. "See that shiny bit, over to the left? That's the top of the great dome on it."

Alec's heart sank further; he'd have to find some way to get Seregil up there, traversing the width of the city. He fingered the packet of jewels inside his tunic, silently resolving to get Seregil to the Orëska House before nightfall even if he had to buy a wagon to do it.

Several men had come on board to speak with Captain Talrien. Alec was just turning to go below when one of them caught sight of him and touched his sleeve.

"Are you the friend of the sick man?" the stranger asked.

Taken by surprise, Alec turned to find a tall, thin old man smiling down on him. His long, good-natured face was seamed with age around the eyes and brow, and his short beard and the curling hair that thickly fringed his balding pate were silvery white, yet he stood as straight and easy as Alec himself. The dark eyes beneath the unruly white eyebrows revealed nothing but friendly interest. By his clothes—a simple surcoat and breeches under a worn cloak—Alec took him for a trader of some sort.

"What business do you have with him?" Alec asked warily, wondering how he'd known of Seregil's presence on the ship.

"I have come to meet you, dear boy," the old man replied. "I am Nysander."

15

RHÍMINEE AT LAST

lec's legs felt shaky as he led Nysander
into the hold.

"It is as I feared," the wizard murmured,
cupping Seregil's face between his hands.
"We must get him to the Orëska House at once.
I have a carriage waiting. Fetch the driver."

Cold with dread, Alec found the driver and
helped him bundle Seregil, well wrapped in
cloaks and blankets, into the carriage.

In the meantime, Nysander spoke briefly
with Captain Talrien, pressing a purse into his
hands. Talrien nodded his thanks and turned to
make his farewells to Alec.

"Many thanks, Captain," Alec said warmly,
wishing he could find better words.

"You've a brave heart in you, Arèn Silverleaf." Talrien clapped him on the shoulder.
"May it bring you luck."

"It has so far," replied Alec, glancing anxiously toward the carriage. "I just hope the
luck holds a bit longer."

As the carriage set off at last, Nysander
knelt beside Seregil and peeled away the
dressing. A single glance was enough; recoiling, he laid the bandages back in place.

"How long ago did this happen?" he asked,
glad that his back was to the boy.

"Five days."

Shaking his head, Nysander began a series of silent incantations. If this was indeed what he suspected, who but Seregil could have survived such an attack?

When he'd finished, he sat back to take a second look at the boy. Pale and grim, he sat clutching Seregil's pack and sword, eyes darting back and forth between his companion and the spectacle of the city passing by the carriage window.

Worn to a shadow, thought Nysander, *and scared to death of me.*

This was a wild-looking lad to be sure, with his rough northern clothes and tousled hair. Nysander noted the ragged bandage bound around the boy's left hand, and how he held it palm up on his knee as if it pained him. Taut lines scored his chapped young face, making him look older than his years. There was a great weariness about him, too, and an air of uncertainty. Yet beneath all that Nysander sensed the ingrained determination that had carried both him and Seregil through whatever evil had overtaken them.

"Another Silverleaf, eh?" Nysander smiled, hoping to put him at ease. "Seregil claims it is a fortuitous name. I hope that you have found it so?"

"At times." The boy glanced up for just an instant. "He told me never to use my real name."

"I am certain he would not mind if you told it to me."

The boy blushed. "I'm sorry, sir. I'm Alec of Kerry."

"A short name, that. They call me Nysander í Azusthra Hypirius Meksandor Illandi, High Thaumaturgist of the Third Orëska. But you must call me Nysander, for that is how friends address one another here."

"Thank you, sir—Nysander, I mean," Alec stammered shyly. "I'm greatly honored."

Nysander waved this aside. "Nothing of the kind. Seregil is as dear to me as a son, and you have brought him back. I am in your debt."

The boy looked up at him again, more directly this time. "Will he die?"

"That he has survived this long gives me hope," Nysander replied, wishing he could be more encouraging. "You did well to bring him to me. But however did the two of you meet?"

"He saved my life," answered Alec. "It was almost a month ago now, up in the Ironheart Mountains."

"I see." Nysander looked at Seregil's still, white face, wondering if he would ever hear his side of the story.

After a moment's silence, Alec asked, "How did you know we were coming?"

"A week ago I was suddenly blinded by a vision of Seregil in some desperate difficulty." Nysander sighed heavily. "But such visions are fleeting things. By the time I had managed to recapture it, the crisis seemed to have passed. I had my first glimpse of you then, too, and sensed that he was in capable hands."

The boy colored again, fidgeting with the hem of his worn tunic.

"I have had other flashes of your progress over the past few days. You are a most resourceful young man. But now tell me what has happened, for I see that you are wounded as well."

Nysander continued his discreet appraisal of the boy while Alec gave an account of their escape from Asengai's domain and subsequent adventures. A bit of gentle magic satisfied him that Seregil had been very astute in his choice of companion, although his friend's reason for taking on the youngster at all remained something of an enigma.

In describing the blind man's house outside Wolde, Alec admitted to his eavesdropping and seemed relieved when Nysander merely smiled.

"They spoke of a man called Boraneus," Alec told him, "but then Seregil called him Mardus. He sounded upset or surprised when he said the name."

Nysander frowned. "As well he should. You saw this man?"

"At the mayor's hall. Seregil got us in there as minstrels, so he could get a look at him, and the other, a diplomat of some sort who was traveling with him."

"This Mardus, was he a tall, dark fellow with a scar under one eye?"

"From here to here." Alec drew a finger from the inner corner of his left eye to his cheek. "You could call him handsome, I guess, but there was something cold about him when he wasn't smiling."

"Excellent! And the other?"

Alec thought for a moment. "Shorter, thin, with the look of a town dweller. Thin, greyish hair." He shook his head. "He wasn't one that you took much notice of. Anyway, we, ah, well—we burgled their rooms that night."

Nysander chuckled. "I should hope so. And what did you learn from your burglary?"

"That's where we found the—"

Nysander held up a warning hand, then pointed questioningly to Seregil's chest.

Alec nodded.

"Then we must speak of that later," warned the wizard. "Tell me everything else, however."

"Well, I was keeping watch most of the time while he worked. He found several maps. He and Micum Cavish talked about those later on, after we left Wolde. There were some places marked, towns in the northlands. Micum's gone to find one marked in the Fens. I'm afraid that's all I know about it. Seregil will have to tell you the rest."

Let us hope you can, thought Nysander again.

His expression must have betrayed his concern, for Alec suddenly exclaimed, "You *can* help him, can't you? He said if you couldn't, then no one could!"

Nysander gave the boy's hand a reassuring pat. "I know what must be done, dear boy. Go on, please. What happened after that?"

Nysander chuckled appreciatively at Alec's description of their hasty escape from Wolde, but grew serious as he tried to explain Seregil's frightening decline aboard the *Darter* and the difficult journey that followed.

"And through all that, he never spoke further to you of what he discovered in Wolde, or of those men?"

"No, Seregil wouldn't talk about any of it much after we left town. He kept saying it was safer if I didn't know certain things."

Nysander regarded Alec in bemusement; even in one so young it was surprising to find such unquestioning trust—if trust it was. Familiar as Nysander was with Seregil's powers of persuasion, he still wondered that Alec should have followed him so far and through so many trials on the strength of little more than a few tales and fewer empty-handed promises.

No, thought Nysander, trust there certainly must have been, and he had no doubt of Alec's loyalty, but there was something else at work here. Seregil would never have involved a green boy in the burglary in Wolde if he himself had not sensed something deeper in Alec's character and been taken with it. Apprentice indeed!

Alec shifted nervously. "Is something wrong?"

"Certainly not!" Nysander smiled. "I was lost in my own thoughts for a moment, a habit we wizards often drop into. Seregil and Micum were both working for me when you met them. At a more opportune time I will explain what that entailed."

Distracted as he was by Seregil's condition, Alec couldn't help looking out at the passing city now and then. Carts, horses, litters, and pedestrians of all descriptions thronged the streets. The road leading up to the citadel was enclosed in curtain walls on both sides and the stonework seemed to trap the noise and amplify it. This road ended at the broad outer gate of the city. Half a dozen blue-clad guards flanked the entrance, armed with swords and pikes, but traffic passed freely. Once through the gate they slowed, moving through an inner barbican, and then passed under the archway of a second gate, its ancient pediment decorated with carvings of fish. Beyond lay the largest marketplace Alec had ever seen.

The stone-flagged square stretched away on all sides, jammed with hundreds of wooden booths. Their colorful awnings rippled in the brisk wind. A broad avenue had been left open through the center of the square to allow for traffic, and narrow side lanes branched out from it into the wilderness of shops.

From all sides came the clamor of the city: voices shouting, animals braying, the pounding of artisans at work, and the rumble of the carts that flowed in a steady line in both directions along the street. Tall, white-plastered buildings, some as much as five stories high, ringed the market square. Everywhere he looked there were people.

Continuing on, they plunged into the maze of streets and neighborhoods that spread over the hills. Structures of all sorts lined the streets, in some cases even overhanging it with walkways and elaborate solariums. Wagons and riders filled the streets; children, dogs, and pigs darted about underfoot.

As the dizzying spectacle flowed by, Alec recalled with horror his original plan to bring Seregil through Rhíminee alone.

The broad avenue they followed opened periodically into broad, stone-paved circles from which other streets radiated like the spokes from the hub of a wheel. Under other circumstances Alec might have asked Nysander about them, but the wizard had grown silent again, watching Seregil's shallow breathing with apparent concern. Holding his tongue, Alec saw that they were entering an area of larger, more elaborate buildings.

Presently they came to another of the open circles, this one centered around a circular colonnade some forty feet in diameter and bordered on one side by a wooded park.

"The Fountain of Astellus, a spring which has never gone dry since the founding of the city," Nysander remarked, indicating the colonnade. "The original city was centered around it. We are nearly to the Orëska."

Halfway around the circle, their driver veered to the left onto another broad, tree-lined avenue. High walls lined the street on either side, presenting blank faces of smooth stone or plaster except for the broad bands of decoration bordering the tops and gateways. Some patterns were painted, others done in mosaics of colored stone or tile. He would later learn that these decorated walls, screening the elegant villas beyond, were not merely decorative; in the Noble Quarter one might be directed to "the house in Golden Helm Street with the red serpent gate" or "the house with the black and gold circles in a blue border."

Small marble pillars stood at intervals along the streets here, each one carved with a figure representing the name of that street. Small gilded helmets marked the way that Alec and Nysander followed.

"Are those all palaces?" Alec asked, catching glimpses of carved and painted facades beyond the walls.

"Oh, no, just villas. Many are owned by members of the Queen's Kin," Nysander replied. "Aunts, brothers, cousins so far removed one must consult the Archives to ascertain from which obscure third brother of what queen or consort they are descended."

"Seregil said it was a complicated place, but that I'd have to learn all about it," replied Alec, looking rather glum at the prospect.

"Quite true, but I am certain he will not expect you to learn overnight," the wizzard assured him. "You could have no better teacher than Seregil for such matters. If you will look ahead, however, you will see a true palace."

Golden Helm Street ended at the huge walled park surrounding the Queen's Palace. The carriage turned onto a cross street and they passed an open gate, Alec glimpsed an expanse of open ground and beyond it a sprawling edifice of pale grey stone decorated along the battlements with patterns of black and white.

Continuing on, they came to another great enclosed park. The gleaming white walls seemed to have been erected for the purpose of privacy rather than defense, however, for the graceful arch through which they passed had neither door nor portcullis.

As they entered the grounds Alec let out a yelp of surprise. Within the embrace of the surrounding walls, it was as if the seasons had suddenly rushed forward into summer. The sky overhead was the same pale winter blue as before, but the air around them was cool and sweet as a spring morning. On every side stretched carefully laid out lawns and beds of brilliant flowers and blooming trees. Robed figures moved among them or reclined on benches. Alec blinked in disbelief as he caught sight of an enormous centaur playing a harp beneath a nearby tree.

The creature had the body of a tall chestnut stallion, but rising from its withers was the hirsute torso of a man. Coarse black hair overhung his brow in a long forelock and grew in a mane down his back. Nearby a woman floated cross-legged ten feet above the ground, lazily tossing globes of colored glass into the air and directing their motion in time to his music.

Nysander waved to the centaur as they wheeled past and the creature returned the greeting with a nod of his great head.

In the center of all these marvels stood the Orëska House itself, a soaring structure of gleaming white stone surmounted by a faceted, onion-shaped dome that flashed brightly in the sunlight. Slender towers topped with smaller domes and studded at intervals with carved oriels stood at each of the building's four corners.

A set of broad stairs led up to the main entrance where half a dozen servants in red tabards stood waiting. Two men hurried forward with a litter as the carriage came to a stop; a third shouldered the battered pack and Alec's meager bundle. At Nysander's nod, Seregil was carried inside.

The main building was centered around a huge atrium lit by the natural light streaming in through the clear glass dome above.

Rising up from a splendid mosaic floor, the inner walls were broken by five levels of balconies and walkways decorated with more elaborate Skalan carving and tile work.

Nysander strode across the atrium and through one of the large archways that flanked it. Beyond lay a staircase that spiraled gently upward, giving onto a landing at each level. At the third landing they walked down an interior corridor lined with doors, found another stairway, and climbed again.

The place was teeming with people in all manner of dress. Those that appeared to be servants or visitors paid them little heed, but Alec noticed that the wizards, whom he distinguished by their long, colorful robes, invariably drew back from them as if in fear or disgust. Several made strange signs in the air as they passed and one, a boy whose white robe had only simple bands of color at the sleeves, collapsed in a faint.

"Why do they keep doing that?" Alec whispered to Nysander.

"I shall explain presently," Nysander murmured. Leading the way along one of the fifth-floor walkways, he stopped at a heavy door.

"Welcome to my home," he said. Opening the door for the litter bearers, the wizard motioned for Alec to preceed him.

Stepping in, Alec found himself in a narrow, tunnel-like space. Stacks of boxes, crates, and sheaves of parchment filled whatever space there was from floor to ceiling. A single, narrow pathway allowed access to the inner rooms; two people might have been able to squeeze past one another, but it would be at the risk of setting off an avalanche.

The room beyond, though cluttered, was bright and spacious by comparison. Looking up, Alec realized they were at the top of one of the corner towers. Colored only by the sun and sky above, the thick leaded panes of the dome were set in swirling patterns interspersed with complicated symbols.

The tower room was filled with an amazing collection of things, the complete order of which was probably known only to Nysander himself. Shelf upon shelf of books, racks of scrolls, hangings, diagrams, and charts covered every inch of wall space. More books were stacked in precarious piles on the floor and on the stairs that curved up to a walkway beneath the dome overhead.

Around the room stood three large worktables and a high desk. Two of the tables were hopelessly laden; among the general clutter Alec noticed braziers, pots, covered jars, several skulls, and a small iron cage. On the third table a thick book lay open on a stand surrounded by a collection of fragile glass vessels and rods. The desk was also relatively clear, though a dusty formation of candle drippings cascaded to the floor from one corner of it where, over the years, one candle had been set into the guttering pool of its predecessor.

Hooks and nails had been driven in anywhere there seemed to be room, and from these were hung an array of things ranging from dried leaves and skins to a complete skeleton of something that was decidedly not human.

Nysander went to a small side door at the right side of the room and sent the litter bearers through with Seregil. Alec followed them into a small whitewashed chamber. In the middle of the room was a rectangular table of dark polished wood inlaid with ivory; a smaller one of similar design stood against the right-hand wall with a simple wooden chair.

At Nysander's command, the servants placed Seregil's litter on the floor next to the long table and withdrew. No sooner had they gone than a thin young man in a spotless blue and white robe hurried in with an armload of leafy branches. His curly black hair was closely cropped and the sparse black beard edging his cheeks accentuated the gaunt planes of his pale, angular face.

Setting his bundle down beside the smaller table, he brushed a few leaves from the front of his robe and glanced down at Seregil, his pale green eyes narrowing with distaste.

"Ah, just in time!" Nysander said. "Alec, this is Thero, my assistant and protégé. Thero, this is Alec, who has brought Seregil back to us."

"Welcome," Thero said, though neither his voice nor his manner evinced any warmth.

"Are the preparations complete?" asked Nysander.

"I've brought extra branches, just to be certain." Looking down at Seregil again, the young wizard shook his head. "It seems we'll need them."

With Thero's terse assistance, Alec pulled off Seregil's filthy tunic and cut away the linen bands covering the dressing. Thero, who'd handled the tunic as if it were smeared with excrement, took a step back, making a quick warding sign as he did so.

"What is it?" Alec exclaimed in growing alarm. "Nysander, please! Why do people keep doing that?"

"You and Seregil have been in contact with a telesm of the most dangerous sort," the wizard replied calmly, bending to scrutinize the wound. "You are both tainted with a miasmal effluence most offensive to any with thaumaturgic powers."

Glancing up, Nysander saw Alec's blank look and gave the boy an apologetic smile. "Forgive me. What I mean is that you two have been in contact with a cursed object of some sort and, while only the physical effects are apparent to the ordinary observer, to a wizard you both smell like you just crawled out of a cesspit."

"I should say so!" Thero concurred wholeheartedly.

Kneeling beside Seregil, Nysander drew a small silver knife from his belt and gently pressed the flat of the blade here and there against the seeping flesh, his unruly eyebrows drawing together as he noted the round mark left by the wooden disk. Setting the blade aside, he sat back on his heels, frowning.

"It is time I saw the cause of all this."

Alec opened Seregil's pack and pulled out the old tunic. He hadn't touched the bundle since the night of the strange attack.

"Place it there, in the center of the small table," Nysander instructed. "We must work with extreme care. Are you ready, Thero?"

Unrolling the tunic, he lifted the disk out with a long pair of silver tongs. "Just as I feared," he muttered. "Thero, the jar."

His assistant placed a small crystal jar on the table and Nysander dropped the disk into it. There was a brief flash of light as he set the lid in place and the jar sealed seamlessly shut.

"That much is done, at least," Nysander said, dropping the jar unceremoniously into his pocket. "Now we must see to the purification. We shall begin with you, Alec, for we will need your assistance with Seregil. Come now, there is no need to look so apprehensive!"

Thero positioned the chair at the center of the room and motioned for Alec to sit. Gripping the arms nervously, Alec watched as Thero fetched a tray.

Nysander patted his shoulder. "There is nothing to fear, dear boy, but you must not speak again until I tell you that I have finished."

Producing a lump of blue chalk from a wallet on his belt, the wizard drew a circle on the floor around the chair and added a series of hastily scrawled symbols around its perimeter. Meanwhile, Thero poured water from a silver ewer into a silver bowl on the side table, then selected three branches from the bundle on the floor, laying them out neatly beside the bowl. The branches were of three different types: white pine trimmed so that the long needles at the tip formed a sort of brush; a simple birch switch; and a straight branch covered in round green leaves that gave off a sharp, unfamiliar aroma.

Adding a shallow clay dish of ink and a fine brush to the arrangement, Thero placed a thick wax candle behind the bowl and lit it with a quick snap of his fingers.

"Everything's ready," he said, moving to stand behind Alec's chair.

Nysander stood over the bowl, hands held palm downward above it, and spoke a few quiet words. Instantly a soft glow radiated up from the surface of the water, followed by a sweet, pleasant fragrance that filled the room. Taking up the small dish and brush, Nysander painted blue symbols on Alec's forehead and palms, taking special care with the wounded hand.

This step completed, he passed one of the aromatic branches several times over the candle flame, dipped it in the glowing water, and sprinkled Alec from head to foot, repeating the flame and water process several times. The droplets glowed with the same magical light as the water in the bowl. They clung to Alec's skin and clothing, winking like fireflies.

Laying aside the first branch, Nysander passed the birch switch through the flame and water and struck Alec lightly on his cheeks, shoulders, chest, thighs, and feet, then snapped the stick in two. Small puffs of brown, foul-smelling smoke rose up from the splintered ends. He uttered a few more, incomprehensible words; the sweet perfume of the water intensified, dispelling the odor.

Finally, he took up the pine branch and repeated the spargefaction. This time the glowing drops vanished as they touched Alec, leaving a faint tingling sensation in their wake. At a final command from Nysander, the painted symbols simply vanished.

"Your spirit is cleansed," Nysander told him, tossing the last branch onto the table. "I suggest you do the same with your body while we prepare Seregil."

Alec glanced anxiously at Seregil.

"There is time," Nysander assured him. "Thero and I have preparations of our own to make. The task before us is an arduous one. I shall need you refreshed and ready. For Seregil's sake, if not for your own, do as I ask. My servant Wethis will conduct you down to the baths. You may also deliver a message for me to Lady Ylinestra on your way. Please tell her that I shall be detained."

Thero paused on his way out with the tray, giving his master a look Alec couldn't quite decipher. "If you'd like to go to the lady yourself, I can begin the preparations."

"Thank you, Thero, but I must keep my mind clear for the ceremony, as must you," replied Nysander.

Thero gave his master a respectful nod. "Come along, Alec."

A lanky, towheaded youth answered Thero's summons.

"This is Wethis," the young wizard said. Turning on his heel, he disappeared back into the side room without a backward glance.

Alec looked back at Wethis just in time to catch him making a sour face at Thero's back. As the two of them exchanged guilty grins, Alec realized how ill at ease he'd been among the wizards.

"We're to stop at the chambers of someone called Ylinestra," he told Wethis as they began the winding descent back down. "I'm supposed to deliver a message to her for Nysander. Do you know who she is?"

"Ylinestra of Erind?" Wethis shot him an unreadable look. "Everyone knows who she is, sir. Come this way, her chambers are in the visitors' wing."

"She's not an Orëska wizard?"

"No, sir, a young sorceress up from the south to study." They walked on a moment in silence, then Wethis stole another sidelong glance at Alec. "You're the one who came in with Lord Seregil, aren't you, sir?"

"Yes," he replied, thinking *Lord* Seregil? "And you don't have to call me sir. My name's Alec."

Continuing down through the warren of stairways and passages, they came out on a gallery overlooking the atrium. From here, Alec saw that the mosaic on the floor below depicted an immense, scarlet dragon crowned with a silver crescent. Its leathery wings were outstretched in flight; beyond its coiling body, as if seen from a distance, lay what Alec took to be the harbor and walled city of Rhíminee itself.

"That must be the dragon of Illior," he observed, leaning over the rail for a better look.

"The very one."

Stopping at the last door on the gallery, Wethis knocked and stepped back to make way for Alec.

A woman opened the door, her welcoming smile one a man could happily die for. It vanished as soon as she saw the two of them, however. Suddenly Alec couldn't have spoken a word if his life depended on it.

Ylinestra was stunningly beautiful. Framed in a mass of raven hair, her face was at once delicate and sensual. Her eyes were the deep, velvety purple of a summer iris. The loose-flowing garment she wore was made of embroidered silk so sheer it did little more than tint the voluptuous body it draped.

Alec, who had never seen a naked woman before, stood rooted to the spot, too shocked to think. Wethis stood to one side in respectful silence.

"Yes?" Ylinestra demanded imperiously, folding her arms beneath her breasts.

"I've come from Nysander," Alec said, finding his voice at last. He wanted desperately to keep his eyes on hers, but the onslaught of her gaze was too much. Knowing that he'd be lost if he looked lower than her shoulders, he finally settled on her chin and blurted out his message. "He—he said to tell you that he'll be late."

"Did he say when he *would* come?" she demanded, her tone ominous.

"No," Alec replied, resisting the strong urge to fall back a pace.

"Thank you," she snapped and slammed the door in his face. A series of loud crashes from behind it quickly followed as Alec and Wethis beat a hasty retreat.

"If I'd known what your message was, I'd have warned you about her temper," Wethis apologized. "She and Nysander are lovers, you see. I think she must have been expecting him in person."

"His lover!"

"The latest one, anyway," Wethis answered with obvious admiration. "Nysander's one of the few Orëska wizards who doesn't hold with celibacy. Far from it, in fact. Still, I'm not certain even he is a match for Ylinestra, if you know what I mean."

Lowering his voice, he added with a knowing wink, "But I'll warrant she's worth the trouble!"

Reaching the atrium, Wethis led Alec into a long gallery lined with statuary of every size and description.

"This is just the anteroom of the baths," he explained, seeing Alec's look of wonder. "The really unusual things are in the museum across the way. Lord Seregil could show you around there; he knows the place better than some of the wizards."

Steamy air enveloped them as Wethis swung back a large door and ushered him into an immense vaulted chamber. Having always associated washing with chilly streams and drafty bathhouses, Alec wasn't prepared for the opulence that now lay before him.

At the center of the huge chamber lay a broad octagonal pool lined with red and gold tiles. Marble griffins with gilded wings stood at four opposing corners and spewed arching streams of water into it. The tinkling plash of falling water echoed pleasantly around the chamber.

The walls of the room were decorated with frescoes depicting water nymphs and undersea scenes. Beneath these, set into the floor in the same manner as the pool, were individual tubs. Attended by servants, a number of other bathers were already making use of these. Alec could feel the warmth of the heated floor through the soles of his boots.

A carved bench, clothes rack, and the largest looking glass he'd ever seen were arranged around the tub prepared for him. Nearby a servant stood ready with a basket, and another was approaching with a tray of food. The scented water in the tub did look inviting, but Alec felt acutely uncomfortable undressing under so many eyes. Noting his hesitation, Wethis shooed the servants off and turned away himself while Alec slipped hastily into the water.

"Looks like Nysander wants you to eat," Wethis observed, pushing the tray of food over to him.

In spite of his resolution to hurry, the aromas wafting up from the various bowls stirred Alec's empty belly. Taking up a spoon, he hastily wolfed down a few mouthfuls until a fiery red sauce brought him to an abrupt, choking halt.

Grinning, Wethis handed him a goblet of cool water. "You'd better slow down. Skalan food can take you by surprise if you're not used to it."

"I guess so!" Alec croaked, holding out his cup for more water. Taking a last piece of bread, he pushed the rest away. "You want any of this?"

"No," Wethis declined with a bemused smile. "I'll take it away."

Alec ducked his head under, scrubbing his fingers through his hair. When he came up again he found a young bath servant preparing to assist him. Grabbing the sponge out of the startled servant's hands, Alec sent him off with a dark look.

Making cursory use of the soap, he clambered out to find that his soiled clothing had been removed. Clean linen, a loose shirt, soft leather breeches, and a fine scarlet surcoat were laid out on the rack. A broad belt of embossed leather hung over the shoulder of the coat.

"Where's my bow?" he demanded in some alarm as Wethis returned. "Where are my sword and purse?"

"Your purse is here." Wethis handed it to him. "Weapons are not allowed in the Orëska House. They'll be kept safe for you until you leave."

The bath attendant drifted hesitantly back as Alec finished dressing, offering him a tray of oils and combs. Alec was about to wave the boy away again when he caught sight of himself in the glass. For the first time in his life, he saw his entire image at once and scarcely recognized the finely dressed figure he saw reflected there. His hair stuck out in damp disarray. Feeling a little awkward, he accepted a comb and took a moment to smooth it back.

Returning to the wizards tower, Alec found that Seregil had been washed and laid naked on the larger table in the side room. His thin, pale body looked frailer than ever against the dark wood. Angry lines of infection bloomed across his breast like a vile, livid flower.

Nysander was standing on a chair, drawing a blue chalk circle on the ceiling overhead. A corresponding circle had already been drawn on the floor around the table. He'd changed clothes during Alec's absence; the voluminous robe he wore was of the finest blue wool, the breast and sleeves richly patterned with gold embroidery. A wide belt decorated with enameled plaques and silk tassels accentuated the spareness of his frame, making him seem taller than ever. An embroidered velvet skullcap balanced precariously on the back of his head.

"Ah, back so soon? I trust you found yourself well served?" Nysander stepped lightly down from the chair and looked Alec over. Pocketing the chalk, he wiped his hands absently on the skirt of his robe, leaving dusty smudges across the front of it. "Skalan dress suits you, dear boy, although your hair seems to have retained the wild fashion of the north."

He waved a deprecating hand at his own garb. "No doubt you find my appearance more wizardly now? Thero is of a similar opinion, and I find it easiest to humor him. I would be every bit as effective in my ragged old coat, or stark naked for that matter, but he does insist—"

Thero came in just then and Nysander gave Alec a wink that put him very much in mind of Micum Cavish.

Alec was directed to stand at the head of the table. Looking down, he studied Seregil's empty face as Thero quietly arranged the final items for the ceremony. The materials were much the same, with the addition of a slender ivory wand and knife. When he'd finished, he took up his position at Seregil's feet.

Nysander stood beside the table, hands clasped before him. After a moment of silence he looked at Alec. "We shall begin, now. You may find the ceremony disturbing, but remember that we are doing this to save Seregil's life and make him whole again. Once the process has begun, you must not speak or cross out of the circle. Do you understand?"

"Yes," Alec replied, shifting uneasily.

Nysander went to work with the ink and brush, and over the next hour covered Seregil's hands, brow, and breast with an intricate web of interconnected symbols. A particularly dense band outlined the area around the strange wound.

After another invocation, he proceeded with a spargefaction similar to the one he'd performed on Alec. As before, the beaded droplets retained their bright glow against Seregil's skin and by the time Nysander had finished, his body was encased in a gleaming mantle of them.

Nysander took up a birch switch and Alec winced as the wizard brought it down hard enough to raise thin welts across Seregil's skin. At the final blow of the switch, the droplets lost their light, then disappeared.

Chanting in a clear, strong voice, Nysander broke the switch over his knee. Foul brown smoke rose in thick twin columns from the splintered ends, swirling around the confines of the magic circle like a whirlwind in a barrel. It had a fearsome stink and Alec and Thero choked, half blinded, in the midst of it.

Unaffected, Nysander purified the ivory wand in flame and water and drew a glowing sign in the air above Seregil. The sigil writhed in a quick succession of patterns and disappeared with a loud pop, taking the smoke with it.

Motioning for Alec's attention, Nysander raised one hand and made a brief gesture. It took the boy a moment to realize that he was using Seregil's silent hand language.

Hold him.

Thero joined Nysander in a fast, rhythmic chant as they scattered water over Seregil with pine branches. The droplets danced and sizzled across his bare skin like water on a hot griddle, then disappeared. Points of reddish light winked into existence where they had been. Alec thought at first that they were drops of blood, but they quickly swelled to fingertip size, taking on an uncanny, spiderlike shape. They moved like spiders, too, and Alec felt a keen revulsion as the glowing things skittered over Seregil's helpless body, across his mouth, his eyelids and lips.

Around the wound they swarmed out in such numbers that Alec stepped back, instinctively raising his hand in a warding sign. Before he could complete it, however, Nysander's hand closed over his. With a stern gesture, the wizard firmly indicated that Alec should not repeat the gesture.

By the time they'd finished, Seregil was scarcely visible beneath a seething mass of the spidery things. His breathing had grown harsh in his throat and he stirred restlessly, rolling his head from side to side. Signing for Thero and Alec to hold him down, Nysander raised the ivory wand over Seregil's chest and traced another intricate series of patterns on the air. When he was satisfied with the design, he drew a final circle around it. A swirling breeze sprang up above them.

Seregil's breathing quickened to short, painful panting as the glowing things were pulled off his body and drawn up into a small, tightly twisting column. When the last of them had been lifted away, Nysander and Thero cried out in unison, their voices booming in the confines of the tiny room. The very air reverberated in a manner transcending the mere power of a human voice. The swirling cloud of red lights winked out; and blackened husks fell from the air crackled underfoot like tiny shards of glass.

They carefully cleared the remains from Seregil's body and the surface of the table, then began again from the beginning.

Seregil grew increasingly restless as they continued. Within an hour he was physically resisting their efforts; by the fourth cycle of spargings Alec and Thero had to use all their strength to hold him down. During the worst of his throes, Seregil clawed at his own chest, shouting unintelligibly. Nysander paused to listen, then shook his head.

Another hour and they were all to the point of exhaustion. Alec's face and neck were scored with the marks of Seregil's nails. Thero had a bruise darkening over his left eye and his nose was bleeding from a sudden kick. The black cinders lay almost three inches deep on the floor and broken branches were piled around Nysander's ankles.

At last the wound opened, draining thick, bloody pus. They were soon all smeared with it as Seregil continued to arch and struggle. When Nysander paused to sponge the area clean, they saw that the mark of the disk had reappeared. Alec could make out some of the enigmatic pattern and the mark of the square hole at its center.

Late-afternoon light was shining down through the tower dome by the time they completed the last of the purifications. A few of the red lights sprang up under the sprinkling of the pine tip, and finally none at all. Seregil grew quiet again, his breathing a soft, steady moan. Using the ivory knife, Nysander gently pricked the skin where the pulse throbbed at the base of Seregil's throat. A drop of bright blood welled up, nothing more.

Reaching overhead with the wand, he broke the blue chalk circle on the ceiling, then bent and scratched across the one on the floor. Straightening wearily, he kneaded at the back of his neck with one hand.

"He is cleansed."

"Will he get well now?" Alec asked uncertainly, seeing little improvement.

Nysander stroked Seregil's damp hair back from his forehead with a fond smile. "Yes. He would not have survived the ritual, otherwise."

"You mean he could have died from this?" Alec gasped, grasping the edge of the table to steady himself.

Nysander clasped him by the shoulders, looking earnestly into his face. "He would certainly have died otherwise, and perhaps gone on to something far worse after death. I did not tell you that before because I did not want you distracted by such concerns."

"Shall I send for Valerius now?" asked Thero.

"Please do. I believe you will find him in the atrium."

"Who's Valerius?" asked Alec.

"A drysian. Seregil is damaged in body as well as in spirit. That will require special healing."

This, at least, was something Alec understood. He set to work clearing away the remains of the ceremony. Gingerly picking up a few of the blacked stars, he found them as brittle as the dead spiders they resembled.

"What are they?" he asked, dropping them in disgust.

"A corporeal manifestation of the evil that came into him through the disk," Nysander replied, sifting a handful through his fingers. "It is very difficult to affect anything of insubstantial nature. By means of the procedure you just witnessed, I was able to draw the evil from Seregil's body bit by bit, binding it to a small amount of matter to lend it a tangible form. I could then act upon it by magic to dissipate it. These ashes are simply the residue of the temporary physical form I imposed upon it."

"Is it difficult?"

"More draining than difficult. But you must be exhausted, wrestling with our poor friend here for so long. How do you suppose an old fellow of nearly three centuries must feel?"

Alec blinked. "Micum said you were the oldest of the wizards, but I never—"

"I am hardly the oldest of all, my boy, merely the eldest in residence at the Orëska," Nysander corrected. "I know of several others half again as old as myself. As wizards go, I am in my prime. Please do not go making an antiquity out of me just yet!"

Alec began a stammered apology, certain he'd given offense, but Nysander chuckled and reached to ruffle his hair. "If Micum spoke of me, he must have told you not to fear me. Speak your mind honestly, and I shall like you the better for it."

"I'm still getting used to all this," Alec admitted.

"I am not surprised. Once Seregil is settled, you and I shall have a nice, comfortable chat."

Alec went back to his task in silence, wondering what he would have to say to a wizard, even one as friendly as Nysander. He was soon startled out of his reverie, however, by the sound of someone entering the front room.

"What's the brat gotten himself into this time?" a brusque voice bellowed.

The owner of the voice, a wild-looking man in rough clothing, strode into the room, bringing with him the smells of fresh air, wood smoke, and wild growing things freshly gathered. Thero trailed in the newcomer's wake, his thin mouth pursed into a vaguely disapproving line.

"Valerius, old friend!" Nysander greeted the man warmly. "How fortunate to find you in Rhíminee today. I have dispelled the magic, but he still requires considerable healing."

Tossing a battered satchel onto the table, the drysian scowled down at Seregil. Valerius' unkempt black hair stood out in violent disorder beneath the cracked brim of his disreputable felt hat. His beard bristled belligerently, and the rich black thatch that covered the backs of his hands and forearms and curled forth from the unlaced neck of his tunic gave him a bearish look. His clothes, like those of most drysians, were plain and stained with hard travel. His heavy silver pendant and smooth-worn staff, together with the pouches of every size and description hanging from the belt girding his ample middle, marked him as a drysian. Deep lines bracketing his mouth warned of a formidable nature.

"I believe it was curse magic of some sort," Nysander informed him.

"I can see that," Valerius muttered, brown eyes glittering as he ran his hands over Seregil's body.

"What's this?" he asked, tapping a finger under the open wound.

"The imprint of a wooden disk Seregil wore next to his skin for several days. I do not know whether the mark is the result of magic, or happened when this boy inadvertently pulled the thing off. Alec, you did say you noticed a reddening of the skin there a few days before the final incident?"

Pinned by the drysian's sharp attention, Alec nodded.

"Never seen anything like this, but it stinks of sorcery." Valerius wrinkled his nose as he examined the faint tracery still visible. "Best to have it off."

The wizard cupped a hand over the mark for a moment, then shook his head slowly. "I think it would be better to leave it as it is for the time being."

"The last thing Seregil wants is another scar on his pretty

skin," Valerius glowered. "Especially one as distinctive as this! Besides, who knows what this thing means?"

"That was my first thought," Nysander concurred, unperturbed by the drysian's manner. "Nonetheless, I feel it would be best to leave it as it is."

"Some mystical presentiment, no doubt?" Valerius gave a derisive snort. "Suit yourself, then. But *you* explain it to him when he makes a fuss."

Shooing everyone from the room, the healer set to work. Wethis was summoned to assist him, and soon the room was choked with clouds of steam and incense.

Nysander cleared a space at one of the less cluttered worktables and Thero and Alec joined him.

"Illior's Hands, that was thirsty work." He spoke a quick spell and a tall, burlap-wrapped jar appeared on the table before them, a crust of melting snow clinging to the coarse material. Alec reached out a tentative finger to see if it was real.

"Mycenian apple wine is best well chilled." Nysander smiled, delighted with Alec's open amazement. "I keep a supply up on Mount Apos."

The three of them settled down over the mild, icy wine, waiting for the drysian to finish. Poor Wethis scatted in and out on errands for Valerius so often that Nysander finally propped the front door open so they wouldn't have to keep letting him in.

Valerius emerged from the casting room at last, streamers of vapor trailing from his beard. Dropping unceremoniously onto the bench beside Alec, he unhooked a cup from his belt and helped himself to the wine. Ignoring their expectant looks, he drained the cup at one gulp and let out a deep, satisfied belch.

"I've gotten the last of the poison out of his blood. He'll mend now," he announced.

"Was it acotair?" Thero inquired.

Valerius saluted him with his cup. "Acotair it was. An uncommon poison, and very effective. I daresay it leached into his skin from the disk, weakening him so that the magic could work more quickly."

"Or from a distance," suggested Nysander.

"Possibly. The combination would have killed most men, considering how long he wore the damned thing."

"Well, you know Seregil and magic," Nysander sighed. "But

you are fortunate not to have handled it any more than you did, Alec."

"What did you mean, about Seregil and magic?" asked Alec. "He resists it somehow—"

"You mean he fouls it up!" scoffed Valerius.

The drysian's derisive tone bothered Alec less than Thero's discreet smirk; he found he was liking Nysander's assistant less all the time.

"Whatever the case, it has saved his life," said Nysander. "And Alec's as well, judging by his description of Seregil's behavior. Had he decided to kill you, dear boy, I doubt you could have stopped him."

Recalling the look on Seregil's face that night in the barn, Alec knew Nysander spoke the truth.

"He'll sleep for another day, perhaps two," said Valerius. "He should stay in bed a week; knowing him, five days will have to do. But no less than that, mind you. Lash him to the bedposts if you have to. I'll leave some herbs for an infusion. Force as much of it down him as you can, and make him eat. Nothing to drink but water and lots of it. I want him properly purged before we let him go. Thanks for the wine, Nysander."

Rising to his feet, he swung his satchel over his shoulder. "Strength of the Maker be upon you!"

Alec watched him stride out, then turned to Nysander. "He knows Seregil, doesn't he? Are they friends?"

Nysander smiled wryly, considering the question. "I cannot recall hearing either of them use the term in relation to one another. Still, I suppose they are, after their own peculiar fashion. But I suspect you will have an opportunity to form your own opinions over the next few days."

16

DINNER WITH NYSANDER

Exhausted as he was after the ceremony, Alec insisted on helping Wethis carry Seregil down the back stairs of Nysander's tower to the living quarters. A short, curving hallway led past several closed doors to a comfortable bedchamber near the end of the passage.

The room was simply furnished. Two narrow beds flanked an embrasured window on the far side of the room. Thick, colorful carpets covered the floor, and a cheerful blaze crackled in the fireplace near the door.

They laid the unconscious man in the right-hand bed and Nysander bent over him, taking one of Seregil's hands between his own.

"He really is going to be all right, isn't he?" Alec asked, unable to decipher the old wizard's expression. "The same as he was before, I mean?"

Nysander gave Seregil's hand a final pat and laid it gently on the sleeping man's chest. "I believe so. He is strong in ways even he is not completely aware of. But you should sleep now, too. I shall send for you when you are rested and we will talk of anything you like. Look for me in the room across the passage or upstairs if you need me."

When he'd gone, Alec pulled a chair up beside Seregil's bed. It pleased him to see how quietly Seregil slept. His drawn face seemed less empty now, and a faint tinge of color had crept into his sunken cheeks.

I'll just sit here for a few minutes, Alec thought, propping his feet on the edge of the bed.

He was asleep almost at once.

"Alec—"

Alec sat up, glancing around in momentary alarm. He'd been dreaming of the *Grampus* and it took a moment to remember where he was. Someone had brought in a night lamp and by its soft light he saw Seregil regarding him through half-lidded eyes.

"Rhíminee?" It was scarcely a whisper.

"I told you I'd get you here," Alec said, trying to sound nonchalant and failing as he pulled the chair closer.

Seregil's gaze wandered drowsily around the room and Alec saw a flicker of a smile playing about his pale lips. "My old room—"

Alec thought his friend had drifted off to sleep again, but he stirred after a moment and rasped, "Tell me."

He listened quietly, stirring only to look at Alec's scarred hand, and again at the mention of Valerius.

"Him!" Seregil croaked. He groped for more words, then shook his head slightly. "Explain later. What do you think of Nysander?"

"I like him. He's someone you trust right away, like Micum."

"Always trust him, always," Seregil whispered, his eyelids fluttering shut again.

When Alec was certain he was soundly asleep this time, he fell into his own bed, only to be awakened a second time by the sound of soft voices. Pushing the quilt back from his face, he saw Valerius and Nysander bending over Seregil across the room. Sunlight slanted across the carpet.

"Good afternoon," Nysander greeted him. Gone were the embroidered vestments of the night before. His plain robe was frayed at the cuffs and devoid of ornamentation.

"I should have been up before now." Alec sat up and yawned. "How's Seregil? He came around for a few minutes last night."

"Well enough," Valerius replied as he finished with a fresh dressing. Drawing the blankets back over Seregil, he turned and surprised Alec with an almost friendly grin. "How are those scratches today?"

"A little sore."

Placing a hand under Alec's chin, Valerius tilted the boy's head this way and that. "Nothing serious. See you keep them clean. Nysander told me how you brought Seregil here. You must be as stubborn as he is."

Still gripping Alec's chin, he extended his other hand palm down toward the floor. The boy shivered as a pleasant chill ran through him.

"That should take care of anything ailing you." Waving a hand at Seregil, Valerius added gruffly, "I expect you to keep an eye on him for me. He's to stay in that bed until I say otherwise, understand?"

The formidable glint had returned to the drysian's eye, and Alec gave a quick nod of compliance.

"You must not bully the boy," Nysander chided as Valerius took his leave. "You know very well he is quite trustworthy, and a good Dalnan besides."

"Aye, but it's not a good Dalnan that he'll be dealing with when Seregil begins to get his pepper back. Good luck to you, lad, and Maker's blessings."

"And to you!" Alec called hastily after him.

"You must be famished. I know I am," said Nysander. "Come, I have along a meal laid for us in my sitting room."

Alec cast a worried glance toward Seregil.

"Come, you must keep up your own strength if you are to be any help to him," said Nysander, taking him gently by the arm. "It is just across the corridor. We shall leave both doors open and come back with our wine as soon as we have eaten."

Wethis was busy setting out the meal on a round table at the center of the room and nodded pleasantly to Alec as they entered.

After the massive clutter of the upper rooms, Alec was surprised at the orderliness of Nysander's sitting room. The small chamber was furnished for simple comfort; beyond a round dining table, two large chairs faced one another in front of the blazing hearth. Shelves along the walls held neatly arranged collections of scrolls and books interspersed with more arcane objects.

The room's most notable feature was a narrow band of mural running completely around the otherwise unadorned walls. It was scarcely two feet in width but Alec discovered upon closer inspection that it was comprised of a succession of fantastic beasts and birds rendered in superb detail. Here a tiny dragon hovered on scaly outstretched wings over a still smaller castle, blasting it with a glowing stream of fiery breath; there a centaur raiding party bore maidens away in sinewy arms. Farther along the same wall an horrific sea creature reared up from painted waves, spines bristling from its reptilian face as it crushed a ship in its jaws. Near the first corner a creature with the body of a lioness and the breasts and head of a woman held the limp form of a youth between her taloned paws. Interspersed among these scenes were symbols that gave back a silvery sheen in the light.

Suddenly he heard an amused chuckle behind him.

"My little paintings please you, I see," the wizard said.

Alec realized with chagrin that he'd been following the mural around the room with complete disregard for his host. Turning, he found Nysander seated at the table. Wethis was nowhere to be found.

"Forgive me. I didn't mean to be rude," he stammered as he hastily took a seat.

"No need for apologies. It has that affect on most who see it for the first time. As a matter of fact, that is part of its function."

"You mean it's magical?" In spite of his hunger, Alec found it difficult to draw his eyes from the paintings.

Nysander raised one shaggy eyebrow in amusement. "Forgive me, but it is always refreshing to meet someone as ingenuous as yourself. So many who come here expect revelations of mythic proportions—dragons under the wine table, spirits summoned down the chimney! They have no awe left in them for the little marvels. All their wonder has turned to appetite.

"In answer to your question, however, the mural is indeed magical. Its purpose, aside from dazzling my dinner guests, is to protect my rooms. The symbols you see there are each keyed to react to a different sort of intrusion. You will find them throughout the Orëska House. Perhaps you noticed the ones in the dome upstairs? The entire building is protected by an elaborate pattern of magicks— But I am keeping you from your meal! Let us talk of little things as we eat. After dinner we shall converse in a civilized fashion over the wine."

Alec began cautiously, recalling the fiery spices of the day before, but each successive dish was more agreeable than the last.

"Seregil told me that wizards come to Rhíminee to be trained," he ventured at last.

"Wizards, scholars, madmen, they come seeking the knowledge amassed and preserved by the Third Orëska. There is more than magic here, you see. We gather information of all types. Our library is the finest in the Three Lands, and the vaults below contain artifacts which predate the coming of the Hierophants."

Alec laid aside his knife. "Why is it called the Third Orëska?"

"The first mages who came here from Aurënen were the original Orëska," Nysander explained. "It was they who first taught that knowledge is as powerful, in its own way, as any magic, and that magic without knowledge is worse than useless; it is dangerous. Later, they established the Second Orëska at Ero when magical powers became apparent among the half-blood children of Aurënfaie and humans. Unfortunately, the fellowship of the Second Orëska was all but annihilated during the Great War. There have never been as many wizards since that time. Another blow befell it when Ero was destroyed. A terrible tragedy, so many of the ancient writings lost! Queen Tamír bequeathed this site to the surviving wizards at the founding of Rhíminee, with the understanding that they would contribute to the defense of Skala. The new alliance established at that time was deemed the Third Orëska. The Cirna Canal was one of the first demonstrations of their good faith."

"I've heard something of that. How many wizards are there now?"

"Only a few hundred in all the Three Lands now, I fear. Fewer and fewer children are being born with the power; the blood of the Aurënfaie masters has grown thin."

"But don't the children of wizards inherit their powers?"

Nysander shook his head. "There are no children of wizards. It is perhaps the greatest price we pay for our gifts. Magical abilities demand every bit of creative force we possess. We are repaid richly with powers and long lives, but the force of Illior which gives us the ability to recreate the world around us also burns out the natural procreative forces of the body. The Immortal has never revealed why this must be so, even to the Aurënfaie— But I am lecturing you as if you were a novice! Let us return to your room. Seregil is still deep within himself and shall likely remain so for some time, but I believe it will benefit him to have us nearby."

Nysander took down two tall goblets from a nearby shelf and handed one to Alec. The boy turned it about in disbelief, never having seen its like. Carved from flawless rock crystal, it was banded around the stem and cup with heavily embellished gold and polished red gems that glowed like wine in the firelight.

"I could just use my cup from supper," Alec protested, holding it gingerly in both hands.

"Nonsense!" Nysander grabbed up a decanter from the sideboard and headed across to the bedchamber. "I nearly lost my life acquiring them. It would be a waste not to use them."

They found Seregil still sleeping deeply.

"Let us sit close by him." Nysander gave Alec another roguish wink. "You shall surrender the chair to me out of deference to my great age. You can sit on the end of his bed. Some part of him knows we are here and it will comfort him."

Alec settled cross-legged with his back against the footboard. Nysander filled their goblets with red wine and raised his cup at Alec.

"Drink up! This is talking wine and I know you have many more questions. I can see them swarming about like bees behind your eyes."

Alec took a long sip and felt a comfortable warmth spread through him. "I'd like to know more about that disk. What was it you called it?"

"A telesm. A magical object which has an innate power of its own that can also be used as a focus of power by one who understands its function. The poison it was coated with would aid in this, as Valerius and I discussed last night. Unfortunately, there is little more I can tell you of it."

"Well, what about that dark creature Seregil kept claiming to see? Was that real?"

The shadow of a frown flickered across Nysander's lined face. "I shall need to hear Seregil's account to be certain. Whatever the case, someone was taking a great deal of trouble and effort to find both you and the disk."

Alec looked up sharply. "You think they might still be after us?"

"Quite possibly. But you have nothing to fear, dear boy. I have placed the disk beyond their reach. If anyone was following you,

I think that they found a cold trail the moment I contained it in
that jar, or perhaps even when you pulled it from Seregil's neck.
So long as you remain within the walls of the Orëska, an army
could not get to you."

"But if Mardus is such a powerful wizard—"

"Mardus is no wizard!" Nysander fixed Alec with an appraising look. "What I tell you now must go no further, is that understood? I repeat, he is not a wizard. Mardus is one of the most
powerful Plenimaran nobles, also rumored to be a bastard son of
the aging Overlord. Whatever the case, he is a ruthless man of
cruel and dangerous intelligence, a cunning warrior, and a known
assassin. It was most unfortunate for him to have looked upon
your faces that night in Wolde; let us hope he never does so
again. But I did not bring you here to frighten you more than you
have been these last few weeks, so I am going to ply you with
more of this excellent wine and turn to less worrisome topics.
Did Seregil tell you that he was once apprenticed to me?"

"No, but Micum did, back in Boersby." Alec watched the
play of the firelight in the crimson depths of his cup. For all the
days of talking on the Downs and after, Seregil had never once
spoken of his own past. "Micum said something about it not
working out."

Nysander smiled at him over the rim of his goblet. "That, dear
boy, is a magnificent understatement. No wizard ever had so de-
voted or disastrous a pupil! But I shall begin at the beginning.
Seregil came to Idrilain's court as a poor and distant relation, exiled from his family, totally alone. At court they tried to make a
page of him, but that did not last long—as you may well imagine. Next came a position as a junior scribe, I believe. Again failure. After one or two other such fiascoes, he came to my
attention.

"I was delighted to get him, and could not believe my good
fortune. He has the ability, you see, and he was so eager to learn.
But after a few months it became apparent that something was
wrong. He mastered the rudimentary disciplines with an ease
which delighted us both, but as soon as we tried to move on to
the higher magicks, things began to go awry."

Nysander shook his head, remembering. "At first it was simply
that the spells would not come off. Or they would, but with the
most unexpected results. He would try to move a small object,
say a salt cellar; it would overturn. He would try again and the

salt would burst into flames. On the third try it might fly at his head, or mine. One day he attempted a simple messenger spell, and in the space of five minutes every spider, centipede, and earwig in the place came swarming in under the door. We began conducting his training outside after that.

"Attempting to levitate, he blew up an entire grove of trees in the park. A simple summoning, butterflies I think, and all the horses went crazy for an hour. Things soon reached such a state that whenever anything unusual happened within the Orëska grounds, we got the blame for it.

"Oh, but it was frustrating! In spite of all the blunders, all the destruction, I knew the power was there. I could feel it, even when he could not. For he did succeed now and then, but so erratically! Poor Seregil was devastated. I saw him brought to tears just trying to light a candle. Then there was the time he turned himself into a brick."

Caught sipping his wine, Alec choked as he began to laugh. He knew he shouldn't, but the wine was in him to the heart and he just couldn't help it. None of this sounded like the Seregil he knew.

Nysander shook his head ruefully. "The one sort of spell he really took to was shape changing, though I generally had to assist him. This time, however, he was determined to do it by himself and he turned himself into a brick—I believe he was trying for a horse at the time. In any case, there was the usual flash, then a thump, and there he was on the ground at my feet; an ordinary brick!"

Alec pressed a hand over his mouth, quaking with stifled laughter that jostled the bed. Seregil stirred against the pillow.

"No, no, do not trouble to move. It is good for him to sense us with him." Nysander patted Seregil affectionately on the shoulder. "You never like being reminded of that incident, do you? Ah, Alec, we may well laugh now, but I assure you, it was not very amusing at the time. To change another person out of such a self-imposed state, particularly that of an inanimate object, is terribly difficult. It took me two days to get him back! I knew we should stop after that, but he begged me to give him just one more chance. Then he really did it, sending himself into another plane."

"Plane?" Alec hiccuped, wiping his eyes.

"It is like another country or world, except that it does not exist in our reality. No one really understands why they exist at all, only that they do and that there are ways to cross into them. But they are dangerous, for the most part, and difficult to return from. Had I not been with him when he did it, he would have been lost. It was then that I was forced to say 'No more.' "

Nysander looked down at Seregil again, all the mirth gone from his face. "That was one of the saddest days of my life, dear boy, the day you took off your apprentice robe." Taking a deep draft from his goblet, he went on. "You see, Alec, denied children, our apprentices often fill that gap. We give them our knowledge and our skill, and they carry our memory into the future when we die. So it was between my old master and myself. Losing Seregil as my apprentice was like losing a beloved son."

"But you didn't really lose him, did you?"

"No, as it turned out, I did both of us a great service by not allowing him to keep at it until he killed himself. It also forced him to find out what he was truly suited for. But he went away for a long while after that, and I did not know if I would see him again. When he returned, however, he was well on his way to what he is now."

Alec sighed. "Whatever that is."

"Do you not know?"

"I'm still not sure. I want to understand, so that I'll understand better what he's trying to teach me."

"A wise course. And I am certain that when he is ready, Seregil will explain better than either Micum or I could. For now I can tell you that both he and Micum are Watchers."

"Watchers?"

"Spies, of a sort. None of them may speak of it, even among themselves. But as I happen to be the head of the Watchers, I can offer you an explanation."

"You're a spy?" Alec exclaimed in surprise.

"Not exactly. The Watchers are my eyes and ears in distant places. They travel around, talking, listening, observing. Among other things, they have been quite valuable in keeping an eye on certain movements by the Plenimarans. The Queen has her own intelligence service, of course, but my people are often of aid to them. Within the last year there have been rumors of unusual activity in the north, so I sent Seregil and Micum out to appraise the situation."

"Why would a wizard be the leader of that kind of thing, if you don't mind my asking?"

"It does seem odd, I suppose, but it is a tradition which predates the founding of the Third Orëska. My master and his master before him and on back through the centuries, we have always held the post, and my successor shall do the same. The Watchers have contributed much to the libraries of the Orëska over the years. They also keep those of us who take an interest in the wider world well abreast of what is happening beyond our borders."

"But can't you just find things out by magic?"

"Sometimes, but you must never think that it grants one omnipotence."

Alec turned the goblet around in his hands, studying the golden tracery as he weighed his next question.

"Come now, Alec, out with it! I think I know what you are wanting to ask."

Taking a deep breath, Alec plunged on. "You knew that something had happened to Seregil, and you knew we were trying to come to you. Why didn't you just bring us here yourself, like you did with that wine last night?"

Setting his cup down, Nysander laced his fingers around one up-drawn knee. "A fair question, and a common one. In this particular case there were a number of reasons for not doing so. First, I did not know exactly where you were or exactly what had occurred. What little I did know came to me in a fleeting vision, not by any conscious seeking on my part. To search for someone by magic when you do not have many clues is difficult at best, and generally disappointing. Over the next few days I was able to get brief glimpses of you both, but they told me little more than that you were on land or sea until I recognized the Canal.

"That is one reason. The next is that such spells as would have been necessary to bring him here are more difficult than you imagine; all magic takes a certain toll, and translocating him here would have been a thousand times more difficult than bringing down that jug of wine, even for me. Besides that, Seregil, with his own peculiar resistance to magic, has difficulty with translocation spells. They leave him quite ill even under the best conditions. Weakened as he was, he might not have survived. Furthermore, I could not have brought you both, so there you would have been, wondering what had become of your friend. All in all, I decided that it would be safest to await your arrival."

Nysander paused, regarding Alec for a moment from beneath his shaggy brows. "Now those are all valid reasons, but beyond them is one that supersedes all. The Orëska is founded on the principle that the purpose of magic is to *aid* the endeavors of mankind, not to supplant them.

"Despite the hardships you endured, all your worry and care, think of what you have gained. You were braver and stronger and more loyal than you have probably had to be in all your life. And your reward is that you succeeded; you saved the life of your friend. Would you give that up to have had me simply spirit you here from that inn?"

Alec thought of the expression on Seregil's face when he'd awakened in a clean bed in Rhíminee.

"No," he answered quietly. "Not for anything."

"I thought as much."

Alec took another sip of wine. "Micum tried to tell me about you, but you still aren't how I imagined a wizard would be."

"Indeed?" Nysander looked rather pleased. "Most of my colleagues would agree with you. But they have their ways and I have mine. All of us serve the greater good in our own fashion. But I believe you had some point to make?"

"It's just that, with what you told me about Seregil and all, I don't understand about Thero. It seemed to me, yesterday I mean, that he doesn't— Well, he doesn't seem to like Seregil very much. Or me, for that matter."

Nysander grimaced wryly. "If it is any comfort to you, I do not think, in his heart, that Thero cares much for me, either."

"But he's your student!"

"That hardly guarantees affection, my boy, although ideally such regard should exist between master and pupil. Your faithfulness to Seregil after such short acquaintance speaks well of you both.

"It took me many years to find another apprentice. As I said before, there are few who have the inborn power, and those who do vary greatly in their ability. Of those few who did trickle into the Orëska each year, I found none that suited my purposes until Thero. Whatever else you may think of him, he is tremendously talented. There is no facet of our art he cannot grasp. The fact that he was of my old master's family made him seem all the more suitable at the time. All that, together with the fact that I was beginning to feel quite desperately in need of a successor, blinded me to certain aspects of his nature which might otherwise have given me pause. Thero has proven trustworthy in every way, yet his thirst for knowledge borders on avarice—a serious flaw in a wizard. He also possesses no sense of humor and, while you will not find that listed among the requirements of the Orëska, I believe it to be an invaluable trait in those who aspire to power of any sort. And this lack of humor causes him to find me an embarrassment on occasion.

"However, it is his animosity toward Seregil which has most alarmed me over the years, for it reveals envy—one of the most dangerous weaknesses of all. He cannot be content that he replaced Seregil, that he is more gifted in magic than Seregil could ever have been. And though he has little use for my affection himself, he cannot bear that Seregil retains it. Of course, Seregil is little better, as I am certain you shall see for yourself soon enough. But Thero is a wizard. If he acts this way over such small matters, what will he not be capable of over great ones, when he is great?"

Nysander paused, massaging his eyelids with two fingers. "For with or without my teachings, he will be great. And so I keep him with me because I fear to let him go to another master. It is my greatest hope that with time and maturity he will gain compassion, and then what a wizard he shall be!"

Alec was amazed at the old wizard's candor. "Seregil tells me nothing of himself, and you tell me everything."

Nysander smiled. "Oh, hardly everything yet! We all have our secrets, and our reasons for them. I have told you this about Thero and myself so that you may understand him better and perhaps see why he acts as he does. Like Seregil, I also expect and trust in your discretion."

Nysander was just reaching for his goblet again when a yellow globe of light winked into being in front of him. It hovered a moment, gleaming like a tiny sun, then floated gently to settle on his outstretched palm. The wizard inclined his head, as if listening to a voice inaudible to Alec. It disappeared as abruptly as it had come.

"Ylinestra," Nysander explained. "Excuse me for a moment." Closing his eyes, he held up a long forefinger and a similar light, bright blue in color, sprang up there. "Certainly, my dear," he said to it, "I shall be with you shortly."

At a slight flick of his finger, the mote of light shot out of sight.

Anticipating Nysander's departure, Alec stood up and felt the wine rise to his head. "Well, uh, I think I'm beginning to understand a few things. Thank you."

Nysander raised an eyebrow. "There is no hurry. I have sent word."

"No, really. If Ylinestra was waiting for me— Oh, damn!" Alec stammered to a halt, cheeks flaming. "I didn't mean, that is— It's the wine, I guess."

"Illior's Light, boy, what will Seregil ever make of you if you cannot keep a straight face?" Nysander chuckled as he rose to his feet. "Perhaps you are right, though. She can be impatient. Why not take a stroll in the gardens? I should think you would find it most pleasant there after being confined in ships and houses for so long. Wethis can sit with Seregil."

"I don't think I could find my way around," said Alec, thinking of all the twists and turns between here and the main entrance.

"That is easily remedied. Take this with you." Nysander opened his hand to show Alec a small cube of green stone, incised on each side with tiny symbols.

Alec rolled it around on his palm. "What is it?"

"A guide stone. Simply hold it up and speak where you wish to go. It will lead you."

Feeling a bit silly, Alec held out the stone and said, "To the gardens?"

The words were scarcely spoken before the cube took on a pale nimbus and rose to hover in the air just in front of him.

"It will take you anywhere on the grounds you are allowed to go," Nysander explained. "Do remember not to attempt to enter any wizard's chamber unless invited. If you are ready, simply instruct it to proceed."

"Go on, then," Alec told the cube. Floating across the room, it passed though the polished wood of the door in a decidedly unnatural fashion.

Behind him, the wizard chuckled again. "Be certain *you* open the door first."

17

WATCHER BUSINESS

Taking Valerius' admonition to heart, Alec saw to it that Seregil drank the prescribed infusions. Still terribly weak, Seregil slept most of the time, rousing just long enough to take a little nourishment before lapsing back again.

Alec's diligence quickly earned the brusque drysian's respect, and he, in turn, grew comfortable with Valerius' abrasive manner, recognizing the gentle sureness of his healing and liking him for it.

Nysander provided whatever he needed and visited several times a day. When Alec mentioned the writing lessons with Seregil, the wizard brought writing materials and a simple scroll for him to work on.

Alec and Nysander were playing nine stones in Seregil's room the second morning after the purification when an old woman in a travel-stained cloak appeared at the door of the sickroom.

"Magyana!" Nysander exclaimed, rising to embrace her. "You should have sent word. I had no idea you were back."

"I wanted to surprise you, my dear," she replied, kissing him soundly. "Yet it was I who was surprised. Thero says Seregil has been hurt."

Going to the bed, she laid her hand on Seregil's brow.

She must be as old as Nysander, thought Alec. The woman's face was deeply lined and the heavy braid coiled at her neck shone white as moonlit snow.

She sketched a quick, glowing symbol in the air over the sleeping man and shook her head. "Thank the Light he is safe. Who did this to him, and how?"

"He ran afoul of Mardus and his necromancers in the northlands," Nysander told her. "Young Alec here brought him to me just in time. Alec, this is Magyana, a fellow wizard and my dear companion from the days of our youth."

Magyana turned to Alec with a warm smile. "Bless you, Alec. Nysander would have been desolate to lose him, as would I."

Seregil stirred just then, muttering hoarsely as he fought his way out of some panicked dream.

"There now, Seregil," Nysander said, raising his voice as he bent over him. "Open your eyes, dear boy. You are quite safe. Are you awake at last?"

Seregil's eyes flew open. Seeing Nysander and the others, he lay back with a sigh of relief. "I keep dreaming I'm back in Mycena."

Nysander sat on the edge of the bed and took his hand. "You are safe now, and whole, thanks to Alec. He has told me of your adventures and you will tell me more when you are stronger. But for now you must rest. You very nearly destroyed yourself this time."

"I know." Seregil shook his head weakly. "Damn fool that I was, I'd have deserved it, too—"

He shifted to look up at Alec, a shadow of doubt in his eyes. "You all right? I—I wasn't myself for a while there."

"I'm fine," Alec assured him, knowing in his heart that he was damned lucky to be able to say that.

Leaving Seregil to Alec's watchful care, Nysander walked Magyana to her tower at the northern corner of the House.

"My dear, you were away too long!" he remonstrated gently, slipping an arm about her waist and pressing his lips to her cheek again.

"Surely the lovely Ylinestra kept you occupied in my absence?" she shot back, returning the kiss.

"You impossible woman! You with your damnable celibacy.

All these years I have filled my bed with lesser women and not a single spark of jealousy from you. You speak of them as if they were children, or lapdogs."

"Have most of them been any more than that to you, you old rogue? But perhaps I do feel just the smallest spark, as you call it, toward this sorceress. I understand that she is as talented in the casting room as she is in the bedchamber. There, are you satisfied?"

"Perhaps just a bit," Nysander replied, affecting a sulk. "The girl does have a head for magic, but in truth she is beginning to weary me with her demands, in bed and out."

"Ah, the trials of the hot-blooded." Magyana let him into her tower rooms. "You know you shall not have a jot of sympathy from me. But now to Seregil. You still have not told me how he came to be in such a state. It took more than ordinary magic to leave such marks on him."

Pausing in the center of the immaculate workroom, Nysander watched as she set about the familiar ritual of tea making. "Evidently he and the boy stole something from Mardus in the northlands. It appears to be an object of little consequence but, as you saw, it proved to be extremely dangerous. I can tell you no more than that, I fear."

Setting the kettle on the hook, Magyana turned and studied his face; they'd known each other too long and too well for her not to read the import of his silence.

"Oh, my dear," she whispered, a hand stealing to her throat. "Oh, no!"

Seregil's strength returned quickly over the next few days and, as Valerius had predicted, he soon grew restless. On the fourth day he'd had enough of bed rest.

"Valerius said another day at least!" Alec admonished, frowning down at him as he swung his legs over the side of the bed.

"I won't tell him if you don't. Bilairy's Balls, I'm sore all over from lying around so long!"

As soon as he stood up, however, the floor seemed to shift under him. Drenched in a sudden cold sweat, he swayed heavily against Alec.

"There now, you see? It is too soon." Alec helped him back

onto the bed. "Maker's Mercy, there's nothing left of you. I can feel your ribs."

"I thought I heard voices," Valerius rumbled, striding in to glower at the two of them. "Are you going to stay in bed as I ordered, or be tied there?"

"The former, I think," Seregil replied contritely. Pressing a hand dramatically over his eyes, he sank back against the pillow. "I'm sure you know best."

"I certainly do. Not that it's ever made the slightest damn bit of difference to you!"

Still scowling, he lifted the dressing and went about cleaning the wound. "There, this shouldn't give you any more trouble."

Looking down as his chest, Seregil saw the scar for the first time and felt his stomach lurch. The last of the scabs had fallen away and the ridged imprint of the coin's design was visible in the shiny pink circle of new skin.

"What is *that* doing there?" he demanded, fingering the area around the scar.

Valerius threw up his hands. "You'll have to ask Nysander. I was all for having it off that first night, but he said to leave it. It should fade in time. I'm off for Mycena today, so you're in Alec's care now. Try not to drive yourself into a relapse if that's possible, which I doubt. You won't die, but you'll land your ass back in bed for another week if you don't take care. Maker's Mercy be with you both."

Stumping out, he slammed the door after him.

"See? He was angry with you," said Alec, obviously glad not to have been the focus of his displeasure.

"Angry?" Seregil took a last worried look at the mark and pulled the shirt lacings closed again. "He wasn't angry. When Valerius gets angry the furniture catches fire, or walls fall down, things like that. There's no mistaking it when he's upset."

"Well, he wasn't exactly happy with you, either."

"He seldom is." Shifting against the pillows, he settled with one hand behind his head. "Even the other drysians consider him an irascible old bugger. Still, we find one another useful on occasion. How's your hand?"

"Better."

"Let me see." He inspected the circle of tender skin on Alec's palm; it was smooth and featureless except for the small square in the center. "Has Nysander said much about any of this?"

"Only that the disk was something called a telesm."

"Well, that's obvious!" Seregil snorted. "I want more of an answer than that. Fetch him for me, will you?"

Alec found Nysander at his high desk in the workroom.

"Seregil was wondering if you could come down," he told the wizard.

"Certainly." Nysander laid his quill aside. "I was expecting Thero in a moment. Could you wait and tell him where I am?"

It wasn't until the old man had disappeared downstairs that it occurred to Alec to wonder why Nysander hadn't just sent a message by magic.

Minutes passed, and there was still no sign of Thero. Impatient to get back to Seregil, Alec wandered restlessly around the room. The stairs leading up to the little gallery beneath the tower dome soon caught his eye and, climbing up, he looked out through a thick, leaded pane.

With a startled gasp, he caught at the ledge in front of him; the dome bowed out beyond the stonework, affording a view of the ground hundreds of feet directly below. He'd never been this far off the ground and the sensation was not particularly pleasant. Concentrating on the solid floor beneath his boots, he made himself look out over the city. Streets fanned out like spokes from circular plazas, or intersected to form ordered squares and commons. From this height he could also see past the citadel wall to the outer harbor, where boats bobbed at anchor in the shelter of the moles. On the landward side, open country quickly gave way to rolling foothills and jagged, snowcapped mountains beyond.

As he turned to go down the steps again, a blue message sphere suddenly winked into existence in front of him and Nysander's voice said, "Alec, join us in Seregil's room, please."

He found Seregil and Nysander in the midst of a heated discussion when he arrived. Nysander was calm, if solemn, but there was a decidedly stubborn set to Seregil's jaw.

"Are you certain you want him involved?" the wizard was saying.

"Come on, Nysander! He's already involved up to the eyebrows, whether he knows it or not," Seregil retorted. "Besides, you wouldn't have let him stay here if you didn't already trust him."

"Those are two separate issues," Nysander replied, giving Seregil a meaningful look. When the younger man maintained adamant silence, the wizard nodded gravely. "Very well. But the final decision is his to make." He looked up at Alec for the first time. "Would you become a Watcher, Alec?"

A twinge of excitement shot through Alec. "Does that mean you both can tell me more of what's going on?" he asked, guessing the import of this strange exchange.

"Certainly."

"Then yes, I will."

Seregil gave him a wink as Nysander took out his small ivory dagger and waved Alec to a chair. When he was seated, Nysander set the knife spinning end for end in the air mere inches from Alec's eyes.

Alec's mouth went dry as he listened to the angry buzz the blade made as it flickered in front of him; he could feel the breeze of it against his face.

"Alec of Kerry," Nysander intoned solemnly. "A Watcher must observe carefully, report truthfully, and keep the secrets that must be kept. Do you swear by your heart and eyes and by the Four to do these things?"

"Yes," Alec answered quickly, steeling himself not to lean away from the spinning knife.

"Good!" The knife fell out of the air into Nysander's hand.

"That's it?" Alec exclaimed, falling back in his chair.

"You answered truthfully," the wizard told him. "Had you lied, the result would have been rather more dramatic."

"And considerably messier," Seregil added with a relieved grin.

"Considerably," said Nysander. "And now, what have you to report, Seregil?"

Seregil settled his shoulders more comfortably against the pillows. "When I left Rhíminee at the end of Rhythin, I took ship to Nanta and spent two days listening around the docks. Rumor had it that there were an unusual number of ships being refitted at Plenimaran ports, Karia in particular. This confirmed what we'd already heard from Korbin.

"Moving north, I poked around Boersby, learning that a delegation of Plenimaran merchants had stopped there a month earlier to discuss overland trade routes. A contingent of fifty armed riders had continued inland in the direction of the Fishless Sea."

"To what end?" asked Nysander. "There is little in those barren hills but a few nomadic tribes."

Seregil shrugged. "There were all sorts of speculations. Apparently local men were hired on as guides and haven't been heard of since. If the mounted column did come south again, they came by a different route. Thinking they might have followed the Brilith River down toward the Woldesoke, I decided to check in with a friend at Ballton. There'd been no sightings in that area, but she said that similar parties had been seen to the east. The word is that the lords of the various mountain demesnes are being visited, but nobody's certain of their purpose. It boded ill for Plenimar to be so far north, so I decided to work my way along the mountains and see what these riders had been up to. If they went as far as Kerry, there wouldn't be much doubt that they were casting a greedy eye at the Gold Road again.

"I was right, but quickly learned that the Plenimarans had left their new friends with a healthy distrust of strangers. Even as a bard, I had one or two difficulties before Asengai finally caught me. Not everyone was taken in, though. Lord Warkill and his sons gave them the air. Lord Nostor seems to have been noncommittal. My old friend Geriss had just died, and his widow, a Mycenian by birth, would have nothing to do with the envoys."

"Lady Brytha? I knew her as a girl," remarked Nysander. "Her holding is very isolated, as I recall."

"It's a large one, though, and well populated. I spoke to her in private and warned her to be cautious. She has four sons, two of them grown, who seem reliable enough. If worse comes to worst, they'll be able to hold out or flee."

"Let us hope it does not come to that. I have had word already that some advances were made in Kerry, but that they were politely refused."

Seregil laughed darkly. "If by polite you mean no bloodshed. The miners have been content with their situation for hundreds of years and are a hard lot to move. Still, if the mountain lords can be swayed against them, Kerry could be lost."

"And who is leading these Plenimarans? What is their method?"

"Crafty, as usual. It seems that nobody spoke to the same emissary, which means there were either several groups going among the various holdings, or they switched off leaders each time. I have the names, but I doubt they'll amount to much. As for their method, it was the old wishing mirror game."

"The what?" Alec interjected, completely lost by now.

Seregil grinned. "You've never heard the story of the wishing mirror?" You look into it to see your heart's desire. The Plenimarans send a spy or two in advance to sound out the situation, then the grand commander rides in with a great show of soldiers and a saddlebag full of empty promises based on the reports of his spies. Formio, for instance, was informed that the Overlord of Plenimar wishes to arrange a marriage for some distant niece, while old Warkill, whose lands sit at the headwaters of the Silverwind, was promised aid to take the lands clear to the edge of the Woldesoke. Mind you, our friend Mardus is down in Wolde soon after, promising to defend the mayor from just such an incursion.

"I also had the good fortune to be captured by a gang of bandits east of Derila. Their leader happened to be fond of bards, so they decided to keep me on rather than slit my throat. They were a sloppy bunch and I managed to get away when I wanted to, but not before I learned that they'd been foolish enough to attack a party of Plenimarans only two weeks earlier. Instead of obliterating them, as the marines generally would if only for the practice, these blackguards enlisted the bandits to their cause, binding them with oaths, wine, and gold. They even went so far as to offer a bounty for any other freebooters they could bring in."

"What a pack of mongrels they are leashing together up there!" Nysander exclaimed, none too pleased. "They will turn every little faction against its neighbor and let them cut each other to pieces."

"Then march in to sweep up the spoils," added Seregil. "After Alec and I got free of Asengai, we met with Erisa and Micum in Wolde. She'd been along the coast as far as Syr and her news was much the same, including the foray toward the Fishless Sea. She's equally mystified. According to her, Mardus stopped for a week at Sark Island on his way up the Ösk to Blackwater Lake. I've never been there, but Micum says there's nothing but the ruins of an ancient trading colony. Hardly the thing to occupy someone like Mardus for a week."

"And Micum?"

"His news was the strangest of all. He'd been up around Ravensfell and reported a company of marines in full battle dress riding into the pass. Unless they're out to conquer whatever's left of the Hâzadriëlfaie, I can't imagine what they think they'll find except mountains and ice."

Seregil paused, but Nysander simply motioned for him to continue. "That brings us to the mayor's banquet. Alec says he told you about our doings there, but there are a few details I'd better fill in."

"Pertaining to the maps, I assume," said Nysander.

"Yes. I found one in Mardus' campaign chest, quite ordinary, not hidden. Points on it had been marked at Wolde, Kerry, Sandir Point, Syr, and each of the mountain demesnes."

"Rather tidy, that," Nysander remarked.

"But even better, another map locked safely away in his dispatch box was marked with points at Sark Island, another somewhere north of Ravensfell, and one in the Blackwater Fens. The last one was circled. What do you make of that?"

"Most intriguing," Nysander mused, stroking his beard.

"Micum went back to the Fens after Boersby. He meant to head down here when he'd finished."

"How long ago did you last see him?"

"He left us at Boersby; let's see." Seregil thought for a moment, then shook his head impatiently. "Damn! I'm still muddled. Alec, how long has it been?"

Alec counted back. "Just over two weeks now."

"He should be with us soon, then," said Nysander, but something in his expression must have caught Seregil's eye.

"What is it, Nysander?"

"Hmm? Oh, nothing. Is that all you have to report?"

"No. I believe those highwaymen who attacked us below Stook were Plenimaran agents. When we searched the bodies they just didn't have the right look to them. They had new weapons and clothing, all local, little money or possessions. It was as if they'd simply ridden into the Folcwine Forest and set up shop the day before. The whole situation didn't smell right."

"I have had occasion in the past to trust your intuition."

"There'd been a sudden rash of attacks on the caravans around Wolde just before the Plenimaran envoys showed up there," added Alec.

Seregil nodded wryly. "Taken with everything else, it seems

rather too much of a coincidence that these cutthroats should appear out of nowhere just in time to be run off by the able marines."

"I see," mused Nysander. "Then you believe that Plenimar is providing a reason for the northern towns to seek an alliance?"

"I do."

"Anything else?"

"Just this." Seregil pulled the neck of this nightshirt open and cocked his chin at the scar.

Nysander went to the window and gazed out. "I fear I must beg your forbearance regarding that. This matter is not to be spoken of to anyone, at any time."

There was no mistaking the finality in his voice. Seregil's brows drew together ominously over his grey eyes. "I just slept away the last two weeks because of this. Not to mention the madness that went before, or the nightmares and visions and the urge to kill just about every person I came within ten feet of, including Alec!"

"You must be patient."

"What is there to be patient about?" Seregil retorted. "I want to know who did this to me! Do you know or not?"

Nysander sighed as he sat down in the embrasure of the window. "I should say that you did it to yourself, really. You took it upon yourself to steal the thing in the first place, and then to hang it about your neck. Not that I am chiding you, of course. I know that you took it on my behalf. Nevertheless, I—"

"Don't go changing the subject. That's my trick!" Seregil interrupted hotly. "This is *me* you're talking to, not some provincial message carrier. What's going on?"

Caught in the line of confrontation, Alec looked anxiously from one to the other. Seregil's lips were compressed into a thin, stubborn line, his eyes larger than ever in his haggard face as he glared up at the wizard. But Nysander met his friend's smoldering gaze calmly.

"Seregil í Korit Solun Meringil Bôkthersa," he said quietly, rolling the syllables as if they were a spell. "This is a matter which goes beyond any personal vengeance on your part. The mark you bear is a magical sigla, the meaning of which I am bound by the most dire oaths not to reveal."

"Then why didn't you let Valerius take it off?"

Nysander spread his hands resignedly. "You understand better than most the power of prescience. It felt unwise at the time to do so. Now that you are stronger, however, I shall cast an occultation over it."

"But it will still be there," said Seregil uneasily. "I—I had strange dreams after Alec pulled the thing off, different than the nightmares before."

Nysander rose to his feet in alarm. "By the Light, why did you not mention this before!"

"I'm sorry. I only just now remembered, parts of them, anyway."

Nysander sat down on the edge of the bed. "You must tell me what you can, then. By your oath as a Watcher—"

"Yes, yes, I know!" snapped Seregil, rubbing at his eyelids in frustration. "Remembering—it's like trying to grasp a handful of eels. One second I remember a piece of something, then it just goes."

"Nysander, he looks ill!" Alec whispered. The color had fled from Seregil's thin cheeks and a sheen of sweat stood out on his forehead.

"I was terribly sick by the time we reached the crossroads inn," Seregil continued hoarsely. "Alec, you had no idea— Everything had become so unreal. It was like being trapped in a nightmare that I couldn't wake up from. I don't know where in Mycena we were by then. The black creature had been dogging us since the day before. Alec couldn't see it, even when it touched him in the cart, and that scared me worse than anything I've ever encountered. Alec's told you how I attacked him that night, I know, but that's not how it seemed to me at the time, not at all! The thing was attacking me, or rather letting me attack it and sidestepping me. Alec must have come in during all that and I was too crazed to realize. Gods, I could just as easily have killed him—"

"It was magic, dear boy, evil magic," Nysander said softly.

Seregil shivered and ran a hand back through his hair. "After—after I collapsed, I kept dreaming I was on a barren plain. I couldn't move except to turn and there was only the wind and grey grass. I was alone. I thought at first that I was dead."

Alec watched him with rising concern. Seregil was whiter than ever, and his breathing was and labored, as if it took all his strength to keep speaking. Alec glanced anxiously at Nysander, but the wizard's attention was fixed on Seregil.

"After a while, there was someone else there," Seregil said, eyes squeezed tightly shut, one hand raised to his face as if to ward off a blow. "I can't remember who, just—gold. And eyes, something about eyes—"

His chest was heaving now and Alec placed a hand on his shoulder.

"Blue," Seregil gasped, "something so blue—!" With a hollow groan, he fainted back onto the pillow.

"Seregil! Seregil, can you hear me?" cried Nysander, feeling for the pulse at his throat.

"What's happening?" cried Alec.

"I am not certain. A vision of some sort, perhaps, or some overwhelming memory. Fetch a cloth, and the water pitcher."

Seregil's eyes fluttered open again as Alec bathed his temples with a cool cloth.

"You must not try to go on," Nysander warned, stroking Seregil's brow. "You were speaking gibberish just now, as if something was disordering your thoughts even as you tried to voice them."

"Could it have been that black creature again, *here*?" asked Alec.

"I would have sensed such a presence," Nysander assured him. "No, it was as if the memories themselves induced some mental confusion. How very interesting. Can you speak now, dear boy?"

"Yes," Seregil rasped, passing a hand over his eyes.

"Rest, then, and think no more of these things for now. I have heard enough." Rising, Nysander went to the door.

"Well I haven't!" Seregil struggled up on one elbow. "Not nearly enough! What's *happening* to me?"

Alec thought he caught a look of pain on Nysander's face.

"Trust me in this, dear boy," the wizard said. "I must meditate on what we have learned so far. Rest and heal. Shall I send Wethis for some food?"

Alec braced for another outburst, but Seregil merely looked away, shaking his head. He busied himself with the fire for a moment after Nysander had gone, then pulled the chair up beside the bed.

"That black creature you fought with," he began, fidgeting

with the hem of one sleeve. "It really was there in the cart, wasn't it? And in the room with us at the inn. It was real."

Seregil shivered, staring past him at the fire. "Real enough for me. I think you saved both our lives when you yanked that bit of wood from my neck."

"But that was an accident! What if I hadn't?"

Seregil looked up at him for a moment, then shrugged. "But you did, and here we are, safe and sound. Luck in the shadows, Alec; you don't question it, you just give thanks and pray it doesn't run out!"

In the deepest hours of the night, Nysander lifted the wooden disk from its container. The chamber around him vibrated with the thickly woven spells he had invoked in preparation for the examination. Turning the disk this way and that with a pair of forceps, he tried to gauge the quiescent power of the thing. Despite its ordinary appearance, he could feel the energy emanating from it as clearly as waves lapping against his skin.

Heart heavy with foreboding, he sealed the thing away again and pocketed it, then set off for the vaults beneath the Orëska House to take his nightly constitutional.

Alec watched in dismay, if not surprise, as Seregil struggled out of bed the next morning.

"Valerius wouldn't like this."

"Then it's lucky for us he's not here, eh?" Seregil winked, hoping the boy didn't notice how wobbly his legs still were. "Besides, there's nothing more beneficial than a good bath. Just let me lean on you a bit and I'll be fine."

With Alec's grudging assistance, Seregil worked his way slowly down to the baths without mishap.

Winded but triumphant, he let a bath servant assist him into his tub while Alec stationed himself on a nearby bench.

"Illior's Light, but it's wonderful to be back in a civilized city!" Seregil chortled, immersing himself up to the chin in the steaming water.

"I've never met anyone who takes as many baths as you do," the boy grumbled.

"A good soak might improve your disposition," Seregil teased, wondering at the boy's brittleness this morning. He had an edge of anxiety that hadn't been there before, not even during the difficult journey through Mycena.

"For the love of Illior, Alec, relax! No

one's here to see." He swirled the water with his toe. "I think we could do with a walk outside next."

"You barely made it down here," Alec pointed out hopelessly. "Where's your curiosity today? You've been living in the center of the greatest collection of wizardry in the world for almost a week and you've hardly seen a thing!"

"I'm more concerned just now with what Valerius would say if he knew you were wandering around all over the place. I'm supposed to be responsible for you, you know."

"No one is responsible for me except *me*." Seregil jabbed a soapy finger in the air for emphasis. "Nysander knows that, Micum knows that. Even Valerius knows it. Now you know."

To his considerable surprise, Alec stared at him for a moment, then turned on his heel and stalked abruptly away to stare out over the central pool, his back rigid as a blade.

"What is it?" Seregil called after him, genuinely mystified.

Alec muttered something, punctuating the remark with a sharp wave of his hand.

"What? I can't hear you over the fountains."

Alec half turned, arms locked across his chest. "I said I was responsible enough for you while you were sick!"

And I'm a blind fool! Seregil berated himself, the crux of the problem finally dawning on him. Struggling out of the tub, he threw on a towel and went to the boy.

"I owe you a tremendous debt," he said, studying Alec's grim profile. "With all that's happened, I guess I haven't thanked you properly."

"I'm not asking for any thanks."

"But you deserve it nonetheless. And I'm sorry if I insulted you just now. It's just that I don't think in terms of expecting anything of anyone."

Alec turned a bleak eye on him. "That's not what Micum said. He said you demand loyalty and never forgive anyone who betrays you."

"Well—yes. But that's hardly the same thing, is it?"

Color flared in the boy's fair cheeks. "All I know is that I *have* been loyal and if you don't need me around anymore, then what the hell am I doing in Rhíminee anyway?"

"Who said I don't want you around?" Seregil shot back in exasperation.

"No one. Not exactly. It's just that ever since we got here, I

mean since the ship—with the wizards and healers and—" Alec
faltered to a halt. "I don't know, I guess I just don't feel like I
belong here."

"Of course you do!" Seregil sputtered. "Who's been saying
you don't? Thero! That whey-faced son of a bitch—"

"Thero didn't say anything." A gravid pause strung out between them, growing increasingly more uncomfortable.

"I never could carry on an argument naked," Seregil said at
last, pulling a wry face. This elicited a grudging hint of a smile,
at least. "If you figure out what you're so mad about, let me
know. In the meantime, let's go across to the museum. I promised
to show you wonders, and that's as good a place as any to find
them."

Revived by the bath and fresh clothes, Seregil had Alec help
him across the atrium to the opposite archway.

"The vaults under this building are overflowing with treasures
of one sort or another," he expounded, still leaning on Alec's
arm. "I used to go down there with Nysander and Magyana all
the time. You wouldn't believe how much is squirreled away right
under our feet."

Opening the huge door of the museum room, Alec let out a
low whistle.

The vaulted central chamber of the Orëska Museum was
similar in dimensions to the baths. Here, however, every wall was
hung with rich tapestries and paintings, shields, and pieces of armor. Suspended overhead was the skeleton of some horrific creature fifty feet long; the bare teeth jutting from the jawbones were
as long as his forearm. Wooden cases of all sizes, many covered
with sheets of thick crystal, lined the walls and stood in neatly
spaced rows across the room. In the one closest to them lay a
collection of jeweled ornaments and vessels. The one next to it
contained a golden coronet studded with rubies. Another was de-
voted to wizardly paraphernalia.

"How do you like it?" Seregil whispered, grinning at the boy's
gape-mouthed wonder. Alec made no reply as he slowly made his
way from case to case, looking like a thirsty man who just found
an unexpected spring.

The room was very quiet, but not unoccupied. A group of
scholars were there examining a tapestry. Nearby, a girl in

apprentice robes sat on a high stool next to one of the cases, working with wax tablet and stylus at copying a passage from an open book displayed there. Across the room, two scarlet-clad servants were in the process of replacing some items in a crystal case.

"I used to spend a good deal of time here," Seregil told Alec softly. "I've even managed to add a few pieces to the collection over the years. This, for instance."

Steering him to a case near the center of the room, Seregil pointed to a delicate flower carved from translucent pink stone.

"This belonged to the enchantress Nimia Reshal. When the proper words are spoken, it emits a magical fragrance which renders anyone who inhales it a helpless slave to the owner. She'd managed to snare Micum before I got hold of it."

"Why didn't she catch you, too?" Alec whispered.

"I happened to be approaching from a different direction at the time. While she was concentrating on him, I simply held my nose, crept up from behind, and knocked her on the head. Never underestimate the benefit of surprise!"

Nodding, Alec turned to the next case and stiffened. Inside lay a pair of shriveled hands, the skin darkened to the color of old leather.

"What are *those*?" he gasped.

"Shh! A most unusual relic. Look closer."

Jeweled rings still encircled the withered fingers and the long discolored nails were covered with a delicate tracery of golden whorls; the plain iron manacles encircling each wrist looked out of keeping with the rest of the ornaments. Each band was held fast by a long spike driven through the wrist just below the base of each hand. The whole affair was bolted to the bottom of the case.

Alec stared down at the hands with puzzled revulsion. "What in the world are—"

Just then, one of the leathery forefingers slowly raised and lowered, as if scolding his idle scrutiny.

Seregil had been watching closely all the while. As soon as he saw the hand move, he ran a finger lightly down the boy's back, sending him into the air with a startled yelp.

"Damn it, Seregil!" Alec cried, whirling around.

The scholars turned with inquiring stares. The apprentice

dropped her stylus, then began to giggle. The servants merely exchanged disgusted looks.

Seregil leaned against a case, shoulders quivering with smothered laughter.

"I'm sorry," he said at last, feeling anything but repentant as he exchanged a knowing wink with the girl. "That trick has been played on just about every apprentice who ever served here, including me. I couldn't resist."

"You scared me half to death!" Alec whispered indignantly. "What *are* those things?"

Seregil rested his elbows on the edge of the case, tapping a finger idly against the glass. "The hands of Tikárie Megraesh, a great necromancer."

"They moved." Alec shuddered, peering over Seregil's shoulder. "It's as if they're still alive."

"In a sense, they are," Seregil replied. "This necromancer ended his days as a dyrmagnos. Have you ever heard the term?"

"No. What does it mean?"

"It's the ultimate fate of necromancers. You see, all forms of magic exact a certain toll from those who practice it, but necromancy is by far the worst. It gradually wastes the body, draining life even as it increases the force of that person's will. In time, there's nothing left but a walking corpse burning with terrible intelligence—a dyrmagnos. This fellow here was at least six centuries old when Nysander cut these hands off him and, according to him, they haven't changed much in appearance since he took them, which gives you some idea what the rest of Tikárie Megraesh must have looked like."

The left hand stirred, scrabbling softly against the bottom of the case with its blackened nails. Alec shuddered again. "If that's what his hands looked like, I'd hate to have seen the face."

"These hands escaped once," Seregil went on, staring down at the twitching things. "It's nearly impossible to kill a dyrmagnos, once it's reached such an age. All you can do is dismember and contain it. Those symbols you see painted on the nails were part of the original binding spell to break the power of the creature. Eventually the life will fade from them."

Alec frowned down at them. "What if all the pieces were brought together again before that happened?"

"They'd rejoin and the dyrmagnos would live again. As I recall, a few other parts of him are somewhere down in the vaults, but most were carried off for safekeeping by other wizards. The head is the most dangerous part. That was sealed in a lead casket and dropped into the sea.

Seregil savored a shiver of his own, imagining the head locked in darkness beneath the chill waters, dreaming perhaps, or screaming its hatred to the unheeding creatures of the mud. On the heels of that pleasant thought came another, however. When was the last time he'd seen the hands move as much as this?

"Are there any other dead things in here?" asked Alec, moving to another case.

"Not ones that move."

"Good!"

They wandered on awhile longer, but Seregil's strength soon flagged.

There was no use trying to hide the fact from Alec. "You're looking pale again," he said. "Come on, a walk outside in the air might not be such a bad idea after all."

The pale winter sky overhead presaged snow, but inside the walls the gardens were bathed with fragrant breezes, and the soft turf beneath their feet was redolent with chamomile and creeping thyme.

Seregil was leaning more heavily on his arm than he had earlier, Alec noted, wondering if it had been a mistake not going back to their room.

"There," Seregil said, pointing the way to a nearby fountain. Reaching it, he collapsed on the grass and leaned back against its basin.

Alec looked him over with renewed concern. "You're as white as this marble!"

Seregil dipped a hand in the water and pressed it to his brow. "Just let me get my breath."

"He's only doing it to spite Valerius, you know," a familiar voice interrupted.

A pair of women sauntered up. Both wore the green and white uniform of the Queen's Horse Guard. The shorter of the two, Alec realized with a start, was Princess Klia. Her companion, a dark, serious-looking woman, stood at ease beside her.

Klia flopped down unceremoniously in front of Seregil but ignored him completely, addressing Alec as if they were old friends.

"Now, if Valerius had ordered him to get up and about as soon as possible, he'd have clung in bed 'til spring. You're better turned out than when we met last, I must say. What name are you going by today?"

He grinned sheepishly. "Alec."

"Hello again, Alec. This is Captain Myrhini."

The dark woman surprised him with a flashing smile as she joined them on the grass.

"I wondered afterward at meeting another Silverleaf," Klia went on cheerfully. "If I'd known Seregil was with you, the two of you could have ridden back with us."

"I was indisposed at the time," Seregil said, drawing her teasing gaze at last. "How did you know I was back?"

"I met Nysander on his way to a meeting with Mother and Lord Barien last night." Her blue eyes shone fiercely. "From what she said this morning, it sounds like things may get interesting again."

Seregil grimaced. "I should think you'd have seen enough of battle last year. That piece of fun nearly cost you your arm and Myrhini both."

Myrhini gave the toe of Klia's boot a playful kick. "You know her. She's Sakor-touched. It only makes her hotter for the next fight."

"As if you're not just as bad." Klia grinned. "Either one of us could be at home with a babe or two already if we didn't care more for battle than we do for a handsome face! Seregil, come see the horse Alec helped me buy in Cirna. Hwerlu is looking him over for me at the grove."

Klia helped Seregil to his feet, then wrapped a supporting arm around his waist as they set off for a nearby stand of oaks.

"I know one handsome face she favors, if only its owner had the wit to see," Myrhini whispered to Alec, winking in Seregil's direction as they followed the others.

Entering the little grove, Alec was delighted to find that Hwerlu was the centaur he'd glimpsed his first day in Rhíminee.

The creature was even more imposing at close quarters; his chestnut-colored horse body was a good twenty hands tall at the shoulder, while his man parts were those of a giant. Klia's unusual black and white and another Aurënfaie horse stood by him, and he patted them with his large, blunt hands as if they were hounds. Seregil and Klia looked like a pair of children standing next to him.

"Come here!" Seregil called to Alec. "I seem to recall you once referring to centaurs as mere legend."

When Hwerlu bent to greet him, Alec noticed that he had the eyes of a horse, large and dark, showing no white.

"Greetings, little Alec." Hwerlu's voice rumbled richly from the depths of his huge chest. "The light of Illior shines brightly in you. It must please you to see that legends can be real."

"It does," Alec told him. "I never imagined centaurs were so big!"

Laughing, Hwerlu threw back his black mane and pranced in a circle, his broad hoofs shaking the earth beneath their feet. He stopped abruptly, however, and trotted across the clearing.

"And here is another legend! My lovely Feeya," he proclaimed as another centaur stepped into the circle of trees.

Feeya was a sorrel, and only a little smaller than Hwerlu. She had the same coarse mane of hair running down her back, but the skin of her human torso was otherwise as smooth as any woman's. A heavy torque like Hwerlu's was her only adornment, but Alec quickly saw that he had no cause for embarrassment for she had no breasts, centaurs suckling their young in the same fashion as horses. Her broad features were not beautiful by common standards but, taken for what she was, she had a beauty of her own.

Hwerlu gallantly brought his lady to meet Alec. "She does not speak your tongue, but it pleases her to hear it."

Alec greeted the golden centaur. Smiling, she lifted his chin and spoke to him in her own curious whistling language as she inspected his face with apparent interest.

Standing behind Alec, Seregil answered her in the centaur tongue. With a toss of her long mane, Feeya nodded to them both and went to admire Klia's new horse.

"What did she say?" asked Alec.

"Oh, a greeting like Hwerlu's. I thanked her for you." Seregil sat down at the base of a tree with a contented sigh.

"Are there a lot of centaurs in Skala?" Alec gazed at the pair of handsome creatures across the clearing.

"No. They live mainly in the mountains across the Osiat Sea. A few large tribes still roam the high plains there. Magyana brought Hwerlu and Feeya back to Rhíminee with her a few years ago. That's her tower there, to the left of Nysander's."

"Nysander's friend?"

"Yes. Magyana's a great traveler. She went to learn more of centaur ways. Hwerlu was curious about her magic, it being so different from his own, so he came back with her. He'll go home when he's satisfied."

"Are you a wizard, too, then?" Alec asked Hwerlu, who'd returned.

"I cannot make fire without fuel, or fly through the air like the Orëska wizards. My power lies in my music." Hwerlu indicated the large harp that hung in the branches of a nearby tree. "I sing healings, charms, dreams. I think now maybe I should sing a healing for you, Seregil. I still see sickness in your face."

"I'd be grateful. Your cures don't leave a foul taste in my mouth like those of the drysians. In fact, I think I'll spend the afternoon here. Alec, why don't you get a horse from the stables and go for a ride? It'll do you good."

"I'd just as soon stay here," Alec objected, having no desire to go wandering around the city by himself.

"And watch me sleep all day?" Seregil scoffed. "No, I think it's time we got on with your education. Just go around the Ring once, then come back and tell me what you saw."

"The Ring? I don't even know what that—"

"I'll show him," offered Myrhini. "I have to get back to the barracks anyway. It's on the way."

"There now." Seregil blithely ignored Alec's silent appeal. "Already you're consorting with centaurs and wizards and riding about the streets with a captain of the Queen's Horse Guard. Keep your hood well up, though. I'm not ready for either of us to be seen just yet. And be careful! You're not larking about in the woods anymore. Even in daylight, Rhíminee can be a dangerous place. And for Illior's sake, find some gloves! Your hands are in poor enough condition as it is."

Myrhini pulled a pair of gauntlets from her belt and tossed them to Alec. "Come on, boy, before he finds something else to fuss about."

Still dubious, Alec followed her to the stables behind the main building where a groom saddled a spirited horse for him.

Leaving the shelter of the magical gardens for the first time since his arrival in the city, Alec was pleased to feel the cold, sweet winter breeze against his face again.

Golden Helm Street was lined on either side with high garden walls. Craning his neck, Alec caught glimpses of statues, carved pediments, and the tops of columns decorating houses more imposing than any temple he'd seen in the north. After several blocks, the street opened out into one of the paved circles he'd noted during his first ride through Rhíminee with Nysander. Here they turned down a side line.

"What are these for?" he asked, looking around.

"It's a catapult circle, part of the city's defenses," Myrhini explained. "The streets that lead out from them are straight to give the defenders a clear shot at any approaching enemy force. There are circles like this all over the city. The Ring and the market squares by the main gates are defensive positions, too, killing grounds in case the gates are breached."

"Has Rhíminee ever been attacked?"

"Oh, yes. The Plenimarans only got in once, though. The last full-scale attack on the city was over forty years ago, though."

Two Hawk ended at Silvermoon Street, a broad avenue bordering the Queen's Park. Ornate public buildings had been built against the park wall. On the other side stood villas larger than any he'd seen so far.

Blue uniformed guards saluted Myrhini as she and Alec rode under a heavy portcullis and onto the palace grounds.

"Those are the barracks there," she said, pointing out a collection of long, low buildings just visible beyond the dark bulk of the Palace.

At the edge of the broad parade ground that fronted the barracks they reined in to watch a company of riders practicing a battle turn. Tugging his hood back into place, Alec let out a low whistle of admiration.

Each rider carried a lance, and their green pennants snapped smartly in the breeze as the horsemen rode the length of the field in an even rank. Reaching the far end, they wheeled sharply about, lowered their lances, and charged forward with bloodcurdling yells. Wheeling again, they threw their lances down and drew swords to practice cuts to the left and right.

"There aren't many sights finer than that, eh?" Myrhini asked, following them with her eyes. Her horse shifted restlessly, anxious to join its fellows in action.

As they sat watching, a trio of riders rode over from the direction of the barracks—two noblemen and a stern, pale-eyed woman in a green uniform and golden gorget. The older of the two men was imposing in black velvet trimmed with silver and furs. A jeweled chain of office hung across his broad chest. The other man was much younger, perhaps late twenties, with a small blond mustache and a narrow tuft of hair on his chin. Although he was dressed richly in red velvet laced with gold, he struck Alec at once as someone of much less importance than the others.

"General Phoria," Myrhini said, saluting the officer. "And greetings, Lord Barien and Lord Teukros."

"I trust your troop will be ready for inspection this afternoon?" the general asked crisply, returning the salute with a hand lacking the last two fingers.

"At your command, General!"

Phoria's pale stare raked over Alec as if she had only then registered his existence. "And who is this?"

"A guest of the wizard Nysander, General. I'm escorting him to the Ring."

Alec stole a sidelong glance at Myrhini but knew better than to butt in; General Phoria had thawed noticeably at the mention of Nysander.

"You haven't the look of a wizard," she remarked.

"No, General, I'm not," Alec responded quickly, taking his cue from Myrhini. "I've come to study in the city."

"Ah, a young scholar!" The older man smiled approvingly. "I hope you'll stay long enough to see the Festival. It's the great glory of the city."

Alec had no idea what the man was referring to, but nodded politely and did his best to look respectful. Fortunately General Phoria was impatient to move on. With a final curt nod, she and her companions rode on toward the Palace.

Alec let out a slow breath. "Was that the same Barien Klia spoke of?"

"*Lord* Barien," Myrhini cautioned. "Lord Barien í Zhal Khameris Vitulliein of Rhilna, to be exact. He's the Vicegerent of Skala, the most powerful person in the country after the Queen herself. The other one was his nephew, Lord Teukros í Eryan."

"And the general?"

"In addition to being the high commander of all Skalan cavalry regiments, General Phoria is the Queen's eldest daughter. You just met the future queen, my friend. Come on now, I'll write you out a pass."

Dismounting in front of one of the barracks, Alec followed Myrhini into the wardroom. A handful of soldiers sat around a table, intent on a bakshi game. Seeing their senior officer, however, they leapt up to salute. Myrhini returned it and sat down at a nearby desk to write out the pass. After a few curious glances in Alec's direction, the soldiers went back to their game.

Sealing the pass with her signet, Myrhini handed it to Alec. "Show this at any gate of the Ring and you'll have no problem. There's one into the Ring just beyond the last barracks. Get your horse and I'll let you through."

Outside again, she led Alec to a heavily guarded gate near the Palace.

"You can't possibly get lost," Myrhini assured him. "Stay between the two walls and you'll come all the way around the city and back to here. It will be easiest for you to go back to the Orëska House by way of the Harvest Market. Just follow the Street of the Sheaf to the Fountain of Astellus, then down Golden Helm until you sight it again."

Myrhini's directions sounded simple enough, but Alec felt a bit of his original apprehension returning when the postern gate clanged shut behind him.

Looking around, he found himself in a very pleasant park with trees and carefully tended carriage paths. A number of enterprising merchants had set up shop here and many elegantly dressed patrons strolled among the gaily painted booths. Others rode or drove in carriages along the paths, the men in colorful surcoats or robes beneath heavy capes, the women muffled in rich furs, gems sparkling on their gloved fingers and in their elaborately curled and braided hair. Many were accompanied by tame animals and Alec smiled to himself, wondering if he and his father had trapped any of these hawks or spotted cats. They'd certainly sold enough of them to the southern traders.

Riding north at a trot, he soon reached the first gate. The guards inspected his pass briefly, then waved him through into the bustle of the Harvest Market.

This market was considerably smaller than the one by the Sea Gate, and not as busy at this late season. A gate leading out of the city stood open for carts, and numerous inns and taverns faced onto the main square. Checking street markers to satisfy himself as to where the Street of the Sheaf entered the square, he crossed the square and reentered the Ring to continue his assigned ride.

This next section was used as pasturage for livestock. He rode past small flocks of sheep and cattle grazing from hay racks under the watchful eye of the children who tended them. Large cisterns had been sunk into the ground here and there along the inner wall. Although the herds he observed were not large, it was evident that should the city ever be besieged, enough animals could be kept within the walls to feed the defenders for quite some time.

Skirting the northern perimeter of the city at a canter, Alec began to notice signs of human habitation; rough plank shelters huddled at the base of the walls, many of them connected by well-trodden paths. The denizens of this shanty settlement had the sullen air of impoverished squatters. A litter of refuse marked the boundaries of their tiny holdings; thin children and thinner dogs wandered among the shacks, picking through the cast-off belongings of their neighbors and watching passing strangers with a predatory eye.

As he rode past one of these ramshackle hovels, a grimy child in a torn shift popped up almost under his horse's feet, begging for coppers. Alec reined in sharply to avoid trampling her and was instantly surrounded by a crowd of motley little beggars, all clamoring for money. A lank-haired woman appeared in a doorway, beckoning to him in a harsh, lewd fashion. Except for a tattered skirt, she wore only a shawl draped over her shoulders and this she let fall away, calling out something to him.

Alec hastily fished out a few coins and cast them behind his horse to clear the children from his path. But the shacks became more numerous as he rode on, as did the knots of beggars and idlers of all descriptions.

The next gate was in sight when he noticed three men watching his approach with undisguised interest. As he came nearer, they rose from their seats in front of a tattered tent and stood next to the roadway. They were big men, any one of them more than a match for him, and all wore long knives in plain sight.

Alec was considering whether he should turn back or simply kick his horse into a gallop when a group of uniformed riders came into sight from the opposite direction.

The winter sun glinted off their helmets. They wore the same dark blue uniforms he had seen at the gates and carried heavy truncheons and swords. The prospective footpads quickly disappeared among the shacks as the riders came on. Alec rode quickly on to the next gate and into the Sea Market.

The huge square was every bit as overwhelming as the first time he'd seen it. Stopping for a moment to get his bearings, he spotted the open thoroughfare of Sheaf Street in the distance and set out toward it, following one of the wider lanes threading through the marketplace in that direction.

The smell of spiced lamb brought him to a halt. Looking around, Alec quickly spotted an old man grilling skewers of meat over a brazier nearby. A bit more at ease now, he decided to stop and eat. Dismounting, he purchased meat and cider and sat down on a convenient crate to watch the crowd stream by.

This isn't so bad after all, he thought. Six months ago where had he been? Wandering alone through the same mountains he'd known all his life. Now here he sat in the heart of one of the most powerful cities in the world with fine, warm clothes on his back and silver in his purse. He was beginning to enjoy himself after all.

He was just finishing when the dull, uneven clang of a bell rang out over the general noise of the square. Joining the crowd at the edge of the street, he worked his way forward through the press.

A dozen blue-uniformed guards were escorting a tumbrel cart down the avenue in his direction. A tall pike had been set upright in the back of the cart; a man's head was fixed on its point, the slack jaw quivering at every bump and jolt. The glassy eyes had rolled upward, as if avoiding even in death the expressions of scorn and revulsion that greeted this final progress. A placard had been nailed just below it, but the writing on it was obscured by streaks of drying blood.

Alec spat out his last mouthful of meat and lowered his eyes as the cart drew abreast of him. It seemed that no matter where he turned today he was confronted with bits of dead bodies. Suddenly a hand slid under his arm from behind.

"Are you unwell, young sir?"

Unpleasant breath bathed his cheek. Turning, Alec found himself in the supportive grip of a scrawny young ruffian. The fellow's sallow face looked as narrow as an ax blade, an illusion not alleviated by his prominently arched nose and buck teeth. An unruly lock of sandy hair kept falling over one eye and he reached up to push it away with one hand without relinquishing his hold on Alec's sleeve with the other. His garments had once been fine, but judging by their worn appearance and the sour odor that rose from them, Alec suspected their owner to be a denizen of the northern Ring.

"I'm fine, thank you," Alec replied, disliking the stranger's insistent hold on his arm.

"Some don't care for such sights," the other said, shaking his head, though whether it was at the sight of violent death or the lack of stomach for it, Alec could not guess. "When I seen you, I says to myself, 'There's one that might keel right over!' Perhaps you ought to sit down over here, 'til the spell passes. Quite an end for old Lord Vardarus, eh?"

"I'm fine," Alec repeated, pulling free at last. "Who's Lord Vardarus?"

"You was just looking at him. If you'd have looked in the back of that cart, you'd have seen the rest of him headed for the city pit. Executed this morning for plotting to kill the Vicegerent his self, as I hear it." The man paused to spit wetly. "Filthy Leran traitor!"

Vicegerent! thought Alec, recalling the jocular fellow Myrhini had introduced him to at the parade ground. Now, here was something to report to Seregil; Lord Barien must have just been coming from the execution of his own would-be murderer. Alec made a mental note to ask Seregil what a Leran was.

"You all right then, young sir?" his erstwhile rescuer asked again.

"For the last time, yes!" Giving the man a curt nod, Alec stole a glance over his shoulder, looking for his horse. When he looked back, the fellow was gone.

Shaking his head in bemusement, Alec set off again.

The seaward section of the Ring was more heavily guarded; his pass was closely inspected by the watch before he was allowed to enter. Beyond the gate, the open ground had been divided into a series of huge corrals that held the herds of horses belonging to the various military units of the city.

Hundreds of animals milled about beyond the fences on either side of the roadway, their rich odor permeating the air. The workshops of regimental farriers, harness makers, and armorers were scattered among the enclosures, and the craftsmen added their own noises to the din. Signs posted at the gate of each corral displayed the regimental emblem, as did the uniforms of the soldiers standing guard. Alec quickly spotted the helm and saber device of the Queen's Horse Guard, as well as the flame emblem worn by the blue-coated riders he'd noticed around the city. Other uniforms were new to him. Soldiers wearing sky-blue tunics stitched with the shining white outline of a soaring hawk stood guard over several herds made up entirely of white horses. Another group wore deep purple, with scarlet serpents forming a complicated knot as their emblem.

The road was crowded with soldiers, strings of horses, hay racks, and dung carts. To travel any distance afoot was evidently unthinkable in such company. Those having nothing better to do lined the fence rails to watch the activity.

A few of these idlers, both male and female, greeted him with gestures only slightly less suggestive than those of the ragged woman at the hovel. Shocked at the ways of city dwellers, Alec pressed on at a canter to the next gate and emerged gratefully again into the long park behind the Queen's Palace. Nudging his horse into a gallop, he rode to the Harvest Market and the Street of the Sheaf, then east into the city.

People bustled on all sides, jostling each other as they went about their business. Even the buildings seemed to crowd one another, leaning shoulder to shoulder over the street to trap the din of the passing traffic and echo it back. Alec's discomfort at the proximity of so many people began to well up again.

Afternoon shadows were lengthening by the time as he reached the Astellus Circle. He paused at the colonnade. Across the way lay the wooded park, bordering the circle's north side. A single street entered the park through a prettily carved stone archway. Richly dressed riders and fancy carriages were coming and going in a steady stream. Curious, Alec rode over for a closer look.

The park embraced the street on both sides and, together with the arch, gave the place a sheltered, almost magical air, as if it might exist quite separately from the crowded city beyond. The villas here had no screening walls and he marveled at the elegance of the facades and gardens. Despite the early hour, each house had one or more colored lamps burning above its entrance. There were only four colors: rose, amber, white, and green. Although they lent a certain festive tone, their order along the street seemed quite random.

"Excuse me, sir," Alec ventured, catching the eye of a man coming out from under the arch. "What street is this?"

"The Street of Lights, of course," the man replied, looking him over.

"So I see, but what do the lights mean?"

"If you have to ask that, then you've no business knowing, lad!" Giving Alec a wink, the fellow strode off whistling.

With a last curious glance down the intriguing avenue, Alec headed for the Orëska House. Myrhini's instructions brought him safely there, and Nysander's guide stone led him back up to the tower door.

He was just raising his hand to knock when Thero came storming out with an armload of scroll cases. They collided hard enough to knock the wind out of both of them. Scroll cases scattered in all directions, rolling and clattering across the stone floor of the passage. One tube flew over the parapet and several startled voices echoed up the atrium as it shattered on the tiles below. Thero glared at Alec for an instant, then began gathering his scattered documents.

"Sorry," Alec muttered, picking up those that had rolled across the corridor. Thero accepted them curtly and strode off, not bothering to acknowledge that the door had closed behind him.

Much obliged, I'm sure! Alec thought sourly, standing well to one side as he knocked again.

Seregil opened the door this time, and he looked remarkably pleased with himself.

"Gone, is he?" he smirked, letting Alec into the anteroom.

"What was that all about? He practically knocked me over the railing!"

Seregil shrugged innocently. "I came upstairs to borrow a book from Nysander but he wasn't here. In his absence, Thero took it upon himself to tell me I couldn't have it. After reasoning with him at considerable length over the matter, I suggested that it was probably his vow of celibacy that keeps him so irritable all the time. I was in the middle of a detailed discourse—based largely on my own personal experience—on the methods he could employ to alleviate his difficulties when he hurried out. Perhaps he means to put my wisdom into action."

"I doubt it. And isn't it sort of dangerous, teasing a wizard?"

"He takes himself much too seriously," scoffed Seregil, sitting down at one of the work ables. "How was your ride? See anything interesting? Who stole your purse?"

"There was a procession at the Sea Market and I—"

Alec stopped, openmouthed, as Seregil's last questions registered. Checking his belt, he found only the severed strings where his wallet had hung.

"That bastard at the Sea Market!" He groaned.

Seregil regarded him with a crooked grin. "Let me guess: thin, whey-faced, big nose, bad teeth? Got close to you for some reason and wouldn't be shaken off? Relieved you of this, I believe."

Seregil tossed Alec a purse. It was his own, and quite empty.

"His name's Tym." Seregil's grin broadened. "I figured he'd hit you at the market. He can't resist working a crowd, especially if there are bluecoats around."

Alec stared at Seregil, aghast. "You set him on me! He works for you?"

"From time to time, so you're likely to see him again. You can settle up with him then, if you want. I hope you didn't lose too much."

"No, but I still don't understand why you did it. Bilairy's Elbows, Seregil. If I hadn't been carrying that pass in my coat—"

"Consider it your first lesson in city life. Something of the sort had to happen sooner or later. I figured sooner was better. I did warn you before you left to watch out for yourself."

"I thought I did." Alec bristled, thinking of the rough characters he'd managed to avoid in the Ring.

Seregil clapped him on the shoulder. "Well, don't fret. Tym's a professional in his own small way, and you're his favorite sort of victim: just in from the country, green as grass, mouth hanging open as you take in the city. So tell me about your ride."

"Didn't Tym tell you about it?" Alec scowled, feeling he'd been made a fool of.

"Tym isn't you. I want to hear what you saw."

Still smoldering, Alec sketched a terse description of the Ring, pointedly including the ambushers, then moved on to the procession at the Sea Market.

"Lord Vardarus." Seregil frowned, twirling a glass rod between two long fingers. "I did a few things for him in the past. I'd have said he was completely loyal to the Queen."

"That cutpurse of yours said he'd tried to assassinate Lord Barien. Myrhini and I saw Lord Barien before I left, over at the Palace. Maker's Mercy, Seregil, he must have just come from the execution when I saw him, and he was talking of some festival!"

"The Festival of Sakor, at the winter solstice," Seregil replied absently. "I wonder what Nysander knows about all this? I'd never have taken Vardarus for a Leran."

"What are Lerans, anyway?"

Seregil glanced up in surprise. "Bilairy's Balls. You mean I never told you about Idrilain the First?"

"No. That night on the *Darter* you said there was a lot I'd have to learn about the royal lines, but then you got sick."

"Ah, well then, you're in for a treat. Idrilain the First's one of my favorites. She lived four hundred years ago and is the first and only of the Skalan queens to take an Aurënfaie as consort."

"An Aurënfaie?"

"That's right, though this wasn't her first husband. Idrilain was a great warrior, known for her strong will and fiery temper. By the age of twenty, she was already a general. At twenty-two, she married on the day of her coronation and soon produced an heir, a daughter named Lera. Not long after, Zengat declared war on Aurënen. The Aurënfaie appealed to Skala for help and Idrilain led the forces south herself."

"Where's Zengat?" Alec broke in, his head spinning with unfamiliar names.

"West of Aurënen, where the mountains of Ared Nimra reach the Selön Sea. The Zengati are a fierce bunch, most of them warriors, brigands, and pirates. Occasionally they get bored with fighting among themselves and band together to make trouble for their neighbors, especially Aurënen. This time they were laying claim to lands down near Mount Bardôk. Once they got into western Aurënen, they decided they might as well have the rest of it.

"During her campaign there, Idrilain fell in love with a handsome Aurënfaie captain named Corruth. He returned to Skala with her, where nearly caused a civil war by putting aside her first consort to marry him."

"But you said it was common practice for a queen to change lovers as much as she liked," Alec recalled.

"But they usually only did so to gain an heir. Idrilain already had a daughter. But there was also the matter of Corruth being Aurënfaie."

"You mean not human?"

"That's right. Even though the ancient ties from the Great War were still remembered with gratitude, it was quite a different matter for alien blood to be mixed into the royal line.

"As usual, Idrilain had her way in the end and the match produced another daughter, Corruthesthera. Her father, a kind and noble man by all reports, eventually gained acceptance from some of the nobles. But there was also a strong faction, the Lerans, who could not accept the possibility of Corruth's daughter reaching the throne. Idrilain's first consort was at the heart of it from the beginning, and probably involved Lera as well, although it was never proven. Whatever the case, relations between the Queen and the Princess Royal were strained, to say the least."

"So what happened?"

"In the thirty-second year of her reign, Idrilain was poisoned. No connection to the Lerans could be proven, but Lera ascended the throne under the shadow of suspicion. It didn't help matters any that Lord Corruth disappeared from Rhíminee without a trace the day of her accession. To Lera's credit, she didn't have her half sister, Corruthesthera, assassinated right then. Instead, she quietly exiled her to an island in the middle of the Osiat Sea. The people of Aurënen were outraged and relations between the two nations have never been the same.

"Queen Lera was a harsh, tight-fisted woman. She's recorded to have had more people executed during her eighteen-year rule than any queen in the history of Skala.

"Ironically, her half sister survived three different assassination attempts, while Lera herself died in childbirth with a still-born son. In spite of some threat of revolution, Corruthesthera was recalled from exile and crowned as the only remaining heir."

Alec mulled all this over for a moment. "So that means that the queens who came after were part Aurënfaie?"

Seregil nodded. "Corruthesthera favored her father's race; they say she appeared to be hardly more than a girl at age fifty."

"What do you mean?"

"Well," Seregil explained, "in addition to living three or four times as long as humans, the Aurënfaie mature more slowly. A man of fourscore years is close to Bilairy's gate, while an Aurënfaie is still considered a youth."

"They must become very wise, living that long."

Seregil grinned. "Wisdom is not necessarily the product of age. Still, imagine being able to draw on the experience of three lifetimes rather than one."

"How long did Corruthesthera live?"

"She died in battle at the age of one hundred and forty-seven. Queen Idrilain the Second is her great-granddaughter."

"Then if what Tym said is true, the Lerans are still around."

"Oh, yes, though they've never achieved much beyond an assassination or two. But they still boil up to make trouble every now and then. With the war coming, they could be more of a threat. And not only to the Queen, it seems. Was Barien by himself?"

"No, Phoria, the oldest princess—"

"Princess Royal," Seregil corrected, fidgeting with the glass rod. "Though she prefers the title of general. People have been speculating about her and Barien for years now— But go on."

"General Phoria was with him, and his nephew."

"Lord Teukros?" Seregil gave a derisive snort. "Now there's true Skalan nobility for you: nephew and sole heir of the most powerful lord in Rhíminee, scion of one of the oldest Skalan families, not a drop of foreign blood in his lily pure veins. Perfect manners, expensive tastes, and all the brains of a flounder. Quite the gambler, too. I've taken his money more than once."

"He's Barien's heir?"

"Oh, yes. Being childless himself, the Vicegerent has always doted on his sister's son. Barien's no fool, mind you, but love does make excuses, as they say. It just goes to show that the nobles ought to learn what any hog farmer knows, and do a bit more out breeding now and then."

19

UNEASY SECRETS

Seregil inhaled the familiar morning smells of the tower as he and Alec headed up to the workroom the next morning— the mingled incense of parchment, candle smoke, and herbs overlaid with the more immediate aromas of breakfast.

Upstairs, early morning sunlight slanted down through the leaded panes of the dome, giving the jumbled room a comfortable glow. Nysander sat in his usual place at the head of the least cluttered table, both hands clasped around his mug as he conversed with Thero.

A bittersweet pang shot through Seregil. In the days of his apprenticeship, he'd sat in Thero's place each morning, enjoying the early quiet while Nysander outlined the day's tasks. It had been at such moments that he'd felt, for the first time in his life, like he belonged, that he was welcome and useful.

This memory brought with it a momentary stab of guilt at the thought of a certain scrap of parchment carefully concealed at the bottom of his pack. Seregil pushed the thought away.

"Good morning, you two! I hope you are hungry," Nysander said, pushing the teapot their way. Thero acknowledged their arrival with a cool nod.

Nysander's workroom breakfasts were legendary at the Orëska House: fried ham, honey and cheese, hot oat cakes with butter, and good strong black tea. Anyone was welcome and if you wanted anything else you could bring it yourself.

"Valerius will be pleased with you, Alec," said Nysander as they sat down. "Seregil is looking much more himself today."

The boy shot Seregil a pointed glance. "It's none of my doing. He's done just as he pleased ever since Valerius left, but he healed up anyway."

"I daresay you underestimate your influence over him, dear boy." The wizard turned to Seregil with a rather searching look. "Well now, what are your plans?"

Seregil could feel his old mentor watching him as he spooned honey onto a piece of oat cake. Nysander was waiting for another argument over the scar and, under most circumstances, that's exactly what he'd have gotten. But not this time.

Concentrating on his breakfast, Seregil replied, "It's time we headed home. With a war brewing for the spring, there ought to be some jobs waiting for us."

"True," said Nysander. "In fact, I may have a bit of work for you myself."

"About this new Leran upsurge?"

"Precisely. I hope to put what details I can before you within a few days."

Seregil sat back, on safer ground now. "Do you think Vardarus was really mixed up in all that?"

"I must say, I would never have suspected the man. Yet he signed a full confession, and spoke not one word in his own defense. The evidence seemed incontrovertible."

Seregil gave a skeptical shrug. "If he'd contested the conviction and lost, his heirs would lose all claim to his property. By admitting his treason, they were allowed to inherit."

"But if he was innocent, then why wouldn't he have said so?" asked Alec.

"As Nysander said, the evidence against him was irrefutable," Thero answered. "Letters in Vardarus' own hand were produced. He could have pleaded forgery, or that magic had been used to alter them, yet he refused to do so. The Queen had no choice but to pass sentence. With all respect, Nysander, it is possible that he was guilty."

Seregil tugged absently at a strand of dark hair. "And if he was innocent, what could have enforced such damning silence? He was attached to the Queen's Treasury, wasn't he? I'll need a list of the nobles he associated with in that position, and some idea of his personal habits."

"I shall see you have all you need," said Nysander.

Alec found himself studying faces over breakfast. Seregil had been unusually pensive, although he seemed to brighten up once he'd gotten some food in him. Thero was as stiff as ever, and Nysander just as easygoing, yet there was something in the older wizard's expression when he looked at Seregil, as if he were trying to figure him out.

As for himself, Alec realized that he was finally beginning to feel comfortable here. The sense of disorientation that had depressed him during Seregil's recovery had lifted at last. Watching his companion trying to tease Thero into some pointless debate, he sensed that a certain important equilibrium had been reestablished.

"You are quieter than usual this morning," Nysander observed, catching his eye.

Alec nodded toward Seregil. "This is more what he was like when we first met."

"Annoying Thero has always been a favorite pastime of his," the wizard sighed. "For goodness' sake, Seregil, let him eat in peace. Not everyone shares your taste for banter first thing in the morning."

"I doubt there are many tastes Thero and I *do* share," Seregil conceded.

"A fact for which I am continually thankful," Thero parried dryly.

Leaving the two of them to their private battle, Alec turned back to Nysander. "I've been wondering about something you mentioned when we talked that first night."

"Yes?"

"You spoke of shape changing spells. Can a person really be changed into anything?"

"A brick, perhaps?" Thero interjected.

Seregil acknowledged the gibe with a gallant salute of the honey spoon.

"That is correct," Nysander replied. "Transubstantiation—or metamorphosis, if you will—has always been a favorite subject of mine. I made quite a study of it, years ago. Few of the spells are permanent and the risks are often high, but I do enjoy them."

"He turned us into all sorts of things," Seregil told him. "And it still comes in handy now and then."

"There are several general kinds of changes," Nysander went on, warming to his topic. "Transmogrifications change one thing completely into something else—a man into a tree, for instance. His thoughts would be those of a tree and he would exist as one without memory of his former nature until restored. A metastatic spell, however, would merely give a man the appearance of a tree. To alter the nature of a substance—iron into gold, for example—would require an alchemic transmutation."

"And what about that intrinsic nature spell of yours?" Seregil inquired blandly, staring down into his mug.

"I might have known you'd bring it around to that," Thero sniffed. "A trick to entertain children and country peasants!"

"There are those who believe it has some value," Nysander said with a meaningful look in Thero's direction. "Myself among them."

Seregil leaned over to Alec as if to speak in confidence, though he didn't bother to lower his voice. "Thero hates that spell because it won't work on him. He has no intrinsic nature, you see."

"It is true that this particular spell does not affect him," Nysander admitted, "but I am certain that we shall discover the impediment eventually. However, I suspect that it was not Thero's nature you had in mind?"

Seregil gave Alec a playful nudge in the ribs. "How about a bit of magic?"

Nysander laid his knife aside with a resigned sigh. "I see that I am not to enjoy this meal in peace. I suggest we retire to the garden in case Alec proves to be something especially large."

"Me?" Alec choked down a bit of ham. He had no idea what an intrinsic nature spell could be, but it suddenly appeared that they meant to work one on him.

Seregil was halfway to the door already. "I just hope he doesn't turn out to be a badger. I've never gotten on with badgers. Thero will probably turn out to be a badger if you ever get it to work."

They followed Nysander down to the Orëska gardens and into a thick stand of birch surrounding a small pool.

"This will do nicely," he said, stopping in the dappled shade near the water's edge. "I will transform Seregil first, Alec, so that you may observe the process."

Alec nodded nervously, watching as Seregil knelt on the grass in front of the wizard.

Resting his hands on his thighs, Seregil closed his eyes and all expression vanished from his face.

"He attains the suscipient state so readily," Thero muttered with grudging admiration. "Still, you take a chance, trying to work anything on him."

Nysander motioned for silence, then laid a hand on Seregil's head. "Seregil í Korit Solun Meringil Bôkthersa, let thy inner symbol be revealed."

The change was instantaneous. One moment Seregil knelt before them. The next, something was squirming about in a tangle of empty clothing.

Nysander bent over the wiggling pile. "The change was successful, I gather?"

"Oh, yes," replied a small, guttural voice, "but I've lost my way in here. Could you lend a hand?"

"Help your friend, Alec," Nysander said, laughing.

Alec gingerly lifted the edge of the surcoat, then jumped back in surprise as the blunt head of an otter thrust out from under the loosened shirttail.

"That's better," it grunted. Waddling free of the clothing, the sleek creature sat up on its hindquarters with its tail stretched out behind. It looked exactly like any otter Alec had ever trapped, except that its small round eyes were the same grey as Seregil's.

Seregil smoothed his drooping whiskers into place with a webbed paw. "I should've stripped down first, but the effect is more startling this way, don't you think?"

"It's really you!" Alec exclaimed in delight, running a hand over the otter's gleaming back. "You're beautiful."

"Thank you—I think," Seregil clucked. "In light of your former profession, I'm not certain if that was a compliment or an appraisal of the worth of my pelt. Watch this!"

Humping to the edge of the pool, he slid into the water and dove out of sight with sinuous ease. After a few moments he climbed out again to deposit a flopping carp at Thero's feet.

"A cold fish for a cold fish!" he announced with otterish glee before dashing back into the water.

Scowling, Thero nudged the carp back into the pool with his foot. "He never can go anywhere without stealing something."

Nysander turned to Alec. "Ready to give it a try?"

"What do I do?" Alec replied eagerly.

"Remove your clothes first, I think. As you saw, they can be a hindrance."

Excitement overcame Alec's modesty for once and he disrobed quickly. In the meantime, Nysander changed Seregil back; the restoration was as sudden as the initial change.

"It's been a while since we've done that," Seregil said, grinning happily as he pulled on his breeches. "I spent a week as an otter once. I'd like to do that again sometime."

"There is no great trick to this," Nysander assured Alec as he took his place in front of the wizard. "Simply clear your mind. Think of water, or a cloudless sky. Before we start, however, I must know your full name."

"Alec of Kerry is all I've ever gone by."

"He's the son of a wandering hunter, not a lord," Seregil reminded him. "That sort hasn't the use for long names that we do."

"I suppose not. Still, the lad ought to have a proper name if he is going to trail about with you. Alec, what were the names of your father, and his father, and his father before that?"

"My father's name was Amasa. I never knew any of the others," answered Alec.

"In the southern fashion, that would make you Alec í Amasa of Kerry," said Nysander. "I suppose that will have to suffice."

"He's not likely to use his real name much at all if he runs with Seregil," Thero observed impatiently.

"True." Nysander placed his hand over Alec.

Alec thought of clear water as hard as he could and heard Nysander say, "Alec í Amasa Kerry, let thy inner symbol be revealed!"

Alec staggered, found his balance, braced for flight.

Everything appeared in varying tones of grey, yet the slightest movement caught his eye. More overwhelming still were the scents. The pool gave off the sweet message of water and there were horses nearby, mares among them. The countless plants of the garden wove a green tapestry of aromas, some stinking of poison, others succulent and inviting.

Most emphatic, however, was the warning stink of the men. Some new part of him signaled innate alarm. He couldn't understand their ridiculous noise or the strange grimacing that accompanied it.

Then the smallest of the three moved closer, making new, calmer sounds. Watching the other man creatures with suspicion, he stood his ground, allowing this one to come close enough to stroke his neck.

"Magnificent!" exclaimed Seregil, looking over the young stag Alec had transformed into. Its nostrils flared nervously, scenting the breeze as he touched its powerful neck. Tossing its antlered head, it looked at him with wide blue eyes.

"Remarkable," Thero admitted, taking a step closer. "Bring him over to the pool so that he can see—"

"Thero, no! I think he's—" Seregil hissed, too late.

At the young wizard's sudden approach, the stag reared in panic. Seregil threw himself back out of reach of the flailing hooves.

Grasping at the back of Thero's robe, Nysander managed to yank him to safety just as the startled animal leapt forward, lashing out with its antlers.

"Change him back!" yelled Seregil. "He's lost in the shape. Change him back before he bolts!"

Nysander shouted the command, and the stag form shifted and dissolved, leaving Alec in a dazed heap on the grass.

"Easy now," Seregil soothed, wrapping a cloak around the boy's shoulders.

"Did it work?" Alec asked, feeling dizzy and odd. "Things went all funny for a minute."

"Did it work?" Seregil rocked back on his heels, laughing. "Let's see now. First you changed into as handsome a stag as I've ever seen, then you tried to gut and trample Thero. Nysander stopped you, of course, but otherwise I'd call it a grand success!"

"The transformation was rather too complete," said Nysander, less satisfied. "How do you feel?"

"A little wobbly," Alec admitted. "I'd like to try it again, though."

"So you shall," promised Nysander, "but first you must learn to govern your mind."

Left to himself that afternoon, Alec wandered out into the gardens again. He had still not entirely thrown off the morning's disorientation; the world seemed rather muted after experiencing it through the senses of an animal.

As he neared the centaur's grove he caught the sound of harp music and paused. Mastering his shyness, he entered the trees. Hwerlu and Feeya stood close together in the clearing, Feeya leaning languidly on her mate's back as he played. There was an intimacy to the scene that made Alec halt, but before he could withdraw Feeya caught sight of him and broke into a broad, welcoming smile.

"Hello, little Alec," Hwerlu called, lowering his harp. "You have the look of one in need of companionship. Come and sing with us."

Alec accepted the invitation, surprised at how at ease he felt with the immense creatures. He and Hwerlu traded songs for a while, then Feeya attempted to teach him a few words of her flat, whistling language. With Hwerlu's help he managed to learn "water," "harp," "song," and "tree." He was just attempting "friend" when the centaurs suddenly raised their heads, listening.

"That animal is being driven too hard," Hwerlu stated with a disapproving frown.

Seconds later Alec's ears also picked up the distant staccato of a galloping horse. Looking out through the trees, he saw a rider heading for the main entrance of the House. As the man reined in and dismounted, his hood fell back from his face.

"That's Micum," Alec exclaimed, setting off at a run. "Hey, Micum! Micum Cavish!"

Already halfway up the stairs, Micum turned and waved to him.

"Am I glad to see you!" cried Alec, noting as he clasped hands with him that Micum looked haggard, and that his clothing was stained and spattered with mud. "Seregil and Nysander wouldn't say so, but I think they were beginning to worry. It looks like you've had a hard ride."

"I did," the big man answered. "How'd you and Seregil make out?"

"We had some trouble on the way back, but he's fine now. I think he's with Nysander."

"Trouble?" Micum frowned, glancing back at Alec as they hurried toward the wizard's tower. "What kind of trouble?"

"Bad magic from that wooden thing. He got sick, but Nysander put him right. I'm just glad we got here soon enough. I still

don't understand much of it, but Nysander and Seregil can tell
you."

"Let's find them, then. I've something I want you all to hear
and I don't want to have to go through it a dozen times."

Micum felt a rush of relief as Nysander let them in at the
tower door. This was one Watcher report he was anxious to share
the burden of.

"Here you are at last!" said Nysander.

"Is that Micum?" Seregil looked up from something on
Nysander's desk, then hurried over to greet him. "Bilairy's Balls,
man, you look like hell!"

"So do you." Micum inspected Seregil with concern. He was
thinner than ever, and looked tired in spite of his usual grin. "The
boy here says you had some trouble on the road?"

"I think it would be best if we heard your report first," said
Nysander. "Come down to the sitting room, all of you."

"All of them" didn't appear to include Thero, Micum noted as
Nysander shut the study door.

"Seregil, pour the wine," the wizard said, taking a seat by the
fire. "Now, Micum, you have some news?"

Micum dropped into the other armchair and accepted the cup
gratefully. "Yes, and it's not good."

"You found the place marked in the Fens, didn't you?" Seregil
asked eagerly.

"Yes. After Boersby, I rode to the southern end of the Fens.
From what you'd told me, I figured the Plenimarans must have
come up the Ösk and followed the river trail in. I soon picked up
word of them in the villages along that route. Mardus and his
men had been through less than a month before."

"The Blackwater Fens are a bad place to travel," Alec said,
shaking his head. "One minute you're on solid ground, the next
you're up to your waist in mud."

"That's the truth. If the cold weather hadn't firmed the ground
up as much as it had, I'd have lost my horse before I got out of
there," Micum told him. "Mardus had gone clear into the heart of
the Fens. It's a cursed waste of quaking bog in there. The villages
had given out miles back, and I was about ready to turn back
when I came upon a little settlement set up on a rise.

"It was the usual sort of swamp village—just a dirty jumble

of hovels clustered around a muddy track. A wooden causeway led into it and I was halfway across it when I felt something was wrong. There wasn't a soul in sight. You know how it is with these little villages—the minute a stranger turns up the dogs bark and the children run out to see who it is. But I couldn't see anyone around. There was no smoke, either, no sound of voices or work. But there were gathering baskets and nets by the doorways, like someone had just laid them aside. I thought maybe they were hiding at first, until I heard ravens making a racket nearby.

"Looking around, I began to have an idea what I was going to find. The remains of three people were scattered down the other side of the rise below the village. Animals had been at them for days, and what remained was frozen into the mud. Two were adults, a man and a woman. From the way they lay, it looked like they'd been cut down running. The man's head had been knocked twenty feet away and the woman was hacked almost in two at the waist. A young lad lay half in the water at the base of the hill, with an arrow still in his back.

"The signs were easy enough to read. Dozens of tracks led to a depression in the earth halfway down the rise; only a few came back out to cross over them. By the manner that the dirt had been thrown around, I'd say it was a wizard's doing. Going down for a closer look, I suddenly sank into the ground right up to my hip. When I went to wiggle loose, I realized that my foot was in open space down there.

"There was a hollow place in the hill, like a barrow. Digging down, I found a little chamber in the hillside, built low and shored up with timbers."

Micum paused and took another long sip of wine before continuing. "The whole village had been killed and carried in there. The stench was fearsome; I wonder you don't smell it on me still. The torch burned blue when I stuck it through to see. There were bodies sprawled out everywhere—"

Meeting Seregil's level grey gaze, he shook his head. "We've seen some hard things, you and I, but by Sakor, nothing like this. Some they'd just killed, others they'd hacked open, pulling their ribs back until the poor bastards looked as if they'd grown wings. Cut up their insides, too.

"There was a big flat stone in the center of the chamber, like a table. They must have done their butchery on that—it was all black with blood. A little girl and an old man were still laid out there, their faces gone green. I counted twenty-three in all, plus the three above. Must've been the whole damn village."

Micum sighed heavily, kneading his eyelids. "The strange thing, though, was that I found older bones beneath the bodies."

Nysander had been staring impassively into the fire all this while. Without shifting his gaze, he asked, "Were you able to examine the stone?"

"Yes, and I found this." Micum drew a bit of rotted leather from a pouch at his belt and showed them the remains of a small bag.

Nysander took the scraps and examined them closely. Then, without comment, he cast them into the fire.

Micum was too surprised to react immediately, but Seregil leapt up and tried to rake them out with a poker.

"Let it be!" Nysander ordered sharply.

"This is to do with the disk, isn't it?" Seregil demanded angrily, still grasping the poker.

Micum felt a palpable thickening of the atmosphere of the room as Nysander and Seregil faced off. Judging by Alec's startled expression, the boy was feeling it, too. The wizard betrayed no outward sign of anger, but the lamps went dim and the warmth of the fire failed.

"I have told you all I can in the matter." Though Nysander spoke quietly, his voice seemed to reverberate like a thunderclap in the deadened air. "I tell you again that the time is not come when you may know."

Seregil tossed the poker down on the stone hearth with a snarl of disgust. "How many years have I kept your secrets?" he hissed through clenched teeth. "All the intrigues and dirty jobs. Now this touches my own life—Micum's, Alec's—and you won't say a word? Oaths be damned, Nysander! If I'm not worthy of your trust, then I'm not worthy of your roof. I'm going to the Cockerel—today!" And with a final furious glare, he slammed out of the room.

"What the hell was *that* all about?" Micum demanded as he and Alec rose to follow.

Nysander motioned them back to their chairs. "Give him time to calm down. This situation is tremendously difficult for all of you, I realize, but perhaps especially so for him. Curiosity alone will drive him half mad, not to mention his wounded sense of honor."

"Do you mean to say you know something about that business in the Fens but you're not telling us?" asked Micum, none too happy himself.

"Please, Micum, I need your cool head to govern Seregil just now. Should the need for action arise, be assured that I will look to the two of you—" He paused, catching sight of Alec sitting stiff and silent in his chair. "Pardon me, dear boy—to the *three* of you to deal with it. In the meantime, do you think you can prevent him from charging off in a fury? There is another matter I must discuss with him before he leaves the Orëska."

Micum scowled. "It had better be a short fury. I don't fancy sitting in Rhíminee with home so close. I haven't seen my wife in four months."

"Your what?" Alec asked in surprise.

Micum gave a wry shrug. "In the midst of all the running and fighting we did up north, I guess the subject never came up. You'll have to come out to Watermead. In fact, if I let slip that you're an orphan, Kari may just come get you herself."

"Out to where?"

"Our holding," Micum explained. "It lies up in the hills to the west of the city. During my early days with Seregil we uncovered a plot against the Queen. The leader of it was executed and Idrilain offered us part of his holdings as reward. Seregil never cared much for property, so it fell to me. It's really been more Kari's than mine, what with me being gone so much. She and the girls run it."

"Girls?"

Nysander gave Alec a mischievous wink. "This rogue has three daughters, as well."

"Any grandchildren?" Alec inquired dryly.

"I hope not! The oldest, Beka, is only a year or two older than you and she's set her heart on a soldiering life. Seregil's promised to get her a commission in the Queen's Horse Guard, damn him. The other two, Elsbet and Illia, are too young yet to be thinking of husbands."

Yawning suddenly, Micum stretched back in his chair until the seams of his jerkin creaked. "By the Flame, I'm tired. After the riding I did to get here, I could sleep in the middle of the Sea Market and not know the difference. I'd better go after Seregil before I doze off. Before I go, though, there's one thing you must answer me, Nysander."

He fixed the wizard with a serious eye. "I'll accept your conditions of secrecy for now. You know you can always trust me—and Seregil, too, for all his bluster. But if this business is half as serious as you make it out to be, are we in danger? I haven't been easy in my mind since I left the Fens. All the way down here I kept seeing Alec and Seregil stretched back over that stone with their chests torn open. And now you tell me he got hit with bad magic. Could Mardus' people have tracked us here from Wolde? And will they follow me home tomorrow?"

Nysander sighed deeply. "I have had no sign of such pursuit yet. As much as I would like to tell you that there is no danger, that Seregil and Alec eluded their pursuers completely, I cannot be certain of it. But you may believe me, both of you, when I say that—no matter what my vow—I will never endanger any of you with false assurances. I shall continue to keep watch over you all as best I can, but you must also be cautious."

Micum stroked the corners of his mustache, frowning. "I don't like it, Nysander. I don't like it at all, but I trust you. Come on, Alec, let's go find Seregil. If he won't cool off on his own, you can help me dunk him in the horse trough."

They made a quick check of the bedchamber first. Seregil's old pack lay open on the clothes chest, along with an untidy pile of maps and parchment scraps. His traveling cloak lay in a heap next to a chair, along with several tunics and a crumpled hat. The tip of one old boot protruded from beneath the coverlet of the bed like a dog's nose. Combs, a ball of twine, a tankard, and fragments of a broken flint lay along the windowsill as if set out for a ceremony.

"He hasn't stormed off just yet," Micum observed, looking the mess over. "Before we go on, I'd like to hear what happened to you two."

Once again Alec went over the details of their journey and Seregil's strange malady. When he'd finished, Micum rubbed a hand wearily over the coppery stubble on his chin.

"That's not the sort of thing a person just walks away from, I grant you. Still, he ought to know that Nysander wouldn't put him off without good reason. I swear, Seregil is one of the smartest people I've ever known, and the bravest, but he's worse than a child when he comes up against something he can't twist around to suit himself." He yawned again heartily. "Let's get this over with."

"Where do we look?" Alec asked, following him out. "He could be anywhere."

"I know where to start."

Micum led the way out to the Orëska stables. Seregil was in a stall halfway down the mews, currying Micum's exhausted horse.

"You nearly spavined the poor beast," he said, not bothering to look up as they approached. His boots were soiled with barn muck; dust and horse hair clung to his clothing. A piece of sweat-soaked sacking swung from one shoulder as he worked down the animal's flank. A streak of mud down one wan cheek gave him a decidedly mournful look.

Micum slouched against the newel post at the end of the stall. "You acted like a fool back there, you know. I should think you'd want to set a better example for Alec."

Seregil gave him a sour glance across the horse's back, then went back to work.

Micum watched the motion of the curry comb for a moment. "You'll speak with Nysander before you leave?"

"Soon as I finish this."

"Looks like we won't have to toss him in the trough after all, eh?" Micum grinned at Alec. "And I was looking forward to it."

Seregil scrubbed at a patch of dry mud, sending up a cloud of dust. "You off to Watermead tomorrow?"

Micum heard the thinly veiled challenge the question often carried. "At first light. Kari will skin me if I stay away any longer. Why don't you two come out with me? The hunting should be good just now, and we could work on Alec's swordplay. Beka's a perfect match for him."

"I want to get settled at the Cockerel first," Seregil replied.

"Suit yourself. You're no use to anyone when you're like this."

Micum yawned again, then clasped hands with Seregil for a long moment, holding his friend's gaze until Seregil managed a tight, grudging smile. Satisfied, Micum released him and clapped Alec on the shoulder. "I'll be asleep before you get upstairs, so it's farewell for now. Luck to you in the shadows."

"And to you," Alec called after him.

Upending a bucket, Alec sat down to watch Seregil finish with the horse. "He doesn't stay around long, does he?"

Seregil shrugged. "Micum? Sometimes. Not like he used to."

Something in Seregil's voice warned Alec that this, too, was a subject not to be pursued.

"What's this Cockerel place we're going to?"

"Home, Alec. And home is where we're bound tonight." Seregil hung the curry comb on a nail. "Give me a minute to square things with Nysander, then come say good-bye."

Thero answered Seregil's knock. Exchanging their usual terse nods, they strode back through the stacks of manuscripts to the workroom. Walking behind the assistant wizard, Seregil read tension in the set of Thero's shoulders and smiled to himself. There had never been any specific basis for their strong mutual dislike, yet it had sprung up full-blown the first time they'd laid eyes on each other. Out of regard for Nysander's feelings, a grudging truce had developed between them. Nonetheless, they'd never been at ease in the other's presence, though either one would have eaten fire before they'd admit it aloud.

Seregil considered himself to be above such petty emotions as jealousy or envy; so what if Thero had taken his place at Nysander's side, filling it better, in some respects, than he ever had? Seregil had no reason to doubt Nysander's personal regard for him, or the importance of their professional association. His continuing dislike of Thero, he'd long since concluded, must be on a purely instinctual level, and thus irreconcilable and probably justified.

"He's downstairs," Thero informed him, returning to his work at one of the tables.

Nysander was still sitting pensively by the fire.

Leaning against the door frame, Seregil cleared his throat. "I was an idiot just now."

Nysander waved his apology aside. "Come in, please, and sit with me. Do you know, I was just trying to think how long it has been since you spent so many nights under this roof."

"Too long, I'm afraid."

Nysander regarded him with a sad smile. "Too long indeed, if you could imagine that I would keep anything from you out of distrust."

Seregil shifted unhappily in his chair. "I know. But don't expect me to just nod and smile about it."

"Actually, I think you are taking it all rather well. Do you still plan to leave tonight?"

"I need to get back to work, and Alec's feeling a bit lost. The sooner we get busy, the better we'll both feel."

"Mind you pace him in his training," Nysander cautioned. "I should not like to see either of you with your hands on the executioner's block."

Seregil regarded his old friend knowingly. "You like him."

"Certainly," Nysander replied. "He possesses a keen mind and a noble heart."

"Surprised?"

"Only that you would take on such a responsibility at all. You have been solitary for so long."

"It was nothing I planned, believe me. But as I get to know him better, well—I don't know. I guess I'm getting used to having him around."

Nysander studied his friend's face for a moment, then said gently, "He is very young, Seregil, and obviously has great respect and fondness for you. I trust you are aware of that?"

"My intentions toward Alec are perfectly honorable! You, of all people, ought to—"

"That is not what I was alluding to," Nysander replied calmly. "What I am saying is that you must consider more than his mere education. You should be a friend to him as well as a teacher. The time will come when the master must accept his pupil as an equal."

"That's the whole point, isn't it?"

"I am glad to hear you say so. But you must be honest with him, too." Nysander regarded him with sudden seriousness. "I know of at least one thing that he is not aware of. Why have you not told him of his true—?"

"I will!" Seregil whispered quickly, hearing Alec's step on the stairs. "I wasn't certain at first, and then things went to pieces. I just haven't found the right moment yet. He's had enough to contend with these last few weeks."

"Perhaps so, yet I confess I do not understand your reluctance. I wonder how he will react?"

"So do I," murmured Seregil. "So do I."

20

HOMECOMING

Tattered clouds were scudding across the face of the moon when Seregil and Alec set out for the Cockerel. A bitter wind off the sea clattered through the trees along Golden Helm Street. The night lanterns grated on their hooks, making the shadows dance.

Intent on savoring his first night of freedom, Seregil had turned down Nysander's offer of horses, although he did concede to letting Alec carry the pack. As the wind whipped their hair and cloaks about, he was chilled but cheerful.

Rhíminee after dark. Beyond ornate walls and down shadowed alleys lay a thousand dangers, a thousand delights. Passing beneath a lantern, he saw a glimmer of familiar eagerness in Alec's eyes; perhaps, at last, he'd chosen well?

By the time they reached the Circle of Astellus, however, Seregil was forced to admit that his body had not recovered as fully as his spirit.

"I could do with a drink," he said, stepping into the shelter of the colonnade.

The lily-shaped capitals of the marble columns supported a carved pediment and dome. Inside the colonnade, concentric circles of marble formed a series of steps leading down to the clear water welling up from a deep cleft in the rock below.

Kneeling, they pulled off their gloves and dipped up handfuls of sweet, icy water.

"You're shivering," Alec noted with concern. "We should've ridden."

"Walking's the best thing for me." Seregil sat back on the step and wrapped his cloak around him. "Remember this night, Alec. Drink it in and commit it to memory! Your first night on the streets of Rhíminee!"

Settling beside him, Alec looked out at the wild beauty of the night and let out a happy sigh. "It feels like the beginning of something, all right, even though we've been here a week."

He paused, and Seregil saw that he was staring toward the Street of Lights. Across the circle, the dark outline of the archway and the colorful twinkle of lights beyond shone invitingly.

"I meant to ask you about something the other day," Alec said. "I'd forgotten about it until just now."

Seregil grinned at him in the darkness. "Regarding what lies beyond that arch, I presume? The Street of Lights, it's called. I guess you can see why."

Alec nodded. "A man told me the name the other day. Then he made some joke when I asked what the different colors mean."

"Said if you had to ask you were too young to know?"

"Something like that. What did he mean?"

"Beyond those walls, Alec, lie the finest brothels and gambling establishments in Skala."

"Oh." There was enough light for him to see the boy's eyes widen a little as he noted the number of riders and carriages passing under the arch.

"Oh, indeed."

"But why are the lights different colors? I can't make out any pattern."

"They aren't meant for decoration. The color of the lanterns at each gate indicates the sort of pleasures the house purveys. A man wanting a woman would look for a house with a rose-colored light. If it's male company he craves, then he'd choose one showing the green lamp. It's the same for women: amber for male companionship, white for female."

"Really?" Alec stood up and walked to the far side of the fountain for a better view. When he turned back to Seregil he looked rather perplexed. "There are almost as many of the green and white ones as there are the others."

"Yes?"

"Well, it's just that—" Alec faltered. "I mean, I've heard of such things, but I didn't think they could be so—so common. Things are a lot different here than in the north."

"Not so much as you might think," Seregil replied, heading off again in the direction of the Street of the Sheaf. "Your Dalnan priests frown on such couplings, I understand, claiming they're unproductive—"

Alec shrugged uncomfortably, falling into step beside him. "They would be that."

"That depends on what one intends to produce," Seregil remarked with a cryptic smile. "Illior instructs us to take advantage of any situation; I've always found that to be a *most* productive philosophy."

When Alec still looked dubious, Seregil clapped him on the shoulder in mock exasperation. "By the Four, haven't you heard the saying, 'Never spurn the dish untasted'? And here you haven't even had a smell of the kitchen yet! We've got to get you back there, and soon."

Alec didn't reply, but Seregil noticed him glance back over his shoulder several times before they were out of sight of the lights.

Though they kept their hoods drawn, the occasional glimpses Alec got of his companion's face showed that Seregil was delighted to be back in his own element.

At the Harvest Market, Seregil ducked briefly into a potter's shop. A moment later he was out again without explanation, leading the way into a neighborhood of modest shops and taverns crowded together along the edge of the square. Turning several corners in quick succession, they came out on a small lane marked with a fish painted some dark color.

"There it is," Seregil whispered, pointing to a large inn across the way. "We move quietly from here."

A low wall enclosed the inn's small yard and Alec saw that bronze statues of the inn's namesake, a cockerel, were set on either side of the front gate, each clutching a glowing lantern in one upraised claw.

The Cockerel was a prosperous, well-kept establishment, square built of stone and wood, and three stories high. The small windows on the upper levels were shuttered, but the two large windows overlooking the front court let out a welcoming flood of light through their leaded bull's-eye panes.

"Looks like a busy night," Seregil noted quietly, keeping to the shadows as he led the way into the stable that ran along the left wall of the courtyard.

A young man with a disheveled mop of coarse red hair looked up from the harness he was mending as they came in. Smiling, he raised a hand in greeting. Seregil returned the gesture and continued on between the stalls.

"Who is that?" Alec asked, puzzled by the man's silence.

"That's Rhiri. He's deaf, mute, and absolutely loyal. Best servant I ever found." Stopping at a back stall, Seregil paused to inspect a rough-coated bay with a white snip.

"Hello, Scrub!" he said, patting the animal's shaggy flank. The horse nickered, craning his neck around to nuzzle at Seregil's chest.

"Where is it?" Seregil teased, throwing his cloak open.

Scrub sniffed at the pouches at his belt and butted at one on the right. Seregil produced the prize, an apple, and the horse munched contentedly, occasionally rubbing his head against his master's shoulder. A restless shuffling of hooves came from the next stall.

"I haven't forgotten you, Cynril," Seregil said, pulling another apple from the pouch as he stepped around. A large black mare tossed her head and pinned him against the side of the stall as he entered.

"Get over, you nag!" Seregil wheezed, whacking her on the haunch to shift her. "She's half Aurënfaie, but her disposition certainly doesn't give it away." Despite this, he rubbed the horse's head and nose with obvious affection.

At the back of the stable, a wide door let out into a larger yard behind the inn. A smaller wing at the back of the building housed the kitchen; bright light from an open doorway shone across the paving flags, and with it came the inviting smells and din of a busy kitchen. To the left of this door was a second, much broader one where casks and barrels of provender were delivered. The remainder of the ground level, and the stories above, were windowless. A lean-to sheltered a well and a wood stack at the angle of the building. The courtyard walls were much higher here, and the broad gateway was stoutly barred for the night.

Slipping inside, Seregil pointed across the crowded kitchen to a stooped old woman leaning on a stick in front of the enormous hearth.

"There's Thryis. She runs the place," he said, putting his mouth close to Alec's ear.

Thryis' heavy face was deeply seamed with age and her braid was the color of iron. In spite of the heat, she wore a thick embroidered shawl over her woolen gown. The briskness of her voice belied her gnarled appearance, however. Rapping out orders over the hectic clatter from the scullery, she kept servers, cooks, and kitchen maids scurrying about under her shrill direction.

She seemed strangely familiar to Alec; after a moment's puzzled thought he realized that she must have been the model for the disguise Seregil had assumed when he booked their passage in Boersby.

"How many leeks did you put into the stew, Cilla?" she was demanding of a buxom young woman stirring a pot. "It smells weak to me. It's not too late to add another. And a pinch more salt. Kyr, you lazy pup, get that platter out there! Those draymen will box your ears for you if you make them wait any longer for their supper, and so will I! Has the wine gone out to the merchants in the side room? Cilla, has it?"

Everyone in the kitchen seemed accustomed to their mistress' sharp tongue and bustled about their duties with an air of busy contentment. Cilla, the apparent second in command, moved serenely among the servants, pausing occasionally to look into a cradle near the hearth.

Motioning for Alec to follow, Seregil made his way around the long tables without either of the busy women noticing his approach. Coming up behind Thryis, he surprised her with a quick peck on the cheek.

"By the Flame," she exclaimed, pressing her free hand to her cheek. "So here you are at last!"

"It's only been half a year," Seregil replied, smiling down on her.

"If only you'd sent word I'd have had something special for

you! All we have tonight is red fire beef and lamb stew. The bread is fresh, though, and Cilla's made mince tarts. Cilla, fetch a plate of tarts for him to start with while I put together something."

"There's no need for that just yet. Both of you come into the lading room for a moment."

Catching sight of Alec, Thryis paused and looked him over with a sharp eye. "Who's this?"

"I'll explain in a moment." Taking a small lamp from the mantel, Seregil led Alec and the two women through a side door into the lading room. The broad door Alec had seen from the outside stood barred at their left. To the right, a wooden stairway led to the second floor.

"Thryis, Cilla, this is Alec," Seregil told them when he'd closed the kitchen door. "He'll be living upstairs now."

"Welcome to the Cockerel, Lord Alec," Cilla greeted him with a warm smile.

"It's just Alec," he said quickly, liking her kind face at once.

"Is that so?" Thryis said, giving him a decidedly sharp look, though Alec couldn't imagine why she should be suspicious of him.

"Alec's a friend," Seregil told her. "Everyone here will accord him the same respect that they do me, which in your case is little enough. He'll come and go as he pleases and you'll answer no questions about him to anyone. Inform Diomis and the others."

"Just as you wish, sir." Thryis gave Alec a final dubious glance. "Your rooms are just as you left them. Shall I send up wine?"

"Yes, and some cold supper." Turning back to Cilla, Seregil wrapped an arm about her waist, making her blush. "I see you've regained your maidenly shape. How's the baby?"

"Young Luthas is well. He's a sweet one, no trouble at all."

"And the business?"

Thryis pulled a long face. "A bit slack. But Festival time isn't far off. I'll have an accounting ready for you in the morning."

"Don't trouble yourself." Seregil turned to head up the stairs, then paused. "Is Ruetha around?"

"That animal!" Thryis rolled her eyes. "Disappeared soon as you left, same as always. I even put out cream for her this time, but the ungrateful wretch never showed so much as a whisker.

Now that you're back, she'll probably be in by breakfast like always."

"Thryis never changes," Seregil said with a hint of fondness, leading Alec up the back stairs. "Whether I've been gone for two days or six months, she always tells me I should have let her know I was coming, which I never do; apologizes for the menu, which is never necessary; promises an accounting, which I never look at; and then complains about my cat."

At the second floor, the stairs turned sharply and continued up to what appeared to be an attic. A short, dimly lit corridor, broken only by a few closed doors, ran in the direction of the main building.

"That door at the end opens into the main inn." Seregil pointed down the hall. "It's kept locked at all times. This door closest to us is a storeroom, the next are the rooms of Diomis and the women. Diomis is Thryis' son and Cilla is his daughter."

"What about Cilla's husband?" Alec asked.

"No woman ever needed a husband to have a baby. There was talk of conscription last year, and Cilla simply made certain she wouldn't be eligible. She even offered me the honor, which I politely declined. Sometime later she turned up with a big belly. Thryis was a sergeant in her younger days, and none too pleased with her granddaughter, but the damage was already done, so to speak. Now come this way and pay close attention. I have a few things to show you."

The attic stairway was steep. Holding up the small lamp, Seregil went halfway up and pointed to the bare plastered wall on the left.

"Listen and watch the wall," he said softly. *"Etuis miära koriatüan cyris."*

For a brief second, Alec caught the soft glow of magical symbols like those he'd seen at the Orëska House. They were gone too quickly for him to see them clearly or be certain of how many there had been, but as they vanished a narrow section of the wall swung back like a door. Seregil motioned him through, then closed the door firmly after and continued up a precariously steep set of steps ending at a blank wall. At the top of the stairs Seregil stopped and said, *"Clarin, magril, nodense."*

Another door appeared and Alec felt air moving against his face as they stepped into a cold, dusty room.

"Almost there," Seregil whispered. "Watch your step."

Picking their way among the crates and boxes jumbled around the floor, they reached the far wall.

"Here we are. *Bôkthersa!*"

A third door opened in the seemingly blank wall, revealing another dark room beyond.

"Welcome to my humble abode," Seregil said, ushering him through with a crooked grin.

Stepping in, Alec barked his shin against a stone basilisk beside the door. Reaching out to steady himself, he felt thick wall hangings beneath his hand. He could make out little in the darkness, but this place smelled of things more exotic than dust.

"Better stay put until I get some more light," Seregil advised. The little lamp bobbed this way and that as he crossed the room, revealing tantalizing glimpses of polished wood and patterned carpet. Suddenly it jogged to one side and Alec heard the sound of something heavy falling over, immediately followed by a muffled curse. The light bobbed precariously, then came to rest on a cluttered mantelpiece where its light was reflected in a hundred hues by a pile of jewels spilling from a half-open box that stood there.

Rummaging around for a moment, Seregil found a jar of fire stones and shook one out onto the wood laid ready on the hearth. Flames crackled up at once and he went around the room lighting candles and lamps.

Alec stepped forward with a soft exclamation of wonder as the room brightened. The place glowed with the rich colors of tapestries and easily rivaled Nysander's workroom in the variety and disorder of its contents. Slowly turning about, he tried to take it all in.

Shelves packed with books and racks of scrolls covered half the wall opposite the door. More books were stacked on the dining table that stood in the center of the room, and still more on the mantel. An immense carpet woven in patterns of red, blue, and gold lay between the central table and the hearth. Rush matting covered the rest of the floor.

Spaced along the wall to his right were two small windows facing out over the back court; a small writing desk stood under the right-hand one, the pigeon holes in its low back holding a neat collection of pens, inks, drawing quills, rolls of vellum and parchment, and wax tablets. The desk, along with most of the other furniture in the room, was made of a pale wood inlaid with darker bands along the edges. The design, pleasing in its simplicity, was noticeably different from the ornate furnishings of the Orëska.

A long, scarred table beneath the second window was littered with locks, tools, stacks of books, what appeared to be a small forge, and dozens of half-assembled things that defied immediate description. Shelves holding a bewildering assortment of objects framed the window and filled the remaining wall. More locks, more tools, rough chunks of metal and wood, and a number of devices whose uses Alec could not guess were mixed indiscriminately among masks, carvings, musical instruments of all descriptions, animal skulls, dried plants, fine pottery, glittering crystals—there was no rhyme or reason apparent in the arrangement. A broad collar of gold and rubies caught the light from the lamp on the desk, sending ruddy spangles of light across a large lump of baked mud that might have been either a crude bowl or some sort of nest.

On the section of wall that jutted into the room to the left of the entrance hung a collection of weapons, mostly swords and knives, apparently chosen for their unusual design and ornamentation. Beyond it, near the corner, was another door. Trunks and chests stood everywhere—along the base of walls, stacked in corners, under tables. Statues peered out from odd corners some lovely, some grotesque. Eclectic to the point of eccentricity, the overall effect of the room was nevertheless one of warmth and cluttered, haphazard grace.

"This is like the Orëska House museum!" Alec exclaimed, shaking his head. "Where did you ever get all this?"

"Stole some of it." Seregil settled on the couch in front of the fire. "That statue by the front door came from an ancient temple Micum and I unearthed for Nysander, up in the eastern foothills of the Asheks. That one there by the bedroom door was the gift of an admirer." He pointed out a beautifully rendered mermaid of marble and green jade. The sea maiden rose from the crest of a wave that partially covered her scaled lower body, one hand across her breast, the other sweeping her heavy hair back from her face.

"The red tapestry there between the bookcases I found among

the possessions of a Zengati bandit I killed after he ambushed me," Seregil continued, looking around. "Those locks over the table? You'll get to know those well enough before I'm done with you. As for the rest—" He gave a rather rueful smile. "Well, I'm a bit of a magpie. I just can't resist anything unusual or shiny. Most of it's trash, really. I keep meaning to chuck most of it out. The only thing of true value is one you can take away with you in a hurry."

"At least there aren't any crawling hands." Alec glanced over at the shelves again. "Are there?"

"I'm no more fond of that sort of thing than you are, believe me."

Still gazing around, it occurred to Alec that something was wrong with the room.

"The windows!" He leaned over the desk to look out. "I didn't see any windows from outside."

"Nysander did an obscuration on them, like with the scar on my chest," explained Seregil. "The windows are undetectable from the outside, unless you happened to climb out through one. And even then it would look like you were coming out the side of the building."

"There must be a lot of magic in the city."

"Not really. It doesn't come cheap, and the Orëska wizards won't hire out to just anyone. But you do run into it now and then, so it's always wise to be careful."

The room was beginning to warm up now. Dropping his cloak over the mermaid's upraised arm, Seregil picked up a small silver lamp and opened the room's other door. "Come in here, there's something else I need to show you."

The room was a bedchamber, though its dimensions were hard to guess, crammed as it was with wardrobes, chests, crates, and still more books. An ornate bed hung with gold and green velvet stood against the wall in the far corner.

"That's yours?" Alec asked, never having seen the like.

"Won it in a dice game." Wending his way across the room, Seregil looked around for a place to set the lamp, finally balancing it on a pile of books crowding the back of the washstand.

"That's the garderobe there, by the way." He indicated a narrow door barely visible between a wardrobe and a stack of boxes, watching with amusement as Alec explored the wonder of an indoor privy. "Mind you don't drop anything down the hole; if it goes through the grate, it's straight down to the sewers below. Here, this is what I wanted to show you."

Climbing across the enormous bed, Seregil hauled up the velvet curtain and guided Alec's hand between the mattress and the wall. A small knob was hidden in the woodwork of the paneling. Alec pressed it and heard a faint click; the section of paneling in front of them swung back, letting in a puff of cold air from the darkness beyond.

"This is the back door, in case you ever need it." Seregil climbed through the opening into another attic storeroom. "You have to know the command word to get into the bedroom from this side. It's *norásthu caril vëntua*."

"I'll never remember all that!" Alec groaned, following.

"Oh, you'll learn," Seregil assured him, going to a door in the left wall, "or you'll spend the rest of your life sleeping in the kitchen. Damn, I've forgotten the key."

Producing a pick, he threw the lock and stepped out onto an attic landing. A wooden tray lay on a crate at the top of the stairs; on it were two bottles of wine, a plate of tarts, cheese, bread, and an enormous, long-haired cat. At their approach the cat left off gnawing at the cheese and padded over to Seregil with a loud trill. Purring raucously, she wound about his ankles, then rose on her hind feet to thrust her head against his hand.

"So there you are!" Seregil grinned, scooping the cat up. "Alec, meet Ruetha. Ruetha, this is Alec. Don't eat him in the night, he's a friend."

Dumping the heavy creature unceremoniously into Alec's arms, Seregil picked up the tray and headed back the way they'd come. Still purring, Ruetha regarded Alec with lazy green eyes. She was a handsome creature. Her silky coat was striped with black and brown except for a white ruff and feet. One ear was deeply notched; otherwise she was immaculate.

Back in the sitting room Seregil rummaged a moment in his pack, then retrieved his cloak from the mermaid and headed for the door.

"Where are you going?" Alec asked in surprise.

"There's a little matter I need to look into tonight. Make yourself at home. Here's the key to the attic door. You don't know the command words yet, so if you need to leave just use the back way. Don't go out unless you absolutely have to, though. You won't be able to get back in without me. Don't even try. You could get badly hurt. I'll probably be gone most of the night, so don't wait up. Oh, damn!"

Seregil paused, frowning. "I forgot to have them send up a bed for you. Use mine for tonight, and we'll figure out something tomorrow. Good night!"

Alec stared at the door for a moment, stunned by Seregil's abrupt and unexpected departure. For weeks they'd seldom been out of each other's sight, and now this! Left so unceremoniously by himself in unfamiliar surrounding, he felt abandoned.

He wandered aimlessly through the rooms for a while, trying to interest himself in the various oddments scattered about. This pastime only made him feel more like an interloper, however. Under different circumstances, he might have gone down to the bustling warmth of the kitchen again, but Seregil's warning about the glyphs ruled out that slight solace. The thought of lying alone in Seregil's ornate bed was equally intimidating.

The same unsettled loneliness he'd experienced at the Orëska House came flooding back all at once. Blowing out the lamps and candles, he settled morosely on the couch by the hearth. With Ruetha purring contentedly on his lap, he stared into the flames and wondered yet again what he was supposed to do with himself in this incomprehensible place.

Riding through the darkened streets, Seregil was glad he'd resisted the urge to take Scrub on the trip north. He'd gone through half a dozen mounts during his travels and it would have pained him to have lost so good an animal. Scrub's gait matched his nature: solid, dependable, and easy to get along with.

And of course, thinking about Scrub was far more comfortable than acknowledging the growing gnaw of guilt in his belly. Not only over what he was about to do in the way of disobeying Nysander, either. It took several minutes of determined riding before he was ready to face the fact that seeing Alec standing there in his own private sanctuary, he'd suddenly panicked. And fled.

It had nothing to do with Alec himself, of course. But it still wasn't a very pleasant feeling. Better to ignore it, he decided.

He made a quick circuit of several places where word might

be left for the "Rhíminee Cat" that the services of a thief were required.

The first was the Black Feather, a brothel owned by an old sailor who liked gold well enough not to ask questions. A carving of a ship stood on the mantel in the front room of his establishment; if the proprietor was holding a message for the Cat, the prow would be turned to the left. Rhiri usually collected the sealed missives, but Seregil often made the rounds to see if any signals were showing.

As he approached, a group of drunken men came boiling out roaring heartfelt farewells to their weary paramours. Through the open doorway Seregil saw that the little vessel on the mantel faced to the right. Other signals at a Heron Street tavern and a respectable inn near the Queen's Park were equally disappointing.

The wind gusted down the street, whipping his hood back to comb icy fingers through his hair. *No use putting it off any longer,* he thought. Nudging Scrub into an unhurried amble, he headed for the Temple Precinct.

Planning for the long term had never been one of his strengths and he knew it. Certainly he had a talent for gathering facts and implementing tactics; it was his bread and butter, after all. But living by inspiration, seizing the moment for good or bad as it came—that had always been his way in the end.

And what had it brought him this time?

The mysterious mark on his chest. And Alec.

Another twinge of guilt. Nysander's parting words had not been lost on him. What had possessed him to take on the boy? Alec was talented, gifted even, a delight to teach. But he'd found that out after the fact, hadn't he? The orphaned boy's need? His vulnerability? His innate skill?

His pretty face?

Straying again too near truths he didn't particularly wish to deal with, Seregil put an end to that line of thought as effortlessly as another man might snuff out a candle.

That left the scar. In the cool light of reason he didn't doubt Nysander's justification in not telling him more, although that did precious little to assuage his frustration. He'd regretted each bitter word as he'd spoken it; worse yet, the effort had been fruitless.

Oh well, there's always more than one way to pick a lock. He fingered the little roll of parchment he'd smuggled out of the Orëska House in his pack.

At the precinct, he made his way on foot between the minor temples and shrines that surrounded the heart of the district. Passing the healing grove of Dalna's temple, he came out into the huge central square. The city was quiet at this hour; chimes rang softly in the breeze somewhere in the Dalnan grove and a dove called mournfully. From across the square came the soft tinkle of water from the Astellus Temple. In the distance to his left, broad bars of firelight were visible between the black columns of the Temple of Sakor.

The paving stones of the square formed patterns of squares within squares that in turn formed a greater pattern symbolizing the eternal unity and balance of the Sacred Four. Never mind that gangs of young initiates from the various temples frequently punctuated their religious disputes with burst knuckles and cracked heads. Never mind that priests occasionally lined their own purses with gold from temple treasuries, or that the small temples of the lesser deities and foreign mystery cults had been multiplying around the edges of the precinct and around the city over the past few decades. The sacred square with its four temples still formed the heart of every Skalan city and town; even the humblest villages allotted a small square of ground to four simple shrines. Reverence for the Four, in all their complex unity, had for centuries given Skala internal harmony and power.

Crossing to Illior's white domed temple, Seregil strode up the broad stairs. In the portico he paused to remove his boots. Even at this late hour, a dozen other pairs were arranged neatly along the wall.

A girl stifled a yawn in the sleeve of her flowing white robe as she handed him a silver temple mask. Out of habit, he accepted it in such a way that her hand turned palm upward. The circular dragon emblem tattooed there was still only the black outline of the novice. Twelve colors, as well as lines of silver and gold, would be added to that design, marking each of the tests she would have to pass over the coming years in her quest for full priesthood.

"Carry the Light," she said, fighting back another yawn.

"There is no darkness," Seregil returned. Fastening on the mask, he walked into the Circle of Contemplation.

Alabaster pillars ringed the room, and between them braziers sent up the sweet, narcotic smoke of dreaming herbs. Only small amounts were burned here—just enough to free the mind for meditation. Anyone desiring prophetic dreams or spirit journeys spent several days in fasting and purification before entering the small chambers beyond the pillars. Seregil occasionally employed such methods, but recent experience had left him leery of dreams of any sort. In fact, he couldn't recall dreaming at all since waking in the Orëska House.

Other suppliants sat cross-legged on the black marble floor of the central court, anonymous behind the serene silver masks. Others lay on their backs, meditating on the various symbols painted on the dome overhead: the Mage, the Fertile Queen, the Dragon, the Cloud Eye, the Moon Bow.

Leaning over the nearest brazier, Seregil bathed his face in the smoke, then seated himself to wait for an acolyte to notice him. The floor was polished to mirror smoothness and, looking down, his gaze came to rest on the reflected image of the Cloud Eye—magic, secrets, hidden forces, roads to madness. Accepting the symbol, he meditated on it through half-lidded eyes.

Instead of the expected flow of thought, however, he suddenly experienced a dizzying sense of vertigo. The smooth black floor turned to bottomless void beneath him. The illusion was so strong that he pressed his palms to the floor on either side of him and focused on the nearest pillar to clear his head. Soft footsteps approached from behind.

"What do you seek in Illior?" the masked figure asked. His palm, exposed in greeting, showed the green, yellow, and blue detailing of a Third Chamber initiate.

"To make a thank offering," Seregil replied, rising to present a heavy purse. "And to seek knowledge in the Golden Chamber."

The acolyte accepted the purse and led him out through the pillars to an audience room at the back of the temple. With a ritual gesture, he bade Seregil be seated on the small bench in the center of the room, then withdrew.

A carved chair stood on a raised dais at the front of the room. Behind the dais an exquisite tapestry hung suspended between two great pillars, the Columns of Enlightenment and Madness. Worked in the twelve ritual colors, it depicted the Fertile Queen driving her chariot through the clouds of a night sky.

Presently a corner of the tapestry was pulled back and a robed figure stepped into the room. Despite the golden mask covering her features, Seregil recognized the mass of grey hair tumbling over the thin shoulders; this was Orphyria ä Malani, oldest of the high priests and maternal great-aunt to Queen Idrilain.

Regarding him impassively through her mask, the priestess sat down and raised one frail hand to display the completed emblem on her palm.

"Lend me your light, Blessed One," Seregil said, bowing his head.

"What would you ask of me, Seeker?"

"Knowledge pertaining to this." Drawing the little parchment roll from his pouch, he passed it to her.

On it he'd drawn, to the best of his ability, the symbol from the wooden disk. It was not complete, he knew; from the first time he'd seen the thing it had been impossible to reproduce or even memorize. But perhaps it would be enough.

Orphyria unrolled it on her knee, gazed at it briefly, then handed it back. "A sigla, obviously, but what it obscures I cannot tell. Can you tell me something of it?"

"That's not possible," Seregil replied. He had stretched his oath to Nysander far enough for now.

"Then perhaps the Oracle?"

"Thank you, Blessed One." Rising from the bench, he bowed deeply and headed back to the central chamber of the temple.

Orphyria did not rise until the Seeker had gone. It became more of an effort each day, it seemed. Soon she would have to swallow her pride and allow some young acolyte to assist her. Reflecting sourly on the price of a wise old age, she stumbled as she pulled back the tapestry and barked her knee painfully against the Pillar of Madness.

Seregil had always suspected that the stairs leading down to the Illioran Oracle's chamber had been designed to test the fortitude of the Seekers who had to descend it. Wedge-shaped steps scarcely wide enough to accommodate a man's foot spiraled tightly down into blackness below. The steps nearest the top were made of marble, but these soon gave way to speckled granite as the shaft descended into the bedrock beneath the city.

Grasping a ritual lightstone in one hand, Seregil pressed the other firmly against the curved wall of the stairwell as he made his way down in reverent silence. At the bottom a narrow corridor led off into darkness. No light burned there, and it was required that the Seeker leave the lightstone in the basket at the base of the stairs before proceeding. Before he relinquished it, however, Seregil sat down on the bottom step to arrange the necessary items for the Oracle.

Custom dictated that items for divination by the Illioran Oracle must be presented as part of a collection. The Oracle would separate the item of import without being told which it was.

Fishing through various pockets and pouches, Seregil found a harp peg, a bit of Alec's fletching, a ball of waxed twine, a bent pick he'd meant to leave on the worktable, and a small amulet. That should be enough of a challenge, he decided.

Flattening the little scroll on his knee, he scrutinized it again with another twinge of guilt. Working surreptitiously with ink and mirror, he'd made this copy of the strange design on his chest before Nysander placed the obscuration spell on it. He knew it was not exactly right, but it would have to do. Nysander's magic had left his skin unblemished to eye or touch.

With his collection in hand, he dropped the lightstone into the basket beside him and continued on down the chilly corridor.

Of all the many forms of darkness, that found underground—with no faint ray of star or distant lamp to relieve it—had always seemed to him the most complete. The blackness seemed to flow around him in tangible waves. His eyes instinctively strained for sight, aching and creating dancing sparks of false light. Underfoot, a woolen runner deadened the whisper of his cold, bare feet. The sound of his own breathing inside the mask was loud in his ears.

At last, a pale glow appeared ahead of him and he walked forward into the low chamber of the Oracle. The light came from large lightstones, which gave off no crackle or hiss. Only the voice of the seer would break the profound silence here.

Crouched on a pallet, legs drawn up beneath his stained robe, the Oracle stared blankly before him. He was a young man, husky, bearded, and quite insane, but blessed with that special strain of madness that brings bursts of insight and prophecy.

Nearby, two robed attendants sat on benches against the wall, their featureless silver masks framed by the white cowls drawn over their heads.

At Seregil's approach, the Oracle rose to his knees and began to sway from side to side, a peculiar gleam coming into his muddy eyes.

"Approach, Seeker," he commanded in a high, hoarse voice.

Kneeling before him, Seregil cast his handful of objects on the floor. The Oracle bent eagerly, muttering to himself as he sorted through them.

After a moment he tossed the pick away with a contemptuous grunt. The amulet was served in the same manner, and then the twine. Taking up the peg, he held it to his ear as if listening, then hummed a few bars of a song Seregil had composed as a child and long since forgotten. Smiling to himself, the Oracle tucked this under the edge of his pallet.

Finally he picked up the parchment scrap and the fletching, holding them in each hand as if to weigh one against the other. Twirling the bit of feather between thumb and forefinger, he stared at it closely and then handed it back, folding Seregil's fingers tightly around it with his own.

"A child of earth and light," the Oracle whispered. "Earth and light!"

"Whose child?"

The seer's mouth broadened into a sly grin. "Yours now!" he replied, tapping Seregil sharply on the chest with his finger. "Father, brother, friend, and lover! Father, brother, friend, and lover!"

The mad rhyme rang off the walls as the Oracle rocked with childish delight, chanting it over and over to himself. Then, as quickly as he had started he ceased, and his broad face grew still again. Holding the parchment between his palms, he stiffened like an epileptic. The silence closed around them, holding unbroken for a matter of minutes.

"Death." It was hardly a whisper, but the Oracle repeated it, more loudly this time. There was no mistaking it. "Death! Death, and life in death. The eater of death gives birth to monsters. Guard you well the Guardian! Guard well the Vanguard and the Shaft!"

Eyes momentarily sane, the Oracle handed it back to Seregil. "Burn this and make no more," he warned darkly, crushing it against Seregil's palm. "Obey Nysander!"

The mystical intelligence drained away as quickly as it had come, leaving the Oracle as blank as an idiot child. Creeping back to his pallet, he retrieved the harp peg from under the blanket. The sound of his contented humming followed Seregil far down the dark corridor.

As he rode back to the Cockerel, Seregil wondered dourly if he was any further ahead than before. The Oracle's mention of Alec had taken him aback, although the messages seemed clear enough, particularly the reference to earth and light. As for the little rhyme, "father" and "brother" must have been meant figuratively, for such a blood relationship was clearly impossible. But "friend," certainly.

That left lover. Seregil shifted irritably in the saddle; evidently oracles were not infallible.

Shrugging the matter off, he turned his thoughts to the troubling gibberish elicited by the drawing. How was he to heed what was so obviously a warning unless he knew what the "eater of death" was, much less guard who or whatever the Guardian, Shaft, and Vanguard were?

Under normal circumstances, Nysander would be his first recourse for advice, but that was out of the question now. Cursing in frustration, he let himself in through the kitchen at the Cockerel and went upstairs.

One lamp still burned on the mantel, but the fire had gone out. The room was frigid.

"Damn, damn, damn!" he muttered, crossing to the hearth to lay on more wood. As the flames sprang up, he discovered Alec asleep on the narrow couch behind him.

He lay curled up in a tight ball, one arm bent beneath his head, the other hanging down to the floor and pale with cold. Ruetha had tucked herself up against his belly, tail folded around her nose.

What's he doing out here? Seregil frowned down at the two of them, irked to think that Alec would be too bashful to take advantage of a proper bed. As he bent to spread his cloak over the boy, he was surprised to see the traces of dried tears on Alec's cheek.

Something to do with his father? he wondered, mystified and somewhat distressed at the thought of Alec crying.

Retiring to his own chamber, he undressed in the dark and slipped gratefully between the fresh sheets.

But sleep didn't come with its usual ease. Lying there in the darkness, Seregil rubbed absently at the hidden scar and reflected that, on the whole, his life seemed to be in greater disarray than usual.

21

SWORDS AND ETIQUETTE

Seregil stored away the mystery of the Oracle's words and launched back into Rhíminee life. News that the Rhíminee Cat had reappeared spread quickly, and intrigue jobs for various nobles—together with inquiries on Nysander's behalf—were plentiful enough to keep him out most nights.

Alec clearly resented being left behind, but Seregil was not ready to expose the boy to the dangers of the city just yet. Instead, he did his best to make it up to him during the day, showing him wonders and drilling him endlessly in the myriad skills necessary for survival in their precarious profession.

Swordplay was paramount, and they spent most mornings practicing in the upstairs sitting room, bare feet scuffing softly over the rush matting as they circled slowly, moving through the basic blocks and parries with wooden practice battens.

Unfortunately, these proved to be the most grueling lessons. Alec was old to be just starting and, hard as the boy worked, progress was discouragingly slow.

The only other subjects Seregil pursued on any regular basis were reading and lock work. Otherwise, he tended to proceed in whatever direction caught his fancy at the moment. One day they might spend several hours poring over scrolls of royal lineage or sifting through the gems in the chest from the mantelpiece, Alec wide-eyed as Seregil extolled their properties and how to value them. Another day they might traipse off in disguise to practice with a band of market acrobats who knew Seregil as Wandering Kall. Dressed in gaudy tatters and besmudged with dirt, Alec watched gleefully as Seregil juggled, walked ropes, and mugged for the crowd. Alec's own clumsy first efforts were greeted as inspired clowning.

Often they simply walked the labyrinthine streets of the city, exploring its various wards and markets. Seregil had small bundles of necessities stashed in disused attics and sheds all over Rhíminee, kept against the event that he should have to go to ground quickly.

Gradually, Seregil introduced Alec to more clandestine procedures—a little innocent housebreaking, or making a game of evading the notice of the Harbor Watch in the rough byways of the Lower City.

As the weeks passed, Alec realized that aside from certain rapidly diminishing ethical qualms, he had never been happier. The dark days in Mycena were quickly fading to uncomfortable memories and Seregil, healthy and back in his favorite setting, was once again the wry, dashing figure who'd first captured his imagination.

In spite of the odd hours they kept, Alec found it difficult not to break the habit of rising with the sun. Seregil was seldom awake that early, so he'd slip quietly downstairs to break his fast with the innkeeper's family.

The kitchen was an agreeable place at that hour. Whatever misgivings Thryis might have had about him that first night, she had soon taken to Alec and made him welcome in the group that gathered around the scrubbed oak table each morning.

Savoring the fragile peace that lingered before the onset of each day's work, Diomis, Cilla, and Thryis planned the day's meals while Cilla suckled her baby. The sight of her round, bared breast made Alec blush at first, but he soon came to regard it as one of the simple pleasures of the day.

As far as Seregil's "lessons" went, there seemed to be an inexhaustible variety of unrelated matters to master. Reading, lock work, and so forth all made sense, but his insistence on Alec's mastery of such things as etiquette was something of a surprise.

One night, after the shutters were up and the day servants dismissed, Seregil dressed them both in voluminous formal robes and took him down to the kitchen for supper.

"There's more to disguise than changing your clothing," Seregil lectured as they sat down. "You must know the manners proper to any situation, or all the decking out in the world won't carry off your ruse. Tonight we dine among the nobles at a fine villa on Silvermoon Street, attended by servants."

Cilla and Thryis bowed gravely to them from the hearth. Bluff, bearded Diomis grinned as he dandled his grandson on his knee. "Old mother here was head cook to some of the finest houses in Rhíminee before Lord Seregil stole her away. You won't find better fare at a prince's table. Mind you show appreciation though, young sir, or she's like to crack you on the pate with a ladle. It's a risky thing, I always say, eating in sight of the cook."

"Consider yourself duly warned." Seregil drew Alec's attention to the dishes. "We'll begin with the table service."

The green-glazed plates and bowls seemed thin as eggshell to Alec. Each one was lightly etched with an intricate circular design at the center. Small cups of similar design stood to the right of each plate.

"This is Ylani porcelain. Very delicate, very costly, and made only in a small town in the northern foothills near Ceshlan. Notice how translucent it is, held to the light; the green tint is in the overglaze. The simple design at the center of each piece is the traditional stylized marigold, always considered tasteful and correct. However, it also shows that your host did not spend the extra time and money to have a set made in his personal design. This could indicate several things. He is, perhaps, not as wealthy as he wishes to appear. On the other hand, he might simply be conservative or uninspired in such matters. Or it could be that he's entertaining you on his second-best service, which is another thing altogether. You'd have to investigate further to sort out which.

"The use of this porcelain does portend the sort of dinner you will have, however. Only fish is served on it, never meat. Please note that a table knife is provided in addition to a spoon; never eat with your own dagger. The wine is Mycenian, a very fine variety called Golden Smoke. This betokens shellfish of some sort, for nothing else would be served with such a wine. Send in the first course, my good woman!"

Doing her best to look grave, Cilla set a broad, shallow dish before them. In it half a dozen spherical things roughly the size of a fist sat in a few inches of water. They were a dark greenish-black and bristled with nasty spines that waved slowly about.

"This is a shell fish?" Alec asked, poking dubiously at the closest one.

"There are many types," Seregil replied. "These are urchins. Children pick the smaller varieties from the tide pools along the shore and sell them by the basketful in the markets. These larger ones are brought in by fishermen who lower traps for crabs and lobsters. Just about everyone in Rhíminee eats them; the trick is to do it the right way according to your surroundings. First, let's see how you'd do it."

Alec looked at him in disbelief. "As they are? Seregil, those things are still moving!"

Thryis snorted derisively from the hearth, but Seregil motioned her to silence. "Cooking spoils both the flavor and the texture. Go on! I wouldn't give it to you if it wasn't edible."

Still doubtful, Alec pulled the smallest urchin gingerly from the bowl by one of its spines. Halfway to his plate the spine pulled loose and he ended up juggling the prickly horror the rest of the way with both hands. Once he had the thing where he wanted it, he rolled it this way and that with his spoon, wondering how to proceed. Discovering an opening of sorts on the underside, he tried prying at it with the tip of his knife. The shell immediately crushed into fragments under the blade. Water, broken spines, and bits of soft grey and yellow matter splattered up the front of his robe.

"Excellent!" Seregil laughed, tossing him a napkin. "Whenever you present yourself as an inland noble on his first visit to the coast, do it just that way. I've never yet seen anyone get through their first urchin without smashing it to bits. Now, if you were in some local tavern, posing as a workman or farmer in for market day, you'd do it like this."

Picking an urchin out of the dish with a light, sure touch, Seregil cracked it against the edge of the table and pulled back the fragments of shell to expose the contents.

"These grey bits here are the body. You don't eat that," he

explained, scraping them out with a finger. With them came a conical ring of white fragments that looked like tiny carved birds. "And those are the teeth. It's the yellow parts you're after, the roe."

Plucking out several slender, gelatinous lobes, Seregil ate them with apparent relish.

"I got them at the docks early this morning," Cilla told him. "I made the fisherman give me a bucket of seawater and kept them down the well all day."

"Lovely flavor!" Seregil tossed the emptied shell into the fire behind him. Wiping his hands and lips with a napkin, he said, "Those are tavern manners and they'll serve well anywhere outside the Noble Quarter, provided you want to be taken for a common sort. However, we are dining in Silvermoon Street, as you recall, and here they will not do at all. Observe.

"First, the hanging sleeves of a formal robe are pushed—never rolled—halfway back to the elbow, no farther. You may place your left elbow on the table, never the right, although it's generally acceptable to rest your wrist on the edge. Food is handled with the thumb and first two fingers of each hand; fold the others under, like so. Good. Now pick up the urchin with your left hand, handling it lightly, and hold it so you can see the mouth. Now, crack the shell with a single sharp stroke of your knife. Once it's open, clean out the waste with the tip of your knife, then use your spoon to scoop out the roe. The empty shell goes on your plate. Never speak with a full mouth. If anyone addresses you, simply curve a finger in front of your lips and finish what's in your mouth before answering."

Alec managed to puncture himself badly on the spines before he mastered the art of handling the things, and his fingers kept cramping from being held back so unnaturally. The roe, when he finally managed to extract a few intact lobes, had an unpleasantly viscous texture in his mouth and it's salty sweet flavor was revolting. Relying heavily on the pale, oak-flavored wine, he managed to get two down before his stomach rebelled. Grimacing, he pushed his plate away.

"These are awful! I've found better eating under rotten logs."

"You don't care for them?" Seregil deftly split his fourth urchin. "We'll have to cultivate your tastes, I'm afraid. In Rhíminee, just about anything that comes out of the sea is considered a delicacy. Perhaps you'll find this next course more to your liking." He motioned to Cilla. "Have you ever tried octopus?"

As the weeks passed, Seregil remained frustrated by Alec's poor progress at swordplay. The situation finally came to a head during one of their morning sessions a month or so after their arrival.

"Keep your left side *back!*" he chided for the fifth time in half an hour, giving the offending shoulder a sharp poke with his wooden blade. "Stepping forward like that after you block gives your opponent twice the target. Your enemy has only to do this—" Seregil slapped Alec's blade smartly aside and feigned a cut across the boy's belly. "And there you are, holding your guts in your hands!"

Alec silently positioned himself again, but Seregil could see the tension in his stance. The boy turned his next feint clumsily, then brought his shoulder around again as he tried a counter-attack.

Before he could stop himself, Seregil parried and gave him a sharp tap across the neck. "You're dead again."

"Sorry," Alec mumbled, wiping the sweat out of his eyes.

Seregil cursed himself silently. In all the time he'd known him, this was the first time he'd seen the boy look defeated. Fighting down his own impatience, he tried again. "It's not natural to you yet, that's all. Try imagining how you'd hold yourself pulling a bow."

"You hold the bow with your left hand and draw with your right," Alec corrected. "That puts your right shoulder back."

"Oh, yes. Well, let's hope that you end up better at swordplay than I ever did at archery. Now, once again."

Alec managed to parry an overhead swing but followed it with another unsuccessful counter. Seregil's wooden blade caught him hard at the base of the throat and drew a few drops of blood.

"By the— Oh, damn!" Breaking his batten in two over his knee, Seregil tossed the pieces aside and inspected the jagged scratch on the boy's neck.

"Sorry," Alec repeated, staring over Seregil's shoulder. "I turned again."

"I'm not angry with you. As for that—" He motioned toward the fragments of the batten. "That's just to break the bad luck.

'Cursed be the weapon that tastes the blood of a friend.' Let's have a look at the rest of the damage."

Alec tugged the sweat-soaked jerkin off over his head and Seregil inspected the bruises scattered darkly over his chest, arms, and ribs.

"That's what I thought. Illior's Fingers, we're doing something wrong! You've caught on to everything else so quickly."

"I don't know," Alec sighed, dropping into a chair. "I guess I'm hopeless as a swordsman."

"Don't say that," Seregil chided. "Clean yourself up while I fetch lunch. I've an idea or two how we can help you."

Seregil returned from the kitchen with a steaming platter of tiny roasted birds stuffed with cheese and currants and some darkly mottled mushrooms that looked vile and smelled delicious.

"Clear a spot, will you?" he puffed, resting the heavy tray on the corner of the dining table.

"Thank the Maker, something that lived on dry land," Alec exclaimed hungrily, pushing books and rolls of parchment aside; Thryis had served another variety of raw shellfish the night before and he'd gone to bed hungry.

He had thrown on a clean shirt while Seregil was gone, neglecting in his haste to tuck it in or do up the lacings. The linen swirled loosely around his lean hips as he hurried to fetch cups from a shelf. His fair hair, properly trimmed at last, shone when he passed through a patch of sunlight.

Seregil caught himself staring and hastily turned his attention to the food.

"This isn't going to be another lesson in manners, is it?" Alec asked, eyeing the array of eating utensils suspiciously as he reached for one of the tiny birds.

Seregil rapped him smartly over the knuckles with a spoon. "Yes it is. Now watch."

"Why is all the food in Skala so hard to eat?" Alec groaned as Seregil demonstrated the tricky business of eating the tiny auroles without lifting them from the plate or disturbing the bones.

"I admit I've had Thryis make us some of the more difficult dishes, but if you master those, the rest will be simple," Seregil assured him with a grin. "You mustn't underestimate the importance of such customs. Say you've managed to gain admittance to some lord's house by posing as the son of an old comrade he knew in the wars. You've studied the battles, you know the names of all the pertinent generals, your accent is correct, and you're dressed perfectly. The minute you reach out of turn into the common platter, or spear a fried eel with your knife, you're under suspicion. Or imagine you're trying to pass yourself off as a sailor down in the Lower City. If you mistakenly call for a wine that would cost a month's wages, or eat your joint with fingers folded daintily back, it's highly likely you'll next be seen floating face down in the harbor."

Chastened, Alec took up his spoon again and began picking at the bird before him. "But what about my sword training?"

"Ah, yes. Well, I suspect the problem may be more me than you."

Alec eyed him skeptically. "Micum said you're one of the best swordsmen he's ever known!"

"That's the problem. With me, it's all here." Seregil tapped a finger over his heart. "Swordplay comes as naturally to me as breathing; it always did. It's all aggression and skill and intuition. So every time you drop your guard or turn your shoulder forward, I lunge in and exploit the mistake. All I've managed to do so far is make you doubt yourself. No, this is the one thing I can't teach you. That's why I've decided to send you out to Watermead."

Alec looked up sharply. "But we've hardly—"

"I know, I know!" Seregil interrupted, hoping to forestall another argument over Alec being left out of his work. "It's only for a week, and the rest of it can wait that long. I have to deliver Beka's commissioning papers anyway, so we'll ride out today."

Just then a brisk rap sounded at the door, startling Alec.

"Don't worry," said Seregil. "Anyone who can still knock after climbing my stairs is a friend. That you, Nysander?"

"Good day to you both." The scent of magic clung around the wizard as he strode in, though he was dressed in the same ordinary clothing he'd worn the day Alec had first seen him on the docks. "Ah, I see I am in time for one of Thryis' excellent meals!"

Seregil raised a questioning eyebrow. "I thought we were to meet tonight?"

"In truth, I have rather missed seeing Alec. You have been keeping him very busy. Unfortunately, that is not my only reason for coming. I should like your opinion on this."

Drawing a small scroll tube from his pocket, he handed it to Seregil. A wax seal still dangled from one of the ribbons tied around it.

"It's one of mine," Seregil remarked in surprise, examining the seal. His look of puzzlement deepened as he extracted a sheet of creamy vellum from the tube and glanced over it. "This is a note I wrote to Baron Lycenias last spring, thanking him for a week's hunting at his estate. You sent me there yourself, remember? That business about Lady Northil."

"I suggest you read it over carefully."

"Let's see; the crest is in order, and it's dated the third day of Lithion. That should be right. 'My Dear Lycenias í Marron, allow me to again proffer my heartfelt thanks for a most enjoyable—' Yes, yes, the usual rubbish; fine hunting, laudable companionship, what a—"

He broke off with an incredulous laugh. "Bilairy's Balls, Nysander! It appears I'm thanking him for several nights of *carnal* pleasure, as well. As if I'd take on that reeking tub of guts!"

"Keep reading; it gets worse."

Seregil read on, eyes flashing indignantly, but an instant later he went pale. Carrying the letter to the window, he inspected it closely, then reread it.

"What's wrong?" Alec demanded.

"This isn't good." Seregil tugged at a stray strand of hair as he studied the note. "For all intents and purposes, this is my handwriting, right down to the great flourish connecting the final word of the letter to my signature—which I always do to prevent exactly what has somehow happened here."

"Someone's changed what it says?"

"They certainly have. 'Regarding Tarin Dhial, you may rest assured of my complete support.' No, this isn't good at all!"

"I don't understand. What's wrong?" Alec said, turning to Nysander.

"Tarin Dhial is an encrypted form of the name of a Plenimaran spy caught buying information from several Skalan nobles," Nysander explained. "They were all executed as traitors two months ago."

"Argragil and Mortain," said Seregil, nodding thoughtfully.

"Both guests of Lycenias that same week I was there. I had no idea what they were up to at the time! I suppose you've checked this for magic?"

"Not a trace. Unless you can prove forgery, this could be most damaging."

"But how did you come into possession of it?"

"It was sent anonymously to Lord Barien this morning."

"The *Vicegerent*?"

"Oh, yes. Fortunately I have several Watchers among his staff. One of them recognized your seal and waylaid the document before it was seen. There may be other copies, however. I shudder to contemplate the colossal scandal that could arise should one of these fall into the wrong hands. Such embarrassment for the Queen is unthinkable, a perfect coup for the Lerans!"

Unnoticed by the others, Alec looked up sharply at this last comment, then stole a quick glance at Seregil's face. Certain suspicions he'd been nursing for some time were beginning to take clearer shape.

"There are only three forgers capable of this quality," Seregil mused. "Fortunately, two of them are right here in the city. It shouldn't take long to find out if they're involved. I've already tried to tie them into the Vardarus business with no success. Still, for something as large as this, I can't imagine the Lerans going too far afield. They're better organized than usual but probably still fiercely insular. That's always been their undoing in the past."

"I shall leave it to you for the time being," said Nysander, standing to go. "Keep me closely informed and if things should turn ugly, depend on me to remove you from harm's way. Farewell, Alec."

"If things turn ugly for me, then you'll have problems of your own!" Seregil warned, accompanying him to the door.

"Seregil? Is all this because you're Aurënfaie?" Alec blurted out suddenly.

Thunderstruck, Seregil turned to stare at him. "Where did you hear that?"

"You mean after all this time you *still* had not told him?" exclaimed Nysander, equally shocked.

"Then it's true?" Alec was grinning now.

"Actually, I was waiting for him to figure it out for himself," Seregil countered, shifting uncomfortably under Nysander's displeased gaze. "Well done, Alec. I'm just surprised it took you so long."

"Indeed?" Nysander said, giving him a last dark look. "Then the two of you have *much* to discuss. I shall leave you to it. Farewell!"

Returning to the table, Seregil sank his head in his hands. "Really, Alec. Of all the moments to choose!"

"I'm sorry," Alec said, coloring hotly. "It just came out."

"Who told you? Thryis? Cilla? Someone at the Orëska?"

"I figured it out myself, just now," Alec admitted. "It's the only explanation that makes sense. The way your friends speak of you, all the stories—after a while I began to wonder how someone so young could have done so much. I mean, looking at you I'd say you were no more than twenty-five, but Micum's older than that and he spoke once of meeting you when he was a young man, so you must be a lot older than you look. Once I figured that out, then things you'd told me or refused to tell me came back and I started wondering even more. Like why half the books here are written in Aurënfaie—"

"How in the world did you know that?"

"Nysander showed me some Aurënfaie writing while we were staying at the Orëska House. I can't read it, but I recognize the characters. I've had plenty of time to poke around, you know, all these nights you've been gone."

"Very enterprising of you," said Seregil, wincing a bit as the barb struck home. "But why didn't you ask earlier?"

"I still wasn't sure until Nysander said it would be a terrible scandal if the Lerans could make you out to be a traitor. Micum and Nysander both said you're related to the Queen. The best thing for the Lerans would be if a relative of the Queen who is also a friend to her daughter, former apprentice to her favorite wizard, and an Aurënfaie was caught selling information to the Plenimarans."

Alec hesitated. "You're not angry, are you? I'm sorry I just blurted it out like that in front of Nysander but suddenly it was all—"

"Angry?" Seregil laughed, raising his head at last. "Alec, you constantly exceed my highest expectations!"

"Except at swordplay."

"But we've settled that. Go on now. Pack whatever you think you'll want." Jumping up, Seregil headed for his room. "I've got an extra saddle somewhere. And be sure to take your bow. Beka's quite an archer herself."

"You're not still sending me away?" exclaimed Alec, crest-fallen.

"And why wouldn't I?"

"With everything Nysander just told you? How can we just ride off like that with you in trouble?"

"I can be back in town by tomorrow evening."

"So you're getting me out of the way!"

Going to Alec, Seregil clasped him gently by the back of the neck and looked earnestly into his eyes. "This is dangerous work. How can I concentrate on the task at hand if I'm constantly worrying about losing you down some dark alley during a chase? I won't feel right taking you along until I think you have some way of protecting yourself. That's why it's so important for you to learn to use your sword. Go to Micum; learn from him. He can teach you more in a week than I could in half a year, I promise."

"You never thought I was so helpless before we got to Rhíminee," Alec grumbled, trying to pull away.

Seregil tightened his grip slightly, holding him in place. "Oh, you're anything but helpless, my friend. We both know that." Releasing him, he added, "But trust me when I tell you that you haven't yet seen the Rhíminee I know."

"But what about the Lerans? Can you leave with all that going on?"

"That letter was delivered this morning, so it will be at least a day or two before they begin to guess that it's missing. Even then, I doubt they'll act right away."

"Why not? If they have another copy they could just deliver it to someone else."

"They won't do anything until they learn what happened to the first copy, and that's not going to happen until *I'm* ready to let them," Seregil assured him with a grim smile. "Now go get packed. The day's half over already and we still have to buy you a horse!"

22

ONE HORSE, TWO SWANS, AND THREE DAUGHTERS

The livestock marketplace lay just outside the city walls by the Harvest Market gate. Mounted on a borrowed horse, Alec looked around eagerly as they rode among the horse traders' enclosures there.

"That's who we want," Seregil said, pointing out a woman in a dusty riding kirtle and boots. At the moment she was engaged in a heated discussion with several of her fellows beside one of the corrals. Dismounting, Seregil led Scrub over and joined the circle of conversation. The trader nodded to him and hooked a thumb at a large wooden building a few hundred yards away.

"Damn fool thing to do," she grumbled. "Look at my poor beauties, what it does to them!"

"The new Butcher's Hall, you mean?" asked Seregil, wrinkling his nose. A faint breeze carried the sickly sweet smell of the place and the cries of ravens and gulls fighting over the piles of discarded entrails in the pits beyond the slaughterhouse.

Leaning on the upper rail of the corral, the horse trader watched her horses stamping nervously as they scented the wind. "We've petitioned before to have a market of our own, farther away from the damned butchers, but the Council can't be bothered with us, it seems! Cows, pigs, sheep; they're too dim to mind the smell of blood if they was swimming in it. But my poor beauties there— look at 'em! How am I supposed to show you a steady beast when they've all got that stench up their noses?"

"Petition the Queen's Court directly," Seregil advised. "Idrilain understands horses a good deal better than the fat merchants on the Council of Streets and Markets."

One of the other traders nodded. "Aye, that's not a bad idea."

"You and I, Mistress Byrn, we've done enough business for me to trust the quality of your beasts." Seregil pointed to Alec, who was already scrutinizing the herd. "I think my friend here favors them, too. Let's have a closer look."

With a pleased nod, the trader tucked the hem of her woolen skirt up into her belt and climbed over the rail.

Seregil waded into the herd beside her, rubbing necks and rumps and crooning softly to them. Following in his wake, Alec marveled at how the animals seemed to calm under his hand. Other horses crowded up to their mistress.

"They're just a pack of great colts, as you see," she said, grinning at Alec over their backs. "Northern stock mostly, with a few drops of 'faie mixed in here and there. They're strong and they're smart. I doubt you'd find better between here and Cirna."

Alec wandered among the shifting herd, trying to sort out those that showed the best natures and conformations from those he only liked the looks of. He was just reaching out to stroke a pale sorrel filly when a shove from behind nearly knocked him off his feet. A dark nose pushed under his arm and he found a brown mare nipping at his belt pouch.

"You, Patch!" the horse dealer shouted. "Get out of that, you hussy!"

The mare, a plain-looking beast, looked longingly back at Alec as she sidled away. Despite her unremarkable appearance, he was taken with the disdainful set of her ears. He put a hand out to her and she butted him under the arm again, nuzzling at his belt.

"It's the leather she's after," the dealer confessed. "Crazy for it as others are for apples. She's a losel with the tack, I'll warn you."

"All the same, she's not half bad," Seregil remarked, coming over to see.

Running a critical eye over joints and hocks, Alec noticed an irregular spot of white hair the size of a child's hand just behind her right flank.

"How did she come by this scar?" he asked.

The woman smoothed a hand fondly over the mark. "Wolves got into my enclosure last winter. Killed three foals before we got out with the torches. One tore at her here, as you see, before she brained it with a kick. She's a feisty one, my Patch, and stubborn, but she has a smooth, strong gait and she'll go all day for you. Saddle her, young sir, and see what you think."

A gallop across the open ground around the marketplace was enough to win Alec over. The mare showed no skittishness, and took the reins well.

"That's settled, then," Seregil said approvingly as he paid out the money.

Moving his saddle and pack onto Patch, Alec slung his bow over one shoulder and followed Seregil onto the Cirna highroad.

Several miles out from the city they turned onto a road leading up into the hills. Seregil seemed to be in no particular hurry and they rode easily, giving the horses their head and enjoying the crisp, clear afternoon.

Winter was beginning to take hold in Skala now, though the breeze still carried the stinging scent of smokehouse meats, yellowed hay, and the last sour tang of the cider presses from the farmsteads they passed along the way.

They'd ridden for some time in comfortable silence when Seregil turned to Alec and asked, "I suppose you're wondering why I didn't tell you sooner?"

"You never say much about yourself," Alec replied with a touch of reproach. "I've gotten used to not asking."

"Delicate manners will get you nowhere with me," Seregil advised, nonplused. "Go on, ask away."

"All right. Why didn't you tell me sooner?"

"Well, at first it was because you had so many misconceptions about the 'faie," replied Seregil. "You seemed to think we were all great mages or nectar-sipping fairy folk."

Alec's cheek went hot as he recalled the childish fancies he'd shared with Seregil in their first days.

Seregil shot him a sidelong grin. "Oh, you northern barbarians do have some strange notions. Anyway, I decided I'd better let you get used to me first. Then I got sick."

He paused, looking a little sheepish himself. "I've been mean-ing to tell you since we got to the city, really, but— I don't know. The right moment just didn't seem to come. What I said to Nysander is sort of true; I am proud of you for figuring it out on your own. What else would you like to know?"

What wouldn't I like to know! thought Alec, wondering how long this strange humor of Seregil's would last. "How old are you?"

"Fifty-eight, come Lenthin month. In the reckoning of my race, that doesn't make me all that much older than you, though I've certainly had more experience. It's difficult to draw compari-sons between Aurënfaie and human ages; we mature differently. Under Aurënfaie law, I'm not old enough yet to marry or hold land." He chuckled softly. "For the most part, I've done very well for myself in Skala."

"Because you're related to the Queen?"

"To some degree, though it's a very distant and threadbare tie. Just enough to have gotten me an introduction and a place as a high-class servant. Lord Corruth, consort to Idrilain the First, was a cousin of my grandmother's mother. My claim to Skalan nobility is a tenuous one at best."

Alec'd had hints enough from both Micum and Nysander to know better than to ask Seregil why he'd left Aurënen in the first place. "What's it like there, in Aurënen?"

Seregil rode on in silence for a moment, his face half turned away. Alec feared he'd taken a misstep after all and was about to take back the question when Seregil began to sing.

The language was unfamiliar, yet so liquid, so graceful in the ear that it seemed Alec could almost grasp it—and that if he did it would reveal a depth of meaning his own language could never achieve. The melody, simple yet haunting and full of longing, brought tears to his eyes as he listened.

Seregil sang it a second time, translating so that Alec could understand.

> *"My love is wrapped in a cloak of flowing green*
> > *and wears the moon for a crown.*
> *And all around has chains of flowing silver.*
> > *Her mirrors reflect the sky.*
> *O, to roam your flowing cloak of green*
> > *under the light of the ever-crowning moon.*

Will I ever drink of your chains of flowing silver
and drift once more across your mirrors of the sky?"

Looking out across the empty winter fields, Seregil said in a husky whisper, "That's what Aurënen is like."

"I'm sorry." Alec shook his head sadly. "It must be painful, thinking about your own country when you're so far away."

Seregil shrugged slightly. *"Yri nala molkrat vy pri nala estin."*

"Aurënfaie?"

"An old proverb. 'Even sour wine is better than no wine at all.' "

Afternoon shadows were creeping down the hills as Seregil turned from the highroad and led the way onto a stone bridge over a large stream. A flock of swans grazing in the bordering field took flight at their approach, rising into the air with a great beating of wings.

Unslinging his bow with surprising speed, Alec brought down two of the great birds and nudged Patch into a canter to retrieve them.

"Well shot!" Seregil called after him, turning his horse loose to drink. "Just yesterday I was wondering if you were out of practice."

Alec rode back with the birds slung from his saddlebow. "Me, too," he said, dismounting to let Patch drink. "At least I won't come in empty-handed. Are we almost there?"

Seregil pointed up the valley. "That's Watermead. We'll have missed supper but I'm sure Kari won't send us to bed hungry."

A few miles above them they could see open meadows and a cluster of buildings nestled against the edge of the mountain forest. Below the main house flocks of sheep wandered like clouds across the face of the hills. Darker herds moved across some of the other meadows.

Alec squinted at the distant house, wondering what his reception would be.

"Don't worry. You'll be part of the family in no time." Seregil reassured him.

"How many of them are there again?"

"Three girls. Beka's the oldest. She'll be eighteen in Lithion,

I think. You'll spend a good deal of time this week looking down her sword. Elsbet's fourteen and has the makings of a scholar. I expect she'll be entering the school at the Illior Temple soon. The youngest girl is Illia, just six years old and already the mistress of the whole estate."

"I hope Micum's wife doesn't mind having me underfoot," Alec said, still feeling shy.

"Kari?" Seregil laughed. "By now Micum's told her all about the poor orphan boy I've dragged south. I'll be lucky to get you back! As for being underfoot, I doubt there'll be much time for that."

Seregil whistled and Scrub splashed up from the stream. Patch, however, had waded out into the middle and seemed content to remain there despite any urging from Alec. Whistle and call as he might, the mare staunchly ignored him. Giving up at last, he stood scowling on the bank.

"Dark looks won't do it," Seregil chuckled. "I think you're going to have to get your feet wet."

"I'll wet more than that," Alec grumbled, looking at the brownish slime that coated the rocks of the streambed. Suddenly, however he broke into a grin. Taking an archer's tab from his purse, he held the bit of leather out and called, "Hey you, Patch!"

The mare's head came up at once, ears forward. Snuffling loudly, she came close enough to nip at it and Alec snagged her by the head stall.

"You'll spoil that beast," Seregil cautioned, splitting an apple for his own horse. "Teach her to come at your whistle, or you'll have to buy a tannery to keep her."

When they reached the summit of the hill they found the gate of the wooden palisade that surrounded the main house open to them. A pack of enormous hounds bounded out of the shadows as they entered the walled yard, growling suspiciously until they caught Seregil's familiar scent. He dismounted and one of them, a grey-muzzled old male, rose on his hind legs and rested his paws on his shoulders, looking him in the eye. Others milled happily around Alec, slapping him with their plumed tails and sniffing hopefully at the swans hanging at his saddlebow.

"Hello, Dash!" Seregil rubbed the hound's head affectionately before pushing him off. Wading through the pack, he led the way to the door.

• • •

Kari was the first to see them as they entered the main hall. The tables had been pushed back against the walls for the night, and she and her women sat spinning around the central fire. Meeting her eyes across the room, Seregil caught a fleeting glimpse of the old apprehension: *No, it's too soon, we've only just gotten him back.*

That look had given him a degree of satisfaction in the early days, before the rivalry between them had mellowed into friendship. Now it saddened him a little that his sudden appearance still evoked the same flash of resentful alarm.

Before he could reassure her, however, a bundle of dark braids and flying skirts streaked from the direction of the kitchen. Dropping his saddlebags, he scooped Illia up and received a resounding kiss on the cheek.

"Uncle! Look, Mother, Uncle has come after all!" she cried, kissing him again. "But you can't take Father away with you, you know. He's promised to take me riding tomorrow."

Seregil looked down the length of his nose at her. "Now, that's a fine welcome."

"Illia, where are your manners?" Kari laid her distaff aside. She was dark like her daughter, with a gentle oval face that belied her brisk manner. "Seregil hasn't ridden all this way just to have you hang on him like a burr."

Undeterred, Illia peered over Seregil's shoulder at Alec. "Is this the brave boy who saved Father from the bandits?"

"It is indeed," Seregil answered, pulling Alec forward with his free hand. "Alec's the best archer in the whole entire world, and he shot two enormous swans on the way here especially for your mother. They're outside on his saddle if your dogs haven't eaten them already. He's come to learn sword fighting from your father and Beka, but I'm certain he'll be a fine playfellow for you, in between lessons. You may have him for a week if you promise not to maul him to death. What do you say to that?"

Looking over at Kari, Seregil answered her look of relief with a wink.

"Oh, he's handsome!" Illia exclaimed, climbing down to take Alec's hand. "You're almost as handsome as Uncle Seregil. Can you sing and play the harp like he does?"

"Well, I can sing," Alec admitted as the little girl hauled him toward the hearth.

"Let the poor boy catch his breath before you take at him," her mother chided. "Run out to the stable and fetch your father and sisters. Scat!"

With a last beaming smile for Alec, Illia dashed off.

"Come and sit down by the fire, both of you," Kari said, motioning for her women to make room. "Arna, find some dinner for our friends, and see that a fire's laid in the guest chamber."

The eldest serving woman nodded and disappeared out a side door; the other women retired to a smaller fire at the back of the hall. Turning to Alec, Kari took his hands in hers.

"You're welcome in our home, Alec of Kerry," she said warmly. "Micum told us about the ambush in Folcwine Wood. I owe you a great deal."

"He's done as much for me," Alec replied, feeling awkward. Just then, however, Micum burst in with Illia on one shoulder and an older girl in tow. In his woolen breeches and leather vest he looked every inch the country squire.

"Well, this is a happy surprise!" he cried. "The little jackdaw here says Alec's looking for a real swordsman."

Swinging Illia down, he clasped hands with the two of them. "Beka will be in as soon as she cleans up. One of her mares had a bad foaling this afternoon." Drawing the older girl to his side, he said, "And this quiet one here is Elsbet, the family beauty."

Elsbet touched Alec's hand in a quick greeting. Dark hair framed a face very like her mother's, soft and gentle.

"Welcome to Watermead," she murmured, her hand trembling against his for an instant. Blushing to match Alec, she hastily sat down by her mother.

"You must be thirsty after your ride," Kari said, giving Seregil a mischievous look. "If I know you, you talked the whole way. Would you dare sample this season's beer? For once I think it's almost fit to drink."

Micum nudged Alec playfully as she went out. "This is the first season since we came south that I've seen her satisfied with her beer. Mind you, she's the finest brewer in the valley, but she's never left off saying that northern hops give a finer taste."

"I think I've heard her mention it a few times," Seregil

concurred wryly. "Illia, do you think you could fetch my saddle-bags there by the door?"

The little girl's eyes went round. "Presents?"

"Who knows?" he teased. "But here's Beka at last."

A tall girl in a stained tunic and breeches burst in, her face lit by an expectant smile.

"Any news, Seregil?" she cried, stooping to hug him.

"Patience, Beka. At least say hello to Alec first."

Of all the girls, Beka alone had taken after her father. Freckles peppered her fair skin, and an unkempt mare's tail of coppery red hair tumbled over her shoulder as she leaned forward to clasp hands with Alec. She had rather too much of her father's features to be beautiful, but her sharp blue eyes and ready smile would never let her be called homely either.

"Father says you're quite an archer," she said, looking him over in friendly appraisal. "I hope you brought that bow of yours. I've never seen a Black Radly."

"It's there by the door," Alec replied, suddenly more at ease than he'd been since their arrival.

"Here they are!" Illia puffed, dragging the saddlebags over to Seregil. "Did you remember what I asked you for?"

"Illia, you beggar!" her mother scolded, returning with a pitcher and mugs.

"Why don't you reach in and see what's there while I try your mother's excellent beer?" Seregil suggested, taking a long sip. "Sheer delight, Kari. Better than that served at the royal table of Mycena."

Alec sampled his own and didn't doubt Seregil's sincerity, though Kari obviously did.

"Well, it's better than last year's," she allowed.

Illia, meanwhile, had worried open the first bag. "These must be for Beka," she said, pulling out a pair of glossy cavalry boots. "She's going to be a horse guard."

"A rider in the Queen's Horse Guard," Beka corrected, looking hopefully at Seregil.

Micum shook his head in mock despair. "We haven't had a moment's peace since she heard you were back."

Seregil drew a scroll case from his coat and presented it to her. Prying off the seal, she shook out the papers inside and scanned quickly down through them, her grin broadening by the second.

"I knew you could do it!" she cried, giving Seregil another exuberant hug. "Look, Mother, I'm to report in a week's time!"

"There's not a finer regiment," Kari said, slipping an arm about Beka's shoulders. "And think how much quieter it will be without you crashing in and out!"

As Beka sat down to try on the new boots, Micum reached to take his wife's hand; her smile did not match the sudden misting of her eyes.

"She's your daughter, right enough," Kari sighed, clasping his hand tightly.

Illia burrowed deeper, finding a tobacco pouch for Micum and a larger bag for her mother.

"Oh, Seregil, you needn't have—" Kari began, then broke off as she pulled out a handful of papery hop cones and a knot of wizened roots.

"Cavish hops!" she cried, holding the cones to her nose. "This brings my father's hop yard back to me as if I were standing in it! All the cuttings I brought with me here died out years ago. Oh, Seregil, how good of you to think of it. Someday perhaps I'll be able to brew a proper beer again."

Seregil saluted her with his cup. "I want to be the first to broach a keg of the batch that pleases you."

Rescuing a finely bound book from Illia's impatient pillaging, he handed it to Elsbet.

"The dialogs of Tassis!" the girl breathed, examining the cover. Any trace of shyness fled as she opened the volume and ran a finger down the first page. "And in Aurënfaie! Where did you ever find it?"

"I'd rather not say. But if you look toward the middle, I think you'll find something else of interest."

Elsbet's eyes widened as she drew out a small square of parchment and read Nysander's invitation to visit at her earliest convenience.

"Someone must have mentioned your interest in the Orëska library to him," Seregil said, affecting innocence.

Torn between terror and delight, Elsbet stammered, "I wouldn't know what to say to him."

"He's pretty easy to talk to," Alec told her. "After a few minutes you feel as if you've known him all your life."

Elsbet returned to her book, blushing more hotly than ever.

"Uncle!" Illia rocked back on her heels with an indignant look. "There's nothing else in here!"

"And my lady supposes herself forgotten! Give me your kerchief and climb up in Alec's lap. Don't be shy—he has lovely young ladies sitting on his lap all the time. You're quite used to it, aren't you, Alec?"

Alec gave Seregil a dark look over the top of Illia's head, not appreciating the gibe.

"Now," said Seregil, pinching the corners of the kerchief together and holding it up, "what was it you asked for last time I was here?"

"Something magic," Illia whispered, dark eyes fastened on the kerchief.

Making a great show of incantations and gestures, Seregil handed it back to her. She unfolded it to find a small ivory carving on a chain.

"What does it do?" she asked, hanging it about her neck at once. Before Seregil could reply, however, a swallow fluttered in through the smoke hole and lit on Illia's knee. Blinking in the firelight, the little bird began to preen.

"It's a drysian charm," Seregil told her as she reached out to stroke its shiny blue wing. "You must be very gentle with the birds it brings to you and never use it for hunting. Study them as much as you like, but put the charm away when you're finished so that they can fly away."

"I promise," Illia said solemnly. "Thank you, Uncle."

"And now it's time for your swallow to fly off in search of its supper," said her mother fondly, "and for you, my little bird, to fly off to your bed."

With a final kiss for Seregil, Illia went out with her mother. Elsbet retired to a quieter corner with the new book.

"Alec, I bet Beka would like a look at that black bow of yours, before it gets too dark," Micum suggested. "Get her to show you her horses in return."

"I've got some beauties," Beka said proudly as he fetched his bow and quiver. "Pure Aurënfaie blood, and some mixed. You'll have to try them out while you're here."

Micum turned to Seregil and raised an eyebrow when they'd gone. "He's just the thing to occupy her while she waits to report. But what am I supposed to teach him that you couldn't yourself?"

Seregil shrugged. "You know me. I have no patience with beginners. Can he ride in with you and Beka at the end of the week?"

"Of course," Micum said, sensing something in the wind. "Something going on back in Rhíminee?"

Seregil pulled out the damning letter Nysander had intercepted. "Seems Lord Seregil has run afoul of the Lerans at last. I've got a forger to track down."

Micum quickly scanned the letter. "Does Alec know?"

"Yes, and he's none too happy about being put out of the way. Keep him occupied and make a swordsman of him for me. It's the only thing holding him back. By the Light, Micum, you've never seen such a sponge for learning. It's all I can do to keep ahead of him!"

"He puts me a great deal in mind of you at that age."

"I could do worse, then. Now, assuming this week goes well, I'd like to arrange a little something special for him when he gets back."

"Smooth his feathers, eh?" Micum asked with a knowing look. "What did you have in mind?"

"I think you'll settle in quite well here," Seregil said with a yawn as he and Alec settled down for the night in the broad guest chamber bed.

Alec watched the play of the firelight across the whitewashed walls of the little room, arms crossed beneath his head. "Do you think Micum will really have better luck teaching me?"

"Would I have brought you all the way out here if I didn't?"

"And what if you're wrong?"

"I'm not."

Alec fell quiet, but Seregil sensed something was still worrying him.

"Go on, speak out."

Alec sighed. "I still feel like you're getting me out of your way."

"I am. But only for the week, just as I told you."

Rising on one elbow, he looked down at Alec. "Listen to me now. I may make my living lying and tricking, but I'm always honest with friends. There'll be times I choose not to tell you something, but I won't lie to you. That's a promise and there's my hand on it."

Alec clasped it sheepishly, then settled back against the bolsters. "What are you going to do when you get back?"

"I'll check with Nysander first, see if his sources have found anything else. Then there's Ghemella, a gem cutter in Dog Street, who's known to do a tidy little side business in forged seals."

"How will you get her to talk?"

"Oh, I'll manage something."

23

A LITTLE NIGHT WORK

Seregil woke well before dawn the next morning. Alec had gravitated to the far edge in the night, and lay now curled in his usual tight ball, one arm sticking stiffly over the side, fingers half curled. Resisting a wayward impulse to touch the tousled mass of yellow hair scattered over the pillow, Seregil dressed in the hall and set off for the city at a gallop.

He reached Nysander's tower rooms before noon and found the wizard at work with Thero over a scroll.

"Any new developments?" asked Seregil.

"Not as yet," replied Nysander. "As we expected, they were wise enough not to send more than one of the forgeries at a time. I think we may still have a bit of leeway before their next attempt."

"Then this is all I have to work with." Seregil pulled the forged parchment from his coat again and fingered the wax seals on the ribbons. "These have to be Ghemella's work. I don't know anyone else capable of this quality. Look at this."

Taking his own seal stamp from a pouch, he held it next to the wax imprints; they were indistinguishable. He'd designed the original himself: a griffin seated in profile, wings extended, one forepaw upraised to support a crescent. The forger had caught every nuance of the design, as well as several tiny imperfections Seregil had specified in the original to make such a forgery easier to catch.

"She knew very well whose seal it is, too," he added wryly. "Lord Seregil has had a number of over-the-counter dealings with her."

"There's no chance these were somehow struck with the original?" asked Thero, examining the seal. "I seem to recall you breaking into noble houses to steal impressions."

"Which is why I make a point of not letting my own seal out of my possession," Seregil replied curtly, tucking it away.

"You will look into this yourself, I trust?" said Nysander.

"Oh, yes indeed."

"Very well. In the meantime, I must ask you to leave the letter with me."

Surprised, Seregil met the old wizard's level gaze for a moment, then handed the document over without comment.

Ghemella's first thought was to ignore the hesitant rapping at the door. The gold had just reached the proper color for pouring, and if she left off now she'd have to start all over again. The shop door was shut and the shutters put up; any fool could see she'd closed for the night.

Reaching into the forge with her long tongs, she gently lifted the crucible from its ring over the coals. The troublesome knock came again just as she bent to pour it into the mold. It disrupted her concentration, and a few precious droplets spilled uselessly onto the sand packing the wax form. She set the crucible back on its iron stand with a hiss of exasperation.

"I've closed!" she called, but the rapping only intensified. Heaving her great bulk up from the stool, the jeweler lumbered to the small window and cautiously cracked a shutter. "Who is it?"

"It's Dakus, mistress."

A hunched old man shuffled into the slice of light from the window, leaning heavily on a stout stick. His crippled back kept him from raising his face to the light, but Ghemella recognized the gnarled hand clamped over the head of the stick. Like most craftsmen, she always noticed hands. A wave of revulsion rippled over her slack flesh as she unbarred the door and stepped back to admit the dry little grasshopper of a man.

Against the rich backdrop of the shop he was more hideous than she recalled. Pointed spurs of bone sprouted from his knuckles, wrists, and the prominent bones of his ravaged face, looking as if they would burst through the taut yellow skin at a touch.

Hobbling toward the warmth of the forge, he settled himself on the stool and turned his one good eye to her. It had always offended her sensibilities, the way that bright, clear eye glittered in such a face, like a precious Borian sapphire glittering up from a clod of dung.

"So many pretty things!" the old relic wheezed, fingering a half-finished statuette on the workbench. "You're looking prosperous as ever, dearie mine."

Ghemella kept her distance. "What are you selling tonight, old man?"

"What would I have to sell to such a rich woman?" replied Dakus, giving her the ruins of a leer. "What except the occasional bit of information that these old ears glean as I beg at the back doors and waste heaps of the more fortunate? Are you still in the market for secrets, Ghemella? Fresh, shiny secrets? I've offered them to no one else as yet."

Slapping a few sesters down on the bench in front of him, she stepped back and folded her arms across her broad leather apron.

The old man pulled a copper vial from his pouch. "Baron Dynaril has murdered his lover with poison bought from Black Rogus. His manservant made the purchase at the Two Stallions a week ago."

Ghemella produced a gold coin for this and Dakus placed the vial on the workbench.

"Lady Sinril is with child by her groom."

The jeweler snorted and shook her head.

Nodding agreeably, Dakus reached into his tattered tunic and produced a sheaf of documents. "And then there's these gleanings of a poor beggar's wanderings. More to your taste, I think."

"Ah, Dakus!" the jeweler purred, taking the sheets eagerly and sorting through them. The pages differed in size and quality and several were wrinkled or stained. "Lord Bytrin, yes, and Lady Korin. No, this is worthless, worthless, perhaps this—and this!"

Choosing out seven documents, she set them apart. "I'll give five gold sesters for these."

"Done, and the blessings of the Four be showered on you for your generosity!" cackled the beggar. Sweeping up the small pile of coins and rejected papers, he shuffled out into the night without a backward glance.

Ghemella barred the door after him and allowed herself a sly smile. Nudging aside the stool Dakus had sullied with his deformed backside, she drew up another and settled down to peruse the stolen papers more closely.

Meanwhile, the crippled beggar hobbled down Dog Street and into the deeper shadow of a deserted alleyway. When he'd made certain that no one else lurked there, he pulled a flat clay amulet from around his neck and knocked it against the wall until it shattered. A wrenching spasm gripped the frail old body for an instant as the magic drained away, leaving Seregil young and whole again.

Retching dryly, he rested his hands on his knees and waited for the accompanying wave of nausea to pass. A number of major magicks had this residual effect to one degree or another, just one more delightful side effect of his baffling magical dysfunction.

Straightening at last, he felt for the reassuring smoothness of his face and limbs, then took out a shielded lightstone and shuffled through the papers Ghemella had rejected.

He'd provided a tempting selection: documents, personal correspondence, declarations of illicit love, all from various influential persons. Most were old, things he'd picked up on various nocturnal excursions. Salted through these, however, were three half-finished letters from the pen of Lord Seregil. Knowing the method of his would-be detractors, he'd taken care to make them suitably ambiguous. Ghemella had taken all three.

Smiling darkly, Seregil headed back to the jeweler's shop to begin his patient vigil.

24

WATERMEAD

Alec slid his blade away from Beka's and jumped back, leaving her off balance. For the first time in half an hour, he managed to get past her defense and score a touch.

"That's right! Hold her, hold her!" Micum cried. "Now pull back the way I showed you. Just right. Again now!"

It had been snowing heavily since early morning, so they'd cleared the hall for a practice area. Alec had made good progress over the last three days and neither he nor Micum wanted to chance losing ground.

Kari had been patient about it all, merely insisting that the tables be moved to protect the tapestries. She and Elsbet had then retired to the kitchen for the morning, but Illia remained perched beside her father, cheering gleefully every time Alec bested her sister. It hadn't happened often so far.

Beka rubbed her side with a rueful grin. "You're improving, all right. I think Seregil will be pleased."

Her face was flushed under its freckles and her eyes sparkled with the same gleam Alec had seen in Micum's and Seregil's during mock battles. She looked older with her hair braided back, and the close-fitting jerkin showed the gentle swell of her breasts more than the shapeless tunics she usually wore.

As she raised her sword again, he found himself so distracted by the deadly grace with which she moved that her sudden over-hand swing took him completely off guard and cost him a new bruise on his shoulder.

"Damn, I did it again!" Grimacing, he assumed a more wary stance.

"Concentration," Micum advised. "Watch your opponent, look wide, see everything. A flick of the eye, a change in balance, the way she holds her mouth, anything that can tell you what she's thinking of doing next. And don't tense up; it makes you slow."

Trying to keep all this in mind, Alec worked backward, draw-ing Beka, making her follow him. The bound wire grip of the hilt felt warm and familiar against his palm as he executed a respect-able attack of his own. Catching her blade in the curve of one quillon, he twisted hard and almost succeeded in disarming her.

"Hooray for Alec!" Illia crowed, clapping her hands in delight as her champion pressed his advantage.

Beka knew that trick, however, and quickly taught him one of her own. Hooking his ankle with her foot, she pulled one leg out from under him. Alec fell heavily backward as his sword spun away across the flagstones.

Beka pinned him none too gently with a foot on his chest and rested the tip of her blade lightly against his throat. "Cry mercy!"

"Mercy!" Alec dropped his hands in submission. When she released him, however, he grasped her other ankle and brought her tumbling down beside him. Leaping astride her, he pulled the black dagger from his boot and rested the flat of it against her throat.

"Cry mercy yourself," he gloated.

"You cheated!" sputtered Beka.

"So did you."

"Seregil *will* be pleased!" Micum groaned, shaking his head.

"It sounds like someone's slinging anvils around out here!" Kari laughed, striding in with an armload of trenchers. "The pack of you go find somewhere else to make your racket. I've got a meal to get on."

Servant and laborers quickly filled the hall for the midday meal. Stamping snow from their feet, they pulled out the tables and soon everyone was seated over a hot meal.

Micum spent most of the meal planning a new saw pit with the reeve. It did not escape his notice, however, that Alec and Beka had their heads together in some discussion of their own. Judging by the evident disinterest of Elsbet, who sat on Alec's other side, the subject probably revolved around swordplay or archer's tack.

Kari leaned close, following her husband's eye. "You don't suppose she's falling in love, do you?" she whispered.

"With a commission to the Queen's Horse in her pocket?" Micum chuckled. "Our Beka's too hardheaded for that."

"Still—he's a good lad."

"Don't give up hope," Micum teased. "He's too wild for Elsbet's taste, but Illia would have him in a minute. She says so at least twice a day."

Kari gave her husband a good-natured nudge in the ribs. "Get on with you! The last thing I need in this family is another man with wandering feet. And if Seregil's taken this boy up, you can bet your head he's got them."

Micum hugged her close. "You'd be the best judge of that, my patient love."

At the meal's end, Micum pushed back from the table. "I should be getting over to Lord Quineas' soon. I promised him a game of nine stones the other day. You'll come with me, won't you, Kari? You haven't seen Lady Madrina in weeks."

"Me, too! Me, too!" Illia shouted, jumping into her father's arms. "I want to show Naria the charm Uncle Seregil brought."

"Well, let's just take the whole bunch of you, then," Micum cried, swinging the little girl into the air.

Beka exchanged a glance with Alec. "We were going to hunt along the river trail."

"She doesn't want to see Ranik," Illia taunted.

"Let him fawn over Elsbet for a change," Beka shot back. "She's the one who thinks he's such a fine gentleman."

"And he is," Elsbet retorted primly. "He's a scholar, *and* a poet as well. Just because he isn't always out shooting at things the way you are—"

"That's a lucky thing for the neighborhood," Beka scoffed. "That donkey-handed looby couldn't shoot a bull in the arse if it was standing on his foot. Come on, Alec. You can ride Windrunner again."

• • •

Horses nickered expectantly as Alec and Beka entered the stable. Going to Windrunner, he heaved the blanket and saddle over the chestnut stallion's glossy back. He felt a bit guilty when Patch craned her neck over the stall at him; still, the chance at an Aurënfaie mount was something he wasn't about to turn down.

"There's something special I want to show you," Beka said, giving him a mysterious look as she buckled her horse's saddle girth.

Setting out across country, they gave their mounts free rein. Plumes of new snow trailed after them as they galloped and wheeled over the bare fields. Alec tried to explain the maneuvers he'd seen Captain Myrhini's riders perform and they dashed back and forth, yelling and tilting their bows for lances.

"I can hardly believe it!" Beka cried, reining in beside him. "In a few days I'll be with them."

"Won't you miss your family?" ventured Alec. His short stay at Watermead had shown him a life he'd never known. It was a noisy, bustling household with servants, dogs, and Illia underfoot much of the day but, like the Cockerel, there was an air of warmth and security about it that he liked.

Beka looked away over the hills, watching the last of the ragged clouds scudding across the sky.

"Of course," she said, heading her mare toward the river. "But I can't stay here forever, can I? I'm not cut out to be like Mother, raising a family and waiting around for a man who goes off for months at a time. *I* want to be the one who's gone. I should think you'd understand that."

Alec smiled. "I was just thinking how nice your life must have been, being in one place all the time. Still, I know what you mean. My father and I wandered around in the same forests my whole life. Then along comes Seregil with his tales of far-off places, wonders I could hardly imagine—I guess I didn't take much convincing."

"You're lucky, being with him the way you are," Beka said with a trace of envy. "He and Father—all they've done together? Someday I want to ride with them, but first I need to make my own way. That's why I wanted so badly to join the Queen's Horse."

They rode for a moment in silence, then Beka asked, "What is it like, anyway, being with him?"

"You'd like it. It's never the same from one day to the next. I don't think there's anything he doesn't know at least something about. And then there's Nysander. I've tried telling Elsbet about him, but it's hard to explain how someone can be so powerful and so ordinary at the same time."

"I've met him. Do you know it was he who first suggested I join the Guards? Then he laughed and made me promise never to tell Mother he said so. Isn't that odd?"

Alec thought he could see what the old wizard had been up to; Beka would make a fine Watcher.

The swans had abandoned the frozen stream. Turning upstream, they rode a mile or more without seeing any sign of game. Giving up the hunt, they challenged each other at clout and wand shooting. Beka's grey-and-white fletched shafts seldom came closer to the mark than his red ones.

"Come on," she said at last, noticing how low the sun had fallen, "we'd better gather our arrows. I want to show you my surprise."

Following the stream again, they reached the wooded hills and rode into the trees. At a bend they dismounted and Beka led the way to a broad, half-frozen pool. Signing for Alec to keep quiet, she settled behind a fallen tree and pointed across to the other side.

Two otters were playing in the open water. Paddling to shore, they humped up the snowy slope and launched themselves back down again, sliding merrily on their smooth bellies into the water. Clucking and grunting all the while, they repeated the performance over and over while Alec and Beka watched in silent delight.

"They remind me of Seregil," Alec whispered, propping an elbow on the tree trunk. "Nysander turned him into an otter once when we were at the Orëska House. There's this special spell—I can't remember what he called it—but Nysander says the kind of animal you turn into has something to do with what kind of person you are."

"An otter, eh?" said Beka, considering the matter. "I would've taken him more for a lynx or a panther. Did he do it to you, too?"

"I turned into a stag."

"I guess I can see that. What do you suppose I'd be?"

Alec considered the matter. "A hawk, I bet, or maybe a wolf. A hunter, anyway."

"Hawk or wolf, eh? I'd like that," she murmured.

They watched the otters in silence, each one savoring the sense of companionship that had grown up so easily between them.

"Well, come on, we'd better get back," Beka whispered at last. As they headed back to the horses, she turned to him and asked, "You're fond of him, aren't you?"

"Who? Seregil?"

"Of course."

"He's been a good friend," he replied, puzzled by the question. "Why wouldn't I be fond of him?"

"Oh." Beka nodded as if she'd expected a different answer, then, "I thought maybe you were lovers."

"What?" Alec stopped dead, staring at her. "What put *that* in your head?"

"I don't know," Beka bristled. "Sakor's Flames, Alec, why not? He was in love with Father once, you know."

"With Micum?" Alec leaned against a slender alder. The tree swayed under his weight, sifting snow over the two of them. It dusted Beka's hair with a veil of sparkling crystals and filtered down the neck of Alec's tunic to melt into points of coldness against his skin.

"How do you know that?" he demanded, flabbergasted.

"Mother told me ages ago. I'd heard things growing up and finally I asked. It was pretty one-sided, according to her. Father was already in love with her when he and Seregil met, but Seregil didn't give up for a while. He and Mother didn't care much for one another in those days because of it, but they're friends now. She won out, and he had to accept it. Still, I remember once when I was very young, hearing Mother and Father arguing. Father said something like, 'Don't make me choose, I can't do it!' Mother told me that it was Seregil he was talking about. So I guess he loves Seregil, too, in his own way, but they were never lovers."

Alec chewed over this unexpected revelation; the more he learned of southern ways, the more incomprehensible they seemed.

• • •

Watching the girls trying to teach Alec a country dance in the hall one snowy afternoon toward the end of the week, Micum realized he was going to miss the boy when he was gone.

Just as Seregil had predicted, Alec had settled in well with his family and already seemed a part of it. Kari's heart had gone out to him at once, and the girls treated him like a brother. He'd picked up swordplay damn fast, too, without Seregil's impatient jousting to contend with.

Kari stole up behind Micum and clasped her arms around his waist as she watched the progress of the dance lesson. The steps were complex and there was a lot of good-humored chaffing as Alec jostled to and fro between Beka and Elsbet.

"I wish I'd given you such a son," she whispered.

"Don't let Beka hear you say that!" Micum chuckled.

Kari was doing her end-of-the-week mending by the kitchen window when Alec wandered in with his bow.

"Do you have any beeswax?" he asked.

"It's there on that shelf by the herbs," she said, pointing with her needle. "There are some clean rags over there if you need them. Why don't you put the water on to heat and sit with me awhile. You go home tomorrow and I haven't had you to myself all week."

Alec swung the kettle hook into the fireplace and sat down on a stool beside her, bow across his knees.

"It's good having you here," she said, her needle flashing in the sunlight as she stitched up a tear in one of Illia's kirtles. "I hope you'll come back to us often. Seregil doesn't come out as much as we'd like. Perhaps you can influence him for me."

"I don't think anyone influences him very much," Alec said dubiously, then added, "You've known him a long time, haven't you?"

"More than twenty years," Kari replied. "He's part of the family."

Alec rubbed wax into his bowstring and smoothed it over with his fingers. "Has he changed much since you first met him? Being Aurënfaie and all, I mean."

Kari smiled, thinking back. "It was before we'd married that

I first met Seregil. Micum came and went as he pleased, just like now, but always alone. Then one fine spring morning he showed up at my father's door with Seregil in tow. I remember seeing him that first time, standing there in the kitchen door, and thinking to myself, 'That's one of the most beautiful men I've ever seen, and he doesn't like the looks of me one bit!' "

Kari took up a new piece of mending. "We got off to a rather rough start, Seregil and I."

"Beka told me."

"I thought she might have. How mature he seemed to me then. I was only fifteen. And now look at me." She smoothed a hand over her hair, where scattered strands of silver were mingled with the dark. "A matron and mother of three girls, and Beka older than I was then. Now he looks so young to me, still the handsome boy. In the reckoning of his own people he *is* young and will be long after I've been tilled into these fields."

She looked pensively down at the vest on her lap. "I think it troubles him, to see Micum getting older, knowing sooner or later he must lose him. Lose us all, I suppose, except perhaps Nysander."

"I never thought of that."

"Oh, yes. He's lost friends already that way. But you asked me how he's changed. He has, but more in his manner than in his looks. There was a bitterness in him back then that I seldom see anymore, though he's still a bit wild. He's been a good friend to us, though, and brought Micum safely back to me more times than I can say."

She left unsaid the fact that more often than not it was Seregil who had led her husband into danger in the first place. This boy was cut from the same cloth as they, and Beka, too, to her mother's sorrow. What could you do but love them and hope for the best?

25

RETURN TO RHÍMINEE

Alec rose before dawn his last morning at Watermead, but found that Beka was up before him. Dressed for riding, she sat mending a broken catch pin on her bow case in the hall. Beside her lay a few small packs containing all she would take with her to the Guard barracks.

"You look ready to go," he said, setting his pack down next to hers.

"I hope so." She worked an awl through a stubborn piece of leather. "I hardly slept last night, I was so excited!"

"I wonder if we'll see much of each other in the city. Where we live isn't too far from the palace grounds."

"I hope so," replied Beka, inspecting the new catch. "I've only been in Rhíminee a few times. I'll bet you could show me all kinds of secret places."

"I guess I could," Alec said with a grin, realizing how much of the city had become familiar to him since his arrival.

The rest of the family soon appeared and they settled down to their last breakfast around the fire.

"Can't Alec stay a little longer?" begged Illia, hugging him tightly. "Beka still beats him a lot. Tell Uncle Seregil he needs more lessons!"

"If he can beat your sister just some of the time, then he's a pretty fair swordsman," said Micum. "You remember what your Uncle Seregil said, little bird. He needs Alec back."

"I'll come back soon," Alec promised, tweaking one of her dark braids. "You and Elsbet haven't finished teaching me to dance yet."

Illia cuddled closer, giggling. "You *are* still awfully clumsy."

"Guess I'll go check on the horses," Beka said, setting her breakfast aside half eaten. "Don't dawdle, Alec. I want to get on the road."

"You've got the whole day ahead of you. Let him eat," chided her mother.

Beka's restlessness was infectious, however, and Alec hurried through his porridge. Shouldering his pack and bow, he carried them out into the courtyard only to find that Beka had put his saddle on Windrunner. Patch shifted resentfully behind the Aurënfaie horse, tethered on a lead rein.

"What's this?" he asked. Turning, he saw the others beaming at him.

Kari stepped up and kissed him soundly. "Our gift to you, Alec. Come back to us whenever you can, and keep an eye on this girl of mine in the city!"

"You'll see me at the Sakor Festival," Beka said gruffly, embracing her. "That's just over a month away."

Kari pressed a handful of Beka's wild, coppery hair to her cheek. "As long as you remember whose daughter you are, I know you'll be fine."

"I can't wait to join you there," exclaimed Elsbet. "Write as soon as you can!"

"I doubt barracks life will be much like what you'll get at the temple school," Beka said with a laugh. Swinging up into the saddle, she gave a final wave and followed Alec and her father out through the palisade gate.

They reached the city just after midday. It was Poulterer's Day in the outer market, and every sort of fowl—from auroles to peacocks, quail to geese, live or plucked—were on display. Each poultry dealer had a bright pole standard mounted over his wares and these, together with the usual strolling vendors of sweetmeats and trifles, gave the market a festive look despite the low-

ering sky overhead. Drifts of multicolored feathers blew in the
breeze as the three travelers rode through the honking, cackling,
twittering din.

Alec smiled quietly to himself, recalling his fears the first
time he'd entered Rhíminee. This was his home now; he'd
learned some of its secrets already and would soon know more.
Gazing about, he suddenly caught sight of a familiar face in the
market crowd.

Same protuberant teeth, sly grin, and moldy finery. It was
Tym, the young thief who'd cut his purse at the Sea Market. Taking advantage of the slowed traffic by the Harvest Gate, he'd
latched on to a well-dressed young man, evidently cozening him
with the same tricks he'd used on Alec. A girl in a tattered pink
gown clung to the mark's other arm, aiding in the distraction.

I owe him a bit of trouble, thought Alec. Dismounting, he
tossed his reins to Beka.

"Where are you going?" she asked.

"Just saw an old friend," he replied with a dark grin. "I'll be
right back."

He'd already learned enough from Seregil to approach the
thieves unnoticed. Biding his time, he waited until they'd lifted
the unwitting victim's purse, then came up behind them and
grasped Tym's arm. His triumph was short-lived, however, and it
was Micum's recent training that saved him.

Newly honed instincts read the thief's sudden movement just
in time. Alec caught at his wrist, halting the point of Tym's dagger scant inches from his own belly.

Tym's eyes narrowed dangerously as he tried to jerk free; easy
enough to read the message there. The girl stepped in to screen
her compatriot's knife hand and Alec prayed that she wasn't
ready with a blade of her own. In the press of the crowd, she
could easily stab him and disappear before anyone was the wiser.
She made no attack, but Alec felt Tym tensing.

"We have a mutual friend, you and I," Alec said quietly. "He
wouldn't be very pleased if you killed me."

"Who's that?" Tym spat back, still pulling against Alec's
grasp.

"It's a trick, love," the girl cautioned. She was scarcely older
than Elsbet. "Do 'im and move on."

"Shut up, you!" Tym growled, still glaring at Alec. "I asked
you a question. Who's this friend of ours?"

"A comely, openhanded fellow from over the sea," Alec replied. "Handy with a sword in the shadows."

Tym glared an instant longer, then grudgingly relaxed his stance. Alec released his wrist.

"He should've told you never to grab a brother from behind like that unless you mean to deal with him!" Tym hissed, yanking the girl to his side. "If you'd done that in a back alley, I'd have you lying dead right now." Sparing Alec a final scornful look, he and the girl disappeared into the crowd.

"Did you catch your friend?" Beka inquired when Alec reappeared.

"Just for a moment." Alec mounted and wrapped the reins around his hand. It was still trembling a little.

From the market they turned south to the barracks gate of the Queen's Park, where Beka showed her commissioning papers to the guards. Giving her father and Alec a final farewell embrace, she rode in without a backward glance.

Micum watched through the gateway until she was out of sight, then heaved a deep sigh as he turned his horse back toward the Harvest Market. "Well, there she goes at last."

"Are you worried about her?" asked Alec.

"I wouldn't have been, a year ago when there wasn't a war brewing for spring. Now I don't see any way around it, and you can bet the Queen's Horse will be some of the first into the fray. That doesn't leave her much time to get used to things. No more than five or six months, maybe less."

"Look how far I've come with Seregil in a few months," Alec pointed out hopefully as they headed for the Cockerel. "And he had to start from practically nothing with me. Beka's already as good with a bow and sword as anyone I've seen, and she rides like she was born on horseback."

"That's true enough," Micum admitted. "Sakor favors the bold."

In Blue Fish Street, they slipped in through the Cockerel's back gate and went through the lading-room door and up the stairs with hoods well drawn up. Micum took the lead on the hidden stairs, speaking the keying words for the glyphs with the same absent ease as Seregil.

Following him in the darkness, it occurred to Alec that Micum, too, had come and gone here freely over the years, always certain of welcome. Everything Alec had learned of the friendship between these two seemed to come together and spin itself into a long history in which he had only the most fleeting foothold.

Reaching the final door, they stepped into the cluttered brightness of the sitting room. A crackling fire cast a mellow glow over the chamber. The place seemed more disordered than usual, if that was possible. Clothing of all sorts hung over chairs and lay piled in corners; plates, papers, and scraps of wizened fruit rind cluttered every available surface. Alec spotted a mug he'd left on the dining table a week ago still standing undisturbed, as if to anchor his right of presence until his return. A fresh litter of metal fragments, wood chips, and scattered tools ringed the forge on the workbench beneath the window.

The only clear spot left in the room was the corner containing Alec's bed. A suit of fine clothes had been neatly laid out there, and against the pillow was propped a large placard with the words *Welcome Home, Sir Alec!* written on it in flowing purple letters.

"Looks like he's been busy!" Micum remarked, eyeing the mess. "Seregil, are you in?"

"Hello?" A sleepy voice came from somewhere beyond the couch.

Stepping around, Alec and Micum found him sprawled in a nest of cushions, books, and scrolls with the cat on his chest.

Seregil stretched lazily. "I see you left each other in one piece. How did it go?"

Grinning broadly, Micum settled on the couch. "Just fine, once I managed to undo all your wrongheaded teaching. You may get a few surprises next time you cross blades."

"Well done, Alec!" Pushing the cat aside, Seregil stood up and stretched again. "I knew you'd get the hang of things. And not a moment too soon, either. I may have a job for you tonight."

"A Rhíminee Cat job?" Alec ventured hopefully.

"Of course. What do you think, Micum? It's just an over-the-sill-and-out-again sort of thing in Wheel Street."

"I don't see why not. He's not ready to storm the Palace yet, but he should be able to look out for himself on something like that if he doesn't attract too much attention."

Seregil ruffled Alec's hair playfully. "Then it's settled. The job's yours. I guess you'd better have this."

With a dramatic wave of his hand, Seregil produced a small, silk-wrapped parcel and presented it to Alec.

It was heavy. Unwrapping it, Alec found a tool roll identical to the one Seregil always carried. Opening it, he ran his fingers over the ornately carved handles: picks, wires, hooks, a tiny lightwand. On the inner flap of the roll a small crescent of Illior was stamped in dull silver.

"I thought it was about time you had one of your own," said Seregil, clearly pleased with Alec's speechless delight.

Alec glanced back at the forge. "You made these yourself?"

"Well, it's not the sort of thing you see in the market. You'll be needing a new history, too. I've been giving it some thought."

Micum nodded toward the placard. "Sir Alec?"

"Of Ivywell, no less." Seregil dropped Alec a slight bow before collapsing into the couch opposite Micum. "He's Mycenian."

Alec went to the bed and looked more closely at the clothing.

"So Lord Seregil will be returning to the city in time to prepare for the Festival of Sakor, as usual?" observed Micum. "And not alone this time?"

Seregil nodded. "I bring young Sir Alec, only child and last surviving heir of Sir Gareth of Ivywell, a genteel but impoverished Mycenian baron. In hopes of giving his scion a chance in life, Sir Gareth has left his son ward to an old and trusted friend, Lord Seregil of Rhíminee."

"No wonder he died poor," Micum threw in wryly. "Sir Gareth seems to have been a man of questionable judgment."

Ignoring this, Seregil confined his attention to Alec. "By situating the now defunct and completely fictitious estate of Ivywell in the most remote region of Mycena, we kill several birds at a shot. Any unusual mannerisms you might display will be put down to your provincial upbringing. There's also less chance that anyone will expect to know a common acquaintance. Thus Sir Alec's background is at once suitably genteel and safely obscure."

"The fact that he's neither Skalan nor Aurënfaie would make him a tempting target for any Leran hoping to get at Lord Seregil," added Micum.

"A jilt!" said Alec.

"A what?" laughed Seregil.

"A jilt, the bait," he explained. "If you want to trap something big, like a bear or mountain cat, you stake out a kid and wait for your beast to show up."

"All right, then. You'd be our jilt. If any bears do show up, just be your sweet, innocent self, feed them everything we want them to know, and report everything they say back to me."

"But how would they get to me?" asked Alec.

"That won't be difficult. Lord Seregil's a social sort. His house in the Noble Quarter has already been opened and word's getting around. I'm sure the news will reach the right ears sooner or later. In a few days we'll throw a big party to introduce you to society."

Micum favored his friend with an affectionate grin. "You scheming bastard! So what else did you get up to while we were gone?"

"Well, it's taken until today, but I think I've found our forger. You recall Master Alben?"

"That blackmailing apothecary you burgled a few years back during that business for Lady Mina?"

"That's the one. He's moved his shop to Hind Street since then."

"How'd you find him?"

"I was pretty certain Ghemella was our seal forger. Since she also buys stolen papers, I planted some of mine with her and last night she led me straight to him. It's only a matter now of finding his cache to see if there's anything useful to be had. If he is the one who forged the letter from me, then my guess is he's probably made a copy or two for himself just to hedge his bets. And if we can get our hands on those we can squeeze him for names."

"Is that the job tonight?" asked Alec, an eager gleam in his eye. "The sooner we clear your name, the better."

Seregil smiled. "Your concern for my tattered honor is deeply appreciated, Sir Alec, but we'll need another day or so to prepare for that one. Don't fret, now. Everything's under control. In the meantime, however, I think you'll find tonight's little exercise worthy of your new skills."

Wheel Street, a quiet, respectable boulevard of modest back garden villas, lay on the fringe of the Noble Quarter. Well dressed so as to attract no attention, Alec strolled along beside

Seregil and Micum just after dark—three gentlemen out enjoying the night air.

The narrow houses were decorated Skalan style with mosaics and carvings. The ground level of some had been converted into shops; in the dimness Alec made out the signs of a tailor, a hat maker, and a gem dealer. The street ended in a small circular court in front of a public stable. Riders and carriages bustled in all directions; the sounds of entertainment could be heard here and there as they walked past.

"That's ours, the one with the grapevine pattern over the door," whispered Seregil, indicating a brightly lit house across the way. "Belongs to a minor lord with some connection to shipping. No family, three servants: the old manservant, a cook, and the maid."

Several horses were tethered in front and they could hear the noise of pipes and fiddles being tuned.

"Sounds like he's having a party," whispered Micum. "Suppose he's engaged extra servants for the evening?"

"Those can be the worst sort, forever bumbling into places the regular staff can be counted on not to go," Seregil warned Alec. "And guests, too! Keep your ears open and remember, all we're after is a correspondence case. In and out, nothing fancy. According to my information, he keeps the case in a desk in his study, that room there at the left corner of the second floor, overlooking the street."

More carriages rumbled by, destined for houses up and down the cobbled street. "It's too busy out here," said Alec. "Is there a back way in?"

Seregil nodded. "The house backs onto a walled garden, and a common beyond. This way."

Crossing the street a few houses down, they went through a narrow alley into the little common. Such areas had been left open throughout the city to assure pasturage in time of siege. At the moment it was occupied by a flock of sleeping geese and a few pigs.

Creeping softly along, they counted gates until they found the one leading into the back garden of the house in question. The wall was high, the gate stoutly barred from within.

"Looks like you'll have to climb," Seregil whispered, squinting up. "Be careful going over; most of these places have the walls topped with spikes or sharp flints."

"Hold on!" Alec tried to make out Seregil's expression through the darkness. "Aren't you two coming with me?"

"It's a one-man job; the fewer the better," Seregil assured him. "I thought this is what you wanted, a first trial on your own?"

"Well, I—"

"Would I send you in alone if I didn't think you could handle it?" Seregil scoffed. "Of course not! Best leave me your sword, though."

"What?" Alec hissed. "I thought I had to be armed so I could *do* jobs!"

"Generally speaking, yes. But not this time."

"What if someone sees me?"

"Honestly, Alec! You can't just go hacking your way out of every difficult situation that arises. It's uncivilized," Seregil replied sternly. "This is a gentleman's house; you're dressed as a gentleman. If anyone catches you, just act chagrined and drunk, then claim to have stumbled into the wrong house."

Feeling a good deal less confident all of a sudden, Alec unbuckled his sword and started up the garden wall. He was halfway to the top when Micum called softly, "We'll meet you back here when you've finished. Oh, and look out for the dogs."

"Dogs?" Alec dropped down again. "What dogs? You didn't say anything about dogs!"

Seregil tapped himself sharply between the eyes. "Illior's Fingers, what *am* I thinking of tonight? There's a pair of Zengati hounds, snow-white and big as bears."

"That's a fine detail to forget," growled Micum.

"Here, let me show you what to do." Taking Alec's left hand, Seregil folded down all the fingers except the index and fourth, then turned the palm downward.

"There. All you have to do is look the dog in the eye, make the sign by snapping the little finger down—like this—and say 'Peace, friend hound' as you do it."

"I've seen you do that trick. That's not what you said," Alec remarked, repeating the hand sign.

"*Soora thasáli,* you mean? Well, you can say it in Aurënfaie if you like. I just thought it might be easier for you to remember in your own language."

"Peace, friend hound," Alec repeated, performing the hand sign. "Anything else I should know?"

"Let's see, the spikes, the dogs, the servants— No, I think we covered it that time. Luck in the shadows, Alec."

"And to you," Alec muttered, starting up the wall again.

The top of the wall was indeed set with spikes and thick shards of broken crockery. Clinging to the edge of the wall, he pulled his cloak up from behind and wadded it up on top of the sharp points in front of him. Hooking an elbow over the thick material, he tugged the cloak strings loose from his neck.

The garden below appeared to be empty, though muffled sounds of the familiar kitchen variety issued from a half-open door at the back of the house. Hitching himself swiftly over the top of the wall, Alec lowered himself by his fingertips and dropped down the other side.

The garden centered on an oval pool. Graveled walkways showed pale in the darkness between planting beds and leafless trees. An especially large tree growing close to the carved balcony running the length of the second story looked to provide the easiest way in.

The shadows closed in around Alec as he stole toward the tree. He moved silently, careful to avoid the gravel paths. He was in reach of the trunk when something large stirred just beside him. Hot, wet jaws closed firmly on his right arm, just above the elbow.

The white hound might not have been quite as large as a bear, but Alec was not about to argue the point. The beast did not growl or tear at him, but held him fast, regarding him with eyes that shone yellow in the dimness.

Fighting down the impulse to struggle or cry out, Alec quickly made the left-handed sign and croaked, "*Soora*, friend hound."

Not seeming to mind the mixed translation, the dog obliged immediately, padding off into the darkness without a backward glance. Alec was up the tree and reaching for the marble balustrade almost before he realized he was moving again.

Dry leaves had collected in little piles on the balcony. Stepping over these, he inspected the two windows that flanked an ornate door leading into the house; the door was locked, the darkened windows covered with heavy shutters.

With a silent nod to Illior, he set to work on the door. Sliding a wire along the edge, he found three separate locks. Moving on to the larger window, he found two equally stubborn mechanisms there. The third window, scarcely large enough to admit a child, was secured with a single shutter.

During a lesson on housebreaking, Seregil had once remarked that the way least likely was often least barred. Alec pulled a thin strip of limewood from the roll and worked it around the edges of the shutter. In less than a minute he found the two hooks securing it. These yielded readily and the shutter swung back to expose a small panel of leaded glass. The room beyond was quite dark.

Praying that any occupant would have set up an alarm by now, he went to work with the wire again and threw the single hasp lock with no difficulty at all. The pane swung in on silence. Slipping the tools back into his coat, Alec pulled himself up by the window frame and wriggled in feet first. Lowering himself into the room, his foot struck something that overturned with a clatter.

He dropped in with his back to the wall and listened for an outcry; none came. Groping in the darkness, he pulled out the lightstone.

An overturned washstand lay on the floor beside him. *Thank the gods for carpets!* he thought wryly, righting it and replacing the basin and pitcher.

The spacious bedchamber was plainly furnished by Rhíminee standards. A broad bed with hangings of translucent silk took up much of one end of the room. A dressing gown draped carelessly across the foot and a thick book propped open against the bolsters, together with the remains of a fire on the marble hearth, all warned of recent occupation.

There were several tall wardrobes and chests against the other walls. A gaming table stood next to the single deep armchair drawn up before the fireplace. Thick, patterned carpet gave underfoot as Alec moved across to an interior door. Finding it unlocked, he pocketed the light and took a cautious peek through.

A corridor ran the length of this level, with several other doors on each side. Halfway down the right-hand wall was a staircase leading down. Light came up from below, and with it music and the sounds of lively conversation.

Alec stepped out into the corridor and closed the door of the bedroom behind him. Picturing the location of the study, he moved quickly down the corridor to a pair of doors at the far end. The one in question was secured with a complicated lock.

Feeling nervous and exposed, Alec tried one pick and then another. Twirling a third in, he closed his eyes and explored the wards by feel.

The master of the house evidently set great value on privacy; like those on the windows, this was no common device. The endless lessons at Seregil's workbench paid off, however. The lock gave and he was in.

A writing desk and chair stood between two tall windows overlooking the street. A glance outside found the avenue busier than ever. Pulling the drapes shut, Alec took out the lightstone and sat down to begin his search.

A few items lay arranged in orderly fashion on the polished desktop: ink wells, a bundle of uncut quills, and a sand shaker stood ready on a silver tray beside a tidy stack of parchments. Next to these was an empty dispatch box. Finding nothing of note, he moved on to the drawers.

The wide central drawer was flanked by two narrow ones. The central one was locked but yielded readily. Inside were packets of correspondence tied up with silk cord, a stick of sealing wax, a sand brush, and a penknife.

The left drawer was lined with silk and contained four locks of hair. Each had been carefully tied up with ribbon and one, a thick curl of raven black, was adorned with a jeweled pin. Reaching over these tokens, Alec found a velvet pouch containing a thick golden ring and a small ivory carving of a nude man.

The third drawer held a more mundane collection—used blotting paper, wax tablets, styluses, a tangled skein of twine, a litter of gaming stones—but nothing resembling a correspondence case. Going to the door, Alec checked the corridor again and then continued with his task.

Pulling out all three drawers, he lined them up and discovered the narrow ones to be a full hand's-breadth shorter than the central.

The desk was a casework piece, enclosed on the bottom as well as the sides. Peering in, he saw that the cavity for the central drawer ran to the back of the desk, separated from the side drawers by thin wooden dividers on either side. These also ran the depth of the desk. Small leather-faced blocks were fixed to the bottom of the cavity to keep the drawer flush with the front skirt when closed. Similar stop blocks were in the side drawer tracks, but there was a difference. Just behind these, the cavities ended in wooden panels that sealed off whatever space lay beyond. In-experienced he might be, but the whole costly, overly compli-cated structure of the piece seemed to promise at least one secret compartment.

Sliding his arm into each of the three spaces, Alec pressed and tapped with no success. As he sat back in exasperation, won-dering what Seregil would do, his gaze wandered to the dispatch box. A memory leapt to mind; Seregil toying with a similar box during their burglary in Wolde, finding a secret mechanism.

Running his hands slowly over every surface of the desk, he finally located a tiny lever concealed next to the right front leg. When he shifted it, however, nothing seemed to happen, not even a telltale click. Perspiration beaded his upper lip as he knelt and inspected the interior of the desk again.

This time he noticed something he'd missed before. The un-finished wood on the bottom of the central drawer track showed the parallel wear marks that one might expect to find; these he'd seen. But halfway in, toward the center of the panel, a faint, curving scuff could just be made out, arcing from a point mid-way between the two more pronounced marks and terminating abruptly at the right-hand divider. Looking closer, he realized that there was also the tiniest hairline gap between the lower edge of the partition and the bottom of the desk. If not for that arcing scratch, he might have passed it off as nothing more than the re-sult of the wood shrinking in the dry winter air, causing a joint to pull apart.

He pressed the hidden lever again, at the same time pushing firmly against the edge of the partition closest to him. Pivoting on unseen pins, the partition swung into the central opening and out over Alec's lap, revealing a small triangular compartment at-tached to the far end. Grinning in silent triumph, Alec lifted out a leather folder and heard the muffled crackle of parchment. Cramming it into the front of his coat, he quickly put everything else back the way he'd found it.

Back in the corridor, he locked the study door again for thor-oughness' sake. No sooner had the last ward fallen into place, however, when he heard footsteps on the staircase behind him. There was no time to unlock the door or retreat to the bedchamber at the far end of the hall; the light of a candle was brightening rapidly toward the head of the stairs.

In desperation, Alec tried the door of the room next to the

study; the handle turned smoothly under his hand. Ducking inside, he put his eye to the crack of the door.

Two women had just reached the top of the stairs. One carried a candelabra and by its light he could see that both were expensively dressed and quite beautiful.

"He said to look on the second shelf to the right of the door, a thick folio bound in green and gold," the younger one said, peering around the hallway.

"This is a lucky night indeed, Ysmay," remarked her companion. "One so seldom has a chance to visit his library. But which room is it? It's been so long since I was last up here."

Jewels winked in the dark coils of the young woman's hair as she turned Alec's way. More jewels sparkled in the intricate necklace that covered her chest. In fact, Alec saw, the necklace was very nearly the only thing covering her breasts. The bosom of the dress was cut so low the top of one nipple peeped out from the fretwork of gems and gold.

"I must thank you again, dear aunt, for bringing me tonight!" the girl exclaimed. "I nearly swooned when you presented me to him. I can still feel his lips on my hand."

"A fact I pray your esteemed father never learns," her aunt replied with a low, musical laugh. "I felt just the same the first time I met him. He's one of the most charming men in Rhíminee, and so handsome! But take care, my dear. No woman has ever held his fancy for long, or man either. But now for that excellent manuscript. Which room is it?"

"This one, I think," replied the girl, making straight for the room where Alec was hiding. He pressed back against the wall behind the door, hoping for the best.

"La, this isn't it," the aunt exclaimed as the candles illuminated a bedchamber similar to the one at the back of the house.

"Is it *his* room?" breathed Ysmay, stepping toward the bed.

"I shouldn't think so. See that painted chest there? Mycenian work. Not his sort of thing at all. Come, my dear, I think I have my bearings now."

As soon as the women had disappeared into a room down the corridor, Alec bolted silently for the first bedchamber. Not daring to chance the lightstone again, he found the dim outline of the little window and made for it.

He hadn't gone three paces when a large, callused hand

clamped over his mouth. Another seized his right arm, pinning it behind his back as he twisted and struggled.

"Hold him!" a voice hissed from somewhere across the room.

"Got him!" a deep voice rasped next to Alec's ear. The hand across his mouth clamped tighter. "Not a sound, you. And quit yer wigglin'!"

A lightstone appeared and his captor swung him roughly about to face it. Alec gave another convulsive twist, then froze with a strangled grunt of astonishment.

Standing there, one arm propped on the corner of the mantel, was Seregil. At his waved command, the man holding Alec released him and he spun to find himself facing Micum Cavish.

"By the Flame, boy, you're worse than an eel to hang on to!" Micum exclaimed softly.

"Did you get the case?" asked Seregil.

"Yes, I got it," Alec whispered, casting a nervous glance in the direction of the door. "But what are you doing in here?"

Seregil shrugged. "And why shouldn't I be in my own bedroom?"

"Your own— *Yours?*" sputtered Alec. "I went through all that to burgle *your* house?"

"Not so loud! Don't you see? We wanted to make sure you had a proper challenge."

Alec glared at the two of them, cheeks aflame, all his careful work reduced to a ridiculous charade. "By breaking into your own house? What kind of a challenge is that?"

"Don't take on so," Seregil said in honest consternation. "You just got into one of the most difficult houses in the city! I admit, I removed a few of the more deadly wards, but do you think just any common tickler could have gotten past those locks you found?"

"This is the last place we'd send you into if we didn't think you were ready," added Micum.

Alec chewed this over angrily for a long moment, arms locked across his chest. "Well, it was pretty hard. The study door was nearly the end of me."

"You see!" Seregil cried, throwing an arm around Alec's shoulders and giving the boy a rough hug. "For plain housebreaking I'd say you acquitted yourself boldly. In fact, you surprised us both by weaseling in through that little window. Remind me to see to that tomorrow, will you? And that was a quick bit of thinking when the ladies wandered through."

Alec pulled back, eyes narrowing suspiciously again. "You *sent* them!"

"Actually, that was my idea," said Micum. "You were having such an easy time of it. Admit it now, it will make a better story later on with that."

"So what now?" asked Alec, still wary. "Tonight, I mean."

"Tonight?" Seregil's grin went crooked. "Why, tonight we have guests to attend to."

"The party? This party? Now? You said before you were doing that in a couple of days!"

"*Did* I? Well, it's a lucky thing we're already dressed for the occasion. By the way, how did you like your new room?"

Alec grinned sheepishly, recalling the woman's remark about the painted Mycenian chest in the room where he'd hidden. "From what little I saw of it, it seems very—useful."

Reluctantly following Micum and Seregil downstairs, he found himself faced with a room full of elegant strangers.

Dozens of thick candles lit the room, their honeyed scent like the distillation of long-dead summers. Their radiance was given back everywhere in the flash of jewels and the sheen of silks and polished leather.

The salon itself was no less elegant than those who occupied it. The high walls of the room had been painted to look like a forest glade, the tops of life-size oaks extending up across the vaulted ceiling overhead. Garlands of brightly flowering vines adorned the trees, and between their trunks distant mountains and ocean vistas were visible. Musicians played on a carved balcony overhead.

Seregil paused halfway down the great staircase and laid a hand on Alec's arm.

"Most honored guests!" he called, assuming the formal manner he'd used while playing Lady Gwethelyn aboard the *Darter*. "Allow me to present my ward and companion, Sir Alec of Ivywell, lately of Mycena. Make yourselves known to him, I pray you, for he is new to our great city and has made few acquaintances."

Alec's mouth went dry as dozens of expectant faces turned to him.

"Steady now," whispered Micum. "Just remember who you're

supposed to be." Slipping the boy a covert luck sign, he moved off into the crowd.

At the bottom of the stairs, a servant stepped forward with a tray of iced wine. Alec took a cup and drained it in a hasty gulp.

"Go easy with that," Seregil murmured, propelling him gently forward. Playing the gracious host, he made a circuit of the room, moving smoothly from one knot of conversation to another.

The guests seemed to be mostly minor nobles and wealthy merchants associated with "Lord Seregil's" business interests. There was much talk of caravans and shipping, but the most popular topic was clearly the possibility of war in the spring.

"I hardly think there can be any question," sniffed a young nobleman introduced to Alec as Lord Melwhit. "Preparations have been going on since summer."

"Indeed," a portly lord grumbled over his wine cup. "You can hardly come by a decent stick of lumber these last few months with the requisitioners snapping up everything in sight. I doubt I shall be able to complete my solarium before spring!"

"Wolde cloth?" a woman exclaimed nearby. "Don't speak to me of Wolde cloth! With all the new tariffs, I can scarcely afford a new riding mantle. And gold? Mark my words, Lord Decius, before this is over we shall all be reduced to wearing beads and feathers."

"And what a delightful fashion that would prove," exclaimed her companion.

Trailing along with Seregil, Alec suddenly found himself face-to-face with the two women he'd seen upstairs.

"Allow me to introduce a very dear friend of mine," said Seregil with a hint of his wicked smile. "Lady Kylith, may I present Sir Alec of Ivywell. Sir Alec, Lady Kylith of Rhíminee, and her niece, Lady Ysmay of Orutan."

Executing his best courtly bow, Alec felt his cheeks go warm. Lady Kylith's velvet gown draped a form still slender and elegant; like those worn by most other women of fashion present, it left her bosom nearly bare beneath a tissue of thinnest silk and a heavily jeweled necklace.

"What a fortunate young man you are!" purred Kylith, enveloping the boy in a languorous dark-eyed gaze that sent his heart knocking again. "Our friend Lord Seregil is one of the most cultured gentlemen in the city, well versed in all the pleasures

Rhíminee has to offer. I am certain you will find your time with him most enjoyable and instructive."

"You flatter me, dear lady," murmured Seregil. "But perhaps I might presume on our friendship? Would you partner Sir Alec in the first waltz? I believe the musicians have just struck up one of your favorites."

"A pleasure," replied Kylith with a curtsey. "And perhaps you would return the boon by partnering my niece. I did, after all, promise her an evening of wicked pleasures, and I cannot think of a greater one than to dance with you."

Blushing prettily, Ysmay accepted Seregil's arm. At this signal, the other guests formed couples and assembled for the dance.

Kylith extended her hand to Alec with a dazzling smile. "Will you do me the honor, sir?"

"The honor is mine, I assure you," Alec replied. The words sounded wooden and foolish to his ears but he pressed on as best he could. "I must warn you, though, I've never been called a graceful dancer."

Taking her place in front of him, she gave him another melting look. "Think nothing of it, my dear. The instruction of inexperienced young men is one of life's unrivaled pleasures."

Seregil set about a playful flirtation with Ysmay while keeping one eye on Alec. As expected, Kylith put the boy at ease in no time. Another dance or two under her influence, and Alec would feel like he'd moved in such society his whole life. She'd had that same affect on Seregil years before.

Beginning as a courtesan in the Street of Lights, Kylith had risen to nobility when a headstrong young lord had brooked the strenuous opposition of family and class to marry her. Over the years her beauty, discretion, and lancing wit had earned her a degree of acceptance and drawn in the best of Rhíminee society to her famous gatherings. The finest artists and musicians of the day were to be found in her house, mingling with adventurers, wizards, and ministers of the highest offices. Few outside of the Queen's Park knew more than she of what went on in the council chambers and bedrooms of Rhíminee.

It had been for just such a reason that Nysander had introduced Seregil to her after the end of his ill-fated apprenticeship.

Charmed by his mysterious past and questionable reputation, Kylith had drawn him into her bright circle and, for a brief time after the death of her husband, into her bed. He'd never been certain if she'd guessed him to be the faceless, unpredictable "Cat" of Rhíminee fame rather than a mere intermediary, but she often relayed requests for services to him, knowing that results were generally swift.

Whatever the case, she was one of the few nobles in whose discretion he had any faith. If Alec should falter in his role tonight, she would not broadcast the fact. And Alec did appear to be enjoying her company.

Keeping up his side of the agreement, he turned his full attention on Ysmay and flirted outrageously with her until she quivered in his arms.

Alec was midway through his second dance with Kylith when Micum laid a hand on his shoulder.

"Forgive me, lady, I must borrow your partner for a moment," he said, bowing to Kylith. "Alec, a word?"

Trouble? Alec signed as Micum walked him toward the front entrance of the hall. The big man's grim sidelong glance was answer enough.

In the small entrance chamber at the front of the house they found Seregil boxed in by four bluecoats. Another was binding his hands in front of him. Seregil's old manservant, Runcer, stood wringing his hands and weeping nearby.

An officer wearing the chain of a Queen's Bailiff rolled up a black-ribboned scroll as Micum and Alec approached. Seregil's stony expression revealed nothing.

"What's going on here?" Micum demanded.

"And who might you be, sir?" replied the bailiff.

"Sir Micum Cavish of Watermead, friend of Lord Seregil. This boy is his ward, Sir Alec of Ivywell. Why are you arresting this man?"

The bailiff consulted another scroll and took a second look at the two of them. "Lord Seregil of Rhíminee stands accused of treason. I am also charged to instruct Sir Alec not to attempt to leave the city."

Eyeing the man with chilly dignity, Micum asked quietly, "Am I to understand he is under suspicion as well?"

"Not at present, Sir Micum. But those are my instructions."

"Seregil, what's happening?" asked Alec, finding his voice at last.

Seregil gave a grim shrug. "Some sort of misunderstanding, apparently. Make my apologies to the guests, would you?"

Alec nodded numbly. Glancing down at Seregil's bound hands, he saw him give the sign of Nysander's name, one long forefinger curled tightly over his thumb.

"Come along, my lord," said the bailiff, grasping Seregil's elbow.

"Where are you taking him?" Alec demanded, following as the guards led Seregil out to an enclosed black cart.

"That's not for me to say, sir. Good evening." Climbing in behind Seregil, the bailiff motioned to the driver and the cart rumbled off down the cobbled street.

"Seregil said to go to Nysander," Alec whispered, feeling Micum beside him.

"I saw. We'd better go."

"But what about the guests?"

"I'll have a quick word with Kylith. She'll manage things."

Alec watched miserably as the cart disappeared into the night. "Where do you think they're taking him?"

"It's a Queen's Warrant arrest, so it'll be Red Tower Prison," Micum said, looking bleak. "And that's one place not even Seregil can get out of on his own."

26

PLANS AT THE COCKEREL

Alec and Micum were halfway to the Orëska House when a tiny message sphere winked into being in front of them.

"Alec, Micum, come to the Cockerel at once!"

Alec blinked in surprise. "That was Thero."

"Bilairy's Balls!" muttered Micum, changing direction.

At the Cockerel they found Thero waiting for them, but not his master.

"Where's Nysander?" Alec asked, somewhat taken aback that Thero also knew how to enter Seregil's closely warded rooms.

"With the Queen," the young wizard replied, looking stiffly out of place in the midst of Seregil's mess. "He sent me to meet you. He'll join us here as soon as he's able."

"I take it he was as surprised by the arrest as we were?" asked Micum, tossing Seregil's sword belt onto the table.

"Events have moved more rapidly than any of us anticipated. Nysander is quite worried over the fact that Idrilain did not consult with him before ordering the arrest."

"But what happened?" fretted Alec, pacing in frustration. "Nysander stopped the letter! Seregil said they'd never dare to send another without knowing what happened to the first."

"I have no idea. The Queen sent word that he'd been taken to the Red Tower, nothing more. Was the arrest carried out discreetly?"

"If it hadn't been for Runcer, we might have missed it altogether," glowered Micum.

Thero rubbed his chin pensively. "That's a hopeful sign, anyway."

For the first time in their brief acquaintance, it occurred to Alec that Thero must be a Watcher, too. With this revelation came the certainty that it was this fact, rather than any personal feelings for Seregil, which engaged his interest now.

"Do you think they'll—" Memories tightened coldly in Alec's chest. "Do you think they'd torture him?"

Thero arched an eyebrow, considering. "That would depend on the severity of the charge, I suppose."

"The bailiff said treason."

"Ah. Yes, I'd say it was quite likely."

"Damn it, Thero, show some sense!" Micum growled, catching at Alec's arm as the boy went pale. "Steady now, there's no use thinking like that. Nysander would never allow it."

"I doubt Nysander could interfere," Thero countered, oblivious to Alec's distress. "The Red Tower is protected by magic as well as bars; Nysander and I did some work in there ourselves. Not only that, but given Nysander's close association with Seregil, he can't afford any suggestion of interference with the law."

"What are we going to do?" asked Alec.

"We're going to sit here and wait for Nysander, as ordered," Micum said calmly. Giving Thero a dark look, he added, "Meanwhile, there's no use wasting time in idle speculation."

Nysander felt a certain relief when the royal messenger led him to the Queen's private audience chamber rather than the Great Hall. There had always been little need for ceremony between them; he had known Idrilain since infancy, and though he had always afforded her the respect due her station, their ties of mutual affection generally allowed them to drop formality in private. Something in her cool greeting, however, conveyed a warning.

Even in her evening robe, greying hair free over her shoulders, Idrilain looked like the warrior she was. Joining her at the small wine table, Nysander did his best to mask his rising uneasiness. Neither spoke until they had saluted each other with their wine cups and taken the ritual sip, signifying their pledge to speak honestly.

"You have arrested Seregil," Nysander said, getting directly to the point. "On what charge?"

"Treason."

The wizard's heart sank; somehow, their enemies had outflanked them. He must proceed with caution and respect. "Upon what evidence is he being charged?"

"Lord Barien received this earlier today." Idrilain pushed a rolled document across to him.

He recognized the opening lines; it was based on one of the half-finished letters Seregil had sold to Ghemella. Like the last, it had every mark of being authentic except its contents. Handwriting, signature, ink—all were consistent.

"It appears genuine, I admit," Nysander said at last. "And yet I do not believe that it was composed by Seregil. May I inquire as to your opinion?"

"My opinion is irrelevant. It's my duty to deal in facts," she replied. "So far no evidence of tampering, magical or otherwise, has been discovered on that parchment."

"And yet you must have doubts or I would not be sitting here with you now," Nysander suggested gently.

The regal mask slipped just a bit at that. "I don't know Seregil well, Nysander, but I know you. I know that you've been worthy of my trust, and that of the three queens before me. It's difficult for me to believe that anyone you hold in such esteem could be a traitor. If you know anything about this, you'd better tell me now."

Nysander drew the forged letter he'd intercepted from his coat and handed it to her. "I came into possession of this a week ago. Believe me when I tell you that I would have spoken to you at once if I had the slightest doubt as to Seregil's innocence. The initial content is based on a letter Seregil did in fact write, but the damning lines were added by the forger. I have spoken with Seregil about it and have every reason to believe that he speaks the truth."

Idrilain's face darkened again as she compared the two letters. "I don't understand. If these are false, then they're masterpieces of forgery. Who would go to such lengths to discredit a person of such small importance? Forgive the bluntness of an old soldier, Nysander, but aside from his friendship with you and my children, what is Seregil but an exiled wastrel noble with a bit of trader's sense? He has no power at my court, no influence."

"True. Which leaves nothing of significance except his rather tenuous connection to you, or perhaps even to me. And who but the Lerans would find this of value?"

"The Lerans?" Idrilain said derisively. "A bunch of narrow-minded malcontents mouthing the empty threats even their great-grandparents didn't believe! By the Four, Nysander, the Lerans have been nothing more than a political bugbear since the time of Elani the Fair."

"So it is generally believed, my lady. Yet you must remember that I was a boy at the wedding of your ancestor and namesake, Idrilain the First, when she took the Aurënfaie, Corruth, as her consort. Seven generations later, who but a handful of old wizards recall the shouts of anger outside the temple during the ceremony? Yet I tell you, my Queen, that at this moment I hear them as clearly as I did then. 'A Skalan lord for the Skalan people!' they screamed as the Queen's Horse rode out with swords and clubs. And it was not only the rabble who protested, but nobles, as well, who felt their honor usurped by foreign blood. I saw these same nobles stand by Queen Lera through her oppressive reign. I watched the public protests when her half sister Corruthesthera took the throne after Lera's death."

"And yet my ancestor Corruthesthera reigned unchallenged by any revolution, and her descendants after her."

"And two of those queens died under questionable circumstances."

"Rumors! Elani died in the Great Plague, and Klia was poisoned by Plenimaran assassins."

"So history has decided, my Queen. Yet there was talk to the contrary at the time."

"Nothing was proven in either case. And without proof to the contrary, you're left standing on smoke," Idrilain asserted stubbornly. "Which brings us back to Seregil. Perhaps it *would* be to the Lerans' advantage to embarrass me through him. Sakor knows, I can't afford division among my own people with the threat of war hanging over us. Still, you realize that by giving me this second letter, you have doubly damned him unless you can produce proof that they're not genuine?"

"I do," replied Nysander. "And I give it to you as a pledge of my good faith, knowing I must prove him innocent or watch a man I love as my own son executed in the most horrible fashion. You have him in custody. Word will spread, just as the Lerans intend. All I ask of you is time to produce proof of his innocence."

Pressing her palms together, Idrilain rested her forehead against her fingertips. "I can afford no show of leniency. Barien is planning to pursue the matter personally."

"And his loyalty to you is unclouded by any regard for Seregil?"

"Precisely."

Nysander hesitated an instant, then reached across the table and clasped her hands in his. "Grant me two days, Idrilain, I beseech you. Tell Barien whatever you wish, but give me time to save a man more loyal and valuable than you know."

Astonishment dawned on Idrilain's face as the implication struck home. "Seregil, a Watcher? Sakor's Flame, can I be that blind?"

"He is a master of his craft, my dear," Nysander said rather sadly. "Regardless of what I would have wished for him, Illior has set him a path all his own. With your permission, I would prefer to say no more, except that I gladly stake my own honor on his loyalty to Skala and to you."

Idrilain shook her head doubtfully. "I hope you never have cause to regret those words, my friend. He was a traitor once; we both know that. What you've just told me—that could be a double-edged thing."

"I stand by him, nonetheless."

"Very well, then. Two days. But I can't give you any longer, and your evidence must be irrefutable! I don't suppose I need to warn you that any interference in the due process of the law would be most unwise?"

Nysander rose and bowed deeply. "I understand perfectly, my lady."

Riding at once to the Cockerel, Nysander made no effort to hide his concern from the others waiting there.

"It is as we feared," he told them. "A second forged letter has been delivered to the Vicegerent, this one dated the sixth of Erasin. Ironically, the original was one that Seregil handed over to Ghemella as part of his scheme to entrap the forger."

"The sixth of Erasin?" Alec counted back. "That's just after we met. We were still out on the Downs then."

"Bloody hell!" growled Micum. "Either the bastards know about Seregil's work or they struck lucky in the dark. Either way, they've fixed it so he either has to rig up some lie or reveal himself. And *that* could prove a death sentence in itself."

"I could say he was at Ivywell," Alec offered. "We've already set up the story that he brought me down from there. He was telling everyone at the party about it."

"I fear not," said Nysander. "That tale serves well enough in some circles, but would not bear up under the scrutiny of the Queen's inquisitors. At the very least, witnesses would be sent for from Mycena. When none appeared, you would find yourself as deeply implicated as Seregil. Besides, there is no time. Idrilain has given us just two days' grace. I fear our best recourse is to pursue Seregil's original plan regarding Hind Street."

"I've been thinking about that," mused Micum. "It took Seregil a week to find Alben, and he's not even certain he's the right one. Assuming that we do find a cache—that there is one—what if he's not our man after all? It could take us weeks to run down information that Seregil could come up with in a few days' time."

Nysander spread his hands resignedly. "True. Yet at the moment I can think of no other option."

"If only he'd had another day," Alec exclaimed bitterly. "He was all smiles about it tonight, as if he had all the time in the world."

"It occurs to me," said Thero, who'd been quiet for some time, "that Alec's absence at Wheel Street this evening will surely have been remarked upon. Perhaps an appearance at the prison would not be out of place—expressions of outrage, bewilderment, and the like? While it would not be politic for Nysander to be seen there, who would question Lord Seregil's young ward bringing his protector a few necessities for the night? A blanket, perhaps, and some clean linen—"

"A lock pick!"

Thero spared Alec a withering glance. "Only if you want to guarantee your place on the gibbet beside him. My thought was that if they allowed you to see him, he might be able to pass along some helpful information. If not, what have we lost?"

"You've a bit of the spy in you after all," said Micum.

Thero looked slightly offended. "It's simple logic. My thinking is unclouded by emotion in this matter."

"Nonetheless, it is a fine idea," said Nysander, giving the young wizard an approving look. "Well done, Thero."

Alec rose and reached for his cloak. "I'll go right now! Are you coming, Micum?"

Nysander raised a warning hand. "A moment first, both of you. It is imperative that you recognize the magnitude of our actions. Should anything go awry, we will have forfeited any credibility we have left with the Queen. We could all find ourselves in the Red Tower, or worse."

Having said what was necessary, he was proud to see no signs of wavering in the others. "Very good. I must add that any misstep will reflect most disastrously on the Queen; that must be the final consideration in any decision. If this does stem back to the Lerans, any cock-up on our part would play right into their hands. Nothing would please them more, I am certain, than the appearance of a widespread conspiracy that includes myself. With that in mind, I pray for Illior's favor to grant us all luck in the shadows."

"I'll second that," said Micum. "Come on, Sir Alec. We've got work to do."

A dank wind whipped up from the harbor as Alec and Micum rode up to the prison near the southern wall of the city. The main tower was a squat, ugly structure ringed by a bailey wall. Dismounting in the outer yard, Alec wrinkled his nose at the dismal stench of urine and burning tallow that hung over the place.

"It's hard to believe I woke up at Watermead this morning," he whispered, clutching the little bundle he'd thrown together.

"More like yesterday morning now," sighed Micum.

"What if they don't let us in?"

"Just be as persuasive as possible and have some gold ready. Throw back your cloak so they can see you're a gentleman."

Following Micum's advice, Alec pounded at the gate.

A bearded face appeared at the door grille. "What's your business at this hour?"

"A man was brought in tonight," said Alec. "His name is Lord Seregil. He's my protector and I've brought some clothing and blankets for him. May I see him, please, just for a moment?"

"That dark-haired blade?"

"Yes, that's him."

"It's damned late, you know."

"Inconvenience has its price." Alec held up a gold half sester. "We'd be very grateful."

Micum stepped closer behind him. "They haven't given an order against visitors, have they?"

The guard eyed Alec's coin, then turned to confer with someone else. The gate soon swung open.

"I suppose there's no harm in the lad going up," the guard said, taking the coin and leading them into the warder's room. "But just him and only for a minute. You can wait here by the fire if you like, sir, while he goes. And I'll have a look through that bundle first."

Satisfied with the contents of the parcel and a second coin, the chief warder turned Alec over to another guard, who led him into the depths of the chilly edifice.

The walls seemed to press in around Alec as he followed the warder up flight after drafty flight of stone stairs. His time in Asengai's dungeon had left him with an indelible hatred of such places.

Stopping at one of the low cell doors, the guard peered through the tiny grille. "Visitor, your lordship!"

A muffled reply came from within.

"You'll have to speak to him through here," the warder told Alec. "Don't pass nothing through, not even your hand. I'll see to it that he gets this package."

Taking Alec's bundle, he moved off far enough to give them a modicum of privacy.

The grille was set deep in the thick wooden door. Light from the nearest lantern in the corridor slanted through the bars, illuminating a crescent of profile and one glittering eye.

"Are you all right?" Alec whispered anxiously.

"So far," Seregil replied. "It's damn cold, though."

"I brought a blanket, and some fresh clothes."

"Thanks. Any news?"

Leaning as close as he dared, Alec quickly told him the details of their conference at the Cockerel. "Nysander thinks finding evidence against your forger may be our only chance. Micum and I'll have to do it, I guess, but we're not certain how. God, I wish all this hadn't happened!"

"I know how you feel. Is the guard still well away?"

"Yes."

"Then pay attention." Seregil cautiously reached the fingers of one hand through the bars, signing something about Micum.

It was too quick. Alec shook his head. "I can hardly hear you. What did you say?"

"I said it's a dead end. Nothing to be gained," Seregil said, raising his voice for the guard's benefit as he signed again, more slowly this time.

His fingers were somewhat hampered by his bars, but Alec got *Tell Micum silver fish.*

"I don't understand!" Alec whispered, convinced he must have gotten the nonsensical message wrong. "I won't leave you here to rot!"

"Don't fret," Seregil replied, locking eyes with him. "There's a lucky moon tomorrow night. Fortify yourself with prayers to the Lightbearer and all will be well. In the meantime, I entrust you to the care of Micum Cavish. Heed his wisdom; he's a man of many parts."

"Sorry, young sir, that's all the time I can give you," the guard called.

"Damn!" muttered Alec, still convinced he'd misinterpreted a crucial message. Pretending to brush back a stray strand of hair, he signed *Silver fish?*

To his surprise, Seregil nodded emphatically.

"Come along, sir!"

Alec held Seregil's gaze a moment longer, heart pounding painfully in his chest. What he could see of Seregil's mouth tilted up suddenly in the old reassuring grin.

"Why the long face?" Seregil whispered. "You're not alone in this, you know. Everything's going to be fine!"

But Alec felt anything but fine as he followed the guard back down the stairs. Much as he wanted to believe Seregil's brave assurances, he thought he'd heard a hollow note in his friend's voice. They were in a bad spot, and a good deal of it was up to him to solve. The consequences of failure were too awful to bear thinking about.

His face must have given something of this away, for the

guard said kindly, "There now, sir, perhaps it'll all come right in the end. He seems a good enough fellow."

Sensing a potential ally, Alec managed to work up a few tears by the time they reached the bottom of the stairs. In fact, they came with surprising ease.

As soon as they were out of sight of the prison Alec passed on Seregil's strange message. For a moment Micum looked disconcertingly blank.

"Silver fish?" Stroking the corners of his mustache, he shook his head. Then suddenly he broke into a broad grin. "By the Flame, he must have meant *silverfish,* like the insect!"

"That means something to you?" Alec asked, still doubtful.

"Oh, yes! In fact, our sneaky friend has given us our whole plan of attack. I'll explain when we get home—home being Wheel Street tonight."

Runcer met them at the door. "The guests have departed, Sir Alec, and I have laid a fire in your chamber. Will you be requiring anything else tonight?"

"No, thank you," Alec replied, feeling a bit confused. The elderly servant's manner conveyed the impression that he had served Alec all his life. He was hovering in a manner that suggested he expected further orders. "Well, I think I can manage. You should go to bed, ah—"

"Runcer," Micum whispered behind him.

"Runcer, yes. Go to bed. It's late. Thank you."

Runcer's wrinkled face betrayed nothing but respectful attention as he bowed good night. Retreating hastily upstairs, Alec found his new bedchamber brightly illuminated.

"He's refurbished it," Micum remarked dryly, looking the place over. "It's very—Mycenian."

"Is that what you'd call it?"

The cabinets, chests, chairs, and tall, carved bedstead were all brightly painted with garish fruit and game motifs. The bed hangings, though faded, were richly embroidered with a pattern of pomegranates and wheat. The overall effect was rather overwhelming, even to Alec's untutored eye. The only familiar objects in the room were his sword and bow, which lay across the bed.

"I supposed I'll get used to it," he sighed, drawing a chair up to the fire. "Now tell me about the silverfish."

"Old Silverfish was a name we gave to a slippery customer Nysander had us track down a few years back," explained Micum. "He was another blackmailer and, like his namesake, he had a talent for disappearing into the woodwork. Seregil had a hell of a time finding his cache. He finally did, though, and I never saw a prettier bit of coggery."

"How did he do it?"

"We'll get to that. What else did he tell you?"

"To depend on you, and that there'd be a lucky moon tomorrow night when I should pray to Illior. I think he means we do the burglary then."

"Right. We'll pay a daylight visit to Master Alben's shop, look the place over, then do the real work after dark."

"And if he's right? The bailiff who arrested Seregil had my name, too. If *I* show up with evidence they'll never believe us!"

"Probably not. Which means we have to make certain it gets to the Queen some other way. The City Watch, for instance. I daresay they'd welcome the opportunity to arrest a traitor."

"Sure, but why would the Watch believe us any more than the Queen's Bailiff?"

"They wouldn't," Micum said with a sly smile. "But Myrhini will."

"Who?" Alec was too tired to place the name immediately.

"Princess Klia's friend. She's a captain of the Horse Guard."

Alec, rubbed his eyelids with the heels of his palms. "Oh, yes, the one who took me to the barracks for a pass that day Seregil had me robbed."

"The day he what?"

"Never mind. You think Myrhini will help us?"

"For Klia's sake, if not for Seregil's. I'll send a message, but I don't expect we'll see her before dawn. You try out this new bed of yours in the meantime. I have an idea tomorrow will be another long day."

Alec gave a humorless laugh. "I don't think I've seen a short one since I met Seregil!"

27

HIND STREET

Opening his eyes the next morning, Alec was startled to find Runcer bending over him.

"Forgive me for the intrusion, Sir Alec, but Sir Micum sent me to wake you." Moving with fossilized dignity, the old man set a steaming pitcher on the washstand.

The promise of a watery grey dawn filtered in at the window. He couldn't have been asleep more than a few hours. Sitting up, Alec watched the old servant moving about the room at what were apparently his morning duties. After laying out the bath items, he fetched clean linen and a fresh shirt from a clothes chest and laid them out on the foot of the bed.

Unaccustomed to such ministrations, Alec watched with growing unease. His experiences at the Orëska baths had left him wary of servants. What if the man wanted to help him dress? It was unnatural, having another person doing things for him as if he were a child or an invalid. The man's respectful silence only made matters worse.

"You manage the household, don't you?" Alec asked as Runcer proceeded to brush his cloak. How much, he wondered, did this wrinkled old man know of his real background—or Seregil's, for that matter?

"Of course, sir," Runcer replied with no discernible change of expression. "Lord Seregil has left instructions that you be made comfortable. Breakfast has been laid in the dining room and Captain Myrhini is expected shortly. Shall I lay out your clothes, sir?"

"I suppose so."

Runcer went to another chest for breeches, then creaked to a halt at the wardrobe. "And which coat would you prefer today, sir?"

Having absolutely no clue as to the contents of the wardrobe, Alec hazarded a guess. "The blue, please."

"The blue, sir." The old servant took out an outrageously ornate coat stitched with gold beading.

"Well, maybe not the blue," Alec countered hastily. "I'll decide later."

"Very good, sir."

To Alec's dismay, Runcer did not leave but instead gave him another of those expectant looks. After a long, chagrined moment Alec realized he was waiting to be dismissed.

"Thank you, Runcer, I don't need you."

"Very good, sir." The old man bowed and left the room.

"Bilairy's Balls!" Jumping out of bed, Alec stalked to the wardrobe and inspected the surcoats hanging there. The blue was by far the gaudiest. Pawing through the others, he found a plain russet and hurried into his clothes. Not surprisingly, they all fit as if he'd been measured for them, even down to the boots.

Seregil did this while I was in Watermead, Alec thought with a pang. *And none of it will be worth a damn if we don't get him out of the Tower.*

He headed downstairs and followed the smell of sausage to a pleasant room overlooking the garden. Micum was seated already, with Scregil's two Zengati hounds lying to either side of his chair. Apparently they held no grudge over his recent burglary. At his approach they merely raised their gleaming white heads, heavy tails brushing the floor in welcome.

Micum pushed a plate of sausage his way. "You'd better eat something. Myrhini will be here any minute."

They'd barely finished their hasty meal when Runcer ushered in the tall captain.

"This had better be fast. I've got inspection in an hour," she warned, mud-spattered cloak billowing about her legs as she joined them at the table.

"How's Klia taking the news of the arrest?" asked Micum.

"Oh, she's livid, but worried, too. Queen's Kin or no, Vicegerent Barien's out for blood, and pissed as hell that Idrilain granted a grace period before the questioning starts."

"Nysander expected that," said Alec. "Does Barien have a grudge against Seregil?"

Myrhini held up her hands. "Who knows? According to Klia, he thinks Seregil's a bad influence and has never liked his being friends with her and the twins."

Elesthera and Tymore, thought Alec. Seregil had drilled him mercilessly on the royal family. The twins were Klia's older brother and sister, Idrilain's other children by her second consort.

"Did you tell Klia you were meeting us?" asked Micum.

"No and she'll ream me for it when she finds out. But I agree with you that it's best not to involve her until we know which way the wind's going to blow. So, how can I help?"

Micum poured more tea and settled back in his chair. "There's a man in Hind Street, a forger, who probably fabricated the false documents that put Seregil in the Tower. Seregil had planned to go after him himself tonight; he wants us to go ahead without him."

"But the evidence can't come from us," added Alec. "Barien could say we made it up just to clear Seregil's name."

Myrhini looked out at the grey sky brightening above the muddy garden. "What you need is someone to tip off the bluecoats. Someone who won't ask too many questions."

"That's about the size of it," said Micum. "Of course, there's a certain amount of risk involved. I'd understand if you wanted no part of it."

Myrhini waved the warning aside with a disgusted look. "As it happens, there *is* a certain captain of the Watch who'd be happy enough to do me a favor. And Hind Street just happens to be in his ward—to catch a forger squeezing nobles would be a proper feather in his cap."

Micum grinned knowingly. "Enough said. We'll send word as soon as we're certain of our man. When we do, you speak to your bluecoat captain. Alec and I will play the flushing hounds and he can have the kill. We'll need you there, though. Your captain can't see us or know we're involved."

"I'll be there." Myrhini rose to go. "Having one of the Queen's daughters as best friend and commander does have its occasional advantages, you know."

Alec made his way through a cold winter drizzle to Hind Street an hour later. It was a neighborhood of plain, respectable tenements: five-story wood and stone buildings constructed around small interior courtyards.

Dressed as a country lad of good family, he made a show of great agitation as he asked directions along the street. He was directed to a whitewashed building in the third block. Hurrying into the courtyard, he spotted a brass mortar hung over a door on the ground level. The shutters were open. With a silent prayer to Illior of the Thieves, he lifted the latch and burst into the little shop.

The low room reeked of herbs and oils. A young boy stood heating something over a lamp at a table near the back of the shop.

"Is this the apothecary's?" Alec asked breathlessly.

"Aye, but Master Alben's still at his breakfast," the boy replied without looking up from his work.

"Call him, please!" cried Alec. "I've been sent for medicine. My poor mother's had an issue of blood since last night, and nothing seems to stop it!"

This galvanized the apprentice. Setting his pan aside, he disappeared through a curtain at the back of the room, returning a moment later with a balding man with a long grey beard.

"Master Alben?" asked Alec.

"That's me," the man answered brusquely, brushing crumbs from the front of his robe. "What's all this fuss about, first thing in the day?"

"It's my mother, sir. She's bleeding terribly!"

"Durnik told me that much, boy. We've no time to waste on hysterics," snapped Alben. "Does the blood come from her mouth, nose, ears, or womb?"

"From the womb. We're in from the country and didn't know where to find a midwife. They said at the inn that you might have herbs—"

"Yes, yes, Durnik, you know which jars."

The apprentice fetched three jars from one of the crowded

shelves and the apothecary set to work measuring the herbs and powders into a mortar. Alec wandered to the window, wringing his hands with simulated impatience.

In the courtyard outside he saw other tenants of the place setting out for their day's business. Micum was just across the way, strolling around the court as if looking for a particular address. Seeing Alec at the window, he sauntered over in the direction of a refuse pile in a corner of the yard.

Alec paced back to the worktable. "Can't you hurry?" he implored.

"A moment!" snapped Alben, still grinding. "It's of no use at all if it isn't correctly mixed— By the Four! Is that *smoke*?"

At that moment a cry of "Fire!" went up in the courtyard, followed by a scream and the sound of running feet. Dropping his pestle, the apothecary rushed to the door. The rubbish heap was in flames.

"Fire! Arson!" he shrieked, going white. "Durnik, fetch water at once! Fire, fire in the courtyard!"

By now the shout had been taken up through the building and doors flew open as people hurried out to douse the blaze.

Young Durnik ran for the well, but his master disappeared back through the curtain. Following him, Alec discovered a comfortable sitting room behind the shop. Alben was hovering at the hearth, gripping one of the carved pillars supporting the mantel with one hand, and pulling nervously at his beard with the other.

Seeing Alec in the doorway, he snarled, "What are you doing in here? Get out!"

"The medicine, sir," Alec ventured meekly. "For my mother?"

"What? Oh, the medicine! Take it, take it!"

"But the price?"

"Bugger the price, you idiot! Can't you see there's a fire?" Alben gasped furiously, making no move to abandon the hearth. "Get out, damn you!"

Backing out through the curtain, Alec dumped the contents of the mortar into a parchment cone and hurried out past the crowd that had gathered in the street. A few blocks from the tenement Micum stepped from an alley to meet him.

"Well?"

"I think it worked," Alec told him. "As soon as it started he went right to the room behind the shop and wouldn't be moved from the hearth."

"We've got him, then! It's just as Seregil said the first time we pulled that trick on Old Silverfish: 'Shout "Fire" and a mother will race to save her child, a craftsman for his tools, a courtesan for her jewel box, and a blackmailer for his hoard of papers.' "

"So now we tell Myrhini?"

"Yes, and pray to Illior this is the *right* forger!"

That night, Seregil found himself with nothing to do but worry. The cell's tiny slit of a window was too high to look out of; he gauged the passage of time by listening to the prison go quiet around him. Hunched miserably on the hard stone sleeping shelf with his blankets pulled tight around his shoulders, he worried.

Have they gone out yet?

In truth, he had no way of knowing if Alec and Micum had understood the import of his message.

Surely Micum would have found some way to get word in to you if he hadn't?

Unless the Lerans found some way to gather Alec and Micum up in their web, too.

The two of them were certainly tempting targets: both foreign born, both known friends of an accused traitor. Even Nysander could be implicated on the basis of their long relationship. Seregil's imagination, not always a kind companion at such times, was soon busy painting alarming scenes of forged letters, sudden arrests, and worse.

Throwing aside the blankets, he stretched his stiff muscles and paced the now familiar confines of the cell—three strides and turn, three strides and turn again. It was doubtful that word would come before dawn even if things went as planned.

He paused at the door, rising on his toes to peer out the grille. Was it midnight yet? An hour before? Two hours past? The blank, silent corridor told him nothing.

Damnation! he raged silently, resuming his restless vigil. *By now I'd have done the job and be back home in front of the fire!*

Unless, of course, he'd been wrong about the apothecary's involvement in the first place.

. . .

Alec and Micum met Myrhini in a darkened square near Hind Street. She'd wisely put aside her uniform in favor of a plain tunic and breeches under a dark cloak, though she'd kept her sword. Unrolling an awkward bundle, she handed them two pot-brimmed helmets like those worn by the City Watch.

"Where did you come by these?" asked Micum, trying his on.

"Don't ask. If things do go wrong, you can pass for some of Tyrin's men in the dark."

"This Tyrin of yours, he's up to this?"

Myrhini nodded. "He has ten men in an alley across from your man's tenement and two lookouts in the courtyard. They've been told to move at the first sign of disturbance inside. I just hope Alec can manage it without getting caught."

"If I can get in, then I can get out again," Alec said quietly, tucking his helmet under his arm.

Leaving their horses tethered in the square, the three set off together for Hind Street. Slipping into a narrow alley beside Alben's building, they took stock of the situation.

The lower floor showed no light between the shutters, nor was any apparent on the upper level, where Alben's chamber would be. A small window overlooking the alley appeared to be the best point of entry.

Pulling off his boots, Alec climbed onto Micum's shoulders and peered through a crack in the shutters. The room beyond was quite dark and no telltale sounds of breathing or snoring warned of anyone within. Jiggering the latch inside as quietly as he could, Alec opened the shutter and climbed through.

He smelled candle smoke in the darkness, felt bare floor beneath his feet. Faint candlelight showed at the top of a stairway across the room. As his eyes adjusted, Alec realized with relief that he was in the very room he'd come to burgle. But someone, presumably Alben, was still awake upstairs after all. A creak of floorboards came from overhead, followed by a muffled cough. The sitting room fire had been banked, however, meaning the master of the house was not coming down again before morning.

Alec took a lightstone on a handle from his tool roll and shielded it with one hand as he crept to the door leading to the shop. It had been closed and bolted for the night.

Alec fumbled a leather cone out of his pouch and fitted it over the stone to shield the light.

It didn't take long to find what he was looking for. Running his fingers over the carved moldings that framed the fireplace, he soon struck a loose edge on the thick square base of one of the decorative posts. Working the tip of his dagger under it, he uncovered a deep, narrow cavity in the stonework of the fireplace. Inside lay a long iron box secured with a heavy lock. Hunkering down, he picked the lock and opened the box. Inside were several bundles of documents. His skill at reading was by no means great but he knew Seregil's large, flowing script and signature well enough to recognize them among the others. One entire packet was made up of letters in Seregil's hand, some complete, some half finished. There were eleven in all, and several were clearly duplicates of others.

Got you, by the Maker! Replacing the documents, he returned the casket to its hiding place, carefully leaving the concealing bit of stonework slightly askew.

This accomplished, he picked up a small footstool and went back to the window. With one leg hooked over the sill, he tossed the stool into the center of the room with a loud thump and dropped down into the alley. Poised for flight, he and the others listened for an outcry to be raised.

Nothing happened.

"How could they not have heard that? *I* heard it!" whispered Myrhini.

Micum shrugged. "You'd better give it another try."

With another boost from Micum, Alec peeked over the sill. The faint glow of candlelight still showed in the stairwell but there was no sign of life.

Climbing in, he briefly considered setting another fire but dismissed the thought; at this time of night the whole place might go up before enough water carriers could be roused. Casting around, he spotted a glazed jar on the mantelpiece. That would do nicely. He smashed it against the fire irons.

This produced an admirable crash and drew startled shouts from upstairs and down. Satisfied, he lunged for the window, caught his foot on the overturned footstool, and went sprawling.

"Is that you, Master Alben?" a quavering voice called from beyond the shop door.

"Damn and blast you, Durnik!" an outraged voice screeched somewhere above. "What in the name of Bilairy's Bitch are you doing down there?"

Scrambling to his feet, Alec glimpsed a pair of bony ankles at the head of the stairs. He threw himself out the window and tumbled into Micum's waiting arms.

"That did the trick!" Micum chuckled, clapping the helmet on Alec's head as the boy hastily pulled on his boots. Together, they hustled off down the alley, while Myrhini disappeared in the opposite direction to make sure of Tyrin's support.

Stopping at the far end of the alley, Micum and Alec heard Alben cursing his befuddled servant. The shuttered window banged open, then slammed shut again. A moment later they could hear soldiers hammering at the front door of the shop.

The alley window opened again and this time an ungainly figure in a long nightshirt clambered out.

"Bloody hell!" Micum exclaimed in disgust. "Don't tell me every damn bluecoat is going in the front door?"

The street running behind the building did appear to be unguarded.

"Quick, draw your sword!" Alec whispered, doing the same. His left hand found the lightstone he'd jammed in his pouch and he held it over their heads, hoping the helmet brims would shade their faces.

"You there, stop where you are!" he shouted in the deepest voice he could muster.

Alben clutched the damning strongbox to his chest as he blinked wildly at the sudden light. Panicked by the sight of swords and helmets, he turned tail, rushing down the alley and into the arms of several of Captain Tyrin's more enterprising men.

Alec quickly covered his light again as Micum called out, "We caught him shinnying out the back window!"

In the ensuing confusion, they slipped away with no trouble at all.

28

A Midnight Inquisition

Thero answered the summoner's knock just before midnight. Accepting the rolled message, he carried it downstairs to Nysander, who was dozing in the sitting room armchair.

Thero shook his master gently by the shoulder. "The Queen's sent for you."

Nysander's eyes blinked open, instantly alert. "Was there a message?"

Thero handed him the little scroll.

Nysander read through it quickly, then rose and brushed the wrinkles from his blue robe. "Nothing of use here, only that I should come at once. Well then, we must simply hope for the best."

"Shall I come with you?"

"Thank you, dear boy, but I think it best for you to remain here for the moment. If something has gone awry, I shall need you available to Micum and Alec."

At the Palace Nysander made his way alone through the familiar corridors. Despite its rich tapestries and murals, the place had none of the Orëska's spacious ambience. Part royal residence, part fortress, the walls were thick, the corridors labyrinthine, the doors heavily strapped with ornate metalwork.

The judgment chamber was more forbidding still, and intentionally so. The long room was empty of furnishings except for a black and silver throne on a raised platform at the far end. To approach it, one crossed a chill expanse of polished black floor under the marble gaze of the royal effigies lining the walls. Iron cressets cast a grim, shifting light over the small group already gathered around the throne.

Idrilain acknowledged Nysander's bow tersely. She wore the crown and breastplate of office tonight, and her great sword lay unsheathed across her knees. The Vicegerent and General Phoria stood on either side of her, looking equally dour.

"We have come into possession of certain documents which may clear Lord Seregil's name," Idrilain informed Nysander, laying her hand on a long iron box that lay open on a small table at her elbow. "I thought you should be present at the proceedings."

"Many thanks, my lady," Nysander replied, taking his place at the foot of the dais.

Looking up at her eldest daughter, Idrilain motioned for her to proceed.

"Bring the first prisoner!"

At Phoria's shout, a side door swung open and two guards dragged in a querulous old man in a stained nightshirt. Nysander allowed himself a brief brush across the surface of the accused man's mind and read a panicked craftiness, a fury to survive.

They were followed by three others: an officer of the Watch, a woman in the robes of the Queen's High Bailiff, and a young wizard of the Second Degree named Imaneus. Nysander knew this last one well, a talented mind adept frequently called in as verifier at such trials.

The Vicegerent stepped forward and turned a bleak eye on the prisoner.

"Alben, apothecary of Hind Street, you stand accused of forgery and possession of personal papers belonging to a member of the Royal Kin. How plead you?"

Cowering on his knees, Alben mumbled a whining plea.

"Repeat yourself," the bailiff ordered, leaning closer to listen. "My Lord Barien, the accused maintains that there has been some mistake."

"A mistake," Barien repeated tonelessly. "Alben the Apothecary, were you not apprehended by Captain Tyrin of the City Watch while fleeing through a back window in the dead of night with this box in your arms? A box found to contain letters, documents, and missives penned by members of the nobility."

"A mistake," Alben whispered again, trembling.

Lifting a sheaf of papers from the box, Barien continued, "Among the documents in this box found upon your person at the time of your arrest are letters and copies of letters. In short, forgeries. Specific charges against you are as follows: first, that you were instrumental in the slander and wrongful condemnation of an innocent and loyal servant of Her Majesty, Queen Idrilain the Second." Barien paused to select two letters. "Found in your possession is the duplicate of a letter purportedly written by Lord Vardarus í Boruntas Lud Mirin of Rhíminee, the very letter which sent Lord Vardarus to the block. With it, secured with a wax seal identified as your own, was found another, nearly identical letter entirely lacking in the details which damned him."

Barien lifted another bundle of papers from the box. "Secondly, you are charged with collusion to perpetrate the same heinous crime against Lord Seregil í Korit Solun Meringil Bôkthersa. I myself received a letter identical to the one which I hold here, a letter bearing Lord Seregil's signature and sealed with Lord Seregil's mark. In this letter are statements which suggest he was plotting sedition and treason against Skala. Yet here, in addition to the duplicate, I find another letter bearing the identical salutation, signature, and seals, which is in every way innocent in content."

Honed by years of practice, the Vicegerent's voice echoed around the cold chamber. "I caution you to speak the truth, Alben the Apothecary. How plead you in the face of this evidence?"

"I—I heard a noise. Last night I heard a noise!" stammered the wretched man. "I went down and found that box. Someone must have thrown it in my window! When I heard the soldiers I panicked, great lord, most honored Queen!"

Standing behind the accused man, Imaneus shook his head.

Impassive as the marble statues of her ancestors, Idrilain signaled to the bailiff, who strode to a side door and knocked. Two warders escorted in an immensely fat woman in a garish brocade night robe.

"Ghemella, gem cutter of Dog Street," announced the bailiff.

Catching sight of Alben, Ghemella screeched out, "You tell

'em, Alben, you tell how I only did the seal work! You miserable bastard, you tell 'em I didn't know no more of it than that!"

The accused man buried his face in his hands with a loud moan.

"Bailiff, speak the sentence for forging the documents or seals of a noble," the Queen ordered, looking sternly at the miserable pair trembling before her.

"The sentence is death by torture," announced the woman.

Alben groaned again, rocking miserably on his knees.

"My Queen, I am here at your own summons. Might I speak?" asked Nysander.

"I always value your council, Nysander í Azusthra."

"My Queen, I suggest that it is unlikely that these two acted on their own, but at the behest of another," said Nysander, choosing his words carefully. "It is certain that Lord Seregil was not approached for the purpose of blackmail, nor was there any such evidence in the case of the late Lord Vardarus. Had these two been acting on their own, surely that would have been their motive."

Phoria bristled visibly. "Surely you're not suggesting that it would in any way mitigate the severity of their offense?"

"Certainly not, Your Highness," Nysander replied gravely. "I only wish to point out that the person who would orchestrate such a deception represents a far greater threat. Should it be determined, as I suspect it will, that the same person is behind the slandering of both Lord Vardarus and Lord Seregil, then we must learn what motivated them to so desperate a course of action."

"We shall have that information out of these two soon enough!" Barien said, glowering.

"With all respect, my Lord Vicegerent, information gained under torture is not always reliable, even with a wizard in attendance. Pain and fear cloud the mind, making it difficult to read with any certainty."

"I am quite aware of your theories regarding torture," Barien returned stiffly. "What is your point?"

"My point, Lord Barien, is that this whole matter is far too grave to trust to such methods. Reprehensible as I find the actions of these creatures, they are inconsequential pawns in a greater game. It is their master whom we must run to ground at all costs."

As he'd expected, Barien and Phoria still looked dubious but Idrilain nodded approvingly.

"And what is your alternative?" she asked.

"Your Majesty, I humbly suggest that should you, in your great mercy, commute the sentence of the condemned to banishment in exchange for a full and free confession, then we may be a good deal better off in the end. Imaneus can validate whatever information they give."

Idrilain looked to the younger wizard.

"I have always concurred with Nysander's opinions regarding confession under torture, my Queen," said Imaneus.

With a humorless smile, Idrilain turned back to the accused, speaking directly to them for the first time. "What will it be, you two? Full confession for the loss of your right hand and exile—or a red-hot pike up your miserable backsides?"

"Confession, great Queen, confession!" croaked Alben. "I don't know the man's name and I never asked. He had the look of a noble but I'd never seen him before and he hadn't a Rhíminee accent. But it was the same one both times, for the letters—forgeries, that is—against Vardarus and Lord Seregil."

"The truth so far, my Queen," announced Imaneus.

"What other forgeries did you execute for this man?" demanded the Queen.

"Shipping manifests, mostly," quavered Alben, staring miserably at the floor. "And—" He faltered to a halt, trembling more violently than ever.

"Out with it, man. What else?" barked Barien.

"Two—two Queen's Warrants," whispered Alben, naming the document that allowed the bearer access anywhere in the land, including the Palace itself.

"You admit to forging the signature of the Queen *herself*!" Phoria burst out furiously. "When was this?"

Alben quailed miserably. "Three years ago, it must be now. They weren't any good, though, when I delivered them."

"Why not?" Barien's voice betrayed nothing, but Nysander was surprised to note that the Vicegerent had gone quite pale. Phoria also seemed shaken.

"They hadn't any seals yet," whined the wretched man. "I don't know where he meant to get them. I never kept any copies of the warrants, Your Highness, I swear! Let this wizard be my witness, I knew better than to mess with those!"

"And they never got no Queen's Seal from me, I swear by the

Four!" Ghemella chimed in. Again, Imaneus indicated that the truth had been spoken.

"When did this occur?" Barien asked again.

"Three years ago last Rhythin, my lord."

"Are you certain? Surely you've done hundreds of forgeries. How is it that you recall this particular one so clearly?"

"It's partly the warrants, my lord. It's not every day you get a chance at something like that," Alben quavered. "But there was the manifest business, too. One of them was for a ship called the *White Hart*, registered out of Cirna. I recall it because I did a favor for my neighbor, putting his lad's name on the crew list. Only, you see, the ship went down with all hands in the first of the autumn storms less than a month later. The boy was lost."

"You're certain of the name? The *White Hart*?" asked Phoria.

"Yes, Highness. I don't recall the other vessels, but I know that one. I watched the port lists for months, hoping she'd turn up and the boy with her. My neighbor's never spoken to me since over it. Anyway, this man who came to me? He wanted a few other things over the years, manifests mostly, until last spring. Late one night in Nythin he came saying he had a letter he wanted altered and could I do it? The very letter you have there, Majesty, belonging to Lord Vardarus. For one hundred gold sesters I made him two copies with the changes. Ghemella did the seals, like always."

"And you made copies for yourself," interjected Nysander. "In case you might use them yourself for future gain?"

Alben nodded silent admission.

"And did this man provide you with the letters of Lord Seregil?"

Alben hesitated. "Only the first one my lord. The rest came to me from Ghemella just recently and I sold them to that same man."

"I bought them off chars," the gem cutter put in hastily.

"What's she saying?" asked Phoria.

" 'Char' is the street parlance for a dealer in stolen papers," explained Nysander.

"That's so, your lordship," Ghemella said, determined not to leave out any detail. "I got them from an old cripple named Dakus."

Ah, Seregil, you outfoxed yourself that time! Nysander thought resignedly, knowing well enough who this "Dakus" was and where the second damning letter had originated.

"This fellow doing all the buying, he was pleased with the work I did," Alben continued. "He said he'd pay well for any letters from nobles whose lineage went outside Skala."

"Lord Vardarus' great-grandfather was a Plenimaran baron." Idrilain frowned, tapping the hilt of her sword. "And Seregil—well, that was certainly no secret!"

"And so you made the forgeries for him and once again kept copies for yourself," Barien said. "What was his purpose in securing these documents?"

"He never said, my lord, and I never asked," Alben replied with a hint of skewed dignity. "You'll pardon me for putting it so, but a forger doesn't last long without discretion."

"That is all you can tell us, then?" Barien looked to the wizard still standing over the accused pair.

"It's as much as I know of the matter, my lord," Alben assured him.

Imaneus nodded again but Nysander forestalled him. "A few salient points remain to be established, the first being when the latest forgery was to be delivered and to whom. The second is whether or not the prisoners know of any Leran connection with this whole affair."

"Lerans!" Barien grasped angrily at his heavy chain of office. "What have the Lerans to do with this?"

"I don't know anything about Lerans," Alben cried out, looking imploringly up at Idrilain. "I'm loyal to the throne no matter what your blood is, great lady! I wouldn't have anything to do with that sort of thing."

"Nor I, your ladyship, nor I!" Ghemella sobbed.

"They speak the truth," said Imaneus.

"Their loyalty is so noted," Idrilain observed sarcastically. "But what of Nysander's first question? When are these new forgeries to be delivered, and to whom?"

"Tomorrow night, my Queen," said Alben. "There were three this time, those you have there done up in the yellow ribbon. There's a letter of Lord Seregil's, one from a Lady Bisma, and another from Lord Derian."

"All with foreign connections," noted Phoria.

"I wouldn't know about that," Alben maintained. "The gentleman only said I was to give them to no one but himself, just as before. He always comes alone at night. That's the end of it, my Queen, and by the Hand of Dalna, I can't think of a thing I've left out now!"

Idrilain turned her icy gaze on the jeweler. "Have you anything to add?"

"I bought the papers and made the seals," Ghemella whined, tears dripping down over her quivering jowls. "I swear by the Four, my Queen, I knew nothing more than that of the whole business!"

When the prisoners and officials had been dismissed, Barien rounded on Nysander.

"What's all this about Lerans?" he demanded. "If you have any evidence of such activity in the city you must share it with me at once!"

"I should certainly have done so," Nysander replied. "At this point it is simply a theory which makes a great deal of sense."

"Poor old Vardarus," Idrilain said sadly, pulling a letter from the box. "If only he'd spoken up—"

"You had no choice, given the evidence," Phoria insisted staunchly. "It all seemed irrefutable. At least Lord Seregil's come to no harm."

"Ah yes, Seregil. And what of him, Nysander? By rights I can't hold him. Yet if I release him the traitorous bastards who've concocted all this will surely bolt."

"That is certain," the wizard agreed. "He must remain where he is for now and we must hasten to allay suspicion at the apothecary's house. The neighbors will be gossiping of the night's events, and word travels all too quickly to evil ears. Our only hope lies in tracking this buyer of forged papers when he comes for the next packet. Alben could be put back in place—with all suitable restraints, of course—for the time it takes to apprehend our man."

"It must be done quietly," cautioned Barien. "If word of this business should get out to the people, especially about Vardarus, I shudder to think of the reaction."

Idrilain waved a hand impatiently. "It's the tracking I'm concerned with. There's no room for failure. Barien, Phoria, leave us."

Accustomed to such peremptory dismissals, the Princess Royal and Vicegerent withdrew at once. Nysander watched them go, troubled by something in Barien's manner.

"He's been terribly upset by this whole business," said Idrilain. "I wish you'd mentioned your concerns about the Lerans to him before. He's always found the whole idea so upsetting."

"My apologies," Nysander replied. "It was simply a stab in the dark."

"But a good one, the more evidence I see. Damn it, Nysander, if those traitors have grown strong enough for something like this, then I want them destroyed! This delivery has to be handled perfectly, and anyone who can get their hands on a Queen's Warrant may well know the faces of my spies. Your people are another matter; even I don't know who most of them are."

Nysander bowed deeply, relieved that she'd reached the desired conclusion on her own. "The Watchers are at your command, as always. Have I your permission to pursue the matter in my own fashion?"

Idrilain clenched a fist around the hilt of her sword. "Use whatever means you see fit. Whoever this traitor is, I want his head on a pike by week's end!"

"As do I, my Queen," replied Nysander, "though I will be surprised if there is only one."

29

AN ABRUPT CHANGE
OF SCENERY

Caught in midpace, Seregil ran headlong
into something in the darkness. Backing
up hastily, he could just make out two tall
forms that had somehow materialized in
the cell. For a chilling instant, his mind
skipped back to the lonely Mycenian inn and
the dark presence he'd grappled with there;
then he caught the familiar smell of parchment
and candle smoke.

"Nysander?"

"Yes, dear boy, and Thero." Drawing
Seregil to the back of the cell, he spoke close
to his ear. "Thero has come to take your
place."

"How?"

"No time for explanations. Join hands with
him."

Biting back a flood of questions, Seregil
did as Nysander asked. Thero's hands were
cold but steady in his as Nysander took them
firmly by the shoulders and began a silent
incantation.

The transformation happened with dizzying
swiftness. For an instant the shadows of the
cell seemed to brighten, swirl, engulf them
all—and when Seregil's vision cleared, he
found himself on the wrong side of the room
facing a slim, all-too-familiar figure.

Raising a hand to his face, he felt a coarse mat of beard covering a gaunt cheek.

"Bilairy's Balls and Kidneys—"

"Quiet!" hissed Nysander.

"Take care with my body," Thero warned, touching his own new face.

"I'm more anxious to trade back than you, believe me!" Seregil shuddered, swaying a little in his new, taller frame. He could guess what was next and dreaded it.

Nysander slipped a firm hand beneath his arm and led him to the back wall of the cell. Reluctantly, Seregil took a deep breath, squared his shoulders, and stepped forward into the aperture that yawned, blacker than darkness—

—and staggered out again, blinking and gagging, into the sudden brightness of Nysander's casting room.

"Steady now, I've got you," Micum said, catching him as his knees gave way. "Alec, the brandy. And the basin, too, by the looks of him."

Seregil crouched over the brass basin for a moment, fighting down the intense nausea brought on by the spell; translocation spells had by far the worst aftereffect. Settling back on his heels, he gratefully accepted a cup of brandy.

Alec stared at him, goggle-eyed. "Seregil, is that really you in there?"

Seregil examined the pale, bony fingers wrapped around the cup, then knocked back the fiery liquor in a single gulp. "Gruesome, isn't it?"

"Thero was no more pleased than you by the prospect," sighed Nysander. "He *was*, however, a good deal more gracious."

"Forgive me," Seregil retorted. "I'm just not myself tonight."

Alec was still staring. "You've got Thero's voice, but somehow—I don't know, it still *sounds* more like you. Is it different than when you changed into an otter?"

"Decidedly." Seregil looked down at his new body warily. "It's like wearing an ill-fitting suit of clothes you can't take off. He wears his linen rather tight, too. I didn't know you could do this, Nysander!"

"It is not a practice of which the Orëska particularly approves," replied the wizard with a meaningful wink. "As it was successful, however, I should like to undertake a brief experiment. Do you recall the spell for lighting a candle?"

"You want me to try it while I'm in this body?"

"If you would."

Nysander placed a candlestick on the casting table. Getting to his feet, Seregil held his hand over the candle.

Micum gave Alec's sleeve a surreptitious tug, whispering, "You might want to stand back a bit, just in case."

"I heard that," Seregil muttered. Centering his concentration on the blackened wick, he spoke the command word.

The results were instantaneous. With a rending groan, the polished table split down the middle and fell apart in two neat halves. The candle, still unlit, clattered to the floor.

They all regarded the wreckage in silence for a moment, then Nysander bent to finger the splintered wood.

Seregil sighed. "Well, I hope that answered your question."

"It has answered several, the most significant being that the transformation of magical power was complete. Thero should be fairly safe, providing we proceed with all possible haste. There is a great deal to discuss before Alec returns to Wheel Street."

"I have to go back tonight?" Alec asked, clearly crestfallen at the prospect. "But Seregil only just got—"

Seregil gave him a playful cuff. "Appearances, Alec, appearances! You're the master of the house in my absence, as well as a possible suspect by the sound of things. We can't have you dropping out of sight with no explanation."

"Quite right," Nysander agreed. "But we shall lay our plans before you go. Come down to the sitting room, all of you. I expect Seregil would like a decent supper. Thero ate almost nothing tonight."

"I can feel that!" Seregil patted his lean belly wryly. Following the others downstairs, he touched his face again. An unruly hair on his upper lip tickled a nostril and he smoothed it impatiently.

"Amazing," he muttered. "I've never cared much for all this hair you people have sprouting out of your faces anyway, but now that I've got it myself—it's absolutely revolting!"

Micum proudly stroked his heavy red mustache. "For your information, we consider it a sign of virility."

"Oh?" Seregil snorted. "And how many times have I sat waiting in the middle of nowhere while you scraped away at your chin with a knife and cold water?"

"It's my fashion," Micum said, giving Alec a wink. "Kari likes it this way—smooth cheeks with a bit of tickle thrown in."

"It itches," Seregil complained, scratching under his nose again. "Teach me to shave, will you?"

"You most certainly will not!" Nysander said sternly.

During supper the others outlined their recent activities for Seregil. He chuckled appreciatively over their adventures in Hind Street but grew serious at Nysander's report.

"Forging a Queen's Warrant? No wonder Barien was upset. Except for the Queen and Phoria, he's the only person with access to the necessary seals."

"Rightful access," Micum amended. "What do you suppose this ship, the *White Hart*, ended up with in her hold?"

Seregil looked to Nysander. "I could probably find out. Three years is a long time, but records would be kept in the shipping master's offices at her port of call. It won't show us her real cargo, I'm certain, but it would be a start."

"It will probably prove unrelated to the business at hand, yet I should prefer to leave no avenue untried," mused Nysander. "And now let us lay our plans for tomorrow."

Dawn was only a few hours away when they'd finished, and Alec suddenly gave in to a cavernous yawn.

"Sorry," he said, yawning again.

Seregil grinned. "No wonder you're tired. You've been busy!"

Thero would be a lot better-looking if he'd smile more, Alec thought, surprised at the difference it made. What must Seregil's face look like now, with Thero's mind behind it?

"I'm done in myself," Micum said. "If we're all in agreement on tomorrow's work, Alec and I had better go find our beds before the sun comes up."

"You're getting old," Seregil scoffed, following them upstairs. "Used to be we'd be up for two or three days before you'd begin to flag."

"By the Flame, you've got that right! Another few years and I'll be happy to spend my days in a sunny corner of Kari's garden spinning lies for the servants' children."

At the workroom door, Alec turned for a last look at Seregil in Thero's body. He couldn't imagine a more unlikely combination. Shaking his head, he said, "It's good to have you back— sort of."

"Sort of good or sort of back?" Seregil countered, managing a semblance of his familiar lopsided grin in spite of the beard.

"Sort of both," said Alec.

"And I sort of thank you, all of you, for your good work tonight on my behalf," Seregil said, clasping hands with them. "Things were beginning to look a bit grim in that cell. Between the four of us, we should be able to sort things out soon enough."

A crushing weariness settled over Seregil as he went back downstairs. Collapsing gratefully on Thero's clean, narrow bed, he hadn't the strength left to pull off his shoes.

It's the magic, he thought, drifting off to sleep. *Damn stuff always wears me out.*

Exhausted as he was, the night was not a peaceful one. Tossing restlessly, he fought his way through a parade of uneasy dreams. At first they were only fragmented glimpses of the past few days—a distorted event, repetitious snippets of conversation, faces of no consequence looming again and again. Gradually, however, the images began to coalesce.

He was still in Thero's body, riding on horseback through the city. It was dark and he was lost. The street markers were gone, the lamps unlit on their hooks. Frustrated and a little frightened, he pushed on at a gallop.

His horse had no head; the reins passed over a smooth, glossy hump and disappeared somewhere underneath the animal's chest.

I can't stop it anyway, he thought. *Letting go of the reins, he clung to the saddlebow.*

Flecked with sweat, the strange creature thundered for hours, carrying him down one unfamiliar street after another until an owl flew up beneath its feet. Startled, the horse reared and threw him, then disappeared into the surrounding darkness.

Looking up, he found himself at the gate of Red Tower Prison.

Enough! I'm getting my own body back right now! he thought angrily, floating up from the ground and soaring to the roof of the prison.

It felt wonderful to fly, and he circled the Tower a few times, savoring it. The ships in the harbor were all on fire, however, and this disturbed him greatly. Diving like a swallow, he darted in through a hole in the prison roof.

It was dark here, too. Stumbling through the blackness, he spied a glimmer of light ahead. It came through the grille of a cell door. The door was locked but the wood turned to red butterflies at his touch. Passing through their gentle resistance, he stepped into a fiery brightness and threw his arm up to shield his eyes.

His true body stood in the center of the room, naked except for the crawling mass of tiny, spider-shaped flames that encased it from the neck down.

They should be gone! *he thought, repulsed by the sight.*

His body raised a hand to its chest, saying with Thero's voice, "They're coming from here."

"I'll stop them."

Approaching cautiously, Seregil brushed at the flame creatures on the chest. They fell away at his touch, revealing a bright blue eye glaring balefully from a bloody hole in the chest just over the breastbone. Recoiling, Seregil watched in mounting horror as the skin around the eye began to twitch and stretch. The flame creatures crumpled and fell away and he could see the writhing motions beneath the skin of his body's chest and belly, as if something hideous was clawing its way out from inside.

Tears of blood streamed down from the unnatural eye but his face—Thero's now—smiled calmly. Still smiling, Thero leapt at him, arms outstretched as if to embrace him. With a strangled cry, Seregil fell backward through the red butterflies—

He sat up with a gasp. Pulling free of the tangled sheets, he went to the hearth and poked up a fire bright enough to light the room. His clothes were soaked through with cold, sour sweat. Stripping them off, he looked down at the pale, angular body he inhabited. Little wonder he was dreaming of his own! The details of the nightmare were already skittering away, but he recalled the image of the eye with a shudder.

Tossing a few more logs on the fire, he climbed back into bed and pulled the covers up to his nose. As he drifted back to sleep it occurred to him that this was the first time in weeks that he'd dreamed at all.

• • •

Late-morning light was streaming in at the open window when he opened his eyes again. Lying quietly for a moment, he discovered that he'd forgotten most of the nightmare. His second sleep had been filled with dreams of a lascivious nature quite unlike his usual fare and he'd awakened to find Thero's body in an uncomfortable state of arousal. Cold water soon put a stop to that. He pulled on a clean robe and went up the tower stairs two at a time.

"Good morning!" Nysander smiled at him over a cup of morning tea, a familiar, reassuring sight. "Are you feeling more at—dear me, you appear to have slept badly."

"I did," Seregil admitted. "I had some nightmare about going after my body. It had that eye in the chest, where the scar is. It was all sort of familiar, in a way, like I'd dreamed it before."

"How unpleasant. Do you recall any more of it than that?"

"Not really. Something about flying, I think, and fire—? I don't know. Later on there were other, different images. Is it possible for me to have Thero's dreams?"

"A mental link through his body? I should not think so. Why?"

Seregil rubbed his eyelids and yawned. "Oh, nothing. First night in a new body and all that. Just between you and me, though, a few days in the Street of Lights wouldn't do Thero any harm."

"He seems to be celibate by nature."

Seregil chuckled cryptically. "By practice, perhaps, but *not* by nature!"

They kept to Nysander's tower all day, avoiding anyone perceptive enough to detect a change in "Thero"—not an easy task in a house full of wizards.

Wethis appeared to notice nothing amiss, and Seregil noted with amusement the guarded dislike that lurked behind the young servant's deferential mask as he went about his daily duties in Thero's room.

At midday Nysander went out to attend to some business elsewhere in the House. Seregil was poking restlessly around the workroom when a sharp rap sounded at the tower door. It was

House etiquette to open the door to all callers, so Seregil had no choice but to answer. Peering out, he found Ylinestra waiting impatiently in the corridor.

Her green silk gown was gathered tightly beneath the breasts, setting off her ravishing loveliness in a fashion that Seregil could not help but note.

He did not know her well, and her behavior toward him had always been civil to the point of coolness. It was quickly apparent now, however, that this reserve did not extend to Nysander's assistant.

"Ah, Thero! Is Nysander in?" She flashed a radiant, violet-eyed smile.

"Not just now, my lady," Seregil replied, wondering how Thero comported himself around such beautiful women. He soon had an inkling.

"So formal today!" Ylinestra chided playfully, sweeping past him. The crowded confines of the entrance might have explained the generous brush of silk-clad breast and thigh against his side; something in the lilt of her voice warned otherwise. Following her back to the workroom, Seregil felt a pleasant tug of anticipation. Both of them, he suspected, were about to put on excellent performances.

"Out chasing around on behalf of his pretty Aurënfaie friend, is he?" she sighed, turning back to him with a conspiratorial pout.

"Not at the moment." Seregil gave a credible rendering of Thero's customary disdain at any mention of himself. "He's gone to see Mosrin í Argavan. Something about the library."

"And left you here to solitary toil, eh? How lonely for you. And me, as it turns out." Ylinestra drifted closer, and Seregil was suddenly aware of the light, spicy scent she wore. With it came a sudden mental image of the perfume rising invisibly from the warm cleft between her breasts. That put him on his guard. It wasn't his usual sort of thought at all, and smacked of magical machination.

"I hardly see Nysander anymore," she sulked, just inches away now. "You tell him for me that if he doesn't mend his ways, I'll look elsewhere for inspiration. I daresay he neglects you as well when that Seregil fellow is around. It makes one wonder—"

Arching a perfect eyebrow, she let the thought hang unfinished between them, then surprised him with a brisk, almost maternal pat on the arm. "If you find yourself at loose ends, my offer still stands."

"Offer?"

"Oh, shame on you!" she twinkled, coy again. "Those Ylani levitation chants I promised you? You still haven't come to learn them and you seemed so eager when we spoke last. I've a few other bits of magic that I think you'll enjoy, too, things Nysander can't teach you. I'd show you one now, only I need my own things. You must come to my rooms. You wouldn't want me to lose patience with you, would you?"

"No, not at all," Seregil assured her. "I'll come as soon as I can. I promise."

"There's a good boy." Brushing his cheek chastely with her own, she swept out leaving a light drift of scent in her wake.

Illior's Fingers! Seregil thought, impressed. What she hoped to gain by seducing Thero was beyond comprehension, but the sooner Nysander knew what was going on, the better.

To his disappointment, Nysander was more amused than outraged.

"What are you so upset about?" he asked. "Only this morning you were advocating just such a course of action yourself."

"Well, yes, but not with his master's lover!" sputtered Seregil.

"It is not like you to be such a prig," countered Nysander. "I appreciate your concern, but it is quite unwarranted. The lovely Ylinestra and I claim no more hold on one another than we do on the wind. Though I flatter myself that she does take some genuine pleasure in my company, it is my magic that interests her most. She has shown me a few interesting aspects of her own art, too, but it must be apparent to you of all people where my real interest in her lies."

"A good lay?"

"Beyond *description,* dear boy! And as neither she nor I have asked more than the other is prepared to give, we are quite satisfied with the arrangement. At heart, Ylinestra is a vain creature whose sexual tastes run more commonly to the conquest of virginal young men."

"She's a man-eater, all right. She's always very cool with me though."

Nysander let out a dry chuckle "I would hardly describe *you* as virginal. I suspect she also prefers her lovers to be more singular in their tastes than your reputation suggests. It is Alec I would keep an eye on, if I were you. She would have him—what is that colorful phrase of Micum's?"

" 'On a platter with boiled leeks'?" Seregil snorted. "Thanks for the warning."

30

DOWN TO BUSINESS AT LAST

By nightfall, suitable explanations regarding the previous night's disturbances had been carefully spread among Alben's Hind Street neighbors. The forger, chastened and anxious to be of service, was temporarily reinstalled in his shop under strict but indiscernible supervision.

An icy drizzle misted down, making for a clammy vigil. Seregil stationed Micum on watch in the alley beneath Alben's window, while Alec monitored the street fronting the building. Seregil took up his own position in the shadows of the courtyard.

As the hours dragged by, he noted grudgingly that he seemed to mind the cold less in Thero's body. The man's night vision was rather poor, however, and his sense of taste was hopeless. Overall, Seregil reflected, the habitation of another person's body was nothing to be taken lightly. In fact, there was something rather obscene about it; he couldn't scratch without feeling like he was taking liberties, and trips to the privy were decidedly disquieting. It was, he concluded, rather like being forced into bed with a lover you didn't fancy. And it was certainly closer contact with Thero than he ever hoped to experience again.

What Thero might be experiencing in his body he didn't care to speculate.

He was just wondering if he dared risk a stretch when he caught the sound of rapid footsteps from the street. Striding into the courtyard, a cloaked figure rapped softly at Alben's door. The apothecary answered at once, lighting the visitor into the darkened shop with a candle. In the instant both men were framed in the doorway, Seregil got a clear look at the newcomer—a well-dressed man of middle years. In spite of his clothing, however, the unconscious bob of the head he gave Alben in greeting betrayed him; this was a servant out of livery for the purpose of the evening's assignment.

Alben hung back for an instant, giving the candle a slight sideways jerk before he closed the door. This was the signal. Creeping silently to the courtyard gate, Seregil passed it on to Alec.

He was about to resume his hidden position when he heard the rattle of Alben's latch. Caught in the open, Seregil made a show of heading up one of the tenement stairways. The emissary seemed unconcerned at being observed, even nodding to him as they passed in the yard.

Seregil waited a slow count of five after the man left the courtyard, then slipped out to see which way he'd gone. Alec motioned to the left. Micum had already been signaled, and together the three set off in pursuit.

Their man sauntered along at his ease for a few streets, then went into a tavern.

"You'd better go in. He's already had a glimpse of me," Seregil whispered to Micum. Nodding, Micum sized the place up, then sauntered in.

Micum Cavish had a particular aptitude for blending into tavern crowds. Settling near the door, he ordered a pint and kept a surreptitious eye on their quarry.

The fellow sat alone near the hearth, slowly nursing a mug of ale as if waiting for someone. Presently a young servant woman joined him. Sitting down with her back to Micum, she greeted her companion with a heartfelt kiss. Though Micum saw nothing amiss, it was certainly the perfect opportunity for a parcel of some sort to change hands. A moment later the pair left together.

Strolling out behind them, Micum loitered a moment under a street lantern and made a show of adjusting his cloak as he noted the direction the couple took. Alec and Seregil ghosted off in silent pursuit, and he followed.

The couple walked along arm in arm, heads together, to a small fountain circle where they suddenly disappeared down a dark side way. Hurrying to catch up, Micum nearly fell over his friends crouched at the mouth of an alley. From beyond came the muffled but unmistakable sounds of a hasty coupling in progress.

Leaving Alec on guard, Seregil and Micum went back to the fountain for a whispered conference.

"What do you think? Did he pass anything to her?" asked Seregil.

"He could have, but I didn't see it happen." Micum jerked a thumb in the direction of the alley. "Given this business, we can't be sure the girl's in on anything, or if they're just lovers."

"Damn! We'd better watch both of them. They're certain to part ways sooner or later."

"You take her," said Micum. "Alec and I will stay on him. I'll meet you back at Nysander's."

A few moments later the sighing lovers reappeared and continued on in the direction of the Noble Quarter. There were more lanterns as they went on, and a good deal more traffic; Seregil and the others spread out so as to be less conspicuous.

They nearly came to grief at the Astellus Circle. The Street of Lights was alive with activity, and the Circle was crowded with patrons coming and going from the various establishments. Slipping through the crowd, Seregil suddenly lost sight of the lovers. A few yards away, he saw Alec casting around in alarm. A sharp whistle brought them both around. Standing on steps of the colonnade, Micum gestured in two directions at once.

Seregil caught a quick glimpse of the girl heading off down Eagle Street by herself. Trusting the man to Alec and Micum, Seregil hurried after her.

He had no problem keeping her in sight. There was enough activity in the street to cover his pursuit and she seemed to have no qualms about her own safety as she strode past the walled gardens of the villas. Eagle Street ended in Silvermoon and she turned left toward the Palace. As he reached the Queen's Park, Seregil began formulating a plan for following her onto the grounds. Instead, however, she ducked down a side lane to the servants' entrance of a grand house across the broad avenue from the Park.

Seregil waited until he was certain she wasn't coming out again, then returned to the street. With a growing sense of foreboding, he scowled up at the gilded bulls rearing protectively over the gates of the eminent and all-too-familiar residence.

Alec and Micum dogged their man through a succession of fashionable avenues to a house in the Street of Three Fountains, which was not far from Wheel Street. Unlocking a side gate, he disappeared into a fashionable villa.

"One of us should go in," Alec whispered. "The other can stand watch in case anything goes wrong."

"I guess we both know who's better at that sort of thing. Go on."

Scaling the wall, Alec dropped down into the garden. The layout of the place was similar to Seregil's house, but on a larger scale. The garden surrounded the house on three sides, and there were an encouraging number of windows overlooking it. Keeping an eye out for dogs and watchmen, he crept forward.

Starting at the right side of the building, he worked his way from window to window, pulling himself up by the sills to peek in. Most of the rooms were dark or unoccupied, except for a salon toward the front where two pretty young women sat before a blazing hearth. One was working at an embroidery frame while her companion plucked listlessly at a lyre.

Leaving off, he gave the kitchen door a wide berth and set to work on the left side of the house, though with no more success than before. He was about to give up when he noticed a faint glow of light from a balcony just overhead. The ornate stonework surrounding a first-floor window afforded ample fingerholds. Climbing up, he eased himself over the balustrade. There was a small table on the balcony. Two wine cups stood there, and a warm pipe.

The balcony door had been left ajar; peering in, Alec discovered an elegantly appointed bedchamber lit by a single lamp. Another door stood open across the room, and through it came the sounds of a heated argument. There were two male voices involved, one strident with anger, the other shrill in its protestations of innocence.

"How can you accuse me of such a thing?" the higher voice demanded.

"How can you look me in the face and deny it?" boomed the other. "You greedy, bungling idiot. You've destroyed me! You have destroyed this family!"

"Uncle, please."

"Never let me hear that word in your throat again, you viper!" shouted the other. "From this day forth you are no kin of mine."

A door slammed forcibly, and Alec shrank back as a young man entered the bedchamber and collapsed into a chair. His elaborate surcoat showed him to be the master of the house. He was fair-skinned, with a small blond chin tuft that he fingered nervously as he sat.

A nagging tingle of recognition stirred in the back of Alec's mind as he studied the haggard profile. He couldn't immediately place the man, but he felt certain he'd seen him before.

The man was clearly agitated. Gnawing at a thumbnail, he lurched to his feet again, then beat a fist against one thigh as he paced up and down the room.

The significance of the balcony table occurred to Alec almost too late. The man swerved suddenly, heading out to settle his nerves with wine and tobacco. Clambering back over the railing, Alec caught hold of two carved balusters and hung by his fingers. The evening drizzle had thickened to sleet and the polished marble felt slick as lard in his hands as he clung doggedly on, feet dangling twenty feet above the ground. Glancing sideways, he saw that he could probably reach the cornice of the downstairs window with his left foot but he didn't dare chance the noise. To make matters worse, his side of the balcony overlooked the street; it would be the most natural thing in the world for the man to lean on the railing just there, glance down—

Looking up, Alec could see the side of the man's silken slipper less than a foot from his rapidly whitening knuckles. Cold fire ached down through his wrists and arms, weakening his grip, numbing his fingers. Melting sleet trickled down over his face and ran down his sleeves into his armpits. Biting his lip, he gripped the posts harder, scarcely daring to breathe.

Just when it seemed he'd have to chance dropping and running, a knock came at the chamber door. Tappng his pipe out on the railing above Alec, the man disappeared back into the room.

Alec shook the hot ashes from his hair and found a foothold

on the window cornice. Bracing his shoulder in the angle of the balcony, he flexed his stiffened fingers. The balcony door had been left open again and he could hear the conversation inside quite clearly.

"Any difficulty with Alben?" This was the nobleman, calmer now and speaking with authority.

"Not exactly, my lord," replied the newcomer. "Though he didn't seem quite himself, somehow. But I did get the documents and these, as well, while I was out."

"Well done, Marsin, well done!"

Alec heard the metallic clink of coins changing hands.

"Thank you, sir. Shall I deliver it now?"

"No, I'll go. My horse is already saddled. See to it that the house is locked up for the night and inform Lady Althia that I'll be returning tomorrow."

"I will, sir, and a good evening to you."

Alec heard the servant leave, and a moment later the light was extinguished. Climbing down, he hurried back to the street in time to see a man galloping out the front gate on a white horse.

"We're losing him!" he exclaimed as Micum appeared out of the shadows beside him. "I think he's off to deliver the forged letters!"

"Deliver them where?" Micum asked, scanning the neighborhood for quickly obtainable horses. There were none.

"I don't know," Alec replied in an agony of impatience. The rider had already disappeared around a corner and the sound of hooves was fading rapidly. "Damn it, now we've lost him!"

"Can't be helped. At least we've got a connection to work with and that's a start. And you'll never guess who else came riding out of that gate a short while ago."

"Who?"

"Only the Lord Vicegerent himself. You should have seen him! I didn't know the old fellow could ride like that."

"Barien?" Alec's eyes widened as a memory snapped into place. "Maker's Mercy, that's it! This is Lord Teukros' house. The Vicegerent's *nephew*! I knew I'd seen him before, that day I rode around the Ring."

"The nephew, eh? By the Flame, that looks bad—though I can't imagine Barien mixed up in anything disloyal to the Queen!"

"He was cursing Teukros when I first got there," Alec told him. "He called him a viper and disowned him."

"Well, that's a strike in the old man's favor. Come on, we'd better go let the others know."

Still smarting over the loss of Teukros, Alec was in a dour mood by the time he and Micum reached Nysander's door.

"Good hunting?" the wizard inquired, letting them into the workroom.

"In a manner of speaking," Micum replied. "Is Seregil back?"

"No, he was up to something in the vicinity of the Palace when I last checked. Come downstairs and warm yourselves. You both look quite damp."

Standing before the sitting room fire, Alec carefully recounted their evening's work. Nysander made no effort to hide his dismay over what they'd learned and sat silently for some moments after he'd finished.

"What do you think?" Alec ventured. "Could Barien be mixed up in something like this?"

"It is difficult to imagine. Young Teukros is another matter, however. In spite of his obvious wealth, Teukros í Kallas is not known for his perspicacity. Whatever his involvement in this, I would wager that he is acting at the direction of another."

"We'd have found out if we could have followed him tonight," grumbled Alec.

"Patience, dear boy. It should not be difficult to obtain that information. You said Lord Teukros' pretty wife is at home tonight?"

"Yes, but we can't just knock on the door and ask her."

"Of course we can! What do you say, Micum? An urgent message carried by a servant of the Orëska House, one which must be delivered into Lord Teukros' hands at all costs this very night?"

Micum grinned wolfishly. "That should do the trick."

Going to his desk, Nysander quickly penned a cordial dinner invitation for the following evening.

"What happens when he shows up for dinner?" asked Alec, peering over the wizard's shoulder.

Nysander chuckled darkly. "Assuming that he does, I shall be afforded an opportunity to give closer attention to this enterprising young spy." Sealing the missive with an impressive array of ribbons and wax seals, Nysander sent Wethis off to deliver it.

Seregil arrived soon after. He was smeared with mud, and sported torn breeches and a ragged scrape across the back of one hand.

"Illior's Eyes, Seregil, what have you been doing with poor Thero's body?" asked Nysander, handing him a clean robe.

"You'd think he could at least climb a garden wall!" Seregil said in disgust, shucking the filthy breeches off to show them an angry bruise on one of Thero's pale, hairy knees. "Never mind that, though. Micum, Alec, you'll never guess where our little serving maid led me! Straight to the house of the Vicegerent."

He paused. "What? What is it? Neither of you look very surprised."

"That's because our man led us to Teukros' villa," Micum informed him. "Alec overheard him and his uncle having quite an argument."

"The man we followed tonight was Teukros' servant, by the name of Marsin. He brought the forged documents to Teukros," said Alec. "Then Teukros took off on horseback to deliver them, but we don't know where. Nysander's sent Wethis off to find out."

"I hope he does," said Seregil. "That prat Teukros certainly can't be at the bottom of anything like this! Incidentally, Barien came home after you saw him. I hung around to make certain the girl wasn't coming out again and saw him arrive. Anyway, a few minutes later a messenger goes across to the Queen's Park gate and tells the guards there he has a message for the Princess Royal. This same messenger is out again a few minutes later with someone wrapped up in a dark cloak and hood. I couldn't see her face, but it was Phoria; I know that stiff-legged stride of hers. I went over the wall to see what was up—that's when I fell—but I couldn't get a look at them."

He was interrupted by Wethis, who'd returned from his errand.

"Lord Teukros wasn't home to receive the message," the young servant reported. "Lady Althia says he's gone out to Lady Kassarie's estate and isn't expected home until tomorrow afternoon. Shall I ride out?"

"That is not necessary, Wethis, thank you. I shall not be needing you again tonight."

Micum raised a skeptical eyebrow as Wethis went out. "Kassarie? What would she want with a strutting cowbird like Teukros?"

"They have some common shipping interests, I believe," said Nysander.

"How interesting if Kassarie *was* mixed up in all this," Seregil speculated, looking pensive. "She's rich, powerful, and fairly influential among the more conservative nobles. To my knowledge she's not part of the Queen's inner circle, but—"

"Who's Kassarie?" asked Alec.

Seregil steepled his fingers before him in a manner that generally presaged one of his encyclopedic recitations. "Lady Kassarie ä Moirian is the head of another of Skala's oldest families. Like Barien, she can trace her lineage back to the Hierophantic migration. And, I should add, without a drop of foreign blood sullying her august veins. Her ancestors made their fortunes in stonework at Ero, and prospered again providing Queen Tamír with stone and masons to build her new capital. Her estate lies up in the mountains about ten miles or so southeast of the city."

Nysander rose to pace the small room. "Be that as it may, I find it inconceivable that Barien should be involved with such a plan. Illior's Eyes, I have known that man for fifty years! And Phoria? That makes no sense whatsoever."

"I can't imagine what she and the Lerans would have to gain from each other," Micum concurred. "In their eyes, her blood is as tainted as her mother's."

"She wouldn't be the first noble to be duped into a betrayal of some sort without realizing it," warned Seregil. "And if her dear close friend Lord Barien was in with the Lerans, he'd be just the man to do it."

"But why would he betray her?" snorted Nysander.

"Who knows? Alec and I could probably slip in and—"

"Absolutely not!" Nysander paused, rubbing his eyes. "I agree, dear boy, that we must examine this matter closely, but you must leave Barien and the Princess Royal to me. For the time being, you three are to confine your investigation to Teukros and Kassarie. It is not yet midnight; could you begin tonight?"

"Oh, I suppose we could drag ourselves out again, if we have to," Seregil drawled, exchanging a wink with the others.

"Excellent. I shall arrange a pass and see that your horses are saddled. Take whatever else you need from here. You must excuse me now, for I have work of my own to begin. Illior's Luck to you all!"

Alec let out a sigh of relief. "At least I don't have to go back to Wheel Street tonight. Runcer treats me like the master of the house, and I don't have a clue what I'm supposed to do."

"l know how you feel," said Seregil, stretching restlessly. "I'll go mad myself if I have to be cooped up in here much longer."

Watching his friend scratch irritably at Thero's bearded cheek, Alec wasn't certain if "in here" meant Nysander's tower or the assistant wizard's body.

31

KASSARIE

Red Orëska livery for Alec and Micum, together with a pass presented by "Thero," got the three of them through the Sea Gate without challenge. Once outside the walls, they followed the highroad south along the cliffs below the city. A few miles farther on, they turned aside onto another route that climbed into the hills.

Just like old times. Everybody knows the way but me, Alec thought resignedly.

This road climbed into forest to twist along the top of a broad river gorge. The ice-laden boughs of fir trees gradually closed in on their left; the rush of the river followed them on the right.

After several miles, Micum motioned for them to halt. Climbing down, he cast back and forth with a lightstone.

"See anything?" inquired Seregil.

"Not much. The mud must have stayed frozen all day up here."

Riding on, they caught a glimpse of watch fires ahead. Lady Kassarie's keep stood on a high cliff overlooking a bend in the river. Sheer cliffs rose behind it, and a high bailey guarded the front. Working their way stealthily around the periphery of the wall, the three spies climbed a wooded slope and climbed into the branches of a tall fir overlooking the place.

There seemed to be nothing amiss: an unremarkable collection of small outbuildings—sheds, wood stacks, and stables—cluttered the yard.

The keep itself was an imposing structure. Tall, square-built, and smooth-walled, it had no windows except for arrow slits below the third level. Square, flat-topped towers stood at each of the four corners, and watch fires burned on all but the one overhanging the gorge.

"Tight as a soaked barrel," Seregil muttered, craning his neck for a better look.

"Appears so," Micum agreed, shifting restlessly on his branch. "Looks like we'll do better tricking our way in."

"Too late for that now," said Alec. "It can't be more than a couple of hours to morning."

"True." Frowning, Seregil climbed down again. "Looks like we're spending a cozy night right here."

Nysander made his way to Silvermoon Street immediately upon leaving Seregil and the others. The streets were quiet at this hour and he met only one other person as he neared Barien's house, a hasty rider whose passing tore at the stillness of the night with a clatter of harness and hooves. The sound passed away with the rider, and he could hear the annoyed grumbling of the guards at the palace gates ahead.

He was surprised to find Barien's gate locked for the night and the lantern over the door extinguished. The Vicegerent shared Nysander's preference for the late hours and seldom retired so soon after midnight. Dismounting, Nysander rapped at the gate until the watchman appeared at the postern.

"Good evening to you, Lord Nysander," the man greeted him, accustomed to the wizard's odd hours.

"Good evening, Quil. I wish to speak with the Vicegerent."

"Sorry, my lord, but Lord Barien's abed already. He left instructions not to be disturbed by anyone but the Queen herself. He was quite firm about it, too. And just between you and me, sir, the chamberlain said the master didn't look well when he retired. He'd been out to dinner but come back early looking right peaked."

"I see," said Nysander. "Poor fellow, I hope it was nothing he ate. Where did he dine?"

"Chamberlain didn't say, my lord, only that Lord Barien wasn't to be disturbed on any account."

"Then I suppose I must call again tomorrow. Please give your master my respects."

Continuing along Silvermoon to a nearby fountain, Nysander sat on its rim and sent a sighting back to Barien's villa.

The Vicegerent was indeed in bed, thumbing listlessly through a small book lying open on the counterpane. Nysander recognized the book with a pang of sadness; it was a volume of bardic poetry he himself had given to Barien some years before. He seemed to settle at last on a page and Nysander shifted his sighting to read it.

"Break, Noble Heart. Dissolve to ashes if thy Honor impugnéd be," Nysander quoted silently, recognizing a line. A swift, tactful brush across the surface of Barien's mind revealed a deep, weary melancholy, nothing more.

It would have been simple enough to translocate himself the short distance to Barien's chamber, but a moment's deliberation left Nysander disinclined to do so. Neither Barien's mood nor current activity warranted such an impertinent intrusion. Tomorrow would be soon enough.

Seregil and the others spent a cheerless night beneath the trees, awakening at dawn to find one of Nysander's blue spheres hovering in the air just over Seregil's head. Passing his hand through it, he released the message.

"Learn whatever you can there, but return to the city as quickly as possible. Come directly to me."

Despite the muted affect inherent in the spell, there was an unmistakable hint of distress in the wizard's disembodied voice.

"What do you suppose that's all about?" yawned Micum, brushing damp leaves from his cloak.

"He must have gotten something out of Barien," said Seregil. "Let's see what there is to uncover here and get back."

A quick reconnaissance up the fir tree showed little change in the keep yard, though by daylight they learned the reason for the one dark tower.

The tower overlooking the gorge was in ruins. One side of its flat top had been struck by lightning and stood open to the sky. Judging by the weathered look of the broken stone, together with an overgrowth of branching, winter-browned tendrils of some creeping vine, it must have been in this condition for some years. It stood out against the solid symmetry of the surrounding structure like a rotten tooth in a sound mouth.

Waiting for a plausible hour of the morning, they proceeded with their first plan. Changing his Orëska tunic for a workman's smock, Alec set off with another fictitious summons for Teukros. Leading his horse back through the trees, he reappeared far enough down the road to give the appearance of having just ridden up the hill.

"I've a message for Lord Teukros," he told the gatekeeper, holding up the letter Seregil had prepared.

"You've wasted a long ride, lad," the man informed him. "Lord Teukros ain't here."

"But I was told he was spending the night here," Alec pressed, trying to act like a servant who'd just learned he'd ridden a long, hard way for nothing.

"Don't know about that," the man grunted, starting to swing the gate closed again.

"Wait," called Alec, dismounting before the heavy door could slam in his face. "I've got to take some answer back."

"That's nothing to me," said the gatekeeper, eyeing Alec's purse meaningfully.

A discreet coin rendered the man instantly more agreeable.

"Perhaps you'd be wanting to speak with our lady?" he suggested.

"I probably should."

Alec followed the man across the yard, taking in as many details as he could along the way. Three fine horses stood saddled and ready near the front door. Two of them had panniers tied behind the saddles. The third was caparisoned for a lady's hunting.

At the keep door, an elderly house servant eyed Alec disdainfully, asked his business, and left him standing in the middle of the hall with a look that said as clearly as words, *Don't steal anything while I'm gone.*

The furnishings of the vaulted hall were costly and in excellent condition. Silver urns and bowls gleamed on the mantelpiece without a hint of tarnish, and the rushes strewn over the floor were crisp and fragrant.

Splendid old tapestries covered the stone walls and these, too, had been lovingly maintained. Alec turned slowly, admiring as he always did the Skalans' taste for fantastic landscapes and creatures. One in particular caught his eye; it was designed to look like a window casement, out of which one could see a pride of griffins prowling an orchard against a mountainous backdrop. The piece was over twenty feet wide and bordered with elaborate designs. Scanning it with admiration, Alec was surprised to find one discordant element embroidered in the lower right-hand corner, the stylized figure of a curled lizard. Looking around, he saw that many of the other hangings had some sort of device in one corner, like a maker's mark—a rose, a crown, an eagle, a tiny unicorn, the curled lizard—a number of the larger ones had several marks together in a row. He was just bending down to study these more closely when he sensed movement behind him and turned, steeling himself to face the old manservant's renewed disapproval.

There was no one there.

It might have been a draft, Alec reasoned, taking a second glance around. Then again, any of the larger tapestries could easily conceal a passageway. Whatever the case, he suddenly had an uncomfortable sense of being observed. Unsure if it was instinct or fancy, he nonetheless did his best to appear as innocuous as possible, just in case.

The old man soon shuffled back in to announce his mistress, the Lady Kassarie ä Moirian. Kassarie swept in behind him, pulling on a hawking gauntlet as she entered. She was somewhere over forty years of age, with a broad, stern face and a manner to match. Alec stooped forward at once in a halting bow.

"What's all this about Lord Teukros?" she demanded impatiently.

"I've a message for him, my lady—" Alec began, showing the packet again.

"Yes, yes," she snapped. "But what possessed you to seek him here?"

"Well, my lady, I called at his house first thing this mornin' and was told by Lady Althia that he'd meant to ride out here last night. That's as much as I know of it."

"Dear me, that doesn't bode well," she said with evident concern. "He certainly never arrived, nor did I receive any word from him that he meant to come. Did you see anyone on the road this morning?"

"No, my lady."

"How very puzzling. I must send word to Althia at once. You can carry it back for me, boy. Who sent you, by the way?"

"Master Verik of Canvass Lane," Alec replied. Seregil had given him the name; Verik, a merchant of genteel but common birth, was a business associate of Teukros'.

"Very good, then. I'll just dash off that note." Having settled the matter to her own satisfaction, Kassarie turned briskly to the old retainer still hovering at her elbow. "Illester, take the lad to the kitchen while I prepare the letter. He ought to at least have a bit of hot food for his troubles."

Illester turned Alec over to a younger servant and sent them both outside again to come in at the back door.

"He's a sour old stick," Alec remarked when they were out of earshot.

"That's not for the likes of you to comment on," the servant returned stiffly.

Passing several small herb beds and a great black kettle hung steaming over an open fire, they came round to the kitchen door. Inside, two women were hard at work over wooden bread bowls.

"Kora, her ladyship wants this messenger boy fed," snapped the manservant. "See to it he stays put until he's called for."

"As if we don't have enough to occupy us this morning, and us up to the tits in flour," huffed the taller of the two women, pushing a lank strand of hair back with her forearm. "Stamie, Stamie girl! Where the blasted hell are you?"

A thin, pockmarked girl of seventeen or so staggered out of a pantry room with an immense ham in her arms. "What is it now, Auntie? I's just out to boil the ham as you told me."

"Put that aside for a moment and set this lad up in the chimney nook with a bite of tucker. There's some rabbit pie at the back of the larder needs eating. That'll do well enough for him."

Retreating meekly to his corner, Alec was quickly ignored by all but plain Stamie, who seemed to be the only friendly inhabitant of the place.

"You just let me heat this up for you," she said, setting the pot of leftovers in the coals. "Do you fancy a pint of beer with your food?"

"Yes, please. It's a long ride all the way up here from Rhíminee."

"Rhíminee, you say?" she exclaimed softly, stealing a glance in her aunt's direction. "Gods, what I wouldn't give to find service in the city! But you've a country accent yourself. How'd you manage it?"

"My position, you mean? Well now, there's not a lot to tell," Alec stammered; he'd been sent in as a simple messenger, for the Maker's sake! It hadn't occurred to any of them that he'd need some detailed history. "Master Verik knew my father, that's all."

"Lucky you. I was born into this lot, stuck out here in the williwags, same old faces day after day." Her callused hand brushed across his as she reached to stir the coals, and hectic patches of color fleeted across her sallow cheeks. "What's your name, stranger?"

"Elrid. Elrid of Market Lane," Alec replied, noting both her blush and the striped bead she wore on a bit of red yarn around her neck. It was a common country charm to attract a lover.

"Well, Elrid of Market Lane, it's a fair pleasure to see someone new for a change. At least someone I don't have to wait on hand and foot!" she added, rolling her eyes.

"Lady Kassarie's got guests, then?"

"Oh, yes, but even they're the same old lot. I spent half last night trying to keep old Lord Galwain's footman out of my skirts, as usual. Why is it never the one you want that takes the liberties, eh?"

This observation, together with the warm look that accompanied it, left no doubt where Alec stood in her estimation.

"You'd best be seeing after that ham now, Stamie," her aunt interrupted gruffly. "I'm sure this great big lad don't need you spooning his food into him. Off with you, now! And no mooning about."

With a resentful roll of her eyes, Stamie hefted the ham again and disappeared into the yard. Bolting down his pot of tepid scraps under Kora's watchful eye, Alec greeted Illester's reappearance with considerable relief.

The old man dourly handed him a sealed scroll and a silver coin. "See that you put that letter into Lady Althia's hands yourself, boy. Your horse has been watered. Off with you now!"

Message in hand, Alec galloped half a mile down the road before doubling back through the trees to where Seregil and Micum were waiting.

"Well?" Seregil demanded.

"I spoke to Lady Kassarie. She claims he never came and that she wasn't expecting him. The watchman said the same when he let me in."

"She didn't pretend not to know him, though?" asked Micum.

"No, she just seemed surprised and a bit worried over the whole business. She gave me this note to carry back."

Lifting the seals with his knife, Seregil read the letter. "Nothing unusual here. She sends her regards and hopes that Lady Althia's husband turns up soon. There's no sign of a hidden message or cipher."

"She did ask me if I'd noticed anyone on the road this morning," Alec told him.

"Nothing suspicious in that," said Micum. "What was the household like?"

"I only saw the hall, kitchen, and part of the yard. She has some other guests, though. I saw two horses saddled for traveling and the scullery maid mentioned a Lord Galwain."

"Well done," Seregil said, clapping him on the back. "What about Kassarie and her people?"

"She's civil enough, I guess. She sent me to the kitchen for something to eat while she wrote out the note. The servants, though! They all treated me like something they'd scraped off the bottom of their boots. Illester, the head manservant, seemed to think I was there to steal the silver and muddy up the carpets. The cooks were the same. The only one who was friendly at all was the scullery maid."

"Took a shine to you, did she?" asked Micum with a knowing look.

"I think she's just lonesome, and no small wonder. She asked how I got service in the city. I had to make up a bit, but—"

"Hold on," Seregil interrupted. "This girl who made eyes at you, did you get her name?"

"Stamie. She's the head cook's niece."

"Good work. She could be our key to the back door if we ever need one."

"So what do we do now?" Micum asked restlessly. "Alec can't show up to romance the girl when he's supposed to be on the road back to Rhíminee."

"I know." Running a hand back through his hair, Seregil encountered Thero's cropped curls and dropped his hand with a grimace. "So far we only have Alec's guess that the papers came here at all. Barien's serving maid could just as well have taken them when she met up with Teukros' man in the tavern."

"That's not what it all sounded like to me," Alec maintained stubbornly, nettled at this sudden doubt.

"Yes, but you only caught a few words. It's unwise to base assumptions on scant evidence. You end up leading yourself into all kinds of blind alleys."

"But what about the horses I saw in the yard?"

"Were any of them white?"

"Well, no. But Teukros could have changed mounts there."

"And ridden home on a different one?" Seregil cocked a skeptical eye at him. "To what end if he's already made no secret of his destination?"

"But the fact remains that we *did* see Teukros ride out last night," Alec insisted. "And he *did* tell his wife he was coming here."

"A lie to cover his tracks perhaps," suggested Seregil. "There's no reason to assume that he'd tell her the truth."

"Maybe we should head back to the city and see what Nysander's turned up," suggested Micum.

"You mean we're just going to leave?" asked Alec. Nysander or not, he'd been inside the place and didn't like the feel of it.

"For now," Seregil said, heading for the horses. "You did a fine job. If nothing else, it was good practice for you."

Thoroughly let down, Alec stole a last resentful look at the keep looming over the gorge, then hurried away after the others.

32

NASTY SURPRISES

As they reached the Sea Gate that afternoon, Seregil was the first to notice that the guard had been doubled.

"Something's happened," he murmured as they rode into the crowded square.

"You got that right," said Micum, looking around. "Let's see what it is."

Tight knots of people stood everywhere among the booths, heads together, faces serious. Ignored by their elders, gangs of children ran about wildly, teasing each other and daring their fellows to nick sweets from the unattended stalls.

Riding up to a small group of gossips, Micum threw back his cloak to show his red Orëska tunic.

"I've been away from the city. What's the news?" he asked.

"It's the Vicegerent," a woman told him tearfully. "Poor Lord Barien's dead!"

Alec let out a gasp of surprise. "Illior's Light! How did it happen?"

"No one's certain," she replied, wiping her eyes with a corner of her apron.

"He was murdered!" exclaimed a rough-looking character beside her. "Them Plenimaran bastards will be behind it, just you wait and see!"

"Oh, shut your hole, Farkus. Don't be

spreading rumors," growled another man, nervously eyeing Micum's livery. "He don't know nothing, sir. All anyone's heard for certain is the Vicegerent was found dead this morning."

"Many thanks," Micum said.

Kicking their horses into a gallop, they rode for the Orëska House. Nysander looked pale but composed when he let them in at the tower door.

"We heard Barien's dead. What happened?" asked Seregil.

Nysander walked across to his desk and sat down, hands folded on its stained surface. "It appears to have been suicide."

"Appears?" Seregil sensed some strong emotion behind his friend's carefully controlled manner, but could not guess what it might be.

"He was found lying peacefully in his bed with his wrists cut," Nysander continued. "The blood had soaked down into the mattress. Nothing appeared amiss until the bedclothes were thrown back."

"Did you talk to him last night?" asked Alec.

Nysander shook his head bitterly. "No. He had gone to bed before I arrived. It was so late and there seemed to be no danger of him bolting. I actually—"

Breaking off, he handed Micum a parchment. "I suppose he was composing this when I looked in on him. Read it out, if you would."

Barien's last, brief missive was as formal as any of the thousands of state documents he'd drawn up over the course of his long career. The handwriting flowed in dark, perfect lines across the page without a blot or waver, devoid of the slightest hint of hesitation.

" 'My Queen,' " read Micum, " 'Know that I, Barien í Zhal Mordecan Thorlin Uliel, have in these last years of my service to you committed high treason. My actions were deliberate, considered, and inexcusable. I offer no justification but pray you to believe that in the end I died the Queen's man.' He's signed it 'Barien, Traitor.' "

"Illior's Eyes, how could I have been such a fool?" groaned Nysander, pressing a hand to his brow.

"But this proves nothing," Seregil exclaimed in exasperation. "There are no details, no names, no specifics of any kind."

"Idrilain is aware of our investigations. I believe she understands the import of this letter," replied the wizard.

"Oh, that's fine then," Seregil snapped, pacing to the far end of the room. "Unless she suddenly begins to wonder why he died *immediately* after you began looking into his activities. Suppose she begins to question whether your loyalty to me is greater than to her? That's still *my* body there in the Tower, you know. I want it back in one piece!"

Micum looked the letter over again. "Couldn't this be a forgery? Sakor's Flames, we've just been dealing with some of the best forgers in Rhíminee."

"And what about Teukros?" added Alec. "It's his word against Kassarie's that he intended to go there at all. He could have gone to Barien's instead. He could have gotten into the house easily enough, being family. Once in, he kills his uncle, drops the note, and slips out again. I told you before, Barien was angry with him over something."

Nysander shook his head. "There were no signs of violence or magic on Barien's person or in the room."

"Doors?" interjected Seregil.

"Locked from within. And as for the matter of Teukros' disappearance, if a man of Barien's stamp believed his nephew had betrayed the family's honor, he himself may have taken steps to remove the young man, a last act of family duty. There is ample precedent for such practices among that class. But the fact remains that whatever Alec heard them arguing about last night, it must surely have contributed to Barien's death."

"What about Phoria?" asked Micum. "It appears she was one of the last people to see him alive, and at his summons, too. Has anyone talked to her?"

"By all reports, the Princess Royal is in deep mourning and is seeing no one," answered Nysander.

"That's vague enough," mused Seregil. "Do you think she's involved?"

"Before Barien's death I should not have thought so. Now I fear we must admit the possibility. If that does somehow prove to be the case, you may be certain it will be dealt with by higher authorities than you or I."

Seregil continued his uneasy perambulation around the room. "Which still leaves us with one man dead and one missing. Have their houses been tossed?"

Nysander nodded. "A small cache of forged shipping manifests was uncovered at Teukros' villa. With them were found copies of several seals, including yours and those of Lord Vardarus, Birutus í Tolomon, and Lady Royan ä Zhirini."

"My seal and that of Vardarus; that's clear enough." Seregil picked up a sextant from one of the tables and fidgeted absently with it. "What about these others? I've never heard of them."

"Minor nobility with minor commissions. Lady Royan oversees the port of Cadumir on the Inner Sea just north of Wyvern Dug. The commission is an hereditary one appended to her holding. Young Sir Birutus was recently appointed to a post with the sutler corps—something to do with meat, I believe."

"They don't sound like the sort to bring the government toppling down," Micum said, perplexed.

"And just where was all this damning evidence found?" asked Seregil, coming to a momentary halt by the desk.

"An interesting point, that," Nysander said with a mirthless smile. "Everything had been concealed beneath the floorboards of Teukros' bedchamber."

"The floorboards," Seregil exclaimed in disgust. "Bilairy's Codpiece, even a green thief knows better than that. You might as well nail it to the front door! This snarl of events just isn't making sense. Barien certainly had access to the royal seal, but to have handed it over to such a dolt as that? It's absurd."

"You said he had a blind spot for his nephew," Alec reminded him.

Seregil stabbed a finger at Barien's letter. "A man who composes as cold-blooded a suicide letter as that would *never* be so careless. Mark my words, there's more to this than we're seeing."

The four fell silent for a moment, mulling the seemingly contradictory evidence.

"What about those servants we followed?" Alec asked at last.

"What about them?" Seregil muttered, still scowling down at the letter.

"Well, I don't know about the girl, but that man of Teukros' seemed to know where to deliver the papers. He offered to go, remember? But Teukros said he'd do it himself."

The others stared at him a moment, then exchanged chagrined glances.

"By the Light, how did we ever overlook such an obvious point?" cried Nysander. "The members of both households have been taken into custody. They are all being held in Red Tower Prison. Come along, all of you!"

"Bless the day I dragged you out of that dungeon," laughed Seregil, throwing an arm around Alec's neck as they dashed for the door.

Nysander had the Queen's authority to question the prisoners and, as Seregil was still in Thero's form, no one challenged his right to accompany his master. Leaving them to their task, Alec and Micum went off to see how the real Thero was faring.

As luck would have it, the warder was the same one whom Alec had met on his first visit to the Tower.

"Poor fellow!" The warder shook his head regretfully. "Prison's been damned hard on 'im, Sir Alec. First day he was gracious as you please, a real gentleman. But he's gone sort of sour since. We've hardly had a word out of him in a couple of days, and what he has said ain't been hardly civil."

Reaching the cell, he took up his post at the end of the corridor. "Visiting rules same as before, young sir. Keep your hands away."

Alec peered through the grille. "Seregil?"

"Alec?"

"Yes, and Micum."

A pale face appeared at the bars and Alec experienced a familiar sense of incongruity. The features and voice were Seregil's; the expressions and intonation were not. The overall effect was reminiscent of Seregil's Aren Windover persona.

"How are you holding up?" asked Micum, standing with his back to the guard.

"It's been a most unusual experience," Thero replied grimly. "They've left me alone for the most part, though, and Nysander sent some books."

"Have you heard about Barien?" whispered Alec.

"Yes. Frankly, I'm not certain—"

"Good news! Good news, Lord Seregil!" the warder interrupted, heading their way with a bailiff in tow.

Thero pressed his face to the bars. "Is that my release?"

"It is indeed, my lord." The warder rattled the lock open with a flourish.

Standing by the cell door, the bailiff unrolled a scroll and droned out, " 'Lord Seregil í Korit Solun Meringil Bôkthersa, now of Rhíminee, the charge of treason laid against you has been rescinded. Your name is cleared of calumny. By the Queen's grace, step forth and be free.' "

"I can't tell you how happy I am, sir," the warder said as Thero stepped blinking into the relative brightness of the corridor. "It would've been damned hard to give you over to the inquisitors, like they was talking at first. Damned hard, sir."

"Harder for me than you, I'm sure," Thero snapped, striding off without a backward glance.

Cocking an eye at Alec, the warder spread his hands. "You see what I mean, sir?"

Alec and Micum caught up with Thero on the stairs.

"You might have handled that a bit more smoothly," Micum whispered angrily. "You're supposed to be Lord Seregil, after all."

Thero shot him a sidelong glare. "After two solid days of rats and platitudes, I doubt he'd have been a great deal more gracious."

For appearance's sake they went directly to Wheel Street. Runcer met them at the door with his usual lack of surprise.

"We had word, my lord," he said gravely. "Your bath has been prepared, if you'd care to go up?"

"Thank you, Runcer, I will," Thero replied, attempting Seregil's easy manner. "Let me know the minute Nysander arrives."

Runcer's wrinkled face betrayed little as he watched Thero march off up the stairs, but Alec thought he caught the hint of a cryptic frown before the old servant doddered off toward the kitchen.

Upon their return from the Tower, Seregil and Nysander found the others just starting on a hot supper at Seregil's bedroom table.

Face-to-face for the first time since the exchange of bodies, Seregil and Thero inspected each other in silence.

Seregil slowly circled his counterpart, amazed by the sight of his own familiar face settled into Thero's guarded expression.

"Say something," he prompted at last. "I want to hear what I sound like with someone else doing the talking."

"This throat's been doing a great deal less talking since

you've been gone," Thero retorted. "I suppose I'll be quite hoarse when I get my body back from you."

Seregil turned to Alec. "You were right. The timbre of the voice is the same, but the speech patterns make all the difference. What an interesting phenomenon!"

"But one which we have no time to explore," Nysander interjected. "You must both be restored to your proper forms."

Joining hands with the greatest eagerness either of them was ever likely to exhibit, Seregil and Thero stood motionless while Nysander performed the spell.

The magic was indiscernible, the effect instantaneous. Restored to his own body, Seregil went a clammy greenish-white. Releasing Thero, he staggered to the fireside armchair and sank down, head between his knees. Alec grabbed up a bowl and hurried to his side.

Thero doubled over, too, grimacing as he grasped his leg.

"What have you been up to?" he demanded, pulling up his robe to examine the swollen knee.

"Up to?" Seregil managed a faint laugh between gasps. "It was—more the down part we had trouble with."

Flexing his long fingers, he rubbed his hands over his smooth cheeks and hair. "By the Four, it's good to get back into my true form! And I've had a bath and clean clothes, too. I'm in your debt, Thero. I just hope you didn't enjoy the soaping up too much."

"You've little enough to be vain of," Thero shot back tartly, returning to his supper.

Still grinning, Seregil tugged at the lacings of his shirt. "I don't know why you have to wear everything so tight, though—"

Alec was the only one who noticed the momentary faltering of his friend's smile. Before the boy could ask what was wrong, however, Seregil locked eyes with him, discreetly motioning silence.

"What did the two servants have to say?" Micum was asking, impatient for details.

"They weren't there," Seregil replied, pulling the lacings shut again. Again his fingers brushed the rough tissue of the scar, which had somehow reappeared. The feel of it made his skin crawl.

"Now there's a surprise," Micum said glumly. "Did you learn much from the others?"

"We had the same story from both households," said Nysander. "The footman Marsin and Barien's maid Callia had been lovers for some time. Their fellow servants assume they have run off together."

Micum raised a skeptical eyebrow. "Bit too coincidental for my taste. What about the wife?"

"Even less helpful," said Seregil. "Lady Althia's a silly, harmless girl, still content after a year's marriage to be her husband's poppet. All she knows of his business is that it keeps her in jewels, gowns, and horses."

"Then we're right back where we started!" groaned Alec. "Marsin, Teukros, and that girl were our only connection, and now we can't find any of them."

"We should check the charnel houses next," said Seregil. "If any of them were murdered in the city, the Scavengers may have found them by now. Alec, Micum, and I will have to handle that since we're the only ones who know what they look like. And speaking of corpses, what's going to happen to Barien?"

Nysander gave a troubled sigh. "According to the law, he will be flayed, disemboweled, and hung on Traitor's Hill, then cast into the city pit."

Micum shook his head. "To end up like that after all the good he's done over the years. It's him I have to thank for Watermead; he suggested it to the Queen."

"At least he's already dead," Seregil said with a shudder, all too aware that he'd faced a similar fate only a few days ago without such benefit. At the moment, however, he had a more pressing concern. "Before we all go our separate ways, Nysander, I'd like a private word."

Leading the way to the library across the corridor, Seregil closed the door carefully, then tugged open his shirt to show Nysander his chest. The circular brand left by Mardus' wooden disk stood out a sinister reddish-pink against his fair skin.

"The transference magicks must have disrupted the obscuration," said Nysander. "Though I have never known such a thing to happen before."

"There's more to it than that and you know it," Seregil said, going to a small mirror on the wall for a better look. The patterns in the scar tissue were more distinct than ever.

"Could Thero have something to do with this?" he demanded. "That dream I had—"

"Certainly not!" Nysander retorted, reaching to touch the tiny ridges of stiffened flesh. "He would certainly have noticed it when he bathed, and told me of it. It must have happened as I performed the restoration. I shall have to cover it again."

Seregil caught Nysander's wrist and held it.

"What is this mark?" he said, searching the old wizard's face. "What does it mean that you want so badly to keep it hidden?"

Nysander made no move to free himself. "Have you recalled anything else of that nightmare? The one with the headless horse?"

"Not really. Only being in Thero's body and seeing the eye in my chest. And flying. For the love of Illior, Nysander, are you going to tell me what this really is or not?"

Nysander looked away, saying nothing.

Releasing him, Seregil strode angrily toward the door. "So, I'm going to go the rest of my life with this burned into my skin and you're not going to tell me a damn thing!"

"Dear boy, you would do better to pray that you never find out."

"That's never been any prayer of mine and you know it!" Seregil spat back. For an instant anger made him reckless. "As it happens, I know more about it than you might think. I'd have told you already if it wasn't for—"

The words died on his lips. Nysander had gone ashen, his face a mask of anger. At his swift incantation, the room went dim and Seregil knew from past experience that Nysander had sealed the room against intrusions of any kind.

"By your honor as a Watcher, you will tell me *everything,*" Nysander ordered and the barely suppressed fury in his voice struck like a blow.

"It was the night Alec and I left the Orëska," Seregil told him, his mouth suddenly dry. "Later that night I went to the Temple of Illior."

"Alone?"

"Of course."

"What did you do there?"

Seregil's skin prickled coldly; he could almost see the black waves of anger radiating out from Nysander. The room went darker still, as if the lamps were dying. Steeling himself, he went on.

"I'd made a drawing of this." Seregil pointed to the scar.

"Before you obscured it that first time I used a mirror and sketched as much detail of the design as I could make out. At the temple I showed it to Orphyria—Nysander, what's wrong?"

Nysander had gone greyer still. Staggering to a chair, he sank his head in his hands. "By the Light," he groaned, "I should have guessed. After all I said—"

"You told me nothing!" Seregil shot back, still angry in spite of his fear. "Even after I almost died, after Micum brought word of the massacre in the Fens village, you told us *nothing*! What else was I to do?"

"You headstrong fool!" Nysander glared up at him. "I suppose you might have heeded my order. My warning! Tell me the rest. What did Orphyria say?"

"She couldn't make anything of it, so she sent me down to the Oracle. During the ritual, he handled the drawing I'd made. He spoke of an eater of death."

Nysander suddenly grasped Seregil's wrist, pulling the younger man to his knees in front of him and staring intently into his eyes. "He said *that* to you? What else? Do you remember his exact words?"

"He said 'death,' and repeated it. Then 'Death, and life in death. The eater of death gives birth to monsters. Guard well the Guardian. Guard well the Vanguard and the Shaft.' "

"Those were his exact words?" cried Nysander, squeezing Seregil's arm painfully in his excitement. The anger was gone now, replaced by something that looked very much like hope.

"I'd stake my life on it."

"Did he explain what he meant by these words? The Guardian? The Shaft? The Vanguard?"

"No, but I remember thinking that he must be referring to specific people—especially the Guardian."

Releasing Seregil, Nysander sat back with a harsh laugh. "Indeed he was. Is there anything else, anything at all? Think carefully, Seregil. Omit nothing!"

Seregil rubbed his bruised wrist as he concentrated. "In the course of the divination he picked up a harp peg and sang a tune I'd composed as a child. He kept that. Then there was a bit of Alec's fletching—he spoke of Alec as being a child of earth and light and said that he was my child now, that I was to be father, brother, friend, and lover to him."

He paused, but the wizard simply motioned for him to continue.

"Then came the eater of death business, and finally he looked me right in the eye, handed me back the scroll, and said, 'Obey Nysander. Burn this and make no more.' "

"Sound advice indeed. And did you heed it?"

"Yes."

"That is a wonder." Have you spoken of this to anyone else? Alec? Micum? You must tell me the truth, Seregil!"

"No one. I told no one. I'll swear an oath on it if you like."

"No, dear boy, I believe you." A little color had returned to the old wizard's cheeks. "Listen to me, I implore you. This is not a game. You have no idea the precipice you have danced along, and I am still bound not to tell you— No, no interruptions! I want no oaths from you now, but a promise made on your honor—on your love for me if nothing else—that you will be patient and allow me to proceed as I must. I swear the wizard's oath to you, by my Hands, Heart, and Voice, there is no doubt now that I shall reveal everything to you one day. You have my word. Can you abide by that for now?"

"I will." Still shaken, Seregil clasped Nysander's cold hands between his own. "By my love, I will. Cover the damned thing up!"

"Thank you, my impatient one." Nysander embraced him tightly for a moment, then placed his hand on Seregil's chest. The scar melted from sight beneath his fingers.

"You must tell me at once if it reappears," he cautioned. "And now you had best be about the business at hand."

"The others must be wondering what happened to us."

"Go on. I shall sit here quietly a moment longer. You gave me quite a turn!"

"I suppose I'll understand that, too, at some later date. Well, we're off to tour the charnel houses now. We'll be back before dawn, but I doubt any of us will be wanting breakfast."

"Probably not. And Seregil?"

"Yes?"

"Watch your back, my boy, and Alec's, too. Now, more than ever, I pray that you will live by your natural caution."

"I generally do, but thanks for the warning." Seregil paused, his hand on the latch. "You're the Guardian, aren't you? Whatever that means—and I'm not asking—but it *was* you the Oracle meant, wasn't it?"

To his great surprise, Nysander nodded. "Yes, I am the Guardian."

"Thank you." With a last thoughtful look, Seregil went out, unaware that his dearest friend had, for a fleeting instant, been his sworn executioner.

33

AMONG THE SCAVENGERS

By virtue of its function, the Scavenger Guild was the caretaker of Rhíminee's unwanted dead. Combing the streets and sewers for refuse, the Scavenger crews were often the first to find the murdered and destitute, the cast-off, cast-out, and abandoned ones.

There were three charnel houses in the city: two in the upper city, one in the lower. Seregil and Micum had often visited them as a final recourse. For Alec, however, they proved to be a harsh new experience.

They began with the closest, which stood near the north wall of the city. Alec had hardly set foot inside the place before he staggered out again, hand clamped over his mouth. Retching, he grasped the top of a street marker to steady himself. He'd gotten a good look at the interior of the plain building, seen the corpses lying face up on the stone floor in rows like bundles of used clothing in the marketplace. Even on such a cold winter night, the smell was appalling, and all the more so to a Dalnan nose.

After a moment, he was aware of Seregil beside him.

"They ought—they should have been burned before now!" he gagged.

"The Scavengers have to keep them for a

few days after they find them, in case they're claimed," Seregil explained. "The ones dragged up out of the sewers are the worst. Perhaps you'd better stay with the horses."

Torn between shame and relief, Alec watched through the open doorway as Seregil returned to his unpleasant task. He and Micum paced up and down the rows, looking into bloated faces and examining clothing until they were satisfied that none of the three people they sought were there. Scrubbing their hands in a basin of vinegar provided by the keeper of the place, they rejoined Alec outside.

"Looks like we get to keep hunting," Micum told him grimly.

The second charnel house was situated a few streets away from the Sea Market. Alec kept silent during the ride, listening to the even rhythm of Patch's hooves as they galloped through the lamp shadows of the Street of the Sheaf. By the time they reached their destination, he'd made up his mind. He dismounted with the others.

"Wait just a second," Seregil said. Ducking in through the low doorway, he came back with a rag soaked with vinegar. "This helps," he told Alec, showing him how to drape it loosely over his nose and mouth.

Clasping the acrid rag to his face, Alec moved among the dozen or so bodies laid out for inspection. The air was uncomfortably damp, and a fetid stench rose from the glistening drainage channels cut into the floor.

"Here's a familiar face," Micum remarked from across the room. "Not one of ours, though."

Seregil came over for a look. "Gormus the Beggar. Poor old bastard—he must have been ninety. His daughter begs over by Tyburn Circle most days. I'll send word to her."

Again, they found no sign of Teukros or the others. Returning gratefully to the fresh night air, they rode down the echoing Harbor Way to the maze of wharves and tenements that clung to the eastern curve of the harbor.

Leading the way into the poorest section, Seregil reined in at a sagging warehouse. It was the largest of the city charnel houses and the stench of the place hit them before they opened the door.

"Sakor's Flame!" Micum croaked, clapping a vinegar rag over his nose.

Alec hastily did the same. None of the evening's activities had prepared him for this place; even Seregil looked a bit queasy.

More than fifty bodies were laid out on the stained wooden floor, some fresh, some with the flesh already slumping from the bones. The cresset lamps set around the room to consume the evil humours burned with a foul, bluish light.

A hunched little woman wearing the grey tabard of the Scavenger Guild limped up to them with a basket of wilted nosegays.

"Posies for you gentlemen? Makes the bitter search so much sweeter!"

Seregil tossed a few coins into her basket. "Good evening, old mother. Perhaps you can make our search a shorter one. I'm looking for three people who'd have come to you within the past day. A young, dark-haired servant girl; a manservant of middling years, also dark; and a young nobleman with a blond mustache."

"You may be in luck, sir," the old woman cackled, hobbling off toward a corner of the room. "I've got the fresh ones over here. Is this your girl?"

Callia lay naked between a drowned fisherman and a young tough whose throat had been cut. Her eyes were open, and she looked vaguely worried.

"That's her, all right," said Seregil.

"Now that's a damned shame," Micum sighed, holding up the hem of his cloak as he squatted down beside the girl. "She can't be more than twenty. Do you see her wrists?"

Seregil fingered the brown bruises circling the pale wrists. "She was bound, and gagged, too. See here, how the corners of her mouth are raw?"

Shivering with nausea, Alec forced himself to watch the examination. The past few hours rolled over him like an oppressive nightmare, leaving him sickened to the core.

The front of the body was unmarked except for the bruises. When they rolled her over, however, they found a single small wound between her ribs just to the left of the spine.

"A professional job," Seregil muttered. "Through the great vessel and straight up into the heart. At least it was quick. Where was she found, old mother?"

"Poor lamb! They pulled her from under the docks, end of Eel Street," the Scavenger woman replied. "I took her for a doxy. Is there family to collect her?"

Seregil laid the body gently back into place and stood up. "I'll look into it. See that she's kept a day or two longer, won't you?"

Outside again, all three sucked in lungfuls of the tar-scented air, but the stink of vinegar on their hands and faces seemed to keep the stench of death about them.

"I want to jump into the sea with all my clothes on!" said Alec, casting a longing look toward the glimmering of water visible at the end of the street.

"Me, too, if we wouldn't come out of that water dirtier than we are now," said Seregil. "A good hot tub will put us right."

"That's your answer to just about everything," Micum observed wryly. "In this case, however, I have to agree."

"At least we know for certain that we're on the right track," Alec said hopefully. "I wonder where Teukros and Marsin will turn up?"

"If they ever do," answered Seregil. "For all we know, it could have been them who did away with the girl, in which case they could be halfway to anywhere by now. Then again, they could both be floating dead in the sewers. Between this and Barien's sudden death, though, I think it's safe to assume that we've got more enemies out there somewhere and, whoever they are, they've got the wind up their tails now. Teukros spilled something to someone!"

34

PHORIA'S CONFESSION

Two days had passed since the Vicegerent's suicide. At noon Barien's body was to be publicly dismembered, a symbolic execution of the self-confessed traitor.

Micum flatly refused to attend. While Seregil finished dressing, he wandered out onto the bedroom balcony to watch Alec at his morning shooting in the garden. Patiently gauging each shot, the boy sent shaft after shaft unerringly into his current target, a sack of straw wedged in the crotch of a tree.

The previous night Alec had halfheartedly offered to accompany Seregil, but they'd managed to dissuade him.

"There's nothing there you need to see," Seregil had told him, kindly leaving unsaid the fact that Alec had shouted himself awake every night since their charnel house tour.

The boy's relief had been obvious, but this morning he'd moped through breakfast in guilty, hangdog silence, then retreated to the garden with his bow.

As Micum watched now, a sudden gust of wind blew a lock of hair across Alec's eyes, spoiling his last shot. Without the slightest show of impatience, he merely brushed it back and went to collect his arrows for another round.

It's a pity you don't have as much patience

with yourself as you do with your shooting, Micum thought, stepping back into the warmth of the bedroom.

Seregil was trying on a broad-brimmed black hat in front of the mirror. Tugging it to a more rakish angle over one eye, he stepped back to judge the effect. "What do you think?" he asked.

Micum ran a critical eye over the plain grey velvet coat Seregil wore under a cloak of darker grey. "No one's going to mistake you for a wedding guest."

Seregil tipped his hat with a humorless smile. "Well turned out but austere, eh? Good. Never let it be said that Lord Seregil doesn't know how to dress for any occasion. Is Alec still shooting?"

"Yes. You know, maybe you shouldn't have talked him out of going. I think he feels like he's let you down."

Seregil shrugged. "Probably, but it was his decision in the end. You saw him the other night; he forced himself into the charnels because he knew it mattered. Today it doesn't and he knows that, too. He's just kicking himself for being squeamish. Hell, *I* wouldn't be going if I didn't have to. The way word has spread around Rhíminee, they're writing ballads about me already; the poor exile unjustly imprisoned and all that sort of horse shit. So it matters and I'm going. At least the poor bastard did us all the favor of killing himself. When the condemned is alive, I have nightmares myself."

The execution site lay a few miles north of the city. Known as "Traitor's Hill," the barren rise was distinguished by a broad stone platform on the crest of the hill. Overlooking a lonely stretch of the Cirna highroad, its gibbet arch and deeply scarred block presented bleak but potent testimony to the Queen's implacable justice.

Riding out under a lowering sky, Seregil clapped his hat on more tightly and silently cursed the duty that forced him out on such a morning. The northern territories had been winter-locked for a month now, but the cold weather was only now settling in solidly here on the coast. A light dusting of snow had streaked the fields just after dawn; in the distance to his right, he could see mountain peaks glistening whitely.

A sizable crowd had already gathered at the execution site. The nobles sat their horses in a tight knot, slightly but definitively separate from the surrounding mob of idlers, ne'er-do-wells, and seekers of morbid thrills.

The latter formed a loose ring around the platform. laughing and jesting as if it were a Fair Day, they took their humble midday meal within the shadow of the gibbet and dared one another to stand close enough to get spattered by the blood.

Ignoring the sudden ripple of excited shouts and pointing his arrival elicited, Seregil rode to join Nysander and Thero on the fringe of the noble ranks.

Thero raised an eyebrow. "Alec's not with you?"

Seregil tensed immediate, forever on guard against some thinly veiled barb from the younger wizard.

"Perhaps it is just as well," Nysander observed quietly. "This is not an aspect of Skalan society of which I am particularly proud. The great pity is that it is so effective a deterrent."

Nysander was looking more careworn than ever this morning. In spite of the irrefutable evidence, the wizard was still finding it difficult to accept Barien's disloyalty. Seregil knew him well enough to understand that it went deeper than mere disillusionment; as an intimate of both the Queen and the Vicegerent, Nysander was reproaching himself for having been blind to a plot of such magnitude. Unfortunately, this was not the time or place to discuss the matter.

Maintaining a somber demeanor, Seregil politely rebuffed efforts by several curious nobles to draw him into conversation. Instead, he listened with a certain sardonic pleasure to the speculations being bantered about nearby.

Lords and ladies who'd feasted at the Vicegerent's own table within the last fortnight now spoke darkly of suspicious circumstances suddenly recalled, or turns of conversation now construed as suspicious or telling.

The crowd grew increasingly restless as the dull sky gradually brightened toward noon. In response, blue-uniformed riders of the City Watch began to make their presence more visible.

Chilled and disgruntled, Seregil shifted in the saddle. "The procession should be in sight by now."

"He's right. Shall I cry for them, Nysander?" Offered Thero.

"Perhaps we —" The older wizard paused, shading his eyes as

he gazed back up the road toward the city. "No, I doubt it will be necessary."

A lone rider had come into view, galloping hard in their direction. As he came closer, they could see that he wore the colors of a Queen's Herald.

"Bloody hell, here comes someone to spoil the fun for sure!" someone shouted.

The assessment seemed a likely one and the crowd parted with a collective grumble to let the rider through. Dismounting, the herald climbed onto the gibbet platform, unrolled a scroll, and in a loud, clear voice proclaimed, "By order of Queen Idrilain the Second, the ritual execution of Barien í Zhal is postponed. There will be no dismemberment today. All hail the Queen's mercy!"

Jeers and catcalls went up from the thrill seekers, but most of the nobles turned their mounts for town with expressions of relief.

"What's this?" muttered Seregil.

"I cannot imagine," replied Nysander. "I suspect, however, that a summons from the Queen may await me upon my return."

Nysander was correct. Hastening to the Palace, he found Idrilain and Phoria waiting for him in the private audience chamber. Idrilain was seated, with Phoria at stiff attention at her left side. Both women looked very grim.

"Sit down, Nysander. There is something I wish you to hear," Idrilain said curtly, motioning him to the only other chair in the small chamber. "Phoria, repeat to Nysander what you have told me."

"Lord Barien was not a Leran," Phoria began, her voice flat as a sergeant's at daily report. "He died believing that he had unwittingly aided them, however, through commerce he and Lord Teukros had with the forger Alben."

"Then he recognized Alben, that night at the inquisition?" Nysander asked, recalling Barien's strange expression.

Phoria shook her head. "No, he'd never met the man or heard his name. The connection was all through Teukros, who'd handled all the dealings with him.

"It all started three years ago. Lord Teukros was involved in that massive land speculation in the western territories which failed so miserably."

"I recall the scandal," said Nysander. "I had no idea Teukros had any part in it."

"He was ruined," Phoria told him. "In the end he owed several millions to the man who'd backed the whole scheme, a Lord Herleus."

"Herleus?" Nysander searched his memory for a face to go with the name.

"Killed during a boar hunt later that same year," Idrilain informed him. "After his death, some evidence was found suggesting he'd been a Leran sympathizer, though nothing could be proven at the time."

"Ah, I begin to see."

"Teukros was ruined," Phoria continued. "Even Barien hadn't the ready funds to save him, and Herleus would not be reasoned with. Barien told me he'd advised Teukros to accept his shame and flee the country, and at first Teukros agreed. A day later, however, he came back to his uncle with a plan to save the family name."

"And this plan involved the forging of certain documents which, after the Queen herself, only Barien had access to?"

Phoria nodded. "Apparently Teukros had gone to plead with Herleus one last time. It was then that Herleus suggested that Barien's position would allow him to divert treasury gold from the Gold Road shipments. Herleus introduced Teukros to Alben, who could forge the necessary papers. The long and the short of it is, poor Barien couldn't bear to see his spineless scoundrel of a nephew disgraced and agreed to it all. They needed my help in rerouting the gold and, for Barien's sake, I agreed. We both regretted it after, but we thought the whole affair was over and done until Alben turned up in this business with Lord Seregil."

Nysander stroked his short beard thoughtfully. "I must hear the details of the plan, of course, but I am still uncertain as to how Barien, whom you say knew nothing of Alben, made the connection between this creature and his nephew during the confession."

Phoria sighed heavily. "Alben spoke of the *White Hart*. That was the name of the vessel the stolen gold was put onto at Cirna."

Ah, and as high commander of the cavalry detachments assigned to guard such shipments, your approval was needed to reroute the gold. As was Barien's to alter the treasury manifest. Both of you needed to know the name of the vessel, if little else."

Phoria met his eye stonily. "I should have refused. I should have stopped him. I offer no excuse for my actions."

Idrilain took a rolled document from the side table and passed it to Nysander. "This is Barien's will, dated three years ago. You'll find he left his entire fortune and holdings to the Skalan treasury. It's more than adequate repayment."

Slapping a hand down on the table, she rose to pace the room. "As if I wouldn't have forgiven him or tried to help! That wonderful, damnable old-fashioned honor of his destroyed him and cost me the most valuable councilor I had, not to mention the trust of my heir apparent. And all on account of a young idiot not worth the price of the rocks to crush him!"

Phoria flinched visibly. "I shall relinquish all claim to the throne, of course."

"You will do nothing of the sort!" shouted Idrilain, rounding on her. "With a war brewing and Lerans in the back pantry, the *last* thing this country needs is the uproar of an abdication. You made a mistake—a stupid, prideful mistake—and now you've seen the consequences. As the future queen of this land, you will accept responsibility for your actions and put the needs of Skala before your own. As the high commander of my cavalry forces, you will remain at your post and carry out your duties. *Is that clear?*"

White-faced, Phoria dropped to one knee and raised a fist to her chest in salute. "I will, my Queen!"

"Oh, get up and finish your report." Turning away in disgust, Idrilain dropped back into her chair.

Rising, Phoria resumed her rigid stance. "As far as I know, the gold was delivered to the *Hart* as planned. Barien never mentioned the matter to me again until the night of his death."

For an instant a small tremor disturbed the masklike composure of her face. It was the first time in years Nysander had seen her show the hint of any strong emotion other than anger. It passed as quickly as it had come, however.

"Barien went to Teukros and confronted him, wanting to

know why he'd continued an association with the forger," she went on. "Apparently Teukros denied everything having to do with the Leran plot and Seregil, but did admit to using Alben's talents to facilitate some shady shipping deals."

"The secret of his fortune, I suspect," said Nysander. "I should hardly have given him credit for such ability, yet it seems we may have underestimated the wretch after all. General Phoria, do you think Barien arranged to have Teukros killed the night of his own death?"

"He said nothing of the kind to me."

"Did you arrange to have Teukros killed?"

"No." For the first time in some minutes Phoria locked eyes with him and Nysander found no reason to doubt her words.

"Is there anything else you can tell me of this business with the *Hart*?"

"Nothing beyond the fact that Barien could never ascertain exactly what happened to the gold. Herleus ceased his demands for money, and a few months later he was dead. Nothing was mentioned of it during the disposition of his estate, but that's hardly surprising. I suppose his heirs have lived rather well off their secret reserve."

"Perhaps," said Nysander, unconvinced that the answer would be that simple.

Armed with Nysander's report from the Palace, Seregil and Alec disappeared for the rest of the day. They returned to the tower before dark, however, still dressed in the hooded robes of professional scholars and smudged with fine bookish dust.

Micum, who'd spent the afternoon with Nysander, exchanged a grin with the old wizard; Seregil and the boy both had the happy look of hounds on a warm scent. It was the most cheerful either of them had looked in days.

"Herleus *had* no heirs!" Seregil cackled happily, warming his hands at the workroom fire.

"None at all?" Nysander raised a shaggy eyebrow in surprise.

"Not only that," the boy added excitedly, "but his entire estate was impounded for debt right after he died. There was no sign of any gold."

"You have been to the city archives, then?"

"And down to the lower city again," said Seregil. "Oh, we've had a busy afternoon, Alec and I. We're off to Cirna tomorrow."

"Hold on now, you've lost me," Micum broke in. "What were you looking for in the lower city?"

"Shipping records," Seregil replied. "The *White Hart* is listed as belonging to a shipping line owned by the Tyremian family of Rhíminee, but it turns out she was based out of Cirna, so that's where all her manifests would be kept. *If* they've been kept."

Micum nodded slowly. "Then you believe there's some connection between that stolen gold and the plot against you?"

"It appears that the same people were involved in both plots, and that they're probably Lerans. If I'm wrong, then we've damn-all to go on."

Micum narrowed his eyes suspiciously. "This is another one of your 'instinct' things, isn't it?"

"Even so, I believe he may be correct," Nysander said. "Teukros' falling into debt with a suspected Leran smacks of a conspiracy. What greater coup for them than to ensnare Barien's compliance through his beloved nephew? We must, at all costs, try to determine the ultimate destination of that gold. Assuming, as Seregil has noted, that the evidence still exists."

"There's always a chance," said Seregil. "You coming north with us, Micum?"

He shook his head. "Doesn't sound like you need me, and I imagine Kari's eager to get me back. I'll ride as far as Watermead with you, though. You can break your journey with us, if you like."

"I'd rather push on, thanks all the same. Depending on what we learn, I may stop by for you on the way back, though."

"I'd better not mention that to Kari." Micum gave a comic grimace. "If you just come calling for me out of the blue, I can lay the blame off on you. How long do you think you'll be gone?"

"Depends on what we find. The *Hart* was a coastal trader working both sides of the isthmus. If we have to go off to some distant port, it could be weeks."

Pausing, he turned to Nysander. "There was one other thing. How many Queen's Warrants would it have taken to reroute that gold?"

"Only one, I suppose. Is there some significance in that?"

"Perhaps," mused Seregil. "As I recall, you said that Alben confessed to forging *two* Queen's Warrants, but nothing of the sort was recovered from Teukros' house. That leaves one very powerful document, probably complete with seals, unaccounted for."

Nysander frowned as he considered the myriad implications of this revelation. "Oh dear!"

35

CIRNA

Alec fought his way out of yet another nightmare, the stench of the charnel house strong in his nostrils. Throwing back the bed curtains, he found the first light of dawn brightening his window. What he'd smelled was nothing more than the scent of sausages frying downstairs.

"Thank the Maker!" he whispered, running a hand over his sweaty face.

He'd slept badly again that night, tossing fitfully through frantic dreams in which a threatening black figure stalked him through the charnel houses. The oppressive feel of the dream dogged him as he dressed and headed downstairs.

Seregil and Runcer were in the main salon discussing the disposal of a collection of traveling cases. "Lord Seregil" was leaving the city on a journey to recover from the shock of his ordeal, taking Sir Alec with him. Luggage sufficient for a lengthy undertaking had to be seen leaving with them.

"We'll leave all this off at Watermead," Seregil was saying as Alec joined them.

"And how shall I respond to those inquiring after you and Sir Alec, my lord?" asked Runcer.

"Tell them that I was too shaken to predict

my return. Oh, good morning, Alec. We'll leave as soon as you get some breakfast. Eat fast."

"And Sir Micum is returning home?" asked Runcer.

"Yes, I am." Micum appeared at the dining-room doorway in his shirtsleeves. "You can tell any callers that I've gone home to the loveliest woman in Skala, and that I'll set the dogs on anyone who disturbs us for the next week!"

Runcer bowed gravely. "I shall convey the sentiment, sir."

Seregil paced restlessly around the dining room as Alec wolfed down his sausage and tea. "We'll set up back at the Cock-erel when we come back."

"Suits me," Alec said happily. He'd had quite enough of fussy manners and overly attentive servants. Finishing hastily, he followed Seregil and Micum out to the street where their mounts and small baggage train stood ready under Runcer's watchful eye.

They'd dressed as gentlemen to be seen leaving the city, and the groom had saddled Cynril and Windrunner, but Patch and Scrub were ready among the pack horses.

It was a brisk, fine day for riding, and they arrived at the by-way leading up to Watermead just after midday.

Crossing the bridge, Alec and Seregil dismounted and ducked into a thicket to change clothes. From here they would travel as merchants.

"You're heading for the Pony tonight?" asked Micum as they emerged again.

Seregil glanced up at the sun. "We should be able to make it if we push on."

"Say hello to Kari and the girls for me," said Alec. Looking up the valley, he saw a pale ribbon of smoke rising from the kitchen chimney at Watermead and imagined the warm scents of hot bread, roasting meats, and drying herbs there.

Changing mounts, Seregil roped the Aurënen horses in with the pack animals.

"Expect us when you see us," he told Micum, handing him the lead rein.

"Good hunting to you," said Micum, clasping hands with them both. "And take care on those damned goat paths they call streets up there in Cirna. One wrong step and it's ass over tippet into the bay before you know what happened!"

Riding back across the little bridge, they turned their horses north and set off along the highroad again at a gallop.

The rolling hills soon gave way to steeper country. Jagged cliffs fell away to the sea on their left, and they could see the dark expanse of the Osiat stretching out past the coastal islands to the horizon.

They reined in at last to rest the horses. Pushing back the hood of his cloak, Seregil let out a happy whoop. "By the Four, it's good to be free of Wheel Street again!"

"You, too?" Alec turned to him in surprise.

"I can scarcely breathe there anymore!" exclaimed Seregil, shaking his head. "I hate to admit it, but I've felt pretty trapped there these past few years. It's a disguise that's taken on a life of its own. Once you've seen how far it all goes, you'll understand."

"Is that why you never told me about it?" Alec asked. The residual mood left by the nightmare, together with some lingering irritation over his first introduction to the place, lent an unexpectedly sharp edge to the words.

Seregil glanced over at him in surprise. "What do you mean?"

"I mean all those weeks we were in the city and you never once mentioned it. Not until you could spring it on me as another of your little tests."

"Don't tell me you're still mad about that?"

"I guess I am," muttered Alec. "You do it all the time, you know—not telling me things."

"Illior's Fingers, Alec, all I've done for the last two months is tell you things. I don't think I've ever talked so much in my life! What haven't I been telling you?"

"About Wheel Street, to begin with," Alec shot back. "Having me break in like a thief and then throwing me into the middle of that party—"

"But I explained all that! You're not going to tell me now you weren't proud of yourself once the shock wore off?"

"It's not that." Alec struggled to put his warring emotions into words. At last he blurted out, "I'd just like to have had some say in the matter. Now that I think of it, I haven't had much of a say in anything since we met. After all we've been through? Bilairy's Guts, Seregil, I saved your life!"

Seregil opened his mouth as if to answer, then silently nudged Scrub into a walk.

Alec followed, still angry but aghast at his outburst. Why was it that strong emotions always seemed to take him by surprise?

"I suppose you're justified in thinking that," Seregil said at last.

"Seregil, I—"

"No, it's all right. Don't apologize for speaking the truth." Staring down at Scrub's neck, Seregil let out an exasperated sigh. "It was different when we first met. You were just someone who needed help and might prove momentarily useful. It wasn't until after Wolde that I was sure about bringing you south with me."

"*After* Wolde!" Alec turned to face him, anger rising again. "You lied to me? All that talk out there on the Downs of Skala, and me being a bard?"

Seregil shrugged, still not looking up. "I don't know, I guess so. I mean, it sounded good to me at the time, too. But I didn't really know how suitable you were until that burglary in Wolde."

"What would you have done if I wasn't 'suitable'?"

"Left you somewhere safe with money in your pocket, and then disappeared. I've done that often enough, with people I've helped. But you were different, and so I didn't do that."

Alec was surprised by an eerie sense of connection as their eyes met; heat like a gulp of brandy sprang up in his belly and spread out from there.

"So yes, I lied to you a little at first," Seregil was saying. "Think of how many strangers you've lied to since you hooked up with me. It's the nature of our work. Since Wolde, though, I swear I've been as honest with you as I could be. I wanted to tell you more, prepare you, but then the sickness came on." He paused. "In your place, I doubt I'd have been as faithful. Anyway, after Wolde and the ambush in the Folcwine Forest I began to think of you as a friend, the first I'd made in a long time. I'd assumed you understood that, and for that assumption I beg your kind forgiveness."

"There's no need," muttered Alec, embarrassed.

"Oh, I think there is. Damn it, Alec, you're as much of a mystery to me as I probably am to you. I keep forgetting how young you are, how different we are. Micum and I were almost of an age when we met. We saw the world with the same eyes. And Nysander! He always seemed to know my thoughts before I did myself. It's so—so different with you! Blundering around the way I do, I seem to end up hurting you without even realizing it."

"Not so much," Alec mumbled, overcome by this unexpected openness. "It's just that sometimes it seems as if—as if you don't trust me."

Seregil gave a rueful laugh. "Ah, Alec! *Rei phöril tös tókun meh brithir, vrí sh'ruit'ya.*"

"What's that?"

Seregil held out his poniard hilt first to Alec. " 'Though you thrust a knife at my eyes, I will not flinch,' " he translated. "It's a solemn pledge of trust and I give it to you with all my heart. You can take a stab at me if you want."

"Do you just make those things up?"

"No, it's genuine, and I'll swear ten others just as dire if it will convince you I'm sorry."

"Maker's Mercy, Seregil, just tell me about Wheel Street!"

"All right, Wheel Street." Seregil slipped the knife back into his boot. "It all started after I'd failed with Nysander. I ran off and lived rough for a few years. That's when I learned thieving and all that. When I came back, I saw at once how I could keep myself nicely employed with the intrigues of the Skalan nobility. I had to establish myself somehow, but that didn't prove too difficult. My checkered past, together with my status as Queen's Kin, the novelty of being Aurënfaie, and my new skills as a thief and general busybody—" He spread his hands comically. "That all pretty much guaranteed success in Rhíminee society. Posing as the reformed exile, Lord Seregil soon established a reputation as a sympathetic listener, a reliable buyer of drinks, a willing roisterer, and a holder of no strong opinions on any subject. Altogether, a person of little consequence and therefore the man everyone talks to.

"I got to be quite a favorite among the younger nobles, and through them I managed to pick up valuable information. After that it wasn't hard to spread the rumor that Lord Seregil, charming as he was, didn't always keep the best company. Word soon trickled out into the right circles that I could sometimes aid in the hiring of a certain discreet but shady character who would carry out any sort of silly undertaking for the right price."

"The Rhíminee Cat?"

"Exactly. Nysander was the only one who knew my secret. I've been more use to him as a spy than I ever was as an apprentice. Even back then, though, I liked my freedom too much to play the noble role all the time. So I bought the Cockerel and fixed up some rooms there. Nysander found Thryis for me. Cilla couldn't have been much older than Illia—"

"Yes, but *Wheel Street!*" insisted Alec, wanting to hear the end of the tale before dark. Once Seregil made up his mind to explain something, he tended not to leave out any details.

"Sidetracked again, am I? Well, as time went on the young nobles I'd rooked around with settled down and had young nobles of their own. Aurënfaie or not, I was expected to do the same. To maintain the confidence of those I depended on, I had to give some outward sign that I was of their ilk. I began by investing in shipping concerns and managed to do fairly well. Small wonder, really, considering the sort of information I was privy to. Aside from the money, my supposed business concerns give me ample excuse to be away for the better part of the year.

"Unfortunately, the charade has grown rather cumbersome. If I didn't love Rhíminee so much, I might just kill off Lord Seregil and start over again somewhere else. What it all boils down to for you, though, is that Sir Alec of Ivywell has a lot of educating ahead of him."

"I'll be an old man with a beard to my knees before I've learned half what you expect me to know!"

Seregil gazed out over the sea a quizzed look on his face. "Oh, I doubt that. I doubt that very much indeed."

They spent that night at the Pony, a respectable wayfarers' inn, then set out again at dawn under a clear sky. By late morning they reached the southern end of the isthmus that linked the Skalan peninsula to the mainland to the north.

Jutting up from the sea like a blanched backbone, the land bridge was scarcely five miles wide at any point. The road ran along the crest of it and Alec could see water on either side: the Osiat steely dark, the shallow Inner Sea a paler blue.

Just after midday they came to the small outpost guarding a fork in the highway. From here the roads diverged to the two bridges, east and west, which led down to the opposing Canal ports of Cirna and Talos. Taking the right fork, they soon came within sight of the east bridge, arching smoothly across the black chasm of the Canal. It was a broad, sturdy structure, wide enough for the heaviest drays to pass without crowding.

"It's an amazing sight from up here, don't you think?" said Seregil, reining in. At the moment several wagons were coming across from the far side, followed by a turma of cavalry.

Alec felt cold sweat break out down his spine as he looked at the precipice beneath it. He'd been at the bottom of that chasm, seen its depth. To him, the great bridge looked as tenuous as a spider's web by comparison.

"Illior's Fingers, you've gone white!" Seregil observed, looking over at him. "Maybe you'd better walk your horse. Lots of people are a bit nervous their first time across."

Alec gave a quick, tense shake of his head. "No. No, I'm fine, I—I've just never crossed anything that deep."

Embarrassed by his sudden weakness, he gripped the reins resolutely and nudged Patch into a walk. Keeping to the center of the road as much as traffic allowed, he fixed his attention on a string of donkeys plodding along ahead of him and did his best not to think about what lay below.

"See, it's perfectly safe," Seregil assured him, riding close beside him. "Solid as the highroad itself."

Alec managed another tight nod. From far below came the faint creak of oars and ropes; sailor's voices rose like the whispering of ghosts.

"There's a good view of the west bridge from here," Seregil said, directing Alec's attention out over the left side of the bridge.

Alec looked and felt his belly lurch. From here, the western bridge looked like a child's construction of dry branches across a ditch, a fragile toy poised over the dizzying gorge. Closing his eyes, he fought off a sudden mental image of the stonework beneath him giving way.

"How did they build these?" he gasped.

"Those ancient wizards and engineers understood the value of forethought. They built the bridges first, then dug the Canal out beneath them."

At the far end of the bridge, Alec unclenched his aching fingers and drew a breath of relief.

A switchback road led down the cliffs to the harbor town below. Cirna was a confusing city of square, closely packed buildings lining a maze of narrow streets so sharply inclined in places that it was difficult for riders going down not to pitch forward over their horses' necks. The local inhabitants apparently favored foot traffic, for many parts of the town were accessible only by narrow stairways.

Clinging to the back of his saddle, Alec looked across the bay and located the shining columns of Astellus and Sakor, his first landmarks in Skala. There were far fewer vessels anchored in the harbor now. Seasonal storms were already whipping all but the most hardy coasters into port for the winter.

By the time they'd wended their way down to the customs house by the harbor, both of them were grateful to set foot on level ground again. Entering the whitewashed building, they found a ruddy woman in salt-stained boots at work over a table cluttered with documents.

"Good day to you," she greeted them, as she finished with a wax seal. "I'm Katya, the harbor mistress. You gentlemen need some assistance?"

"Good day to you," Seregil replied. "I'm Myrus, merchant of Rhíminee and this is my brother Alsander. We've come to track down a shipment that went astray some three years back."

The woman shook her head with a dubious frown. "You've got a job ahead of you, then. Do you know how many ships go through here in a season?"

"We have the name of the ship, and the month she came through, if that's any help," Alec offered. "It was the *White Hart,* a square-rigged trader of the Tyremian Line, Cirna registry. She'd have docked here sometime in early Erasin."

"Ah, well that's a start, anyway." Opening a side door, she led them into a room filled from floor to ceiling with ranks of scroll racks.

"If we've still got the manifest it'll be in the back there somewhere. They'd generally have been chucked out by now, but the old harbor master died in the middle of the job and I've never gotten around to finishing it."

At the back of the room she scanned the racks, then extracted a document at random. The movement disturbed a thick layer of dust that set both her and Seregil sneezing.

"Push open that window just beside you, young sir, before we all suffocate," gasped Katya, brushing at her nose.

Alec threw back the shutters. Shaking the scroll out again, she held it up to the light.

"You see how it's laid out, sirs. Here's the ship's name and the captain's at the top, followed by the date she put in and a detailed listing of cargoes delivered and taken on. These seals at the bottom belong to the captain of the vessel and the various merchants involved. This big one here in the lower right corner is the harbor master's. I'll leave you to it. Mind you close the shutters when you leave and tuck things back where you found them."

There was no system to the storage of documents except a rough chronological layering. Pulling scrolls and checking dates, they narrowed their search down to a few likely shelves. Powdery clouds of dust roiled about them as they sorted and sneezed their way through pile after pile of musty, yellow parchments.

The writing, done aboard ships rolling at anchor, was a challenge to decipher—especially for Alec, whose skill at reading was still far from accomplished. Gnawing absently at his lip, he puzzled his way through a confusing succession of scrawled names: *The Dog, Wyvern's Wing, Two Brothers, Lady Rygel, Silver Plume, Coriola, Sea Mist, The Wren*—

Engrossed as he was in mastering the differing hands, he nearly lay aside one with the smudged entry: *White Hart*.

"Here, I found it!" he exclaimed triumphantly.

Seregil sneezed again and wiped his nose inelegantly on his sleeve. "I've got one, too. The *Hart* was a short hauler, working the northern coasts on either side of the Canal. That means there are likely to be a number of manifests around that date. Keep looking until we're well past the time she was lost. We don't want to miss any."

They found eight in all, and spread them out side by side according to date.

"That's what I was afraid of," muttered Seregil, reading them over. "For the most part the *Hart* had a series of regular runs. Let's see—miscellaneous provisions to these three little towns to the west, with trade cargo back—leather goods, horn, some silver work. The eastern runs seem to have been mostly to mines on the north coast of the Inner Sea: tools and supplies, oil, cloth, medicines. Same here, and here."

"What about odd runs?" asked Alec, hunkered down beside him.

"Good point. There are a few. Poultry to Myl, wine to Nakros, silk, and a load of scented wax. Three large tapestries to a Lady Vera at Areus, one hundred bales of woolen yarn—"

"It would be hard to mistake any of that for a couple hundred weight of gold baps."

"Quite right, and I suspect our Leran friends were wise enough to stick their gold in where something heavy wouldn't attract any attention. Here are iron goods, tools, lumber—"

"That's not much help," said Alec. "After three years, how can we guess which one it was? It's impossible!"

"Probably." Walking to the window, Seregil gazed out over the darkening harbor, then sneezed again. "Bilairy's Balls! No wonder we can't think straight! Pocket those papers, Alec. It's fresh air we need. We'll take a walk to clear our heads, then rinse our dusty gullets with a good deep mug of Cirna ale!"

Night fell quickly in the shadow of the cliffs, but a three-quarter moon lit their way as they meandered through the streets behind the docks. Lost in thought, Seregil was for once disinclined to talk, so they wandered on for nearly an hour in silence. At last they found themselves in an open square with a fine view of the harbor below.

The great signal fires atop the Canal pillars were blazing, and their reflections mixed glints of ruddy light with the pure sparkle of the moonlight like a giant's handful of silver and red gold cast across the dark face of the sea.

"That's the place we want," Seregil announced, steering Alec into a nearby alehouse.

The place was comfortably dim and crowded. Working their way across the smoky room, they settled in a corner with their mugs. Seregil read through the manifests again, then sat back with a frustrated sigh.

"This one has me flummoxed, Alec." Taking a long sip from his mug, he rolled it pensively between his palms. "Of course, we didn't really expect to turn up anything. But to have the damn things right in our hands and not be able to wring the truth out of them— It's worse than finding nothing at all!"

Alec leaned over the sheets. "You really think there's a clue in here, don't you?"

"I hate the thought of missing something if it is there." Seregil took another disgruntled gulp, then sat staring into the mug's depleted depths as if waiting for some oracular answer to float to the surface. "Let's have one more look. No, better yet—you read them out to me."

"That'll take forever," Alec protested. "You know I'm terrible at it."

"That's all right, I think differently when I listen and it's better if you go slowly. Just read the 'Outgoing' columns."

Tilting the parchments to catch the scant light of the nearby hearth, Alec bent dubiously to his task.

Seregil leaned back against the wall, eyes half closed. Aside from helping with a few troublesome words, he showed little sign of interest until Alec was in the midst of the fourth manifest.

" 'Three cases parchment, ten crates tallow candles,' " he read, ticking off each entry with a finger. " 'Sixty-five sacks barley, forty casks cider, thirty coils two-inch rope, fifty iron chisels, two hundred wedges, three score mallets, two crates statuary marble, twenty rolls of leather—"

Seregil's eyes flickered open. "That can't be right. You've wandered into the 'Goods Received' column."

"No I haven't." Alec pushed the manifest across to him. "Says right here, 'Goods Out of Port' and below it 'parchment, candles, barley—' "

Seregil sat forward, squinting where he pointed. " 'Two-inch rope, chisels—' You're right, it does say marble. But this shipment is docketed for a mine on the Osiat coast." His voice sank to a low whisper. "No, a quarry! It's listed here as bound for the Ilendri pits."

"So?"

Laying a hand heavily on the boy's shoulder, Seregil raised a meaningful eyebrow. "So why would anyone pay to ship two heavy blocks of fine carving stone *to* a stone quarry?"

"Bilairy's Codpiece! That's it!"

"Perhaps, unless it really was marble in those crates, shipped back for some reason we have no way of determining. Still, it is suspicious."

"So where does that leave us?"

"At the moment?" Grinning, Seregil gathered up the manifests and rose to leave. "It leaves us in a cheap alehouse with six-to-a-bed accommodations upstairs. I believe we've earned a tidier hostel and a good supper. Tomorrow we'll see what we can turn up at the docks."

"What about the quarry, that Ilendri pit? Shouldn't we go there?"

"As a last recourse, maybe, but it's a week's journey there and back, and it's certain they won't have the gold there now. I doubt they ever knew they had it. No, I suspect we can find our answers a good deal closer to home."

36

TROUBLE ON THE HIGHROAD

They spent the next few days on the wind-swept quays, tracking down ships running the *White Hart*'s old routes. Though they located several vessels, none of their inquiries resulted in much useful information. On their fourth day there, however, a stout little coaster with the unlikely name of *Dragonfly* wallowed into port with a load of stone.

Alec and Seregil lounged against a stack of crates as they watched the dockhands hoisting blocks of various sorts onto the quayside. Rough slabs of building stone were encased in heavy rope nets to prevent them from grinding against one another during the voyage. Finer, more fragile blocks were protected by wood and canvas framing.

"She must have stopped at several quarries on her run," murmured Seregil.

"Let's hope Ilendri was one of them," Alec whispered back.

Strolling up to the quay, they began looking over the various pieces as if considering a purchase. They were still dressed as gentlemen merchants and their respectable coats soon drew the interest of the *Dragonfly*'s captain.

"Are you in the market for stone, sirs? I've got some lovely blocks today," he called from the rail.

"So I see," Seregil replied, smoothing his

palm over a slab of glittering black granite. "I'm looking for marble, statuary grade."

"You're in luck there, sir!" The man clumped down the gangway and led them over to a group of crates. "I've got a good selection today: pink, black, grey, and a lovely white pure as a dove's breast. Let's see now, where was that Corvinar piece? That's an especially good one."

Consulting various emblems branded into the sides of the crates, he pried up lids here and there. "Here's a fine black, sir, and some of the white. Did you have something special in mind?"

"Well," Seregil drawled, peering down into a crate, "I don't know a lot about it, to tell you the truth, but I've heard that Ilendri marble is particularly fine."

"That may have been true in your father's day, sir, but precious little comes out of there now," the captain told him with a hint of condescension. "The Ilendri's mostly played out, though they do still cut some smaller blocks. I've a few pieces back here, as it happens, but I think you'd be better pleased with this other."

"Perhaps," said Seregil, cupping his chin in one hand, "but I'd like to see the Ilendri—if it's not too much trouble."

"Suit yourself." The captain hunted through the crates until he found a small box half hidden behind several others. Opening it, he showed them a small block of greyish marble shot through with rusty streaks. "As you can see, the grade's inferior."

"The quarry's owned by Lord Tomas, isn't it?" Seregil asked ingenuously, inspecting the stone with apparent interest.

"No, sir, an old fellow by the name of Emmer. He and his nephews make a small living out of it, cutting blocks like this. It goes mostly for road markers and such like."

It was a small crate and Alec had to step around the captain to get a look inside. Doing so, he saw for the first time the emblems burned into the side of it; one of them was very familiar—a small, curled lizard.

"What do these stand for?" he asked, trying to mask his sudden excitement.

"Those are shipping marks, sir. We use them to keep track of the cargo. The dragonfly mark is mine, put on when I took the box aboard. The next is from the quarry foreman—"

"And that little lizard?"

Seregil stole a quick glance at Alec, sensing more than casual curiosity.

"That's the quarry's mark, sir. The Ilendri newt, we call it."

"It's an interesting design—stone, I mean." He had to get Seregil away from the captain without attracting undue attention. "I think it would do nicely, don't you, brother?"

"In the garden, perhaps," Seregil said, playing along. Chin in hand, he narrowed his eyes appraisingly. "Though I know Mother had something larger in mind for the niche in the great hall. And you know how she favors the white these days. Suppose we take this piece and the white one the captain recommends?"

Alec hovered impatiently as Seregil paid for the stone and arranged for delivery, then drew him off down the quay.

"What was that all about?" Seregil whispered. "Ilendri or not, that rock isn't worth—"

"I didn't mean for you to buy it!" Alec said, cutting him short. "It was the mark—that Ilendri newt—I've seen it before!"

Seregil slowed to a halt. "Where?"

"At Kassarie's keep. It was on some of the old tapestries in the main hall, like a maker's mark. I don't know why it caught my eye particularly, except that I liked the look of it."

"And you're certain the tapestries were old? Perhaps several generations back?"

"The tapestries?" Alec asked in disbelief, this was no time for one of Seregil's artistic tangents. "Well, I think so. They were like the old ones you showed me at the Orëska, with the fancy patterns around the edges. I remembered you saying you liked that style better than the new ones."

Seregil threw an arm around Alec's shoulders with a delighted chuckle. "Illior's Fingers, you've got the same rat's nest of a memory I do! You're certain this lizard thing was just the same?"

"Yes, but why do the tapestries have to be old?" Alec asked, still puzzled.

"Because new tapestries might have been purchased and the mark would be pure coincidence. Very old ones are more likely to have been made by someone in Kassarie's family, someone who lived in the keep and wove them there and used the newt as her signature. Care to place a wager on who owned this Ilendri quarry before it was clapped out?"

"I'll bet you a block of ugly marble it was Lady Kassarie ä Moirian!"

• • •

A quick word with the *Dragonfly*'s captain proved Alec right. According to him, Lady Kassarie had awarded the failing enterprise to an aging retainer five years ago in appreciation of his long service. The old fellow still used the "newt" out of respect for his former mistress.

"Looks like we're headed south again," Seregil said, rubbing his gloved hands together with a satisfied air as they went back to the inn to collect their horses.

"We don't need to go to the quarry?"

"No. Thanks to your everlasting curiosity, I think we've found the key to our little problem. We can make Watermead before midnight, then it's Rhíminee tomorrow, and on to Kassarie's. Looks like that warmhearted little kitchen maid of yours is going to prove useful after all."

"You're looking forward to this, aren't you?" Alec asked with a grin.

Seregil tilted him a dark smile. "Clearing my name was a relief; giving the Lerans a good kick in the slats is going to be a pleasure!"

In their haste and elation, neither noticed the pair of laborers who detached themselves from a work gang to trail after them through the midday crowd.

Crossing the isthmus again, they retraced their route along the coast. There was little trade on the highroad that afternoon, and in several hours' riding they met nothing but a few wagons and a garrison patrol.

Shortly before sunset they came around a sharp bend in the road to find their way blocked by fallen rocks. It was passable, but it meant riding precariously close to the edge of the cliffs. The way was especially narrow here, with sheer rock face to the landward side and a nasty drop to the sea on the other.

"This slide must have just happened." Frowning, Seregil reined in to inspect the rubble. "That patrol we met would have cleared it, or warned us."

Alec eyed the few yards of open ground between the tumbled rocks and the cliff edge. "We'd better walk the horses."

"Good idea. Throw your cloak over Patch's eyes so she doesn't shy. You take the lead."

Wrapping the reins more securely around his fist, Alec coaxed the nervous mare along with soothing words as her hooves struck loose stones. From behind he could hear Seregil doing the same in Aurënfaie. He was within ten feet of safety when he heard the first telltale rattle of stone against stone overhead.

"Look out!" he shouted, but it was already too late. Rocks came crashing down all around them. Patch let out a frantic whinny, pulling back against the reins.

"Come on!" he cried, wincing as a shard of rock cut his cheek. He could hear Scrub rearing behind him, and Seregil shouting some unintelligible warning.

With a sudden toss of her head, Patch threw off the cloak and bolted. Unable to free his hand from the reins, Alec was jerked off balance and swung out over the cliff edge.

For a sickening instant he hung in space, looking down at the waves crashing against the cliffs a thousand feet below; at the same moment he glimpsed movement out of the corner of his eye as something—man, beast, or boulder—plunged down into the abyss.

Before he had time to do more than register the movement, Patch reared again, snapping him against her neck like a hooked fish against the side of a boat. He grabbed wildly for purchase, found her mane with his free hand, and clung on in numbed terror as she plunged away down the road, miraculously dragging him to safety. He managed to get astride her at last and reined her in.

They'd ridden out of sight of the slide. Heart hammering in his throat, Alec turned Patch and galloped back to find Seregil.

The road was completely blocked now; this last slide had left a great heap of broken rock that slanted down to the very edge of the cliff. Neither Seregil nor his horse were anywhere in sight.

"Seregil! Seregil, are you there?" yelled Alec, praying for some answer from beyond the crest of the heap. He couldn't yet bring himself to look in the more probable direction.

As he cast around in rising desperation, a bit of color caught his eye in the slide where the jumbled rock pile met the cliff face. It appeared to be a scrap of cloth, red cloth, the same as the coat Seregil had been wearing.

Scrambling up, he found Seregil curled on his side, half buried in skree and dust. Blood seeped slowly down over his forehead from a scalp cut; another trickle oozed at the corner of his mouth.

"Maker's Mercy!" Alec gasped, pushing at the rocks on Seregil's chest. "Don't be dead! Don't you be dead!"

Seregil's right hand twitched and one grey eye flickered open.

"Thank the Four!" cried Alec, nearly weeping with relief. "How bad are you hurt?"

"Don't know yet," Seregil rasped, closing his eyes again. "I thought you went over—"

"I thought you did!"

Seregil let out a shaky breath. "Scrub, poor Scrub—"

With a queasy shudder Alec recalled the falling object he'd glimpsed as he swung out over the edge of the cliff.

"Had that horse eight years," Seregil groaned softly, a hint of moisture darkening the dust beneath his eyes. "Bastards! Ambushers killed my best horse."

"Ambushers?" Alec asked, wondering if Seregil was fully conscious after all.

But the grey eyes were open now, and alert. "When the rocks started falling, I looked up and saw a man silhouetted against the sky."

Alec risked an uneasy glance of his own but saw nothing. "When I rode back just now, I noticed a little switchback trail leading up the rocks. It's just around that next bend. He could have gotten up that way, I bet."

"That would explain a lot."

"But if they're still up there they'll have seen me come back! We've got to get out of here."

"No, wait." Seregil lay quiet a moment, thinking. "Whoever they are, they seem to know their business. If we run they'll just track us and finish the job."

"What about the highroad garrisons? We must be within five miles of one by now."

"More than that, I think. With only one horse and night coming on, I doubt we'd make it."

"Then we're trapped!"

"Quiet, Alec, quiet. With a little luck, we can lay a trap of our own right here. It's going to take a bit of acting on your part, though." He shifted slightly, feeling under his left thigh, then gave a soft, anguished groan. "Oh, hell. I've lost my sword. It must've torn loose as I scrambled up here."

"I've still got mine," Alec assured him, fearful that Seregil was in serious pain after all. "I had it strapped behind my saddle."

"Fetch it, but cover your actions. Make it look like I'm dying and you're starting to panic."

"Lure him down to finish us off, you mean?"

"Exactly, though there'll be more than one of them, I suspect. Let them believe they're up against a distraught boy and a dying man. Reach in my boot. Is my poniard still there?"

"It's there."

"Then I'm not completely fangless, anyway. Go on now, we may not have much time."

Alec slid back down to the road, expecting every moment to feel an arrow strike him between the shoulder blades. Doing his best to act panicked, he kept his sword concealed beneath his blanket roll as he carried it and a water skin back to Seregil.

Badly battered as Seregil was, he seemed to have escaped with no broken bones. With the sun sinking into the sea in front of them, they settled down to wait. Alec hunkered down with his back to the cliff, his sword unsheathed and hidden against his outstretched leg. Seregil lay propped up slightly, dagger in hand beneath the blanket.

They hadn't long to wait. As the last ospreys winged off to their nests, they heard the sound of hooves against stone. Riders were approaching from the expected direction, beyond the curve of the road to their left.

A moment later two men rode into sight, coming on at a steady walk. Studying them in the red sunset light, Alec could see that they were hard-faced characters in rough traveling garb. One was lean, with ragged, greying hair and a long, somber face. His companion was round and red-faced, his shiny bald pate fringed with curly brown hair.

"This will be them," Seregil murmured beside him. "Play your role well, my friend. I doubt we'll have more than one chance."

The riders made no pretense as to their intentions. Reaching the edge of the slide, they dismounted and drew swords.

"How's your friend, boy?" The bald one asked, leering up at him.

"He's dying, you rotten son of bitch! Can't you leave him in peace?" Alec spat back, letting some genuine fear show in his voice.

"Wouldn't be kind to let him linger, now would it, lad?" the other replied placidly. He had the same air of dispassionate assurance Alec had seen in Micum Cavish; this was a killer who knew his business. "And then there's the matter of you, isn't there?"

"What do you want with us?" Alec quavered, tightening his grip on his sword hilt.

"I've nothing against you or your friend," the greying man replied, taking a step up the pile. "But there are those who don't like having their business nosed into. Now be a good lad and I'll make a quick job of it. You'll be dead before you know it."

"I don't want to be dead!" Alec rose and threw a rock at the men with his left hand. They ducked it easily and Alec backed away as if to bolt.

"Get the other one, Trake," the grey man ordered, pointing to Seregil who still lay as if dying. "I'll take the whelp here."

Alec moved back a few steps, then froze like a frightened hare. Waiting until his assailant was within sword's reach, he grabbed up the blade and struck at him.

At the critical instant, the loose skree underfoot spoiled his lunge for a killing thrust, but he still managed to hit the fellow hard enough across the ribs to knock him off balance. Scrambling awkwardly, he tried to strike at Alec, but instead fell and tumbled heavily almost to the cliff's edge.

Just then a strangled cry rang out behind Alec, but he didn't dare look back. His opponent had already regained his footing and was starting back up after him.

"Full of tricks, are you?" he glowered. "I'll tie you with your own guts, boy, and ram that—"

Alec was overmatched and he knew it. Hardly pausing to think, he snatched up another fist-sized stone and threw it. It struck the assassin in the forehead. Stunned, the man pitched backward and slid down to the cliff's edge again. He might have stopped there if his fall hadn't dislodged more rocks. With a grinding rumble, an entire section of the pile gave way just below where Alec stood, sweeping the swordsman over the edge.

Flailing desperately, Alec came down hard on his back and slid feet first toward death. Too terrified to cry out, he stared helplessly up at the fiery sky, knowing it was the last thing he'd ever see.

Suddenly a strong hand grasped his left shoulder. Clutching at it, Alec slid a few yards farther before coming to a stop with his feet jutting out into empty air. Scarcely daring to breathe, he looked up and saw Seregil stretched spread-eagle on his belly above him, face white with dust or fear.

Don't move! Seregil mouthed. Then, in the faintest whisper, "Roll sideways, toward the horses. We're only a few feet from level ground. Mind your sword. Try not to lose it if you can help it."

Loose stone shifted treacherously beneath them as they clung together and slowly rolled toward the narrow strip of bare roadway cleared by the last slide. They reached it just as another layer of the pile let go. Hauling each other to their feet, they scrambled forward to safety as another great jumble of stone careened off over the cliff, carrying with it the body of the other assassin, whom Seregil had taken by surprise at the beginning of the attack.

Still clutching each other by the arm, they turned to watch the last stones plummet over the edge.

"I don't know how many times a day I can stand to watch you almost die," Seregil gasped.

"Twice is my limit," croaked Alec, sinking to his knees. As he glanced back at what had nearly been the scene of his death, however, he caught the glint of metal near the top of the remaining rubble. "Seregil, look there. Do you see it?"

"Well, I'll be damned." Seregil limped back to the rocks and gently worked his battered sword free. The hilt was scarred and missing a quillon, but the scabbard had protected the blade from serious damage.

"Aura elthë!" he cried, not bothering to conceal his relief. "My grandfather gave me this sword when I was younger than you. That last slide must have uncovered it. Two fresh horses and now this! It seems our two recently departed visitors did us almost as much good as harm."

Seregil led the way as they rode into the yard at Watermead early the next morning. Micum was there among his hounds.

"Back already?" the big man said, looking up. His grin faded, however, as he got a closer look at them. "What the hell happened to you two?"

"We attracted some attention up in Cirna," answered Seregil, dismounting stiffly and limping inside.

"We got ambushed on the way back," Alec explained. "I think they were assassins."

"You think?"

Seregil raised a wry eyebrow. "We didn't have much time for conversation, but I suspect he's right. Chances are I've been watched ever since Thero came out of the Tower with my body."

"I thought I heard familiar voices!" called Kari, looking noticeably wan as she came out of her chamber into the main hall. "Seregil, you're hurt! Let me get my herbs."

"I'm fine," he assured her, easing down on a bench by the fire. "We slept at a garrison station last night. Their surgeon patched me up. I could do with a hot soak, though."

"I'll have Arna put some birch catkins and arnica leaves in the water to draw out the hurt. Some willow bark tea wouldn't do you any harm, either."

"She looks peaked," observed Seregil. "Been sick, has she?"

"Not sick, exactly," Micum replied, avoiding his friend's eye. "More like—unwell."

Seregil studied Micum's expression for an instant, then broke into a knowing grin. "I know that look. She's pregnant again, isn't she?"

"Well—"

"Oh, go on and tell them," she said, returning with a pair of mugs. "It's no use you trying to keep anything from him!"

"You are, then?" exclaimed Seregil. "Bilairy's Balls, Micum, how long have you known?"

"She told me when I came home the other day. Baby's due at late summer, Maker willing."

"Maker willing," Kari repeated, pressing her palms to her apron front. "It doesn't always go well with me at the best of times, and I'm old now for bearing. I hadn't thought to be with child again, but Dalna must have seen we'd have room for one more." She smiled pensively. "Perhaps this time we've made a son. They say a boy makes you sicker in the first months."

"Poor thing's been vomiting morning and night," Micum explained, rising to slip a supportive arm around her waist.

"And I'm not feeling too pert just now," Kari sighed. "I'd better lie down again. The girls won't be troubling you. They're away for the day."

Micum helped Kari into her chamber and closed the door. When he returned, Seregil made a show of figuring back.

"My, my. Late summer, is it? That must have been quite a homecoming, back in Erasin."

"Better than you got, I'll warrant. If only she can hang on to this one, I wouldn't mind having another little one underfoot."

"Hang on to?" asked Alec.

"Oh, yes." Micum nodded sadly. "She's miscarried as many babies as she's brought to birth. The last time was a year or so after Illia was born. It always happens in the first few months, and leaves her sick for weeks afterward. We're not out of the danger season yet, you see, and it's a great worry to her. But let's get back to you two. What did they use on you, fuller's bats?"

"Rock slide," Seregil replied, serious again. "Two men caught us at a narrow place on the cliffs. We got out, but I lost Scrub."

"That's a damned shame! He was a good old thing. But who were they?"

"We never had a chance to find out. We killed them both defending ourselves and lost the bodies over the cliff. But before that, one of them told Alec that they'd been sent by someone who didn't like us poking around in their business. This was after we'd finished in Cirna and found a link to Lady Kassarie."

Showing Micum the manifest, they quickly outlined what they'd discovered.

"That does seem to bring us right back to Kassarie," Micum agreed. "Do you think she tumbled to Alec that day?"

"I doubt it. At that point, I was still officially in prison and everything appeared to be going according to her plan. I hate to admit it, but they must have kept track of me after my 'release' from the Tower."

"What's your next step?"

"We've got to go back to the keep," said Alec. "We can't give her time to realize her hired killers have disappeared."

"That's a fact," said Micum. "What do you think, Seregil? Will the Queen give you a raiding party, or will she just order Kassarie's arrest?"

"I've been thinking about that. The greatest danger lies in forewarning her. You've seen how that keep is placed; it's a fortress! She'd see an armed force coming miles away and have plenty of time to escape or do away with any incriminating evidence."

"That's true," Micum concurred, looking down at the fire.

It suddenly occurred to Seregil that Micum hadn't once offered to come. *He's needed here,* he thought with a pang of the old resentment. Still, he knew Micum too well not to read the conflict in his friend's face, and it hurt to see it.

"Quick and quiet's the best way," he went on, giving no hint of his own feelings. "With any luck, Alec and I can get in and out again before anyone's the wiser. That servant girl is the key, if Alec can romance her."

"Just the two of you?"

"You and Nysander will know where we are," said Seregil. "I don't want it to go any further than that. We've had enough trouble with spies as it is."

• • •

Stopping just long enough for a bath and a hasty meal, Seregil and Alec were ready to move on by noon. Micum disappeared while they were harrassing the horses they'd left there on the way to Cirna. He returned with a longsword.

"It's not so fine as yours, of course," he said, handing it to Seregil, "but it will do until yours is mended. I'll be easier in my mind, knowing you're armed."

Seregil ran his hand down the flat of the blade and smiled. "I remember this one. We brought it back for Beka from the Oronto raid."

"The very one." Micum looked down at the sword, his discomfort more evident than ever. "You know, I suppose I could—"

Seregil cut him short with a farewell embrace. "Stay put, my friend," he admonished, speaking softly against Micum's shoulder. "It's just a bit of fancy burglary. You know you're no use at that."

"Take care of yourselves then," Micum said gruffly. "And have Nysander send me word, you hear?"

"I hear!" Laughing, Seregil swung up in the saddle. "Come on, Alec, before old Grandfather here worries himself grey!"

As they rode into the Orëska gardens, a familiar deep voice hailed them from the direction of the oak grove. Reining in, Seregil saw Hwerlu cantering out to meet them.

"Greetings, friends!" the centaur boomed. "It's been many days since you've visited me. I trust all is well with you?"

"Tolerably," replied Seregil, anxious to be off again. "We're just here long enough to see Nysander, actually."

"But you've missed him by a day."

"Missed him?" Alec asked. "You mean he's not here?"

"No, he and young Thero accompanied Lady Magyana to another city. Some place on the southern coast, I think."

"Damn!" muttered Seregil. "Come on, Wethis will know."

"They've gone to Port Ayrie with Lady Magyana," the young servant told them. "They shouldn't be gone more than a few days, though. You can put up here until he returns, if you like."

"Thanks, but we can't wait." Seregil pulled out the worn manifest and handed it to Wethis with a hastily scrawled note. "See that he gets this and tell him to contact Micum. Tell him I don't expect to be gone more than a few days myself."

Leaving their Aurënfaie horses at the Orëska, they set off for the Cockerel.

"Shouldn't we wait for Nysander?" asked Alec dubiously. "You told Micum we'd speak to him first."

"The longer we wait, the more chance there is that Kassarie will get suspicious and put up extra defenses."

"I guess so, but it still leaves just you and me—"

"Illior's Fingers, Alec, it's just a simple matter of housebreaking, even if it is a keep. We'll probably get back before Nysander does."

Slipping quietly up the back stairs at the inn, they spent the night in their old rooms and set off the next morning in disguise. Alec wore the same apprentice garb he'd used on their first visit to Kassarie's; Seregil was well muffled in the guise of a one-eyed traveling minstrel. Both carried daggers at their belts, but their swords and Alec's dismantled bow were wrapped out of sight among the gear.

"This all hinges on you, you know," Seregil reminded Alec as they rode along. "It could take a couple of days of wooing before she agrees to let you in."

"If she does at all," Alec replied uneasily. "What do I say?"

Seregil gave him a knowing wink. "With a face like yours, I doubt conversation will be the central issue. From what you saw of her last time, I'd say our Stamie is a restless little bird, only too ready to spread her wings. The offer of freedom may be all the charm we need. It's her fear I'm worried about. That's a suspicious, tight-run household, and she may not dare risk her own skin on your behalf. If that's the case, then you'll have to play the lover for all you're worth."

"Which may not be much," Alec muttered.

"Illior's Fingers, you're not so bloodless as all that, are you?" Seregil teased. "Use a little imagination and let things run their course. These matters have a way of directing themselves, you know."

Reaching the road that led up the gorge, they kept to the trees and climbed into the hills overlooking the keep. They left their horses tethered well out of earshot of the tower sentries and made their final approach on foot. Climbing up the tall fir tree they'd used on their first reconnaissance, they surveyed the keep.

There appeared to be the usual sort of bustle in the courtyard. A groom was currying a fine horse by the stables, and from somewhere below the walls came the sound of a workman's chisel against stone. Presently the kitchen door swung open and Stamie came out with a bucket yoke across her narrow shoulders. Eyes to the ground, she disappeared around the corner of the main building.

"Look there!" whispered Seregil, spying a small postern gate near the kitchen. From it, a well-trodden path wound off into the forest; it would be as simple as lying by a deer track, waiting for their prey to come by.

"Look at what?" asked Alec.

"There, that small door in the wall, near the cliffs. Lean this way and fix your eye on the ruined tower, then bring your gaze down past—"

Seregil broke off, startled by a sudden realization. Gripping Alec by the arm, he whispered excitedly, "The tower! What's wrong with that tower?"

"Lightning, probably," Alec whispered back. "Looks like it happened years ago and—"

He stopped, slowly mirroring his companion's sharp, hungry grin.

"And what?" prompted Seregil.

"And they never *repaired* it."

"Which is pretty damned strange because—"

"Because they employ some of the best masons in Skala," finished Alec. "I knew we'd missed something before, but I just couldn't see it!"

Seregil gazed at the tower with a wry grin. "There it is, right in front of us. Whatever we're here to find, I bet my best horse it's around there somewhere. All we have to do is get inside."

"Which we can't do until Stamie comes out. Maybe we should've waited for Nysander after all."

"Patience, Alec. A good hunter like you knows how to lie in wait for his quarry!"

"You're feeling guilty over not going with them, aren't you?" Kari demanded, lying close to Micum in the darkness of their bedchamber. She knew the signs; in the two days since Seregil's departure, Micum had grown increasingly restless and absent-minded. Today he'd wandered from one small task to another without accomplishing anything.

"Perhaps you should have gone."

"Oh, they'll be all right." Micum shifted to hold her closer. "It's just strange that Nysander hasn't sent word."

"Then send a message down to him. One of the lads could have it there before noon."

"I suppose."

"I don't know why you're so worried. It's not as if Seregil hasn't done this sort of thing before. And two days is no time at all."

Micum frowned up at the candle shadows overhead. "All the same, Alec's so new at these things—"

"Then send word to Nysander. I don't need you moping around like an old dog again tomorrow." Kari kissed him roughly on the chin. "Better yet, go yourself. You'll fidget me to distraction waiting about for it. You can visit Beka while you're there."

"That's a thought. She must be missing home a bit by now. But will you be all right without me?"

"Of course I will!" scoffed Kari. "You'll only be a few hours away, and I've all my women to look after me. Go to sleep, love. I expect you'll want to get an early start."

Feeling a bit guilty, Micum bypassed the Horse Guard barracks and went straight to the Orëska House. Crossing the atrium, he heard a familiar voice hailing him and turned to find Nysander and Thero striding toward him. Both were clad in stained riding clothes and boots.

"Why, good morning to you!" Nysander called. "What brings you into the city so early in the day?"

Micum's heart sank. "Didn't Seregil and Alec tell you?"

"We've been away," Thero told him. "We're just getting back now."

"Indeed," said Nysander, frowning. "I have not heard from either of them since they left for Cirna."

"That little bastard!" growled Micum. "He promised me he'd talk to you before they went. I'd never have let them go off like that if I'd known."

"What has happened?"

"He and Alec came back a couple of days ago with evidence

linking Kassarie to the stolen gold. They'd been attacked on their way back from Cirna and they're convinced that was her doing, too. Seregil was all in a lather to go after her but he said he'd talk to you first."

"Perhaps he left word. Thero, go find Wethis, please. He would be the one Seregil would trust with a message. Come up to my tower, Micum.

"I am not certain I understand your concern," the wizard continued as they climbed the stairs. "Two days is not long for such work and I am certain I should have sensed if either of them had come to any great harm."

"Maybe so," Micum grudgingly agreed. "I guess I'm mostly feeling guilty about not going along with them, but Kari's pregnant again and I hated to leave her."

Thero hurried in with a rolled parchment. "They were here, and they left this for you."

Nysander unrolled the manifest and a terse scrawl from Seregil, explaining its significance.

"Well, he was obviously in a hurry to follow this lead," he said. "I will scry for them."

Seating himself at his desk, Nysander covered his eyes with both hands, murmuring the complex spell. After a moment he sat back. "It is difficult to get an exact sighting on them, but all appears to be well. Would you like to stay here for a few days, see if they turn up?"

"I think maybe I will. You'd better send a message out to Kari for me, though. And keep a weather eye on her, too, while you're at it. I'm off to see Beka now. Her mother's worried she might be homesick."

38

THE KEY TO A POOR GIRL'S HEART

For three days Alec and Seregil kept their cold vigil and at last their patience was rewarded. On watch in the fir tree early the third afternoon, Alec saw Stamie emerge though the postern with a large basket on her back and set off into the woods.

Seregil was napping at the base of the tree. Climbing down, Alec woke him and together they hurried off through the trees to strike the path ahead of the girl.

Seregil remained out of sight among the trees while Alec took up his position on a log near a bend in the trail. In the distance they could hear the girl singing to herself as she approached.

She caught sight of Alec ahead of her and halted abruptly. "Who's that there, and what do you want?" she called sharply.

"It's Elrid. Remember me?" Alec stood up slowly, praying he didn't sound as awkward as he suddenly felt. "I came looking for Lord Teukros a few days back?"

"Oh, the messenger boy from the city." Curious but still on her guard, she stood where she was. "What are you doing back here again? And why are you lurking out here in the forest?"

"You said you wanted a position in the city," Alec replied. "I heard of one—a good one—and come out to tell you. Your aunt didn't strike me as the welcoming sort, though, so I've been waiting out here for a chance alone with you."

Seeing that she softened considerably at this, he added, "It was cold last night. I couldn't get a fire started."

"You poor, simple thing!" Dropping her basket, Stamie hurried forward to chaff his hands between her own. "You're all ice! Don't they teach you nothin' in that city of yours? Imagine being outside on such a night and the stars as sharp as daggers! You'll catch the frostbite."

A patchy flush colored her angular cheeks as she looked up, still holding his hands firmly between her own. "And you came all the way out here for me?"

"I got to thinking about what you said and how lonesome it must be for you out here, and well—" Alec shrugged, feigning shyness to avoid her worshipful gaze. Lying to innkeepers and fat nobles was one thing; deceiving this plain, kind, desperate girl was quite another. Side-stepping his conscience as best he could, he pressed on, carefully doling out the tale he and Seregil had concocted.

"There's a seamstress in the next street from ours wanting a girl to apprentice. It's clean work, and it would get you out of the kitchen." He paused meaningfully. "And it's just in the next street over from mine."

"Is it?" Stamie smiled knowingly. "I've no complaint with that. Do you have a horse? Let's go before I'm missed."

"We can't go now!" *So much for charming her away,* thought Alec. The trick was going to be holding her back long enough to get into the keep.

"Why not?"

"Well—" Alec scrambled for a plausible impediment. "You'll need to gather your things up and give your notice."

"Notice? As if they'd let me go! I've been a slave to them since I was old enough to carry a pan. Just let me nip back and fill a kerchief, then we can slip away tonight!"

Outflanked, Alec had to rethink his strategy again.

"Two servants traveling in the night?" he scoffed. "The patrols would take us for thieves or runaways before we ever reached the city. And that's if the real outlaws and night riders didn't get to us first. You don't want to end up dead in the ditch, do you? Or worse?"

Stamie's eyes widened in alarm. "No, but how do we get away, then? They'll never let me go, not Aunt or Illester or any of them."

"They won't know." Alec slipped an arm around her waist and walked her deeper into the forest. "It's simple enough to manage. You wait until everyone's asleep, then gather your things up and wait until just before dawn. That's the time to travel. Anyone we meet on the road at first light will think we're off to market. Do you see?"

"Oh, yes! I'll do it just as you say. And I'm ever so grateful!"

Turning, she pulled him close with surprising decisiveness and delivered a rough, tooth-knocking kiss. Lips still locked against his, she drew his hand up against her flat bosom with one hand and began rucking up her homespun skirt with the other.

"Here now, there's no time for that," Alec gasped, trying to pull away. She'd been chewing raw garlic to keep away the winter ague.

"It don't take long." Stamie giggled, reaching for the hem of his tunic.

Freeing himself with an effort, Alec held her at arm's length. "Hold off, can't you?"

"What's the matter with you?" the girl demanded indignantly. "One minute you're all sweetness, and the next you act like you don't want me."

"Of course I do," Alec assured her. "But not if it means you getting in trouble. If you don't get back with the kindling or whatever it is you were sent out for, they'll come looking for you, won't they? Or maybe lock you up when you get back?"

"They would, too," Stamie said resentfully. "They done it before."

"Course they would," Alec said, loosening his grip to a caress. "And then where would we be, eh? But if we're careful, we can be in Rhíminee tomorrow night. Together."

"Together!" Stamie whispered, won over anew.

"That's right. Now come on and I'll help you."

Keeping out of sight of the tower sentries, they gathered sticks to fill Stamie's basket. The excited girl chattered readily, and Alec soon turned the conversation to the broken tower.

The tower over the gorge had been in ruins for years, it seemed, though she didn't know how long. No one was allowed there ever, and old Illester said there was even a ghost, some lord who'd been in the tower when it was struck.

"They say he'll push you off to your death if you go up there at night," she confided with a delicious shiver. "And it's true, too. Lots of servants have heard strange sounds from there, and seen lights moving. Aunt says a servant she knew went in once, just a little ways, and felt the touch of a dead hand against his face. He didn't die of it then, but within the week he fell into the gorge and was smashed to bits! Aunt saw him after they carried him up. Ghosts are unlucky things, you know, even just to see one."

"I've heard that," Alec replied uneasily, recalling the strange breeze he'd felt in the main hall.

The basket was soon full. Giving Alec a farewell kiss, she ran her hands down over his hips and whispered, "I won't sleep a wink tonight, I promise!"

"Nor will I." Ready to spring the final ruse, Alec cast a yearning look toward the keep and sighed deeply. "It'll be cold out here again tonight."

"Oh, you poor dear! And it looking like to snow, too."

Alec held his breath, watching her waver. *Let her think of it first,* Seregil had warned.

"It'd be worth both our skins if we was caught." She hesitated, frowning. "But I could creep down and let you in after they're all asleep. If you stayed in the back pantry and didn't make a sound, it might be safe."

"What about the watchmen?"

"They mostly keep an eye on the road. And this side of the yard is good and dark. Oh, but we'll have to be quiet, though!"

"Quiet as ghosts." Alec smiled as he took her hand in his. "Just a warm corner out of the wind, that's all I need."

"I wish I could warm you tonight," she murmured.

"Soon," he promised. "In Rhíminee."

"In Rhíminee!" she sighed. Breathing garlic against his cheek, she kissed him a last time and hurried off.

Alec waited until she was well out of sight, then turned to retrace his steps into the woods. Coming around a fallen tree, he nearly stepped on Seregil.

"Lucky for us she's a lonesome country girl," Seregil said, shaking his head. "A Helm Street maid would've given you the air. 'Here now, there's no time for that!' and 'Hold off, can't you?' A fine, hot suitor you sounded!"

"I told you I'm no good at it," Alec retorted, stung by the criticism. "Besides, it felt rotten lying to her like that."

"This is no time for an attack of conscience. Illior's Hands, haven't we lied to someone on any job we've ever done?"

"I know," Alec grumbled. "But this was different. She's not some footpad or randy ship's captain, just a poor nobody like me. Here I am offering her the one thing in the whole world she wants, and tomorrow all her hopes will be dashed."

"Who says we have to dash her hopes? She wants a position in town; I'll see she gets one."

"You'd do that?"

"Of course I'd do that. I forge a lovely reference. She can have her pick of situations. Think you can live with that?"

Alec nodded, abashed. "I guess I just didn't—"

"Come to think of it, perhaps we could take her on at Wheel Street," Seregil added ruthlessly. "What with you taking such an interest in her welfare and all."

"That's not exactly what I had in mind."

"No?" Grinning, Seregil threw an arm over the boy's shoulders as they headed back up the slope. "Now there's a surprise!"

39

THE TOWER

Alec crouched in the shadows near the postern gate, watching the sky. The stars had wheeled to midnight. It hadn't snowed after all. Instead, the skies had cleared at sunset and the temperature had dropped bitterly. Without a fire, or Seregil to share warmth with, as they'd had to the past few days, he was chilled to the bone. And worried.

The lights in the keep had gone out ages ago and he was beginning to worry that she'd either been caught, or was too scared to come for him. Or had gone to sleep in a warm bed and forgotten her promise to come for him.

But he held his position and finally heard the soft patter of footsteps somewhere beyond the wall. A moment later Stamie inched the postern door open and waved him in. Moving with exaggerated caution, she led him in through the kitchen to a dark pantry.

"I'll come down again before the others wake," she whispered ecstatically, pressing his hand to the bosom of her shift. "Oh, I can't wait to be free of this place!"

Alec felt ribs jutting beneath the coarse fabric, and the rapid tripping of her heart. Determined to play his role better, he took her in his arms. Kissing her just below the left ear, he whispered an endearment Seregil had suggested. The girl gave a happy shiver and pressed closer.

"Where's your room?" he whispered.

She giggled softly. "In the servant's attic, you naughty pup! I sleep on a pallet at the foot of Aunt's bed."

"Have you a window to watch the sky?"

"There's a dormer just over me. I'll prop the shutter open."

"Come to me when the stars begin to fade."

"When the stars fade," the girl breathed. Giving him a last squeeze, she hurried off.

Alec stayed put for a time, fearing she'd find some pretense to come back. The wait was hardly an onerous one; after two days without a fire, even the warmth of a banked hearth was something to be grateful for. The pantry also smelled wonderfully of smoked meats. It was too dark to see, but his groping hand soon found a rope of hard sausage.

Creeping out at last, he spied a long shawl hanging on a peg by the kitchen door. Throwing it on for a bit of extra camouflage, he tiptoed out to the postern and unbolted it. Seregil slipped in with their swords and Alec bolted the door after him.

Safely in the kitchen, Seregil eyed Alec's makeshift disguise and wrinkled his nose. "You been eating garlic, gramma?"

"There's a nice bit of sausage, if you want some." Alec offered, returning the shawl to its peg.

"Take off your boots," whispered Seregil. "Bare feet are quietest for this sort of work. Don't forget your dagger, though. We may need it."

Leaving their boots out of sight behind a row of cider casks, they padded off in the direction of the main hall.

All the stairways of the keep were contained in the towers, so as to be easily defensible in case of attack. It was the southeast tower they wanted, and they soon found a narrow passageway leading in that direction.

An archway at the far end let into a small antechamber. Using a shielded lightstone, they found a heavy oak door at the back of it. Seregil lifted the latch ring and eased it open.

Inside, they found a small, windowless landing. The back portion of the tiny chamber and what must have been the stairwell were completely blocked by broken stone and dusty, shattered timbers.

Alec took a step in, then froze in terror as a light, eerie caress stroked along his cheek. The touch came again, accompanied this time by a low moan and a chill draft of air.

"The ghost!" Alec's voice came out a strangled whisper.

"Ghost, eh?" Seregil waved his hand in the air above his head, then held it to the lightstone for Alec to see. Long black filaments, fine as spider web, hung tangled from his fingers.

"There's your ghost—black silk combed fine and hung in a draft. As soon as I heard Stamie's tale of ghostly touches I suspected as much."

"But the cold draft?"

"We're in the stronghold of master masons, Alec. There are tiny air channels somewhere in the walls here. They let in drafts from outside and those mysterious moans are the sound of it. We'll need to be very careful here."

"What about magic?"

"That's one thing we probably don't have to worry about. If Kassarie's really a Leran, then she'd never stoop to using the unnatural methods of the hated Aurënfaie. But there will be traps, killing traps, and we'd damn well better not get cocky."

A careful search found no sign of any secret openings or traps.

"Looks like we'll have to look elsewhere for our entrance," muttered Seregil.

"But where?"

"Upstairs, I think."

Alec looked over at the pile of rubble. "How could there be anything above us? Look at this! The whole inside of the tower must have been destroyed."

"Yet from the outside it appears that just one side of the top of the tower was broken; it shouldn't have done this kind of damage."

"You mean this mess is just a trick, a fake?"

"Either that or I'm completely wrong." Seregil grinned crookedly. "But why leave the tower broken unless there was some reason?"

"So we go up?"

"We go up."

"Micum! Come here!"

Snapping awake, Micum groped for the lightstone under his

pillow. The room—Seregil's old apprentice chamber—was empty, but Nysander's anxious voice seemed to hang on the air.

Pulling on his breeches, Micum hurried down the corridor to the wizard's bedchamber. Nysander was dressed already in his old traveling coat and breeches; his face was dark with concern.

Micum felt a sudden coldness in his innards. "What's happened?"

"We must go at once!" Nysander replied, throwing on his cloak. "They are in some terrible danger, or were—I pray Illior it was a premonition and not a seeing vision."

"Of what?" demanded Micum. "What did you see, Nysander?"

Nysander's hands shook as he yanked his cloak strings closed. "Falling. I felt them falling. And I heard them scream."

Seregil and Alec crept up the northeast tower stairs to the second floor of the keep and found the door unbarred, though there were brackets set on both sides of the jamb. Covering their lights, they took a cautious peek at what lay beyond.

It was dark here, but there was the feel of open space around them. From somewhere nearby came the buzz and rumble of assorted snores, though it was difficult to judge exactly where the sleepers might be. As their eyes adjusted, they could make out a dim light faintly illuminating a broad archway in a far wall. The acrid smell of a forge, mingled with the tang of metal and oil, suggested that the room was an armory or smithy.

Seregil found Alec's wrist and squeezed it, silently directing him to follow the wall to their left.

This direction proved fruitless, however. There was a door into the ruined tower, but a heavy forge had been set up in front of it. Returning to the other tower, they made their way up to the top floor.

At the top of the stairs they inched the door open and saw a long corridor. Some distance away, a night lamp hung at what appeared to be a juncture with another corridor. By its light they could see that the walls were richly frescoed in the latest style, and that the floors were inset with polished mosaics. Somewhere behind one of the many carved doors that lined the corridor lay their enemy.

Stealing up to the night lamp, they found that this upper story was laid out in four quarters, divided by two diagonal corridors that ran between opposing towers. The corridors looked very much alike, including the doors, frescoes, and patterned floor. Three, including the one they'd come up, ended at tower doors. At the end of the southeast, however, the wall was covered from floor to ceiling with a large tapestry.

As hoped, the hanging concealed another door to the ruined tower and this one had been fitted with a heavy lock. Signing for Alec to hold back the tapestry and keep watch, Seregil began a careful inspection. The ornate mechanism was tarnished, but it smelled of oil, as did the heavy door hinges. Running a finger over the lower hinge, Seregil sniffed at it, then held it under Alec's nose. The boy grinned, understanding at once; why maintain the door to a ruined tower so carefully?

The lock was swiftly dealt with, and cold night air struck their faces as the door swung out onto a moonlit rampart. The square, flat surface they stood had been repaired, but the southern and eastern parapets had been left in ruins. The paving flags sent an aching chill up through their bare feet and ankles.

The wind moaned through the broken stonework, whipping their hair across their faces as they edged over to the remains of the southern parapet. The keep backed directly onto the cliffs; from where they stood, there was a sheer drop into the shadowed river gorge below.

"Caught in a high place again," Alec whispered nervously, hanging back.

"Not caught yet. Here's what we want," said Seregil, poking around in the shadows under the north wall, where the glow of his lightstone revealed another door. Scarred and weathered as it was, it, too, had a stout lock and hinges in excellent repair. Beyond it, a curving staircase spiraled down into darkness.

Seregil felt a familiar tightness in his belly as he peered down. "This place is dangerous—I can feel it. Draw your dagger and watch your footing. Keep count of the steps, too, in case we lose our lights."

The steps here were smooth but narrow underfoot, reminding Seregil of those leading down to the Oracle's chamber beneath the Temple of Illior. The curve of the smoothly dressed walls sliced away the view fifteen feet below at any point. Rusty iron sconces set into the stone at regular intervals held thick tallow candles, but these were dusty. The whole place had an abandoned, disused smell.

Counting softly to himself, Seregil moved down the steps with a wary eye out for trouble. Fifty-three steps down, something caught his eye and he held up a warning hand. A length of blackened bowstring had been fixed tautly across the next step a little above ankle height.

"That could give you a nasty fall," Alec muttered, peering over his shoulder.

"Worse than that, maybe," replied Seregil, squinting into the shadows below. Taking off his cloak, he shook it wide and cast it out in front of him. It floated down a few feet, then caught on what appeared to be another string stretched at an angle across the stairwell. Examining it, they found it to be instead a thin, rigid blade.

Seregil tested the edge of it with a thumbnail. "Fall just right and this could take your head off, or an arm."

They found three more pitfalls of similar design as they continued down. Then, rounding a final turn, they came to the top of the rubble pile blocking the first entrance.

"This doesn't make any sense!" Alec exclaimed in frustration. "We must have missed something."

"We found exactly what we were meant to find," Seregil muttered, heading back up the stairs. "It's another diversion, too obvious and too dangerous. It does prove one thing, though; this tower is in perfect repair. They're hiding something here for certain."

Toiling back up the stairs, they came out again on the rampart.

"We have to work fast now," Seregil warned, glancing up at the stars, which had wheeled noticeably to the west already.

"What if the real way in isn't here?"

"That's a distinct possibility." Seregil ran a hand back through his hair. "Still, everything we've found so far tells me that this is the place. Look around, check every stone. You start there, at that corner. I'll begin here. Look for uneven stones, listen for hollow spots, anything. We're running out of time."

Shielding his light, Alec crossed back to the ruined wall while Seregil remained in the shadows near the door.

• • •

Despite Seregil's confidence, Alec renewed his search with little expectation of success. The mortar was sound, the stones solidly set together. Crossing back and forth, he checked and double-checked his section without finding anything new, and all the while the moon sank lower.

He was crossing to the northern parapet when his bare foot struck a slight declivity he hadn't noticed before. If he'd had his boots on he'd have missed it entirely, but the loose grittiness beneath his chilled toes felt distinctly different from the surrounding flagstones. Dropping to his knees, he found what appeared to be a patch of sand slightly larger than the palm of his hand.

"Seregil, come here, quick!"

With Seregil hunkered down beside him, Alec scooped out the sand and uncovered a square niche sunk into the stone. At the bottom lay a large bronze ring fastened loosely to a staple. It was large enough for him to get a good grip and he pulled up hard, expecting the resistance of a heavy slab. Instead, an irregular section of thin flags lifted easily, revealing the square wooden trap door fastened to their underside. Holding their lights down, they found a square shaft, with a wooden ladder leading down to yet another door.

"Well done!" Seregil whispered. Descending the ladder, they pulled the door closed over them.

The door at the base of the ladder had no lock, just a curved latch, green with age. In his excitement, Alec reached for it but Seregil caught his hand before he could touch it.

"Wait!" Seregil hissed. Pulling a bit of twine from his pouch, he tied a noose in the end of it and looped it over the handle, then stood back and pulled. As the handle lifted, there was an audible click.

Four long needles sprang out, spaced so that at least one would be certain to pierce the hand of an unwary trespasser. Their tips were darkened with a resinous substance. As the door swung open Seregil released the handle, and the needles retracted like the claws of a cat.

"Never trust anything that looks easy," Seregil warned, giving Alec a reproving look.

From here, a steep wooden staircase followed the square shape of the tower walls down in a series of landings and right-angle turns.

"Of course! A double staircase," muttered Seregil, taking the lead again with dagger drawn. "One would have been for the servants, this one a secret escape route for the nobles in case of attack."

"Then we can get out this way, without having to go back through the keep again?"

"We'll see," Seregil replied doubtfully. "It may have been blocked off to keep anyone from wandering in from outside."

Unlike the other stairways, this one was wooden, constructed of thick oak that probably dated from the original construction of the keep. Seregil tested each step as he put his weight on it, yet they seemed sound enough.

There were no trip wires here, no blades. Knowing better than to let their guard down, however, they grew increasingly vigilant, anticipating something more devious in the offing.

This stairway had been used recently and often. The dust that had settled over everything was much thinner at the center of each step and showed footprints on the landings. The tallow candles in the wall sconces smelled of recent burning. There were also spots of finer wax on the stairs, which spoke of someone carrying a taper with them as they descended. Some of the spots were dull with dust, others still shiny and fragrant of beeswax.

"How far down do you think we are?" asked Alec, pausing for a moment to catch his breath. They'd been going up and down stairs for hours, and his legs were feeling the strain.

"We must be past the second floor by now, maybe near the first," replied Seregil, coming to yet another landing. "This is all taking a lot longer than I'd—"

Suddenly the landing floor seemed to fly up in Alec's face. Frozen on the stairs, he watched in helpless amazement as the wooden platform pivoted on diagonally opposing corners, its underside now standing vertically in front of him to reveal a sheer-sided pit of some kind below. A loose board fell free, tumbling into the blackness without a sound.

O Illior, Seregil! The words hammered in Alec's throat as he stared, horrorstruck, into the gaping shaft at his feet. But no sound came out. It had all happened too quickly. His whole body went numb and cold. *First the avalanche and now—*

"Alec!" The hoarse, panicky cry came from somewhere beyond the uptilted floor.

"Seregil! You didn't fall!"

"But I'm about to. Do something, anything! *Hurry!*"

A sickening sense of futility engulfed Alec. The upper corner of the platform was several feet beyond his reach. If he jumped at it, it would tilt back and crush him against the side of the shaft, probably shaking Seregil loose from whatever precarious hold he had managed on his side. If only he had a rope—something long enough to snag the upper corner and pull it down—

"Alec!"

Ripping off his cloak, Alec gathered the hem of it in one hand and tossed the other end at the upthrust corner, hoping to catch it with the hood. It fell mere inches short of the mark.

"Damn it to hell!" Alec could hear Seregil's labored breathing a few short, impossible yards away. Looking wildly around, his eye fell on the rusty sconce set into the wall above the lowermost step.

Without a second thought he grasped it with his right hand and leaned as far out over the pit as his reach allowed, cloak ready in his left for another cast.

He was already overbalanced beyond recovery when the sconce gave beneath his hand. He heard the evil grate of metal against stone as he lurched forward a few inches more over the edge.

He hung a moment, breath dead in his throat, waiting for the final pin or screw or brace to pull free.

It didn't.

It might, if he moved.

Or it might not. He wouldn't know until he tried.

His choices were pretty limited; make a move now or wait to fall when his grip gave out.

"Alec—?"

With sweat pouring down his face and sides, he willed himself to make one last, crucial try with the cloak. Tossing it up with his left hand, he caught the upper corner of the platform with the edge of the hood and felt it hold. Miraculously, the iron sconce held, too, at least for the moment.

Pulling down on the cloak, he dragged the corner of the platform down with every ounce of strength he could muster. Its weight, together with Seregil's—still clinging somehow to its other side—was almost more than he could manage, but slowly, slowly, it tilted back toward level. As it came down he managed to move his left hand up, gripping the fabric in his teeth as he transferred his hold. This process gave him enough leverage to gradually pull himself backward and out of the way of the descending edge. At last he was able to grasp the platform and push.

As the upper side of it came into view, he found Seregil huddled there, grasping the handle of his dagger with both hands. Somehow, even as he'd felt the floor go out from under him, he'd managed to drive the tip of the blade in far enough between two of the floorboards to hold his slight weight as he hung from it.

"Throw me the end of your cloak," he croaked, white and shaken. "It's bound to tip down when I come your way. Can you hang on to me if I drop again?"

"Wait a second." Holding the edge of the platform with one hand, Alec undid his belt with the other and worked the end of it back through the buckle. Securing the loop around his wrist, he flapped the loose end out to Seregil. "Get a good hold on this. I can manage this better than the cloak."

Wedging the dagger more firmly, Seregil gripped the end of the belt and began inching his way toward Alec.

The platform tilted down ominously as he shifted his weight, but Alec hauled him quickly to safety on the stairs.

"Bilairy's *Balls*!" Seregil gasped, collapsing at his feet.

"And Guts!" Alec leaned shakily against the wall. "This candle thing I had hold of nearly came loose! I can't believe it didn't."

Upon closer inspection, however, he found that it hadn't come loose at all. It was still fixed solidly to a rod that ran back into the wall. When he pushed up, it slid smoothly back into place.

"Look at this," he exclaimed, perplexed.

Getting to his feet, Seregil examined the mechanism. Pushing the sconce upright, he drew his sword and pushed on the edge of the platform. It tilted with precipitous ease. When the sconce was pulled down, however, it remained solidly level. They soon discovered two heavy pins that slid in and out of the wall below the platform to hold it steady when the sconce was down.

"Ingenious," Seregil said with genuine admiration. "When Kassarie comes down she pulls this and leaves it fixed. On the way back up she resets the trap. That loose board that fell out must have been some sort of brace that held it in place until I got halfway across. It's more dangerous that way, since there was no chance to jump back."

"How did you ever manage to get your knife set in time?" Alec asked wonderingly.

Seregil shook his head. "I don't even remember doing it."

Moving with redoubled care, they continued down. After a few more turns, the walls of the stairwell changed from masonry to solid stone and they knew they were below ground level. Reaching the bottom at last, they found a short, level corridor leading to a door.

Seregil bent to inspect the lock. "It looks safe enough. You better do it, though. My hands are still shaking!"

Alec knelt and took out his tools. Selecting a hook, he grinned up at Seregil. "After all this trouble, let's hope this isn't just the wine cellar!"

40

FLIGHT

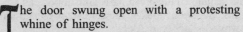

The door swung open with a protesting whine of hinges.

Thrusting in his lightstone, Alec tensed with a hiss of surprise.

"What is it?" whispered Seregil, grasping his sword hilt as he moved to look in.

The light was not bright enough to fully illuminate the room, but they could make out the figure of a person seated in an ornate chair against the far wall. There was no movement or outcry, and stepping closer, they saw that it was the withered corpse of a man.

He was nobly dressed in clothing of antique design. A heavy golden torque hung at his shrunken throat, and several rings glinted on the bony fingers resting on the arms of the chair. His thick, dark hair had retained its living gloss and hung in disconcerting contrast against the sunken cheeks.

"Uven ari nobis!" Seregil exclaimed softly, bending close with his light.

Alec did not understand the words but recognized the reverent tone with which they were spoken. Fighting down his instinctive revulsion, he looked more closely at the corpse's face, noting the fine bones of the skull beneath their thin covering of desiccated skin, the high, prominent cheekbones, the large, sunken sockets where eyes had been.

"Illior's Light! Seregil, this can't be—"

"It is," Seregil replied grimly. "Or was. Lord Corruth, the lost consort of Idrilain the First. These rings prove it. See this?" He indicated the one on the corpse's right hand; it was set with a lozenge of banded carnelian deeply incised with the Dragon of Skala. "It's a Consort's Seal. And this other, the silver with the red stone? Finest Aurënfaie work. This was Corruth í Glamien Yanari Meringil Bôkthersa."

"Your kinsman."

"I never knew him, though I'd often hoped—" Seregil touched one of the hands. "The skin's hard and hollow as the shell of a dried gourd. Someone took great care to preserve him."

"But why?" shuddered Alec.

Seregil shook his head angrily. "I suppose the bastards get some perverse pleasure out of having their enemy looking on as they plot to overthrow his descendants. Perhaps they swear oaths on him, I don't know. Factions like the Lerans don't persist for generations without a good leaven of fanaticism."

The chamber was about the size of Nysander's workroom, and the hand of a master mason was evident in every line; dry, sound, and square, its walls showed no moisture or moss. The ceiling overhead, though not high, was vaulted and ribbed to give the room a less oppressive feel. It was furnished with a round table, several chests, and a few cabinets against the walls. A low dais with a second thronelike chair stood against the left-hand wall. A broad shield hung on the wall behind it.

"Another sacred artifact," Seregil noted grimly, examining the crowned dragon design painted on the shield. "Queen Lera's, no doubt. I wonder who they're grooming to carry it?"

"I thought she didn't have any heirs?"

"She had no daughters, but there are always plenty of nieces and cousins in these Skalan families."

Riffling through the chests and cabinets, they found a carefully organized collection of maps, correspondence, and documents.

"I'll be damned!" Seregil spread a huge, yellowed parchment on the table. "Plans of the Rhíminee sewers. And see here, next to the draftsman's mark?"

Alec recognized the tiny image of a coiled lizard. "Kassarie's family must have built the sewers."

"Parts of them, anyway. It was a huge undertaking. Imagine what this would be worth to enemy sappers!"

Resuming their search, they soon turned up enough damning correspondence to bring nobles of a dozen houses to Traitor's Hill.

Opening a chest, Alec reached to push aside a rumpled swath of wool. Beneath it his fingers encountered cold, rounded metal.

"Seregil, look what I found!" At the bottom of the chest gleamed eight gold baps still bearing the Queen's Treasury mark.

"The *White Hart* gold! Our lady's been busy, though. These are shipped in lots of twenty-four. I tell you, Alec, if Kassarie isn't the head of the Lerans herself, then she's in it up to her ears!"

The gold was too heavy to carry away, so Seregil selected a few of the more incriminating letters and divided them with Alec. Turning to the corpse again, he gently removed the rings from the withered fingers, murmuring something in Aurënfaie as he did so.

He handed Alec the silver ring, and strung the seal around his own neck on a bit of string.

"We're Watchers on this job, and this is Watcher business," he said with uncommon earnestness. "If anything happens to one of us, the other goes on, no matter what. We've got to get at least one of these to Nysander. Do you understand?"

Alec slipped the ring onto his thumb with a grudging nod.

"Good. If we get separated, meet me at the tree we camped under."

"The last time you carried something that way it got us into an awful mess!" Alec noted wryly, touching the seal ring where it hung against his friend's breast.

Seregil dropped the ring down the front of his tunic with a grim smile. "*I'm* not the one this will harm."

Putting the room back in order, they hurried back up to the open top of the tower. Seregil studied the sky with relief; the job had taken far longer than he'd anticipated, but it looked like they still had a little time to spare. As they came out from behind the tapestry into the corridor, however, some instinctive alarm went off in the back of his mind.

Something was different.

He grasped the hilt of his sword, belly tightening coldly again. The light. Someone had turned up the wick on the night lamp. Alec had spotted it, too, and was reaching for his own weapon. They crept up to the intersection of the two corridors, bare feet silent on the smooth floors. The hallways appeared deserted. Bearing right, they headed back toward the northeast tower. They'd nearly reached it when the door swung open and two men with swords stepped out.

There was no time to take cover. Not knowing how many more men might be behind the others, Seregil and Alec turned and bolted back the way they'd come.

"There he is!" a man yelled behind them. "And he's got another with him! Here! He's up here!"

At the juncture of the corridors they cut to the right and made a dash for the northwest tower. More shouts rang out behind them as they flung open the door and plunged inside.

"Go on, I'll follow!" Seregil ordered, and was relieved when Alec didn't stop to argue.

A sizable pack of armed men was coming on at a run. Grabbing the wooden bar from the corner by the door, he slammed the door and rammed the bar into its brackets. A heavy body hit the door from the other side, then another. Muffled curses followed him as he fled down after Alec.

He caught up with him just below the second-floor entrance to the tower. Rounding a corner, however, they saw torchlight coming from below.

"Second floor!" hissed Seregil, scrambling back up the stairs.

Footsteps pounded toward them from above and below as they reached the door. There was no time for caution. Swords at the ready, they threw it open and dashed out into the large chamber beyond.

Its sole occupant was an old woman with a lamp. At the sight of them, she dropped her light and ran off through the workshop beyond, shrieking for help at the top of her creaky voice. Ignoring the flames spreading out from the broken lamp, Seregil barred the door.

"This must be where all that snoring was coming from," said Alec, looking around unhappily.

It was a barracks and there were more empty beds than Seregil wanted to count.

"Everybody's awake now," he noted grimly, heading for the southwest tower. "Come on, let's try this one."

"Up or down?" Alec demanded as they ducked in and barred the door.

"Down."

But rounding the third turn, they ran headlong into another gang of Kassarie's men.

Having the higher ground saved them. Alec and Seregil struck out with their swords before their attackers could get their weapons up. Two men fell, their bodies blocking the stairs long enough for them to retreat. Another man came at them from above, swinging a short club. In the lead, Alec ducked the blow and thrust his sword between the man's ankles. Seregil got in a good jab as the unfortunate man tumbled forward, then heaved the body on down the stairs.

Someone was trying to batter down the second-floor door as they passed. Dashing on, they found themselves back on the third floor.

Alec set the bar across the door, then doubled over panting. "Where now?"

"Let me think!" Seregil wiped his brow with one tattered sleeve. They'd been up and down how many towers? And how many doors had he blocked? No matter, really; by now all of them would be guarded.

Just ahead of them a corridor door flew open and they found themselves faced with four more men.

Falling on the newcomers, Seregil managed to strike down one before the man could draw his sword. The rest put up a savage fight but were no match for their attackers. Seregil ran a second man through, then turned in time to see another stab Alec in the left arm. The boy recovered in an instant and seized the advantage, cutting his attacker across the thigh. The man fell back with a cry and Seregil dispatched him. In the melee, the fourth man took to his heels and escaped down the corridor.

"Let him go," Seregil ordered as Alec started off in pursuit. "You're wounded. How bad is it?"

Alec flexed his bloodied arm. "Just a nick."

Angry shouts interrupted them as a gang of men dashed into view beneath the night lamp. "Here. They're back here!"

"This way!" Seregil bolted through the open doorway the four men had appeared from.

Beyond lay a small storage chamber, and on the far side of it another door stood open. Charging on, they raced up a narrow stairway, threw open the trap door at the top, and came out on the flat roof of the keep.

"We're cornered!" cried Alec, looking around.

A quick circuit of the ramparts proved him right. There was no other way down; looking over the low parapets, they found impossible drops on every side. Behind them, Kassarie's men were already clambering up through the trap door with torches, swords, and clubs.

"We make our stand here," Seregil growled, retreating to the southern rampart.

Back to back, swords at the ready, they stood fast as the grinning mob advanced to form a menacing half circle around them.

"We have them, my lady. The boy and a beggar man," someone called out.

More torches bobbed into view, and the men parted for Lady Kassarie. Wrapped in a dark cloak, hair in a loose braid over one shoulder, she advanced to inspect the interlopers. Alec recognized the old manservant, Illester, at her side.

"Beggar man? Oh, hardly that." She frowned. "Lord Seregil í Korit. And—Sir Alec something, isn't it? Had I known of your interest in my affairs, gentlemen, I would have extended you a proper invitation."

Seregil threw back his tattered cloak and made her a small, mocking bow. "My Lady Kassarie ä Moirian. Your recent interest in *my* affairs was invitation enough, I assure you."

Kassarie gave him an appraising look. "Your reputation fails to do you justice. Your little jaunt up to Cirna exhibited far more initiative than you're given credit for, and now this! Who would have suspected such enterprise? But then, that was foolish of me. The dandified wastrel you're made out to be could never have inveigled himself so skillfully into the chambers of power."

"You flatter me, lady."

"You're too modest, my lord. After all, you've captured the ear of wizards and princesses." Kassarie's mouth twisted with a bitter sneer. "But then, you're one of them, aren't you? Some kin to our mongrel royalty? I trust you enjoyed your reunion with Lord Corruth."

Seregil's jaw tightened. "For that abomination, my lady, you have my family's curse."

"I shall do my best to be worthy of it. Now tell me, on whose behalf have you invaded my home?"

"We're agents of Idrilain the Second, the true and rightful queen of Skala," Seregil replied.

"Bravely spoken!" laughed Kassarie. "And how unfortunate

for me if that were so. Yet I have my own agents, you see, very skillful and reliable ones. If you were working for the Queen I would know. No, I think your Aurënfaie ties go a bit deeper than is generally supposed. Your people would be only too happy, I'm certain, to discredit Skalans loyal to the true line!"

A strange, hectic light came into her eyes as she spoke these last words. Gripping his sword more tightly, Seregil thought with disquieting certainty, *She's going to kill us.*

"It's of small importance, I suppose," she went on darkly. "Your disappearance may cause a certain stir, but few, I think, will mourn you."

"Others will come," Seregil retorted. "Others like us, when you least expect them."

"And find me flown. That fool Teukros did more harm than you could. But you know about Teukros, don't you? This boy came asking for him." Her gaze shifted to Alec. "And repaid my hospitality by seducing my scullery maid."

"She didn't know anything," Alec told her, suddenly fearful for the girl. "I tricked her into letting me in."

"Ah, the gallant suitor speaks." Kassarie gave him a mocking smile. "A position in the great city, promises of passion to come—How pathetically common, but so effective. But she proved a poor choice for your dupe. Her aunt caught her sneaking out with a traveling bundle a short while ago."

"We soon beat the truth out of her," Illester cackled. "The girl never was very reliable."

"Please, don't hurt her," Alec said weakly.

"Of course, I can't help feeling a bit sorry for the poor, homely thing," Kassarie continued. "She was heartbroken to learn of your perfidy. But you'll have a little time to reflect on that. Gentlemen, throw down your swords!"

Seregil felt Alec tense behind him, awaiting his lead. Studying Kassarie's imperious face in the torchlight, he weighed the chances of coming down off this roof alive. It seemed doubtful.

"I've little faith in your hospitality," he replied, stalling for time. *Think, man, think! Find a thin spot in the mob! How far to the stairs, the tower door?*

"You've given me quite enough trouble for one night," Kassarie snapped, losing patience. "Look around! You can't fight your way out. Look behind you. A thousand feet down. Teukros screamed all the way to the bottom when they threw him off. Will you?"

Beside him, Seregil heard Alec's tiny, choked groan. If surrender offered even the sliver of a chance—

Leap, dear boys!

Nysander's shout jolted them both like a war cry, though it was obvious that no one else had heard.

"My lady commands your surrender," Illester barked.

"Did you hear?" hissed Seregil.

"I can't!" Alec whispered back. He was white with fear, eyes wide in disbelief.

"Enough of this," snarled Kassarie, eyeing them with growing suspicion.

"You must!" Seregil pleaded, his own belly lurching at the idea. "No—"

Seregil, Alec, leap! It must be now!

"Seize them!" cried Kassarie. "Take them alive!"

"Alec, go!"

"I can't—"

Now, Seregil, for the love of Illior!

"Now!" yelled Seregil. Flinging his sword aside, he seized Alec around the waist and heaved him over the parapet. Trying not to hear the scream that fell away into the blackness, he vaulted after him and launched himself into the abyss. Kassarie's sardonic laugh lashed out after him.

For a horrifying instant Seregil simply fell, eyes squeezed shut, the insubstantial wind beating up into his face.

Then the magic struck.

A swift, wrenching sensation shot through him, as if his soul were being pulled from his body. This was followed a splendid lightness, though he was still falling, dragged down by some entangling thing. Opening his eyes to a wondrous blaze of stars, he struggled free of his tunic and flung out his . . .

Wings!

Lovely, powerful, striped wings that sliced into the air and found purchase there. Leveling out into a glide, he looked down with his new eyes and saw another bird floundering awkwardly up toward him, hooting wildly all the way. He wouldn't have thought it possible for an owl to look flabbergasted, but Alec did. Their empty clothes tumbled into the darkness as they winged up and over the keep.

Kassarie had moved to the parapet overlooking the road and was gesturing at a body of riders thundering up the road toward her gates. Torches streaked and veered in the courtyard below as her people scattered to meet the attack.

The wind sang deliciously through their feathers as Seregil and Alec spiraled down to meet the riders. Alec let out another excited hoot as his sharp eyes made out the insignia of the Queen's Horse Guard. Klia rode at the head of the party, flanked by Myrhini and Micum.

Diving in low, Seregil flew in front of Micum.

"Seregil, is that you?"

Seregil swooped down again and landed on Micum's out-stretched arm, feeling the roughness of chainmail grating under his talons.

"Is it him?" Klia asked as the large horned owl flapped for balance.

Seregil bobbed his head and winked one great yellow eye.

"It's him!" cried Micum. "Is Alec with you?"

Seregil bobbed again as Alec winged by.

"Go to Nysander," said Micum. "He's back down the road with Thero and Beka. Wait, what's this you've got?"

Micum lifted the ring that hung against the owl's buff breast. The loop of string had held, though Seregil had not noticed the slight weight of it as he flew. Micum pocketed it for him and Seregil spread his broad wings and flapped off to join Alec.

Following the road, Alec soon spotted a small fire below. Nysander and Thero sat cross-legged beside it, watched over by several uniformed riders.

Landing was a far trickier business than flight, it turned out. After several unsuccessful attempts to copy Seregil's smooth descent, he finally ended up in an ungainly heap at a soldier's feet.

"Alec?" asked a familiar voice.

Beka knelt and set him upright, then smoothed his feathers gently. Spreading his toes out for balance, Alec blinked up at her and gave a soft hoot. Something moved under his foot; it was the silver Aurënfaie ring, still around one feathered toe. Raising his foot, he hooted at Beka until she took it.

Seregil, meanwhile, had settled gracefully on Nysander's up-raised arm.

"Thanks to the Lightbearer! We were not certain the spells found you in time," Nysander told him, looking utterly exhausted.

"We were lucky to locate you at all," added Thero. "We nearly didn't, you know, with all your dashing around. Shall I change them back now, Nysander?"

"If you would. I am quite depleted."

This transformation occurred as swiftly as the first, and with the same momentary disorientation.

After an instant's dizziness, Alec found himself standing naked in front of Beka.

"You might want this." Beka handed him her cloak, doing her best not to laugh at the expression of shocked realization spreading hotly over his face.

Mortified, Alec hastily flung it on. In the excitement of the moment he had not anticipated such complications. Taking the ring back from her, he turned to Seregil, who was kneeling beside the older wizard. "I lost the papers with my clothes, but I still have this."

"And another," Seregil gasped, cradling his head in his hands as the usual wave of post-magic nausea swept over him. "The Consort's seal. Micum has it— Nysander, we found it. There's a room below the ruined tower. We have to— We— Tell him, Alec!"

Retching, he staggered off into the shadows.

"Kassarie's a Leran for certain," Alec continued excitedly. "She's still got some of the stolen gold and the body of Lord Corruth!"

"Poor fellow. I always feared something of the sort had happened to him," sighed Nysander. "But what is this about rings and papers?"

"We took Corruth's rings and some papers to prove what we found," Alec explained, handing the wizard the heavy Aurënfaie ring. "Micum has the Consort's seal, but we lost everything else when—" Alec paused with a stricken gasp. "My sword! Oh hell, that went, too, and my black dagger." These, along with his bow, were chief among the very few material possessions he felt any attachment to; they had been the first things Seregil had outfitted him with at Wolde.

"We shall do our best to recover them, dear boy, and all the rest," Nysander assured him.

"We have to get back in there, and quickly," said Seregil, returning to the fire looking haggard but determined. One of the riders held out a cloak and he wrapped himself in it. "She'll destroy everything, Nysander; she may have already. Even with the ring, our word won't be enough against her!"

"He's right," Thero agreed.

"She's the head of the serpent, I'm certain of it," Seregil continued emphatically. "Get her and you get them all! But Klia and the others will never find that room on their own. I've got to go back in!"

"Not without me, you're not!" declared Alec.

Nysander assented with a weary nod. "Sergeant Talmir, please get these men clothing, horses, and weapons."

Beka stepped forward. "Let me go with them."

The wizard shook his head firmly. "It is not for me to countermand Commander Klia's orders. She stationed you here."

"But—"

"You stay put," Seregil warned. "It's worth your commission to leave your post. You haven't even been invested yet!"

Alec stepped away with his usual modesty to dress, while Seregil threw his cloak off with no thought but haste. As he did so, Alec was dismayed to see that the obscuration spell covering the scar had failed again; the strange scar was clearly visible. Nysander saw it, too, and shook his head slightly at Alec. Fortunately, Seregil pulled on his borrowed tabard before anyone else noticed.

Beka, who'd kindly looked away until Alec had gotten his breeches on, offered him her sword. "Take it," she urged. "I'll feel better, knowing you have a blade I trust."

Alec accepted the sword gratefully, hearing the echo of her father's words to Seregil when they'd left Watermead.

Clasping hands hastily with her, he said, "It's one I trust, too." He hesitated, suddenly awkward; he felt as if he ought to say something more, but he couldn't think what.

"Take good care of Nysander and Thero," he said at last, "in case they have to turn us into something else to get us out again."

She gave him a playful cuff on the arm. "Good thing he didn't make you into stags and otters that time, eh?"

Outfitted again, Seregil and Alec leapt onto fresh horses and galloped back to the keep.

The main gate stood open now. Looking around, Seregil guessed that their earlier capture had disrupted the usual discipline of the place, and the garrison had been caught off guard by Klia's attack.

In the courtyard a handful of Guards were standing watch over a knot of captured servants. Stamie huddled miserably among the prisoners and refused to meet Alec's eye when he attempted to speak to her.

The rest of the raiders had stormed inside. Overhead, flames licked out of a second-floor window.

"Looks like we can go in the front way this time," Seregil said with a dark grin, pointing to the shattered doors.

Scattered sounds of fighting rang through the halls as they ran for the northeast stairway. Bodies littered the stairs, but the main battle had been pressed back to the third floor.

Coming out in the upper passageway, they could hear Kassarie's remaining men making a stand at the door to the ruined tower. The halls were impossibly narrow for a pitched battle, and the fighting had spread into side rooms. Passing the open doorways, they caught sight of bodies sagging across costly, overturned furniture. The clash of swords seemed to come from every direction at once. Fresh blood spattered the elegant frescoes and the floor was treacherous with it in places.

They found Micum in the thick of the fight in the southeast corridor.

"Has Kassarie been taken yet?" Seregil shouted, trying to make himself heard over the din.

"Last I heard they were still looking for her," Micum yelled back.

"There's a door behind that hanging." Seregil pointed down the hall at the tapestry. "Pass the word forward; we have to take it!"

A few moments later, Klia's war cry echoed off the walls as the last of Kassarie's fighters threw down their weapons and fell to their knees.

Thrusting his way through the confusion, Seregil reached the princess. "Through here," he called, tearing down the tapestry to expose the door. Trying the handle, he found it locked.

"Braknil, Tomas, get this open!" barked Klia.

Two sturdy Guards threw their shoulders against the door, wrenching it off its hinges, and Seregil and Alec led the way to the trap door. Klia followed with Micum, Myrhini, and several soldiers.

The trap door had been pulled shut again, and the sand smoothed back into place. Seregil found the ring and heaved the door open, then led the way down to the wooden stairs. Careful to avoid the tilting landing, they reached the subterranean corridor to find the final door standing open. The chamber beyond was brightly lit.

Kassarie was waiting for them. She stood by the table at the center of the room, blocking the corpse of Corruth from sight. She held a small lamp in one hand, as if to light their way, and its glow threw her harsh features into imperious relief. The room smelled hotly of wax and oil. Beside him, Alec sniffed the air, frowning.

A prickle of apprehension ran up Seregil's spine; Kassarie looked like a great serpent poised to strike. How long had she stood waiting there?

"So, you're back again, are you?" she observed with a bitter smile as he and Alec stepped into view.

Klia moved up between them. Reckless and pretty as she might be under other circumstances, at this moment she was a commander and moved with her mother's austere assurance.

"Kassarie ä Moirian, I arrest you in the name of Idrilain the Second," she announced with no trace of emotion. "The charge against you is high treason."

Kassarie bowed gravely. "Clearly you have the advantage. I yield, Your Highness, with the understanding that it is to your greater strength and not to your misbegotten right."

"As you will," replied Klia, stepping toward her.

"You will find all that you seek here." Kassarie gestured around her. "Perhaps, like Lord Seregil, you would also be interested in meeting your mutual forebear."

She stepped aside and lifted her lamp with a dramatic flourish. "Allow me to present Lord Corruth í Glamien Yanari Meringil Bôkthersa. Your curs there have already pilfered the body, but I think they will bear out that I speak the truth."

Too late Seregil realized that he had failed to tell Klia what they'd found. She gave a soft, startled exclamation and stepped closer. Micum and the others were equally taken aback; all eyes were fixed on the grisly sight as Klia bent to study the ravaged face.

All, that is, except Alec's.

He'd seen more than enough of corpses over the past few weeks. Avoiding the dried husk in the chair, he looked instead at

Kassarie, and so was the only one to notice the gloating smile that spread across her face as she lifted the lamp still higher.

That smell. It was too strong to be just lamps.

There was no time to warn Klia. Knocking Seregil aside, he lunged forward into the room as Kassarie dashed the lamp to the floor at Klia's feet. The room was doused with oil and something else, something far more flammbale.

Searing heat sucked the air from his lungs and scorched his skin. Reaching wildly, he found Klia's arm and hauled her backward with all his strength. Behind him other hands reached out, yanking him roughly into the blessed coolness of the corridor.

"Get them down!" shouted Micum.

Alec was shoved to the floor and half smothered with cloaks and bodies. Hands pounded down across his back. Somewhere above him, Seregil was cursing frantically.

When they finally uncovered him, Alec saw that they'd dragged him back to the base of the stairs. Heat rolled down the little passage from the open door of the chamber beyond. Inside, solid sheets of flame obscured everything from view. There was no sign of Kassarie.

Klia was lying next to him, her beautiful, heart-shaped face streaked red and black and half her braid singed away.

"You saved my life!" she croaked, reaching for his hand; the back of her own was a welter of angry blisters where oil had splashed.

"While the rest of us had our heads up our arses," Myrhini glowered, wiping a sleeve across her eyes as she knelt by Klia.

Alec shook his head, half dazed. "That smell—It was familiar but I couldn't remember what it was."

Sulfur oil, I think" said Myhini.

The skin on Alec's back and neck suddenly began to hurt and he grimaced.

"Give me this!" Seregil tugged Alec's borrowed tabard off over his head. The back of the garment was burned through in places. "You were on fire, you know! And some of your hair is gone in the back."

Alec raised a hand to the back of his head; it felt rough and his palm came away black.

"Just when we'd gotten you looking presentable, too," Seregil complained, his voice not quite steady. "Bilairy's Cods, you smell like a scorched dog!"

41

SCARS

The sun was just climbing above the eastern treetops as Seregil, Alec, and Micum set off for the city with Nysander. Thero had stayed behind to assist in the search for the lost documents and weapons.

"I thought we'd finally run through our luck that time," Seregil admitted, riding along between Nysander and Alec.

"You damn near did!" sputtered Micum. "Nysander didn't even know you'd gone down here until I showed up."

"And when I realized that you were in danger, I could do nothing at such a distance," added Nysander. "I was not certain if you were dead or alive until after we arrived, and even then I could not fix my attention on you with any accuracy until they had you cornered on the roof. By that point it was too late for any but the most desperate measures."

"It was a lovely bit of work, though," Seregil maintained, unabashed. "You haven't turned me into a bird in years. And never an owl!"

Alec was equally excited. "It was wonderful, at least once I got used to it. But I don't understand why my mind stayed so clear. That time you turned me into a stag I got all confused."

"This was a different sort of metamorphosis," explained Nysander. "The intrinsic nature spell summons an innate magic from the person it is cast upon, and often affects the subject's mind, as in your case. Changing you to an owl was a metastatic spell. Though it demanded far more of my powers, especially at such a distance, it altered only your outward form, leaving your mind unaffected. My greatest concern was whether you would master your wings in time."

"He's a fast learner," said Seregil, resisting the impulse to clap Alec on the shoulder. He could tell from the way the boy sat his horse that his burns were giving him more pain than he was admitting.

"What you didn't learn is who the Lerans were planning to replace Idrilain with," Micum pointed out. "With everything destroyed back there, we'll never track down the others."

"That's not entirely true," said Seregil, tapping his temple. "I got a look at some of those papers before she burned everything. There're a few nobles we can go to for answers. It'll be a start."

Nysander nodded. "I will set some Watchers to it as soon as we get back. I think you three have had enough excitement for now."

"I suppose so," Seregil agreed, stealing another concerned look at Alec riding stiffly beside him.

The day grew brighter as they rode on. They reached a crossroads in sight of the city walls and, bidding them all farewell, Micum turned his horse for home.

"You know where to find me if you need me," he called, kicking his stallion into a gallop.

"I assume you will be at the Cockerel now?" Nysander asked, reining in while Seregil and Alec pulled up their hoods.

Seregil nodded. "Lord Seregil and Sir Alec will be back in town in time for the Sakor Festival. You'll keep our names out of the inquest over this business, won't you?"

"I believe I can. The Queen values the Watchers enough to respect our methods. I must ask you to stop at my tower before you return home, however. There is one last matter to be seen to."

Catching a questioning glance from Alec, Seregil raised a gloved hand to his chest.

Alec flexed his left hand thoughtfully, looking down at the smooth circle of healed flesh on his own palm.

• • •

At the Orëska House, Nysander insisted on breakfast before anything else. Having fortified himself, he led them into the small casting room and closed the door. Instructing Seregil to remove his shirt, the wizard inspected the troublesome scar closely.

"This ought to have stayed covered," muttered Nysander.

"This isn't the first time it's reappeared," Seregil reminded him, staring nervously up at the ceiling while the wizard gently pressed and prodded. A sudden thought occured to him and he reached for Nysander's wrist. "But it didn't when you changed me into old Dakus."

Nysander shook his head. "That was a lesser transformation. I simply altered your existing appearance."

"You mean I could end up looking like that someday?"

"Do be quiet, Seregil! I must concentrate."

Pressing his hand over the scar, Nysander closed his eyes and waited for any impressions to form. Little came: the streak of a falling star; a flash of the mysterious blue; the faint roar of ocean; the hint of an unfamiliar profile. Then nothing.

"Well?" demanded Seregil.

"Just bits and pieces." Nysander massaged the bridge of his nose wearily. "Fragments of memories, perhaps, but nothing to suggest any residual power in these marks. It is most curious. How is your hand, Alec?"

"Nothing's changed," Alec replied, holding it up for him to see.

"Most curious indeed," mused Nysander, unruly eyebrows beetling. "The problem must lie in the markings of Seregil's scar."

Seregil studied them in a hand mirror. "The side of the wooden disk that burned Alec was smooth, no carving at all. But these of mine are getting clearer instead of fainter. Don't you sense any magic at all around it?"

"None," Nysander answered. "So it must somehow be the configuration of the characters themselves, whatever they are."

Seregil looked up. "And you truly don't know what they are?"

"I recognize the sigla, as I have said. What lies beneath it is as much a mystery to me as to you. You have my word on that."

"Then we're right back where we began," Alec exclaimed in exasperation.

"Perhaps not," Nysander said softly, touching Seregil's scar a last time, then casting another obscuration over it. "It reappeared after Seregil changed bodies with Thero, and again when he changed back from the owl form. There must be some significance to that, though I do not yet know what it means."

"It means I'm going to spend the rest of my life trotting back to you to get it covered up again," grumbled Seregil, pulling on his shirt. "I bet Valerius could get it off."

"You must not do that. Not yet, at least. To destroy it before we understand it could prove most unwise. Bear with it awhile longer, dear boy. Perhaps we may yet solve its riddle. In the meantime, it appears to be doing you no harm."

"It's done enough of that already!" Seregil scowled. "Take care, Nysander. We'll be close by if you want us."

Nysander retired to his sitting room after they'd gone. Sinking wearily into an armchair, he rested his head against its back and summoned up the impressions he'd gotten from the scar—the star, the sea sounds, the flash of blue, the hint of a face—

His head ached. He'd had no rest since the raid and he was exhausted—too exhausted to delve further into the matter. A quick nap here in his chair was called for, he decided. Later, after making the proper preparations, he would meditate further on the matter.

The quiet of the room enfolded him like a thick, comfortable blanket. The warmth of the fire was like summer sunshine on the side of his face—so pleasant, so soft, like the touch of a woman's lips. As he sank deeper into the welcome languor, he seemed to feel Seregil's chest beneath his hand again, the tiny ridges of the scar brushing his palm. But now Seregil's skin was cold, cold as a marble statue—

Nysander stirred uneasily in his chair. *A vision is coming,* he thought in vague dismay. *I am too weary for visions—*

But it came anyway.

He was standing in the Orëska's central atrium. Bright sunshine streamed down through the great dome overhead, warming him deliciously. Other wizards passed by without looking at him. Apprentices and servants hurried past at their daily tasks.

But then the Voice spoke and all the people around him turned into marble statues.

The Voice came from somewhere beneath him, a faint, sinister chuckle vibrating up from the depths below the stone floor. He could feel it in the soles of his feet. Looking down, he noticed for the first time that the mortar of the mosaic had crumbled. Large sections of the design, the proud Dragon of Illior, had been loosened and dislodged, the brilliant tiles trampled to powder.

The Voice came again and he turned, striding through the motionless throng to the museum. Across the shadowed room, beyond the ranks of display cases, the door of the antechamber leading to the vaults stood slightly ajar.

As he approached it, he heard something scuttle away into the darkness ahead. It was a scrabbling, clicking noise utterly unlike rats. Something crackled beneath his foot, a fragment of wood. The case that had held the hands of Tikárie Megraesh was empty; a splintered, fist-sized hole had been clawed through the bottom.

Summoning a gleaming sphere of light in his left palm, he continued on. As he neared the door it flew open with such force that it split from top to bottom and hung shattered on its hinges.

"Come, old man," a sibilant whisper beckoned. "Old man. Old man. Old, old man."

Skin prickling with revulsion, he obeyed.

The antechamber was as it should be, but the plain stone stairway beyond was gone. Instead, a terrible black chasm yawned before him, devoid of bridge or pathway. Summoning a second light in his right hand, he spread his arms and launched himself into the fathomless darkness, plummeting like an osprey.

He could not tell how long he fell; it seemed like a very long time. There was no wind, no feeling of passage, only the knowledge that he was descending until at last, in the way of dreams, he came to a gentle landing on uneven stone. In front of him, an archway led into the familiar brick-paved corridor of the Orëska's deepest vault.

The low passage branched out into a warren of corridors and storage chambers. He'd made his solitary way here countless times, passing this corner, turning at the next to make certain that the Place, the unmarked, unremarkable span of mortared wall and all that lay behind it, was as it should be.

But this sojourn, he knew, was not to be a solitary one. The Voice was ahead of him and louder now, shouting to him from the Place.

"Come, old man! Come, Guardian!" The bellowed challenge

echoed coldly through the damp stone corridors. "Come and view the first fruits of your sacred vigil!"

Rounding the final corner, he found himself face-to-face with the dyrmagnos, Tikárie Megraesh. Bright eyes, moist and alive, looked out from the desiccated black face. The hands that he himself—then a young wizard new to his robes—had cut off had found their way back to their owner's arms, visible below the sleeves of the hideous creature's festival robe.

"Pass, O most noble Guardian!" Tikárie bade him, stepping aside with a slight bow. "The Beautiful One awaits. Pass and join the feast." The voice of the dyrmagnos, like his eyes, had retained a terrible humanity.

Passing his ancient enemy, he found the passage blocked by a huge pile of naked corpses. Creatures in colorful rags crawled and scuttled over the dead and he could hear the greedy sounds of their feeding.

Some were human, and among these he recognized many long-vanquished foes, returned now to haunt his dreams.

Others were twisted, monstrous creatures of revolting form beneath their robes.

And all were feasting on the dead. Swarming across the limp bodies, they hunched like jackals over their victims, tearing chunks of flesh out with teeth and talons, crunching through bone.

A tall figure emerged from the shadows, its dark cloak revealing nothing of its form.

"Join the feast," it commanded in a voice like wind groaning down the chimney of an abandoned house. Stretching an impossibly long arm into the heap, it tugged a body loose and cast it at his feet.

It was Seregil.

Half of his face had been cruelly gnawed. Both hands were gone and the skin had been flayed from his chest.

A moan rose in Nysander's throat as grief paralyzed him.

"Devour him," the specter invited, reaching again into the pile.

Micum was next, chest torn open, both strong arms gone at the shoulder.

Then Alec, robbed of hands and eyes. Blood streaked his face like tears, and matted his soft yellow hair.

Others followed, faster and faster. Friends, lords, servants, strangers, thrown about like cord wood until he was ringed in *with an ever heightening wall of bodies. Another moment and he would be immured in a tower of dead flesh.*

Battling grief and horror, he summoned the twin lights he still carried to increased brilliance and hurled them before him, charging over the maimed bodies of his companions. The obscene specter swelled in his vision and was gone, taking the awful pile of corpses with it.

Before him stood the possessor of the Voice, and Nysander's grief crystallized into stony terror. The huge figure was shrouded in shadow except where light fell across one perfect, golden-skinned shoulder.

He stared at it, trying to see his foe in spite of his mounting dread. He could feel the cold power of its eyes upon him; it burned his flesh numb like the water of a winter stream.

Then it raised its hand in greeting and the shining skin of shoulder and arm and hand split like rotten cloth, hanging in dulled shreds from the putrid flesh swelling beneath it.

"Welcome, O Guardian," it said. "You have been most faithful."

Lurching out of the shadows, the thing smashed a fist through the smooth stone wall as if it were a paper screen, reaching into the cavity beyond—

Nysander leapt up from his chair, panting and drenched with sweat. The fire was nearly dead and the room was full of shadows.

"O Illior!" he groaned, pressing a hand over his eyes. "Must I be the one who sees the end of it?"

To Be Continued.

ABOUT THE AUTHOR

Lynn Flewelling grew up in Presque Isle, Maine. Since receiving a degree in English from the University of Maine in 1981, she has studied veterinary medicine at Oregon State, classical Greek at Georgetown University, and worked as a personnel generalist, landlord, teacher, necropsy technician, advertising copywriter, and freelance journalist, more or less in that order. She currently lives in western New York.

And don't miss the riveting sequel to
Luck in the Shadows

Stalking Darkness
by
Lynn Flewelling

Vargûl Ashnazai sat toying with the ivory vial hanging around his neck. Inside were a few blood-soaked slivers of wood, gouged from the floor of the Mycenian inn where he had overtaken the pair of thieves who'd stolen the Eye in Wolde. His chest constricted with anger every time he thought of them, the Aurënfaie bard and his scrawny boy.

"To be so close—!" he hissed, closing his fist around the vial.

Mardus stretched comfortably and refilled his wine cup. "Impatience will be your undoing. Those two are of no consequence. All that matters now is recovering what they stole. Try again."

Clasping the vial grimly in one hand, Vargûl Ashnazai placed the other over his eyes and summoned the image of the thieves. Power flowed through him to the vial and beyond, using the essence of their blood to seek them out.

It was a powerful talisman. With it he'd tracked the pair to Nanta, and then on to Rhíminee, but there the trail had abruptly ended. All attempts at scrying for them had met with fierce resistance.

This time was no different. The moment he focused his concentration on their location, he was blinded by a searing storm of leathery wings and fire. The message was clear enough: *These people are under the protection of the Orëska. You cannot touch them.*

Gasping, Ashnazai pressed both hands to his face. "I'll crush their beating hearts in my hands!" Looking up, he met Mardus' sardonic sneer.

"Vengeance is a dangerous emotion," he cautioned. "Patience is the key now. Our moment will come."

Yes, it will, Ashnazai thought with grim anticipation. *And when it does, I will linger over their deaths, savoring their pain like the finest of wines. . . .*

Available now